> Catrina,
> Thank you supporting me
> Good Reads. I h[ope]
> enjoy my book. Kind Regards,
> L Starla

Crystal's Crucible

A Phoebe Braddock Romance

L. STARLA

Disclaimer: This is a work of fiction. Names, characters, businesses, places, events, locales, and incidents are either the products of the author's imagination or used in a fictitious manner. Any resemblance to actual persons, living or dead, or actual events is purely coincidental.

CRYSTAL'S CRUCIBLE
Copyright © 2021 Laelia Starla.
All rights reserved. No part of this publication may be reproduced, distributed, or transmitted in any form or by any means, including photocopying, recording, or other electronic or mechanical methods, without the prior written permission of the publisher, except in the case of brief quotations embodied in critical reviews and certain other non-commercial uses permitted by copyright law.

To request permission, contact the author:
laelia@starlaarts.com

Graphics & book design by L. Starla
Editing by J. Wake

First edition 2021.

ISBN-13: (paperback) 978-0-6488424-9-1

Self-published.

Note from the Author

Trigger Warning: This book contains situations where consent is dubious, along with graphic depictions of violence, sexual assault, and drug use.

While this book contains scenes with dubious consent and depictions of sexual violence, I do not condone such behaviour. If you are a victim of sexual assault, please consider reporting the crime immediately by ringing emergency services.

For post assault support, I recommend reaching out to a professional, confidential counselling service such as:

1800RESPECT in Australia (Ph 1800 737 732)

RAINN in the United States (Ph 800 656 4673)

SUPPORTLINE in the United Kingdom (Ph 01708 765 200)

And, if you or someone you care about is struggling with substance abuse, please consider reaching out to your local Alcoholics Anonymous or Narcotics Anonymous support group.

Dedication

- This one is for Sarah, a fellow science nerd and friend for life.

Epigraph

'The meeting of two personalities is like the contact of two chemical substances: if there is any reaction, both are transformed.'
— Carl Gustav Jung

Crystal's Jazz Playlist

'Close Your Eyes' by Art Blakey & The Jazz Messengers
'Crystal Silence' by Chick Corea
'Feeling Good' by Nina Simone
'I've Got a Crush on You' by Steve Tyrell
'La vie en rose' by Louis Armstrong
'Let's Fall in Love' by Diana Krall
'Let There Be Love' by Nat King Cole
'The Man I Love' by Miles Davis, John Coltrane
'Moonlight Serenade' by Glenn Miller
'My Favorite Things' by John Coltrane
'Prelude to a Kiss' by Duke Ellington
'Sinnerman' by Nina Simone
'Stolen Moments' by Oliver Nelson
'They Can't Take That Away from Me' by Ella Fitzgerald
'Trust in Me' by Etta James

Playlist available on Spotify.

Personnel

ALUDEL PHARMA ORGANISATIONAL CHART:
Dandenong Chemotherapy Division

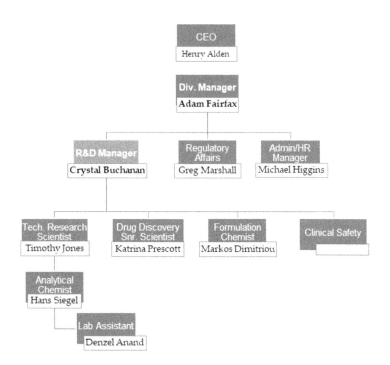

Crystal Buchanan's Family Tree

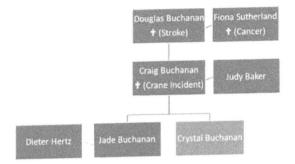

Chapter One

Crystal

C rystal grabbed the employment section and paused when a headline caught her attention: 'Gang Violence on the Rise in Melbourne's Nightclub District.' With a sigh, she wondered if she should warn Jade. Imparting words of wisdom to her older sister had always been a futile endeavour, so she dismissed the idea and returned to the sanctuary of her home office. It was nearly time for the moment of truth.

She ran the comb through her red locks one last time and brushed away the dandruff from her favourite rose-gold blouse. Using a tissue, she dabbed at the perspiration forming on her brow. Summer was just around the corner and, if the last few November days were anything to go by, they were in for a hot one. After smoothing down the creases in her black skirt, she clicked CONNECT on the video conference and forced a smile out of her tense jaw. 'Hello, I'm Crystal Buchanan. Thank you so much for meeting with me online.'

Three pristine businessmen gave her haughty grins. The man on the left—who was wearing a navy suit— shifted forward in his seat. 'It is no problem at all Crystal; we get lots of interstate applicants. I am Nigel Weatherby, the laboratory manager. With me, I have Peter Salisbury, our division manager, and Ethan Van de Brock from HR.' He pointed to the men next to him sequentially. 'Why don't we start with your reasons for wanting this position?'

'Of course.' Crystal caught herself twirling a strand of hair between her fingers. Releasing it, she took a deep breath. 'I have recently graduated from Melbourne University with a PhD in organic chemistry, a field of science I am passionate about, and I believe my expertise would be of value to your research program.'

'What was your thesis focussed on?' Nigel asked.

'Stereoisomer separation techniques.'

'That's great,' remarked Peter. 'Here, at Highgate Industries, you will be expected to work as part of a large team. Can you give us an example of how you have worked well with other group members?'

Crystal's mother, Judy, chose that moment to burst through the door, hiccupping. 'Crissy, darlll, I need a (hiccup) lift to the shop.' She swayed in the doorway and staggered across the room.

'No!' Crystal snapped as she looked up from her computer. 'I told you I'm busy right now.'

Reeking of brandy and stale cigarette smoke, Judy collapsed into Crystal's lap, providing a closeup view of her wrinkled skin and drooping jowls. No one would have guessed the woman was only fifty-two. 'Please, pretty please? I need more ciggies and you never buy 'em for me!' The sound of a throat clearing drew her attention to Crystal's laptop. 'Ooh, aren't you a bunch of handsome fellas? Is my gorgeous girl doin' a strip show for ya?' Giggles erupted from her crude gob.

'Mum!' Every muscle in Crystal's body stiffened as she suppressed her rage. *Great, now I've lost control of the situation.*

Ignoring her, Judy leaned forward, tugging her singlet down to offer the men a view of her bare breasts. 'I'll give ya a two-for-one. My tits are bigger anyway.'

CRYSTAL'S CRUCIBLE

Two large, saggy sacks of crinkled flesh jiggled in front of Crystal, obscuring her view of the interviewers' faces. But she could hear their gasps, picturing the abject horror on their faces as bile ascended her oesophagus. Ducking her head around Judy's side, she glimpsed the screen as the Highgate men disconnected. Her blood reached boiling point.

'Hey, where did they go?' Judy started punching the keyboard and yelling, 'Come back, sexy strangers! We haven't gotten—'

'*Stop it!*' Crystal screeched as she pulled Judy back from the computer and shoved her onto the floor. Wide eyes stared back at Crystal, who jumped to her feet. '*What the hell is wrong with you?* That was my only job interview in four months! You ruined my best chance at decent employment.' Her throat constricted as she fought back the tears swelling in her eyes.

Rolling onto her side, Judy groaned. 'I thought you were fooling 'round on some dating site or something. You should've said you had an interview!'

'I did! Several times in fact. Don't you recall me telling you this morning?'

CRYSTAL'S CRUCIBLE

'Yeah, but I thought you was goin' out to it like a proper interview. What sort of place does 'em on the inta-net?'

'The sort of place that is interstate and would have paid me loads of money,' Crystal snapped.

Judy wheezed. '*You were planning to leave me all alone?* First your dad abandons us, then your sister. You're all I have left!'

'It's not like dad planned on dropping dead.' Crystal let out a sigh of exasperation. 'You need to stop blaming him for everything. If I had been successful in getting that job, I would have paid for someone to look after you.'

Sitting up, Judy crossed her legs and grunted. 'What's Jade's excuse, huh?'

'She grew up, Mum. It's *normal* for children to leave home when they reach adulthood.' Sarcasm dripped from her voice like acid from a pipette.

'I know that!' Her mother glared at her. 'I'm not an imbecile! Would be nice if your sister dropped in to see *me* sometimes.'

'She *does* visit,' Crystal said in Jade's defence.

'Bah!' Judy waved her hand dismissively. 'She only comes for you.'

CRYSTAL'S CRUCIBLE

Crystal shrugged. 'I'm going to run a bath for you, Mum. You need to wash before going out in public.'

Judy's eyes lit up like the neighbour's house at Christmas. 'You'll take me to the store?'

'I may as well. Besides, the fridge could use a restock. But no more booze! I want you to try going sober for a night. And when we get back, I need to focus on job searching.'

Pouting, wisps of ginger hair fell around Judy's face as she rose. 'You're no fun! Why don't we go to the pub for dinner? It's Friday after all, and you could use a night off from your dull life. Maybe even hook up for once.'

Striding out of the office with a huff, Crystal reached the bathroom, turned on the taps, and waited for her mother to catch up. 'My personal life is none of your business, Mum. I'm quite content with my book boyfriends, *thank you very much*.' She spat the response in a defensive tone.

Judy sat on the closed toilet seat and snorted. 'Yeah, right! There's no way that vibrator fulfills all your needs.'

Crystal's cheeks flushed as her mouth gaped open. 'H-how do you know about *that*?'

CRYSTAL'S CRUCIBLE

'I wasn't born in the last shower, darl. I know what it means when a buzzing noise comes from your room at night.'

'Well, it's a lot safer than the multitude of men you bring home. No chance of heartbreak or an S.T.I. Now get in the bath.' Pressing her back to the wall, Crystal crossed her arms and closed her eyes. Water splashed all over the room a few minutes later, spraying her and flooding the floor. 'Are you okay, Mum?' She pried her right eye open a crack to check her mother was still conscious.

'Yeah, I'm all good.'

Reassured by visual and verbal confirmation, Crystal took the seat Judy had vacated, despairing over the rut she had fallen into. *Will I ever escape this hell?*

෨ඥ

Adam

Striding across the tennis court, Adam grabbed one of the Club's white, Egyptian Cotton towels. He brought the plush cloth to his forehead, soaking up his sweat with the soft threads of luxury before tossing it aside. 'Good game.' He shook Greg's hand.

His mate was grinning like an idiot. 'Oh please, that was an amazing game. I finally beat the great Adam Fairfax.'

Adam shrugged. 'About time. Keep this up and we might win some doubles this summer. Come on man, let's hit the showers.'

Greg nodded as he fell in step with Adam. 'You got much planned this weekend?'

Adam sighed. 'Drowning myself at the bottom of a single malt bottle.'

'Yikes. You feeling that bitter about losing?'

Adam glared at his best friend. 'Have you already forgotten? Lucy and I would have been celebrating seventeen years tomorrow.' He flung his duffle bag at the changeroom bench and groaned as the force of his throw sent it sliding across the polished wood. It dropped to the glistening, white tiled floor with a loud *thud*.

'Ah shit! Sorry bro.' Greg frowned. 'Has it really been that long?'

Adam replied with a grim nod before jumping in the shower. Closing his eyes, he focussed on the hot water washing away the anger, the steam clearing the darkness from his mind. He would not let Lucy get the better of him in public. *I am the boss – my thoughts work for me*. After repeating the mantra a few times, he took a deep breath and opened his eyes. Squeezing a generous helping of bodywash into his hands, he lathered up, inhaling the fresh, fruity fragrance of Hugo Boss. He watched as the stream washed the suds of his negativity down the drain.

Revived and relaxed, Adam emerged from the cubicle. He slipped into a clean pair of beige shorts and a designer polo-shirt.

Greg waited outside for him. He offered Adam a half-smile. 'You okay?'

'Yeah. You want a drink?'

'Of course.' As they made their way toward the cocktail lounge, a pair of ladies passed them in a vanilla scented cloud. Greg rubbernecked and whistled through pursed lips. 'Hot damn. God, do I love this club. Nothing but quality.'

Adam's brow creased. 'Don't forget those marriage vows of yours.'

'There's no harm in looking. And you, my friend, are single, so there's nothing stopping you.' Greg gestured toward the women, drawing Adam's gaze toward them.

CRYSTAL'S CRUCIBLE

The pair of tall blondes both looked to be in their early thirties. When they reached the bathroom, they turned. One glimpse of Adam and their faces lit up. With a giggle, they disappeared beyond the solid timber door.

Clamping his heavy hand on Adam's shoulder, Greg snickered. 'I think they like you. You should go for it when they return. Might be good to get your mind off that cheating whore.'

Adam's skin prickled at the mention of his ex-wife. *Maybe a night of meaningless sex is exactly what I need.* An image of burying himself between long legs stirred his blood. *Christ! It's been a while.* Stepping close to the bar, he attempted to hide the growing bulge in his pants and looked at Greg. 'You know, I think I might.'

Greg beamed. 'Good. You've been too tense lately. Especially at work.' He ordered their gin and tonics and led them to a table near the entrance.

After tucking the vacant chairs back into their places, Adam sat opposite Greg. He took a long sip of his drink, savouring the zesty flavour explosion on his palate. Placing the glass carefully on the coaster, he centred it.

'Can I give you a word of advice?' Greg's voice broke Adam's absent-minded trance.

CRYSTAL'S CRUCIBLE

'If you must.'

'When you take one of those girls home, if she rocks your world, you should give her the follow up call. It's been over nine years now. Don't you think it's time to move on?'

'It's not like I haven't tried. It's just…'

Greg pressed his lips together in a half-smile. 'You can't trust them. I know the story.' He scratched his head. 'But, geez man, you've got to find a way past this.'

Adam shifted uncomfortably. 'I know, and I will. When I meet the right woman. Can we… uh… change the subject?'

'Fine,' Greg huffed. 'I've been meaning to talk to you about Brayzon.'

'Argh, are you hell-bent on killing my mood entirely?'

Greg rolled his eyes. 'Sorry boss, but I didn't think it could get much worse.'

'Well, go on. What have the greedy bastards done now?'

Leaning forward, Greg lowered his voice. 'Word has it they are pushing their way into *our* turf with their new chemotherapy range.'

CRYSTAL'S CRUCIBLE

'Jesus! They're not content cornering the market with analgesics and medical devices? Are they applying for any patents yet?'

Greg scowled. 'Yes, and from what I hear, it has the same formula as our latest mitotic inhibitor.'

'What?' Adam sprung to his feet, his chair screeching against the floorboards as he slapped his palms on the table. 'Did it get in before ours?'

'Sit down, Adam, you're causing a scene.'

Glancing around the room, Adam noticed everyone watching him. He slumped into the chair next to Greg. 'When did Brayzon submit their application?'

'Same time as us. From what I gather, it will come down to who has the most advanced research data.'

Adam calmed his breathing. 'How did you learn all this and why hasn't the IP team told me anything yet?'

'I heard it through the grapevine. Nothing official has been said or released. I expect IP will contact you as soon as they know. They'll need you to get the intel from R&D after all.'

Adam leaned back, audibly exhaling. They had spent the last week going through a strenuous regulatory audit. *Now this*. He spotted the two vanilla blondes at the bar and grinned lasciviously. *Greg is right, I do need the stress relief.*

Chapter Two

Crystal

'Ooh!' Esme's monolid eyes opened almost as wide as her thick-rimmed spectacles. 'You brought the new set. Can I have a look?'

Crystal smiled at her bestie. 'Sure.' After closing the boot[1] of her Subaru, she handed the black and rose marble chess set to Esmerelda Kwan.

Esme's arm sagged as she took it. 'Gosh, there's some weight to it.'

'Yep, it's a hefty one,' Crystal agreed as she took the proffered box back.

'It looks so pretty in the picture. I can't wait to try it.'

---

[1] Trunk

CRYSTAL'S CRUCIBLE

'Shall we?' Crystal gestured toward the Royal Botanic Gardens. With a vigorous nod, Esme walked beside her as they entered the southern gate. The sun peeked through the clouds, no longer blazing with the same furious heat as it had the day before. Crystal could almost taste the morning's rain in the air, and the gentle breeze carried the scent of menthol from the surrounding eucalypts. They took their time strolling up the path, listening to various bird calls along the way. Ever since they had discovered this place during their first year of university, the Botanic Gardens had become Crystal and Esme's favourite meeting place. It was a welcome change from their dreary homes and an opportunity to reconnect with nature. 'How's your research going?'

'Absolutely amazing!' Esme gushed. 'I…' she looked ready to spill more but bit her lip. 'I'm sorry, you don't want to hear all the details. How's the job search? You had an interview yesterday, right?'

'It's okay, Ez. Even though I missed out, I'm still fascinated by your work. My search is not going great. My mother ruined the interview for me. By God, you would not believe what she did!'

'Try me. After her speech—about conceiving you in the back of a Combi van, she thinks—at your twenty-first, I don't think Judy could shock me at all anymore.'

'She flashed her tits at my interview panel.'

Esme came to an abrupt stop and gaped at Crystal.

'I told you.' They resumed walking.

'Wow, that's next level. Maybe you should start a YouTube channel and monetize that shit.'

Crystal huffed. 'No thanks. She humiliates me enough. I can't wait to get a job and move out.'

When they reached the Ornamental Lake, Crystal took a moment to admire the black swans gliding across the water, wishing she could possess such style and grace. She captured a few snapshots of them on her phone before retrieving some floating waterfowl food from her pocket: nothing but the good stuff would suffice for these magnificent creatures.

Esme laughed as a family of ducks swooped in to steal the food. 'Too cute.' She sighed as they watched the birds. 'My dad is trying to set me up with another Chinese man.'

Crystal tossed another handful of food directly at the swans. 'Have you met him yet?'

CRYSTAL'S CRUCIBLE

'No, but I've seen pictures. Apparently, he is a successful businessman, but he's really not my type.'

A snort slipped from Crystal's mouth. 'Of course not, he exists beyond the page. Did you tell your dad you're not interested?'

'Yeah, I did. But you're the only person I know who understands my love of book boyfriends, Crissy. Dad is losing his patience. Told me if I don't find a husband soon, he'll disown me.'

'Ouch! Nasty. What are you gonna do?'

'I guess I have to start dating. But where do I look for guys? I don't know the first thing about real men.'

Crystal's brows shot upward. 'And you're asking *me*?'

Esme shrugged. 'At least you've been with a few.'

'Those guys were only after one thing, Ez. Not exactly dating material. Honestly, I'm as clueless as you.' Crystal finished feeding the birds on the lake and found a shaded spot to set up the chess board. 'I figure the heavier board and pieces will work well outside. Less chance of blowing over in the wind.'

CRYSTAL'S CRUCIBLE

Esme nodded as she picked up each of the queens. 'Gosh they are stunning.' She returned the pieces to the board and picked up a pawn of each colour. After hiding them in her palms, she held out her closed fists. 'Pick one.'

Tapping her right hand, Crystal revealed the rose-gold marble piece. 'Nice. I was hoping for my favourite colour.'

'I guess you start.' Esme arranged her side of the board.

After opening with pawn to E4, Crystal leaned back and considered the ultimatum Esme's father had given her.

Esme eventually responded with pawn to E5.

Crystal followed with knight to F3. 'What if we create a profile for you on that dating app?'

Looking up from the game, Esme gave her a sidelong glance. 'You're kidding right?'

'Actually, no, I'm not. If you're serious about meeting someone, why not give it a try?'

'What if I meet some psycho creep?' Esme went for the Petrov's Defence with knight to F6.

Deciding to try the Cochrane Gambit, Crystal moved knight to E5. 'Isn't Dexter like your favourite book boyfriend?'

CRYSTAL'S CRUCIBLE

'Yeah, but he's nice to innocent women. And truth be told, I'd pee my pants if I met someone like that in real-life.'

'I'm happy to chaperone any first dates if you're worried.'

'Really, you'd do that for me?' Black pawn to E6.

'Absolutely!' Knight to F7.

Esme arched her brow before taking the knight with her king. 'I'll do it on one condition.'

'What?'

'You put your profile up too.'

Crystal's eyes bugged out and she swallowed hard against the lump in her throat. *It's only a profile, I don't have to respond to anyone.* 'Okay, fine. Let's do it after this game.'

৩০৫

Jade

Jade could not help but laugh at the messages from her sister, as tragic as their mother's antics were. Thinking of Crystal on Tinder amused her the most. *That girl is adorable. I bet she doesn't even know how popular her profile will be.* Jade tucked her phone inside her purse and locked the car.

The queue to Club Commotion trailed around the block by the time she arrived. Grinning, she strutted straight on past the line of Melbourne's trendiest, collecting a few wolf whistles along the way. Harvey gave her a polite nod as he unhooked the midnight blue velour rope from the stanchion post to let her through. 'Thank you, handsome.' She gave him a wink before stepping inside.

Passing the threshold transported Jade to a vibrant world full of bright colours, hypnotic music, and an abundance of love. Tiësto's 'God is a Dancer' started playing, sending the crowd wild. Jade looked toward the DJ booth and spotted Dieter preparing for his set. She dashed toward the spiral staircase leading to the balcony, gliding her hands along the smooth, brass railing on her ascent.

Sargon, the club owner, rose to greet her when she entered the VIP area. His eyes drank in the sight of her wearing a black, backless bodycon dress. 'Looking as gorgeous as ever, my dear. Come, there's someone I'd like you to meet.' His hand pressed against the small of her back, eliciting a reminiscent spark of desire.

CRYSTAL'S CRUCIBLE

As she reached his table, Jade's breath hitched at the sight of the Greek Adonis standing before her. Designer stubble accented his chiselled jaw, and his form-fitting, gold button-up shirt emphasised his muscular physique. But his dark, deep set eyes, smouldering like buried embers, were his most captivating feature.

'Jade, this is Apollo, my new supplier.'

She reached out to shake his hand, but as he clasped it with his own firm grip, he brought it up to his full lips and brushed it with a soft kiss.

'It is a pleasure to meet you, Jade.' His baritone voice resonated with the deepest, darkest parts of her soul.

'A pleasure indeed.'

Apollo glanced at Sargon; whose arm remained around her waist. 'You did not tell me you had such a beautiful woman.'

Sargon let a short laugh slip. 'I would be so lucky, but alas, Jade is no longer mine.'

The grin on Apollo's face would have put the Cheshire Cat to shame.

'I'll leave you to it, shall I?' Sargon walked off toward the bar.

After taking their seats, Jade leaned in close to him, displaying her ample cleavage. He did not hide his appreciation. Twirling one of her blue braids between manicured fingers, she brought his attention to her lips when she made a show of licking them. 'Your molly[2] must be exceptional if Sargon has taken you on.'

Apollo nodded. 'I guarantee it is the purest stuff because I make it myself.'

Her heartrate spiked at the thought. *I must get some.* She slipped her hand onto his thigh, giving it a slight squeeze. 'I imagine quality like that costs a pretty penny.'

His breath had become short and raspy. 'It's not as expensive as you might think. By dealing it myself, I cut out the middleman.' Apollo's fingers walked along the bare skin of her own thigh as he brought his mouth against her ear. 'And I'd happily discount it for a goddess like you.' Those words sent a shockwave of passion through her body, leaving her nerves humming.

'Is that so?'

'Mhm.' His fingers reached her hemline. 'Would you like one or two?'

'Actually, I'll take four.'

He sat back and cocked his brow. 'Are you sure?'

---

[2] Street name for MDMA (Ecstasy)

CRYSTAL'S CRUCIBLE

Jade nodded. 'I'm meeting a friend later.'

'Tell you what, I'll give you two for free and the other two for a lobster[3] if you dance with me until your friend arrives.'

Yes! The devil on her shoulder was doing a jig. 'You have yourself a deal.' She withdrew her purse and slipped him a twenty.

He replaced it with a baggie while sliding his business card across the table. 'Call me anytime you need more.' His breath tickled her neck as he leaned in. 'Or just call me.' Rising from his chair, Apollo offered his hand. 'Shall we?'

Jade entwined her fingers with his, following him downstairs and onto the dancefloor. Dieter was working his magic on the decks when Apollo drew her close against him. She gulped when his large palms engulfed her backside. After the slightest moment of hesitation, she wrapped her arms around his neck and let the music take control.

After two hours of bumping and grinding against Apollo, Jade felt a familiar arm drape across her shoulder.

Apollo gasped, his wide-eyed gaze lifting to meet the German giant who stood behind her.

---

[3] Slang for Australian twenty-dollar bills, which are red

CRYSTAL'S CRUCIBLE

Dieter kissed her cheek. 'Hallo *Liebling*[4]. I see you made a new friend.' His accent was thick, even after four years of living in Australia.

She moved into his embrace, raising her voice above the thumping bassline. 'Yes, I have. Dieter, honey, this is Apollo, Sargon's new supplier. He gave me a great deal on our party bag.' Stepping aside, she let them shake hands. 'Apollo, this is Dieter, my boyfriend.'

Hope vanished from Apollo's face. 'This is the friend you mentioned?'

'Yep.' Jade hated this moment, but it was a small price to pay for the extra attention she craved. Not to mention the discounted drugs.

Dieter pulled her back into his arms. 'Thank you, Apollo, for the discount as well as for keeping my Jade company. I'm sure you have a busy night ahead of you.'

Having regained his composure, Apollo smirked, his eyes locking with hers. 'It has been an absolute joy.' Stepping closer, he whispered in her ear, 'call me,' before walking off into the crowd.

'Did you have fun playing with your Greek god?' Dieter asked as he spun her around to face

---

[4] Darling (German)

him. His arms snaked around her waist and he kissed her neck.

She sucked in a breath. 'Uhuh.'

'You looked incredibly sexy dancing with him. I want you to do *that* with me now.'

'Of course, baby. But first…' She grabbed the baggie from where she had concealed it in her bra and dropped two of the pills in Dieter's palm. *Time for the real party.* After popping her own, she reached up to kiss her man's luscious lips. Their bodies found the rhythm and within an hour Jade was floating on the clouds. Yet, even in her altered state of mind, she was not oblivious to the two burning orbs staring down at her from the balcony.

Chapter Three

Adam

After attempting to rub the Mondayitis from his eyes, Adam pushed the button on the coffee machine and stared blankly at the cream-coloured plasterboard wall of the breakroom. He winced as the harsh grinding noise started. *God, I'd hate to work in a café.*

'Oh, good, you're here.' Michael popped his head around the door. 'I need to see you in my office.'

Adam groaned. 'I haven't even had my first cup yet, Mike.'

'Sorry boss, but this is kinda urgent. There are some police here to see you.'

'What for?'

'They didn't say.'

Grumbling, Adam poured a splash of milk into his brew and took it with him as he followed

CRYSTAL'S CRUCIBLE

Michael. Being the Administration Manager, Michael Higgins worked near the front of the building. This meant traversing the open plan office area where several people looked up from their cubicle desks to smile and greet Adam. He gave each of them a polite nod and even fended off a couple of questions by pointing to his steaming hot drink.

Two men in suits rose from their seats when Adam entered the room. The older looking of the two stepped forward to offer his hand. 'Adam Fairfax? I'm Detective Edward Draper and this is my partner, Detective Brett Hammond.'

Adam's body stiffened as he shook their hands. *What the hell do the police want?* 'What can I do for you, Detectives?'

Draper gestured for him to sit as Michael closed the door. It was cramped with the four of them squeezed into Michael's poky office.

'We might be more comfortable in the boardroom,' Adam suggested.

Draper shook his head. 'It's okay, we won't take much of your time.'

Perching himself on the vacant chair, Adam took a sip of his coffee before placing it on the desk.

CRYSTAL'S CRUCIBLE

'We found one of your employees this morning.'

Adam exchanged furrowed brows with Michael before returning his attention to Draper. 'Found who and how?'

'Robert Landon was found dead, from an apparent suicide.'

All the blood drained from Adam's face. '*Oh God!* Robert killed himself? Why on Earth would he do that?'

'That's why we wanted to talk to you,' Hammond explained. 'He left a note about the pressures at work being too much.'

'*Seriously?* You're blaming me for this?'

Hammond shook his head. 'We are not looking to assign blame. Just gotta get a few facts straight. What was Mr. Landon's role here?'

'Robert was the R&D Manager.'

After jotting something in his notebook, Hammond returned his gaze to Adam. 'Was Mr. Landon behaving strangely last week? Did he give you any reason to suspect he was unhappy?'

'No. I mean, we had a difficult audit last week, but Robert took it in his stride like usual. He was always a cheerful chap. Ask anyone here.'

CRYSTAL'S CRUCIBLE

'Did you know Mr. Landon was on prescription antidepressants?' Draper piped up again.

Adam felt his eyes pop from their sockets. 'What? No, I had no idea.'

'Are new employees required to submit to a medical when they start here?' Draper asked.

'Yes,' Michael replied calmly.

'We have a subpoena for Mr. Landon's personnel file,' Draper explained. 'Who is responsible for such records at this site?'

Again, Michael responded, 'I am.'

Draper withdrew a large envelope from his briefcase and handed it to Michael.

After reading the enclosed document, Michael rose and unlocked one of the large filing cabinets behind his desk. He withdrew a manilla folder marked ROBERT LANDON and gave it to Draper. 'I can tell you now, you won't find any reference to mental illness in there. I processed his application when we hired him eleven years ago. And Adam is right, Robert never showed signs of depression in all his years here.'

'Thank you, Mr. Higgins.' Draper flicked through the contents of the file and inspected a few of the pages. 'I apologise for the intrusion, but we need to check these things. I'm sure you understand.'

Michael nodded. 'Of course.'

'For what it's worth, I understand it is common for men to hide such matters, especially when applying for work.' He snapped the file shut between his fingers and dropped it in his briefcase. Looking up at Adam, he forced half a smile. 'I am sorry for your loss. We won't take up any more of your time.'

Adam stood to shake both of their hands and show them out. When he returned to Michael's office, he slammed the door and slumped into his seat. Closing his eyes, he imbibed two large mouthfuls of coffee and took a deep breath.

'You okay?' Michael's voice brought him back to the room.

'What do you think? Robert wasn't just my team member. He was my friend.'

'I know. That's why I'm worried. Maybe you should take the day off.'

Adam sighed. 'I can't. This is a critical time, especially for R&D. We need to fill Robert's shoes ASAP. Can I see the CVs from the recent analytical chemist applicants?'

CRYSTAL'S CRUCIBLE

Michael gasped. 'But this role demands a different skill set.'

'Obviously. Still, might be worth a shot.'

Shifting his focus to the computer, Michael clicked away on his keyboard. 'You don't want to promote anyone in the R&D team?'

'I'd have to hire their replacements and we can't afford the time it would take to train a new research scientist. Besides, who would I pick? Katrina has all the people skills of a wasp and Tim would suffer a stroke from the added pressure.'

Michael snorted as he laughed. 'Fair point. What about Markos?'

'Doesn't have the research skills or experience.'

The small desktop printer fired up beside Michael and he grabbed the page it spat out. 'Might I suggest searching these professional databases?' He pushed a list of job seeker websites across the desk.

'Thanks man, I'll give them a look.'

ೞଓ

Crystal

CRYSTAL'S CRUCIBLE

Unlocking the new bolt on her office door, Crystal tiptoed down the hall of her old bungalow house, taking care to avoid the squeaky floorboards. Her mother had been out on a four-day bender and Crystal did not fancy waking the angry dragon.

When she reached the kitchen, she raised the shutters and opened the windows, letting the fresh sea breeze expel the stench of stale cigarette smoke. Sunlight bounced off the beech wood Laminex countertops, illuminating the mint cabinets. She glanced at the wall clock shaped like a ship's wheel and noticed it had stopped. *Oh joy.* Searching the drawer where they kept the spare batteries, Crystal came away empty handed. *Great, just great.* Knowing a clock showing the wrong time would send her nuts, she climbed up on the bench and took it down. After shoving it in the drawer, she wrote *Batteries* on the shopping list.

What was I doing again? Oh right, sandwich. She assembled everything she needed on the island bench. Crouching down, she grabbed a plate from the cupboard. As she rose to her feet, a large, tattoo-covered man walked through the doorway wearing nothing but his ink. Squealing, Crystal dropped the plate, letting it shatter on the floor.

CRYSTAL'S CRUCIBLE

The man, who Crystal had never seen before, smiled at her. 'Oh sorry, I didn't know Judy had a housemate.' He plucked the dustpan and hand broom from the hook by the door and approached her. 'Here, let me help.'

Crystal clamped a hand over her bulging eyes. 'Would you… uh… mind covering up first?'

He laughed. 'Oh right.'

When the room fell silent, Crystal chanced a look and found she was alone again, the dustpan sitting before her on the bench. By the time she had swept up the mess, Judy and her latest hook-up entered the kitchen.

'Crissy, darling, this is Diesel.'

Crystal blushed at the hulking man who was now wearing leathers.

Diesel reached out to shake her hand, crushing it in his firm grip and provoking a tiny squeak from her dry throat. He laughed. 'I think I may have petrified the poor girl with my shameless display.' Swinging one of his long legs over a stool, he sat at the breakfast bar. He tugged at Judy's waist and smacked his lips to her cheek. 'I'd kill for a coffee, sweetheart.'

Biting her lip, Crystal feared the truth behind his words.

CRYSTAL'S CRUCIBLE

Judy smiled at Crystal. 'Be a darll, would ya, and make us some coffee? Oh, and cook us some brekky while you're at it. It's been ages since we enjoyed a Sunday breakfast together.'

'You know it's Tuesday afternoon, right?'

'Really?' Judy looked to Diesel for confirmation, and he nodded. 'Well shit! We've had so much fun this weekend that I lost track of time.'

After flicking on the kettle, Crystal retrieved the jar of instant granules from the pantry.

Diesel gasped, staring wide-eyed at the coffee jar. 'I can't believe you drink such tripe! Don't you have the real stuff?'

'Fraid not,' Crystal replied through clenched teeth.

Leaning into him, Judy sighed. 'Crissy doesn't poison her body with caffeine, and she never buys me anything good, so this is all I get.'

Diesel huffed. 'Well, that's gonna have to change. No woman of mine should have to settle for anything less than quality. I'll buy you a coffee machine, sweetheart.'

Crystal spluttered. 'Since when are you anyone's woman, Mum?'

Judy beamed. 'Since I met Diesel. He has been good to me.'

CRYSTAL'S CRUCIBLE

Resisting the urge to roll her eyes, Crystal gave Judy a sidelong glance.

'Wait,' Diesel interrupted their stare down. 'Crissy's your daughter?'

'Yep,' Crystal answered for her mother. 'The youngest of two in fact.'

He hugged Judy closer. 'I didn't think you were old enough to have grown-arse daughters.' The soppy words followed by the kisses he planted along Judy's neck prompted a fit of giggles.

The scene nauseated Crystal, so she busied herself preparing their brunch. Sliding the scrambled eggs and bacon across the bench put a stop to their make out session.

Diesel grinned at her. 'Thanks, sweet pea.' He scoffed the food down in four massive gulps and let out a thunderous belch. 'Delicious. What are you up to this afternoon, Crissy?'

She collapsed in her seat with her sandwich and cranberry juice. 'More job searching.'

'Crissy is a scientist,' Judy explained after swallowing her mouthful. 'Real smart girl, like her old man. She was always the apple of her dad's eye.' A hint of bitterness laced Judy's tone.

CRYSTAL'S CRUCIBLE

'Is that so?' Diesel's brows rose to meet his receding hairline. 'And what about your sister, Crissy? What is she like?'

'Jade—'

'Is a useless druggie,' Judy cut in. 'Let's not talk about her.'

Crystal's phone rang, giving her a welcome reprieve from the awkward conversation. 'Excuse me.' She took the call in her office, locking the door behind her. 'Hello, this is Crystal speaking.'

'Hi Crystal, this is Adam Fairfax from Aludel Pharma. I'm calling regarding a job opening at our Dandenong branch.'

Aludel Pharma? The name did not ring a bell, but she had submitted an awful lot of applications lately. Her pulse raced out of control. 'Okay, what position was that? Sorry, but I can't remember applying for anything with your company.'

'Because we didn't advertise. I found your CV online. We need a new R&D manager, and your credentials are a good fit for us.'

A management role? 'Oh, um, sounds great.' She took a few deep breaths to calm her nerves.

'When would you be able to come in for an interview?'

'Is tomorrow okay?'

CRYSTAL'S CRUCIBLE

'That'd be great.' Adam gave her all the details she needed before signing off, 'I look forward to meeting you, Dr. Buchanan.'

Crystal's heart leaped into her throat like a startled frog at the sound of Adam Fairfax using her official title. No one ever addressed her so formally. *No one.* But it was more than that. The tone and timbre of his voice were warm and inviting. 'Me too,' she croaked.

Chapter Four

Jade

Jade let her Fitzroy apartment door slam shut and threw her keys at the beige kitchen bench. They slid off and hit the beige, tiled floor where she left them as she collapsed on the beige couch. She slipped her aching feet out of her heels and rubbed them. Work had been worse than normal. After the boss gave her another tardiness warning, a string of shitty customers frequented Jade's checkout, complaining about the rising price of groceries. *Like I have any control over it.* But the fates saved the worst for last. On the tail of an eight-hour shift with five minutes until closing, an elderly lady came through, asking if Jade would mind loading the bags into her trolley. Of course, she obliged, but the old biddy had the nerve to complain about how Jade packed the bags and loaded them into the shopping cart.

CRYSTAL'S CRUCIBLE

'No! You're doing it all wrong, deary,' the woman had snapped. 'Load the heavy items first so you don't crush the bread and fruit. And don't put other items in with meat…' The whole ordeal went on for fifteen minutes, but it felt longer, and none of her colleagues bothered to help when they saw her struggling.

I wish Dieter were home tonight. He had been putting in a lot of late nights at the recording studio, trying to finish his latest album as soon as possible. Reaching into her bag, she retrieved her phone and turned it on for the first time since her lunch break.

There was a message from Crystal: I have a job interview tomorrow! The job sounds A-mazing—wish me luck!

Good for her. Jade meant it—well, mostly. Yet she could not deny the blanket of jealousy smothering her. She typed a quick reply and stretched out on the sofa for a nap. It was no use. Glimpses of her lousy life filled her mind. *I need an escape.* As soon as the thought occurred, she recalled Apollo. Grabbing her purse, she rifled through it for his card, audibly exhaling when she found it. Her fingers were jittery, taking several attempts to type his number correctly.

'Apollo speaking.' His deep voice rattled the cage enclosing her darkest desires.

CRYSTAL'S CRUCIBLE

'Hey, it's Jade here.'

The sound of him sucking in a breath travelled down the phone line. 'Well, hello there gorgeous. I'm glad you called. What can I do for you?'

'I need a hit. Like now.'

'Woah! Are you okay?' His concern touched the hidden depths of her soul in disturbing ways.

'I'm fine! Now can I have the molly?'

Apollo sighed. 'I'm not one to turn down a deal, but I need to know you are okay first, and I'm not convinced. Will you meet me for a drink?'

What harm could one drink do? 'Okay. Where?'

'You pick. What's your favourite local bar?'

'All the good cocktail bars are closed on Tuesdays, so let's go to the pub.' She gave him the directions and arranged to meet in half an hour. When they signed off, Jade's heart was beating out of control. This was not the usual drug deal. She would be spending time with Apollo. Inspecting the state of her armpits, she turned her nose up at the smell. A shower would be essential.

Twenty minutes later, Jade was walking down Brunswick Street in one of her black bodycon dresses and a lethal pair of stilettos. The vintage clothing stores and bric-a-brac shops were closing for the night, but the multitude of cafés and pubs were still drawing a crowd. Fitzroy was buzzing with life on a warm spring night and the aromas of multicultural food filled the air. Reaching the pub with a few minutes to spare, she considered waiting before remembering how eager she sounded on the phone anyway. She entered the pub and headed straight for the bar.

Barry, her favourite bartender, smiled warmly as she pulled up a stool. 'Hi Jade, what can I get ya?'

'Nothing yet. I'm waiting for a friend.'

A moment later he looked up with wide eyes. 'Is that him?'

Turning, Jade gasped at the sight of Apollo in his figure-hugging chinos and another gold shirt, this one revealing a hint of the hairs on his chest. Catching Jade's eye, he grinned and approached.

Barry leaned over the bar and whispered in her ear, 'You didn't mention how hot he'd be.'

With a giggle, she elbowed him before standing to greet Apollo. 'Hi.' Her voice came out soft and breathy.

'It's good to see you again.' Apollo pulled her into his embrace, giving her a whiff of his woody scented cologne.

Jade's toes curled, and she forced herself to break the contact.

'Nice place,' Apollo commented as he sat down and glanced around at all the recycled timber surfaces, his eye lingering on the greenery growing on the far wall. 'Although a tad too hipster for my usual taste.'

Noticing Barry's face droop, Jade laughed. 'Oh dear, I think you may have broken our bartender's heart.'

Apollo looked at Barry and shrugged. 'Sorry, bro, but it was bound to happen. I only have eyes for one person in this place.' He winked at Jade to emphasise his point.

Barry whistled through pursed lips. 'Lucky girl—wins all the good ones. What can I get you both?'

'I'll have a glass of top shelf shiraz,' replied Apollo. 'And I'll cover Jade's drink.'

'What! No—' she began to protest.

'I insist.' His eyes stared sternly into hers, refusing to budge on the matter.

'Okay, fine,' she agreed. 'I'll have a mojito.'

They took their drinks to a private table in the beer garden. Rather than sitting opposite, Apollo settled in beside her. Being on a bench seat

CRYSTAL'S CRUCIBLE

allowed him to get nice and close, robbing Jade of her sanity and some much-needed air.

After a sip of his wine, Apollo scrutinized her. 'You wanna tell me what's going on? Why are you so desperate for my candy[5]?'

'I had a crappy day at work and need to blow off some steam.'

A sly grin tugged at one side of his mouth. 'Can't your boyfriend help?'

She shook her head. 'He's working late tonight.'

'Hmm.' Apollo took another mouthful of shiraz. 'Well I'll do two for forty.'

Jade licked her lips and grasped his muscular thigh. 'Surely you can do a better price for *me*?' She batted her lashes and pressed her chest against his arm.

A guttural groan slipped from his throat. 'Christ, woman. You drive a *hard* bargain. Fine. I'll halve the price. But don't go tellin' anyone how easily I fall for a pretty face.' Once they had made the transaction under the table, he tugged at one of her blue braids. 'You look different without these up in space buns. In a good way, of course.'

---

[5] Street name for MDMA (Ecstasy)

CRYSTAL'S CRUCIBLE

'Um, okay.' She squirmed under his attentive gaze and chugged down the rest of her cocktail.

Leaning closer, he whispered in her ear, 'I'd love to see them sprawled out over my pillow.'

Good Lord!

'Why don't you come back to my place? It'll be a lot more fun to roll *with* me.' His hand slid up her thigh.

Swallowing, Jade suppressed the parts yearning for her to say yes. 'Not gonna happen, sorry. You know I'm in a relationship.'

'Yet here you are, flirting with *me*.'

'For the discount,' she confessed, pulling her bottom lip between her teeth.

Apollo chuckled. 'I'm not stupid, Jade. I know why you were puttin' the moves on me. But I'm not blind either. I can see the desire in your eyes.' His mouth drew close to her ear again. 'I can tell how much you want me to bend you over and fuck that tight little pussy of yours.'

Her panties flooded as his words filled her mind with an array of dirty images. 'It's still a no from me. Thanks for the pills. I need to get going.' Jade sprang to her feet and made a dash for the door before temptation got the better of her.

CRYSTAL'S CRUCIBLE

ಶಿಧ

Crystal

'Please take a seat,' the receptionist gestured toward a row of plush bucket chairs. 'Mr. Fairfax will see you shortly.'

Perching on the edge of one, Crystal studied her surrounds. The lobby resembled something out of a Star Trek movie with the space-aged curves, bright-white walls, and the blue, backlit Aludel logo prominently placed on the front desk. She took a few deep breaths to settle the hurricane in her belly. Her right hand subconsciously fidgeted with the rose-gold swan brooch pinned to her blouse. When she realised what she was doing, she sent a silent prayer to her father: *Wish me luck, Dad.* As she played with the dainty souvenir, memories of him taking her to see *Swan Lake* soothed her.

'Dr. Buchanan?'

Turning toward the smooth, silky voice, her gaze took in the man who had called her name. *Holy moly!* A charcoal business suit accentuated his muscle tone. But it was the handsome face atop his perfect body that caught her attention. The air evacuated her lungs, threatening an asthma attack. Unable to speak, she simply nodded.

Drawing closer, he grinned widely, showing off a mouth full of brilliant pearly whites. 'I'm Adam Fairfax, Division Manager.' He extended his hand once he stood before her.

She rose, entranced by his magnetic chestnut eyes. Slipping her hand into his, she instantly felt the electricity zap through her nerves.

His grip was firm. 'I'm glad you could make it on such short notice.' When Mr. Fairfax released his hold of her, she detected a hint of reluctance, although she might have imagined it.

'Thank you for inviting me, Mr. Fairfax,' she whispered.

'Please, call me Adam. We are meeting in the boardroom. Third on your left.' He tapped a key card against a security panel beside the glass door and held it open for her.

'Thanks,' she whispered as she passed. Several people looked up from their cubicles in the large open-plan office space and smiled at her. When she reached the boardroom, she found it open, and two other men rose to greet her.

Stumbling as her stiletto snagged in the carpet, Crystal cursed herself for trying out new heels on such an important day. Her burning cheeks must have matched the hue of her hair when she tottered through the doorway in front of Adam and the two other men.

Adam caught her, face wiggling in a failed attempt to mask his amusement. 'Please, sit down before you hurt yourself, Dr. Buchanan.'

Part of her wanted to wipe the smirk from the cocky bastard's face, but she pushed 'bitchy Crissy' aside and let him help her into a chair.

'I'd like you to meet two of my associates, Michael Higgins is our Admin and HR Manager, and Greg Marshall oversees Regulatory Affairs at this site.'

Both men reached across the table to greet Crystal. Once they were all seated, Adam opened a file in front of him. Glancing up, he smiled at her, his radiant expression lighting up the room. 'Thanks again for joining us, Dr. Buchanan. Is it okay if we call you Crystal?'

'Yes, of course.' She blushed. 'And it is a pleasure to be here.' *More than you'd know.* Her eyes traversed his gorgeous face, from his full head of mid-length dirty blond hair, parted on the left side, to his chevron moustache and chinstrap beard.

CRYSTAL'S CRUCIBLE

Adam licked his lips and Crystal could have sworn her heart skipped a beat. He cleared his throat. 'So, full disclosure, I read your PhD thesis Crystal, and I was beyond impressed.'

She gaped at him. 'Really?'

'Yes, really. I also spoke to your supervisor and he had nothing but praise for you and your work.' As Adam spoke, his voice was like droplets of rain gliding along glass, and Crystal soon felt herself lulled into a state of serenity.

'I'm glad to hear it. I worried he might have called me a control freak,' Crystal admitted with a chuckle, earning herself a few laughs.

'Tell us a bit more about yourself, Crystal,' prompted Michael. 'What do you like to do with your spare time?'

'Reading mostly. I also love playing chess and listening to jazz music.'

Greg nodded his approval before asking, 'Do you know much about Aludel Pharma?'

'A little. I did some research after Adam rang me yesterday. I know you make a range of pharmaceuticals, although this site focusses on chemotherapy drugs.'

'That's right,' Greg agreed.

CRYSTAL'S CRUCIBLE

'This will be a demanding role,' Michael explained. 'Not only will you need to conduct research, but you will head a department of eleven scientists and technicians. What are you like working in a team?'

She gulped. *Eleven direct reports?* 'Good. I worked well with the other people in my PhD laboratory as well as mentoring the honours students and tutoring undergrads.'

They continued with a series of standard questions about her skills and experience before moving onto some more technical topics. Crystal answered each of them with growing confidence as she came to realise every word she spoke intrigued these men. *They like me! They really like me!*

When the interview concluded, Adam showed her to the front office where he brushed a hand against the small of her back. 'Thanks again, Crystal. I'll call you in the next day or two—regardless of the outcome.' His promise suggested more than a job offer or courtesy call, but she refused to entertain the idea.

Only at night, when alone in her bed, would Crystal let her imagination go on a tour of Sexual Fantasy Land with Adam Fairfax as the guide.

Chapter Five

Adam

Returning to the boardroom, Adam shut the door, threw his jacket over a nearby chair, and rolled up his sleeves. Taking the seat Crystal had vacated, he found it was still warm, and her sweet, musky perfume lingered in the air. 'I like her.' *Understatement of the year.* But he was conscious of divulging the extent of his feelings to the others, especially Michael. 'She has a brilliant mind and I think she would gel well with the others. What do you guys think?'

'I agree,' replied Greg with a big dumb grin on his face.

'Hmm.' Michael tapped his pen against the table. 'I worry about her lack of work experience, especially in a management role. But other than that, she's good.'

CRYSTAL'S CRUCIBLE

Adam reached across the table to grab his notes. 'We've met our minimum quota of candidates for interviews, so head office should be happy. Can we put in our votes and make the call? I'm keen to fill this position ASAP.'

'I say we choose the sexy redhead,' suggested Greg.

'I can't believe you said that, in front of Michael no less,' chided Adam with a laugh.

Michael sighed. 'I think Crystal is the best option. We need the research skills more than the management experience right now. I hope we won't be looking at any sexual harassment charges in the future if we do hire her.' He glared at Greg.

'Woah, man!' Greg threw his hands up in surrender. 'I would never! Besides, I love my dear wife. I think you'll have more trouble with the boss man. Did you see the way Adam was drooling over her?'

'Gee, thanks mate. Throw me under the next tram that passes by, why don't you?' Adam hissed.

Greg's eyes bugged out. 'Christ! I was only joking.'

Michael narrowed his eyes toward Adam. 'Ultimately, the decision is yours, but if you do pick Crystal, I recommend keeping your dick in your pants and refreshing yourself on the Company's Conflict of Interest Policy.'

'You have nothing to worry about,' Adam lied. 'Now scoot, both of you. I need some quiet time to think.'

As soon as they left, Adam hunched over the table and massaged his aching temples. His jaw still hurt from all the bogus smiles he had given the interviewees. *At least I didn't need to fake it with Crystal. But Good God, that woman is something else!* As much as he wanted to give her the job then and there, he was determined to do the right thing, so he worked through his checklist, marking each candidate against the selection criteria. The fates must have been smiling down on him because Crystal still came out the clear winner. Remembering what Michael said, Adam's eyes turned heavenward. *Or maybe this is a curse, and you are laughing at me.* He retrieved Crystal's contact details along with his work mobile and dialled the number.

The tone sounded three times before she answered. 'Hello, Crystal speaking.'

'Hi Crystal, this is Adam Fairfax. I hope I haven't caught you at a bad time.'

She inhaled deeply. 'No, not at all.'

CRYSTAL'S CRUCIBLE

Reclining in the high-back chair, Adam basked in the sound of Crystal's sweet voice. He racked his brain for an excuse to keep her talking more and blurted, 'So, uh, what did you think of Aludel?' *Jesus! That was lame.* He cringed.

'Oh, I think it looks like a great place to work.'

'I was hoping you'd say as much because I'd like to offer you the job.'

'Really?' Her excitement spread across the phone line like a contagion, infecting Adam with her mirth. 'I would absolutely love to accept your offer.'

Joy soon turned to desire, and Adam found himself sporting a full hard-on. *Yep, this is going to be torture.* 'Excellent! How soon can you start?'

'Ah, Friday, if that's okay? I need tomorrow to organise a few things.'

'Perfect. We can get your orientation out of the way and you'll be able to hit the ground running on Monday.' It would have been more sensible to ask her to start next week, but Adam was keen to get things moving. And a perverted part of him wanted to see her plump lips and silky hair sooner rather than later.

'What time do you want me?'

CRYSTAL'S CRUCIBLE

Spluttering, Adam grabbed his glass of water from the table and took a sip of water to soothe his throat. 'Excuse me?'

'What time should I start on Friday?'

'Oh right, eight-thirty is your normal start, but is nine okay for Friday?' he rasped before taking another sip of water.

'Yep, that's fine. I'll see you then.'

'Great. Oh, and Crystal?'

'Yes, Adam?'

'You'll need to bring long pants and enclosed shoes to change into when entering the lab. Save the skirts and kitten heels for the office.' *Christ! I must sound like a massive sleaze!*

She laughed. 'Yes, of course. I haven't forgotten all the safety stuff I learnt at uni.'

At least she did not take offense. 'Good to know. See you Friday.'

The energy-saving switch for the cooling must have timed out because the air in the room was stifling when Adam signed off. Peeling his sweaty arms and neck from the vinyl seat, he gathered his stuff and headed back to his own office. Thoughts of running his fingers through long, red hair plagued his mind, along with images of caressing soft, ivory coloured skin. He collapsed into his chair, determined to shut off the inappropriate thoughts and get some work done.

He glanced at the mountain of documents stacked beside his overflowing IN tray and groaned. When he powered his computer back on, he also found a backlog of emails waiting for him. Methodically, he sorted through his correspondence and paperwork, and prioritised the urgent tasks. By the time he finished, his stomach was grumbling, and sunset coloured the horizon, typical for the end of Adam's workday. Because the lights were off in the main office, he used the torch on his phone to navigate the space, pushing in the stray chairs on his way out.

༄༅

Crystal

Crystal stepped from her rose-gold Subaru into the employee parking area of Aludel Pharma. She took a moment to savour her first time doing so and to come to terms with her new position. *Goodbye academia, hello corporate world!* Spinifex grasses and various shrubs covered in dainty flowers in a rainbow of colours, from blazing red through to vivid violet, filled the garden beds lining the path to the front office. She noticed a couple of benches that would be ideal for tea breaks when the weather allowed. Crossing her fingers, she hoped the sun continued shining for the rest of the day.

'Hi Crystal! Welcome to Aludel,' enthused the receptionist with a bright smile. The African woman's bubbly personality set her at ease.

Crystal glanced at the woman's name tag. 'Hi Jessica, thank you.'

'I popped your name up on the whiteboard there.' Jessica pointed to the board in question. 'You will need to sign-in using the magnet I put next to your name whenever you come on site, and out again when you leave, okay?'

Nodding, Crystal did so.

'I'll let Mr. Fairfax know you have arrived.' Jessica picked up her desk phone and summoned Adam.

Crystal's pulse quickened from the mere mention of his name; her heart pounding when he appeared minutes later.

He was in another figure-hugging business suit, navy blue this time. A wide grin graced his gorgeous features as he stepped forward to shake her hand. 'Hi Crystal, welcome to the team.'

CRYSTAL'S CRUCIBLE

'Thank you, Adam.'

Michael greeted her next. 'Here is your key card and instructions for using the alarm system.' He handed her a white plastic card on a plain black lanyard along with a sheet of paper.

'Michael is your tour guide,' Adam explained. 'Unfortunately, I'm tied up with the IP team all day.'

'IP?' Crystal inquired, trying her best to hide the disappointment punching her in the gut.

'Intellectual Property. They are the guys who look after our patent applications.'

'Right, okay.' Crystal did not know much about patents, but she planned to Google everything about them first chance she got.

As they entered the main office space, Adam's hand found purchase on the small of her back. This time his touch was firmer, electrifying her entire nervous system. His head tilted toward her ear. 'I'm sorry I can't be your tour guide. But I hope to get more time with you next week. I'll leave you in Michael's capable hands for now, okay?'

'Okay.' She smiled up at him, catching his loitering gaze a moment before he disappeared into the boardroom.

CRYSTAL'S CRUCIBLE

Crystal spent the next hour walking through the building and meeting everyone, from the admin and finance staff to the quality department. It was overwhelming and Crystal doubted she would remember most people's names. When they reached the research and development labs, the spacious rooms—all fully equipped with state-of-the-art analytical machines and plenty of quality glassware—filled her with awe. She even had her own fume hood and bench space to work at when she wanted to test her theories.

A short, chubby Indian man looked up from the sink and smiled. 'You must be Crystal.' He took her hand in a vigorous shake. 'I'm Denzel, the analytical lab assistant. I mostly help Hans over there, but if anyone else needs something, I pitch in.'

At the mention of his name, the tall, skinny ginger looked up from his work at the High-Performance Liquid Chromatography (HPLC) machine and grinned. 'Hey boss lady, most people call me Han Solo, or just Solo. Denzel here is an absolute champ. And that sexy Greek man over there is Markos, although most of us call him Mono—short for Monotone.' He pointed to a tall,

CRYSTAL'S CRUCIBLE

handsome man in a lab coat who looked no older than thirty.

Crystal's brows perked up. 'Why?'

'You'll get it as soon as you hear the man talk. Oh, and he only wears shades of brown.'

'Markos is our Formulation Chemist,' explained Michael who went on to introduce everyone else in the labs and attached offices. Most of them were warm and welcoming with the exception of Katrina, the senior drug discovery scientist whose thick-rimmed cat-eye glasses looked ready to take flight from her frosty countenance.

'How about we take a breather?' Michael suggested as they reached the breakroom. 'I'll meet you back here in fifteen?'

'Okay.' A cursory glance through the window ruined Crystal's hopes for an outside tea break as she watched the rain drizzle down the glass. She grabbed her favourite cup and a box of peppermint tea from her office before returning to the empty kitchen. After preparing her drink, she sat down to enjoy a moment of peace.

'Nice cup.' A man's baritone voice drew her attention. He gestured toward her teacup which depicted the periodic table of elements.

'Thanks. It was a high school graduation gift from Mum.' *In one of her rare sober moments.* 'Markos, right?' His name was one of the few that stuck in her mind.

'I see you have a good memory to go with the big brain I've been hearing about.' He gave her a genuine smile, which was helpful because there was no inflection in his monotone voice. His eyes remained fixed on her for an uncomfortable moment.

Feeling her face flush, she blurted, 'You should know, I'm not interested in dating men.'

He arched a brow and filled the air with awkward silence.

Oops! Does he think I'm a lesbian now? Not that it matters, in fact it could be a convenient way of hiding the truth...

The tension snapped with the sound of his deep laugh. 'It's okay Crystal, I'm not trying to chat you up here. But I would like to be friends. I rarely meet an intellectual equal.'

Her complexion must have turned an even brighter shade of red. 'I'm sorry for misreading your intentions—'

CRYSTAL'S CRUCIBLE

'Don't worry about it. You caught me staring, which was terribly rude, I'm sorry. It's just, I feel like I've seen you somewhere before.'

'Oh, well I'm quite certain I'd remember if we had met. I'm actually terrible with most names, but I never forget a face.'

'Fair enough.' He made himself a coffee and sat down next to her. 'Tell me about yourself, Crystal.' They continued conversing for the remainder of their break, discussing safe topics like their hobbies and the joys of Melbourne weather.

After morning tea, Michael escorted Crystal back to her office where he gave her a pile of paperwork and helped set up her computer. 'Feel free to personalise your desktop. Everyone here does and I'm sure I don't need to tell you what images are inappropriate for the workplace.'

Crystal laughed. 'You mean to say there are some here who don't get that?'

He bit his lip a moment. 'You might want to keep an eye on Hans and Peter is all I'm saying.'

She gaped at him. 'Okay, noted.'

Michael left her to settle in and work through her e-learning modules. Reaching her door, he turned back with a final word of advice: 'Please make sure you take a lunch break at some point.'

Chapter Six

Crystal

The calendar alert Crystal had set popped up to tell her it was lunchtime. Unsure of the kitchen facilities available, Crystal had played it safe and packed a sandwich which she retrieved from her chiller bag and took to the breakroom. After setting an alarm to ensure she did not exceed her allocated time, she unwrapped her food and took a small bite. Being later in the day, she had the room to herself, which suited her fine after all the introductions she had struggled through.

'Hi Crystal.' Adam's silky voice broke her tranquil reverie.

She lifted her gaze, bracing herself for the inevitable onslaught of emotions.

He paused in the doorway. 'Mind if I join you?'

CRYSTAL'S CRUCIBLE

Bam! The moment her eyes met his, her stomach churned and her skin sizzled. 'Not at all. Please do.' Her voice was barely more than a squeak. Reaching for her water bottle, she guzzled down the refreshing liquid.

Adam crossed the room in large strides, bringing him to the bench behind Crystal. He placed a container of leftovers in the microwave, unleashing the unmistakable aroma of green curry into the air. 'I see you opted for the pants and sensible shoes today.'

Swivelling in her chair, she caught his gaze travelling along her legs, and staring at them longer than one would consider polite.

Is he checking me out? 'I figured I'd spend time in the labs and decided it would be easier this way.'

'Hmm, it's a pity. I did like those heels.'

Almost choking at the implication, Crystal covered her reaction with a snort of laughter. 'You mean you liked seeing me make a fool of myself in them. That was my first time wearing stilettos. I normally opt for something thicker if I wear heels at all.'

'I guess I'm busted.' He winked at her before taking his meal from the beeping microwave. When he sat next to her, he angled his whole body toward her. 'How are you finding everything so far?'

'Good. Although, if I'm honest, it's been a bit daunting.'

'I'm sure you'll do fine. I have every confidence in you, Crystal. That's why I hired you.' His teeth sparkled as he grinned.

Feeling the warmth of her blushing cheeks, she averted her eyes, and her half-eaten sandwich became the most fascinating thing in the world. 'Thank you,' she whispered.

'I couldn't help but notice the Impreza you rocked up in this morning. You have good taste in cars.'

A laugh tumbled from her belly. 'I bought that because it is my favourite colour. I am actually clueless when it comes to vehicles.'

Adam laughed with her. 'Well colour is an important factor when choosing your ride. I also picked one in my favourite colour.'

'Which is?'

'Ultramarine blue.'

Crystal's jaw dropped. 'That sexy blue sports car out there is yours?'

He nodded. 'You like my BRZ huh?'

CRYSTAL'S CRUCIBLE

'I may be a dunce when it comes to automobiles, but that car's sleek curves even turned me on.' She blurted out the confession before realising her poor choice of words and blushed when hearing herself.

A fire blazed in his eyes, roasting his chestnut orbs as he leaned forward. 'Is that so?'

Hands twitching, Crystal tugged at a strand of her hair and twirled it between her fingers. 'Well… um… figuratively speaking. So… are you into cars in a big way?'

'I'm not what you'd call a complete rev-head, but I do appreciate luxury models and I enjoy watching the rally cars. My biggest passion outside of work is tennis, although, like you, I also enjoy playing chess.'

Her eyes widened. 'How did you know I like chess?'

'You mentioned it in your interview.'
And he remembered. 'Oh right.'

'I'd love to challenge you to a game some time.'

The opportunity to spend time with Adam outside of work was *extremely* tempting. 'I don't know. Your offer presents me with a predicament.'

He cocked his right brow. 'How so?'

'I fear turning you down might offend you, but if we play, my victory could upset you even more.'

Adam burst out laughing. 'You seem sure of yourself.'

'Just stating facts. I was the best player in the university league. Undefeated for the last three years.'

This time Adam gawked. 'That good huh? Well, I'd love to see you in action. And you needn't worry about me. My ego's not so fragile.'

'Okay, fine. I accept your challenge.'

He rewarded her with another breathtaking smile. 'Excellent.'

They resumed eating, filling the room with a comfortable silence while Crystal chanced the odd glance. Thanks to her eidetic memory, she had already committed his face to mind, but there was nothing like basking in his beauty firsthand. When her watch chimed, she scrunched her rubbish into a ball and pushed her chair back. 'My time's up. Back to work.'

'Wait!' His eyes darted from her face to her watch and back again. 'You set a timer for your lunch break?' he asked with an incredulous tone.

CRYSTAL'S CRUCIBLE

She nodded, unable to speak because his stare acted like a vice on her voice box.

'I'm impressed by your work ethic Crystal, but please relax. This is your first day.'

Is he testing me? She took a deep breath. 'I like to be punctual and since I'm back on the clock, I should be returning to work.'

'Punctuality is good. But please, don't rush back to your desk yet. Keep me company while I finish my lunch.'

'Um.' She bit her lip.

'If it helps, you can think of this as a work meeting.'

What is he playing at? 'Okay.' Her eyes locked with his for several long seconds as she searched his soul. *Is my crush that obvious? Is he toying with me? I can't imagine he'd want me. There's no way a nerd like me would be his type. Besides, he is my boss, for crying out loud. It could never happen.*

Adam chowed down on the last of the spicy Thai curry that was mild in comparison to their heated gazes.

A knock at the door startled Crystal, propelling her out of her chair. 'Oh, hi Markos.'

Markos tilted his head, regarding Adam with narrowed eyes. 'I hope I'm not interrupting anything.'

'Of course not.' Crystal threw her rubbish in the bin. 'Are you ready to show me the lab procedure manuals?'

'Yes, are *you* ready?'

'Absolutely.' Crystal followed him.

'I must say,' Markos mused as they marched beside each other. 'I was surprised to see Adam eating lunch in the breakroom.'

'Why?'

'Because Adam always eats alone at his desk or goes out for business lunches.' Markos shrugged. 'I'm sure it's nothing.'

I'm sure Markos is right. But a small part of her wanted him to be wrong.

ಹಲ

Crystal

The next best thing to fish and chips on the beach is dining à la carte at a seafood restaurant with a view of the ocean, which is how Crystal chose to celebrate her new job with her best friend, her sister, and sister's boyfriend.

'Pity about the storm.' Esme sighed as she picked up the menu. 'It would have been nice to sit outside with some takeaway.'

'Cheaper too,' complained Jade. 'I can't afford any of this shit.'

Crystal glared at Jade. 'You forgot your profanity filter.'

Dieter laughed. 'You're forgetting your sister has *no* filter.' He turned to Jade. 'Don't worry, *Liebling*, I'll cover you.'

Jade grinned at Dieter. 'Thanks, babe.' She pecked him on the lips. 'You're the best.'

Crystal's heart melted at the scene before her. Their relationship was beautiful, the stuff of romance novels, and a true story of love at first sight that started five years ago when Dieter was touring for his debut album.

'Maybe next time Crissy can shout us with her hefty pay cheque.' Jade offered Crystal a toothy grin.

Crashing back to Earth, Crystal rolled her eyes. 'You'll be waiting a while. Turns out I get paid monthly and you know my priority is to move out of Mum's, especially now she's dating that Angry Anderson wannabe.'

'Oh yeah, what did you say the loser's name was?'

'Diesel.'

'I wish I could have seen your face when he walked into the kitchen in his birthday suit,' Jade teased. 'Your expression would have been priceless.'

A chill travelled down her spine as images of inked skin filled her mind. *Ick! The hazards of photo recall.* 'Thanks for the reminder, sis.'

'Anytime, Pumpkin.'

A waiter approached the table and took their orders, prompting a welcome change of subject. Once he finished pouring their glasses of water, Esme asked, 'How was your first day of work? What's the place like?'

'Awesome and incredible. You should see the instrumentation they have there!'

'Oh Gawd, please don't start with all that tech speak. You'll bore half of us to sleep,' Jade jibed. 'Tell us the juicy stuff. Like—are there any hot guys working there?'

Her rosy cheeks blossomed as Crystal bit down hard on her bottom lip.

CRYSTAL'S CRUCIBLE

'Oh my God, there totally is!' Esme cried. 'Now you *have* to tell us!'

'There is one man,' Crystal admitted.

Jade threw her arms up in frustration. 'Bloody hell, woman, getting details out of you is like pulling coherent thoughts from Mum when she's on the juice. Who's the hottie?'

Dieter slouched back in his chair, stifling a laugh.

'Adam Fairfax, my boss. He is nearly forty, but he doesn't look his age. He is so fit!'

'Ooh, scandalous!' Esme clapped her hands together, bringing them up to her lips.

Jade exhaled her exasperation. 'Yet another impossible crush. What's with you lusting after older men you can't have? How many uni professors did you have the hots for?'

'Four by my count,' confirmed Esme.

'Being out of reach is the whole point,' Crystal explained. 'That way I'll never end up in an intimate situation with them.'

'Right. The whole sex phobia thing.' Jade's timing could not have been more awkward because the waiter chose that moment to deliver their drinks, interrupting their conversation by clearing his throat. He placed a lemonade in front of Crystal, while everyone else got a glass of champagne.

Her sister dove straight back into the topic when the waiter left. 'You know the best way to combat fears is to face them. Just go out with some random guy and get laid already. You've even got a Tinder profile now, which is like the perfect opportunity.'

'It's not that easy,' Crystal protested.

'Yes. It. Is,' Jade countered.

Dieter clamped a hand on Jade's shoulder. 'Stop pushing her, Jade. Crissy needs to work out her issues in her own time. Now why don't we toast to her employment success?' He lifted his drink.

'Thank you, Dieter.' Crystal raised her own glass, clinking it with each of theirs. As the evening progressed, their conversation lightened, and Crystal was able to relax. It was only when she slipped into bed that her thoughts returned to Adam. Given his recent behaviour, Crystal wondered if he was a safe obsession to have after all.

Chapter Seven

Jade

DJ Dieteronimo's music enveloped Jade, the bass pulsing up through the floor and into her veins, compelling her body to move. She loved watching him lose himself to the magic he created. As the strobe lights flashed around her, she flung herself about amidst the crowd. Several guys approached her, but she only let the regulars get close. They knew a dirty dance was all they would be getting from her.

Halfway through the second hour of her boyfriend's set, she caught a glimpse of Sargon watching her from his balcony, a lecherous grin on his face. She blew him a kiss, which he caught and dropped inside his pants. Laughing, she feigned shock and turned to see another man's gaze fixed on her. Apollo casually reclined against the mezzanine bar, a beer in hand.

CRYSTAL'S CRUCIBLE

Her skin tingled at the sight of him as she recalled the sound of his deep, seductive voice and all the filthy things he had said. It had taken every ounce of her willpower to distance herself from him—not only because she was desperate for that sweet, chemical release—but because she did not trust herself to behave if he so much as touched her again.

Narrowing his eyes on something behind Jade, Apollo moved to the railing.

Hands encircled Jade's hips, bringing her back into contact with a wall of hard muscles. 'Hey, princess.' Tony's voice purred into her ear. He was another regular and one of Dieter's closest friends.

Tucking her head into the crook of his neck, Jade smiled up at him. 'Hey you.' She swayed in time with Tony. When she looked back at Apollo, the heat in his eyes intensified. Imagining Tony's arms were Apollo's, she kneaded his pelvis with her backside.

'Christ, woman!' Tony rasped. 'You're killing me here. Did Dieter get you in the mood and leave you hanging?'

'Hmm, something like that.'

'You wanna return the favour and give him a show?'

CRYSTAL'S CRUCIBLE

'Hell yes!' Jade grabbed his right hand and brought it up to her breast, letting the fingers of his other hand skirt around her inner thigh.

'Shouldn't we face the DJ booth to give him a better view?'

'Not yet.' Seeing the way Apollo gawked at her, she turned on the smoulder. Tony pressed his lips to her neck and Jade almost exploded. 'I need to come.'

'Fuck!' Tony rasped. 'I don't think—'

Jade shoved his left hand between her legs, grinding his thumb against her clit. 'Rub me here for a bit.' She glanced at Apollo once more before closing her eyes. The tension mounted in her core until she unravelled in Tony's arms. Flicking her heavy lids open, she noticed Apollo had left. After taking a deep breath, she spun to face her friend, simpering at his wide-eyed expression. 'Thanks, I needed that.' A knot twisted in her gut when she found the massive tent in Tony's pants. Biting her lip, she looked up at him. 'You want me to return the favour?'

Tony shook his head. 'I'd rather avoid Dieter's wrath. I'll go deal with it myself.'

'I'm so sorry.'

CRYSTAL'S CRUCIBLE

'Hey, don't worry about it. I love lending a hand.' He winked at her before dashing off to the bathroom.

Finding herself alone on the dance floor, Jade took a moment to gather her thoughts and focus on her surrounds. Dieter had finished, replaced by one of the other house DJs, so she scanned the room and discovered him talking to Apollo up on the VIP balcony. *Oh good, he's getting our sweets*[6].

Dieter joined her a few minutes later, wrapping her in his firm embrace and bringing his mouth to her ear. 'Apollo gave me a good deal, so I stocked up.' He snuck two pills into her palm.

Glancing up at Apollo over Dieter's shoulder, she mouthed, 'thank you.'

He raised his drink to her and leered.

After popping the pills, she smiled at Dieter. 'I'm glad he didn't take my rejection to heart.'

'Indeed.' Dieter's hand glided over her backside, inching the hem of her dress enough to slip inside her damp panties. One side of his mouth curled upwards. 'Feels like Tony took good care of you.'

'Mm, only a little. I'm still exceptionally horny.'

---

[6] Street name for MDMA (Ecstasy)

CRYSTAL'S CRUCIBLE

'We should do something about that.' Dieter seized her hand and led her up to one of the private booths in the VIP lounge. He yanked the curtains closed, dropped his pants around his ankles and pulled her into his lap as he sat on the plush, velvet sofa.

Their mouths clashed together, tongues duelling for supremacy as they mauled each other's faces. Jade unbuttoned Dieter's boxer shorts, allowing his erection to spring free. Pushing aside the thin gusset of her lace G-string, she took him between her slick folds and threw her head back to groan as he thrust inside her.

'*Gott, ich liebe dich*[7],' Dieter gasped as she began to ride him.

She touched her forehead to his. 'I love you too, baby.' With one hand gripping his shoulder, she ran the other through his short, spiky hair and lost herself in the depths of his oceanic eyes.

ೞಞ

---

[7] God, I love you

CRYSTAL'S CRUCIBLE

Crystal

Reaching the end of her quiz, Crystal clicked Submit. She sent the certificate to the printer and glanced up to see Adam knocking on her glass door. Waving him in, she removed her reading glasses and smiled. 'Hi, Adam. How was your weekend?'

'Good thanks, and yours?'

Crystal shrugged. 'Okay I guess.'

He circled the desk to peek at her work and whistled. 'I see you are progressing well with your induction program.' His proximity and the scent of his fancy cologne kicked her nerves into overdrive.

'Thanks.' Subconsciously slipping a temple tip of her glasses between her teeth, she chewed on the plastic. When Adam's gaze shifted to her lips, she realised what she was doing and dropped them. 'So… uh… what can I do for you?'

He perched himself on the edge of her desk. 'I thought you might like to take your lunch break now.'

She sucked in a breath. *Is he inviting me to dine with him?* 'I was planning to eat later—'

CRYSTAL'S CRUCIBLE

'I figured you might, but now would be a good time to bond with some of your team members.'

A lead weight dropped in her gut. *That'll teach you for getting your hopes up!* 'Oh, right.' She laughed nervously. 'Here I thought you were simply trying to get another lunch date with me.' *Oh Lord! I need to stop putting my feet near my stupid mouth.*

Mirth lit up Adam's face. 'Sorry to disappoint, but I am heading out with the IP guys.'

'They still here?'

Frowning, Adam nodded. 'There's some serious stuff going down with our latest patent application. I'll be needing your help with it soon, but I want you to get through your training first.'

'Okay.' Closing her internet browser brought her back to her neat and tidy desktop.

'Nice photo.' Adam's head gestured toward the image of the two black waterfowl on her screen. 'I love swans. They are such loyal creatures. Did you know they mate for life?'

'So I've heard, and I love them too. I took this photo in the Botanic Gardens recently.'

Adam rose and headed for the door. 'Well, enjoy your lunch.'

CRYSTAL'S CRUCIBLE

Crystal made her way to the breakroom, finding Denzel and Hans seated at the large, white table. 'Hi guys.' Smiling warmly, they both greeted her. After reheating some left-over pasta, she joined them. 'How's everything going in the lab?'

'Peachy,' replied Hans. 'How are you settling in?'

'Good. Powering through the e-learning. I should finish in record time.'

'That's great news. It'll be good to see you in the labs soon.' The phone in front of Hans lit up, playing the Star Wars Cantina theme. 'Yo, sup Timmy?'

Her brows shot up at the way Hans greeted his supervisor.

'No probs man. I'll get on it first thing after lunch.' He disconnected the call and explained the tests Timothy needed.

'I take it you like Star Wars?' Crystal inquired.

'Yep, love that shi… stuff. What about you?'

'I suppose you could call me a fan. The original trilogy were Dad's favourite movies, so my sister and I thrashed them when we were kids. Jade even styles her hair a bit like Princess Leia.'

CRYSTAL'S CRUCIBLE

'Sweet!' Hans beamed. 'You and your sister should join the rest of us at the cinema release for Episode IX. We're all dressing up.'

'Sounds like fun. Are you going too, Denzel?'

'You better believe it. I already have my jedi costume organised.'

'I still think you should go as Yoda,' insisted Hans. 'You're like the perfect height.'

Denzel laughed. 'I'm not that short! Yoda is barely over two feet tall. You know, with your red hair Crystal, you could go as Mara Jade.'

'Who?'

'Mara Jade, the wife of Luke Skywalker.'

Hans sighed. 'She's not canon, Denz.'

'So? What's wrong with going as an expanded universe character?'

Grinning, Crystal dug into her food while watching the guys debate the finer details of Star Wars and cosplay etiquette.

'What do you think, Crystal?' Denzel asked as they both turned to her.

'I agree with Hans. Official events warrant canon costumes. But I'll keep Mara Jade in mind next time I go to Supanova.'

Both men gaped at her. 'You go to pop culture cons?'

CRYSTAL'S CRUCIBLE

'My bestie drags me along to a bunch of them, but yeah, I enjoy them for the most part.'

'That is so-o rad!' Hans spent the rest of their lunch break drilling her on all the nerdy things she liked.

It was heart-warming to be amongst her tribe. Revived by her break, Crystal returned to her office with a spring in her step and the Cantina band lodged in her brain.

Chapter Eight

Crystal

Slamming on the brakes, Crystal honked at the jerk in the SUV who cut her off and scowled at the impatient bastard behind her who blared his horn at her for stopping. Turning the windscreen wipers to dramatic mode, she continued crawling home through the grid-locked traffic. Two days into December and summer was yet to make an appearance. *Maybe this rain washed away everyone's road sense.*

Sirens started up behind her, forcing everyone in her lane to merge left as two police cars and an ambulance whizzed by. She sighed. *Nothing like a downpour to bring out the crazies.* While she edged forward at an average speed of ten kilometres per hour[8], her mind drifted back to

---

[8] 10km/hr = 6.2 miles per hour

work. Adam had still been there when she left, explaining he preferred working late because it was his most productive time. Given what peak hour was like on these roads, she was beginning to see numerous advantages to staying back at the office for an extra hour or two. She wondered what Adam was doing. *Is he still busy in the boardroom with the IP guys? Or is he sitting alone at his desk?* She had not yet seen the inside of his office. It was one of the few rooms with a solid wood door and the reflective windows only provided a view for those inside.

The lights turned red, giving her a split second to stop microns short of the line. Tyres screeched. *Crunch!* Crystal jolted forward and her chest clenched as the impact propelled her car into the intersection. *What happened?* She took a deep breath and glanced in her rear-view mirror, gasping when she noticed the crumpled bumper of the ute behind her.

A man with long hair, ripped jeans, and a flannelette shirt jumped out of the vehicle, slamming the door before storming toward her. He pounded against her window.

After another deep breath, she lowered the glass barrier protecting her from untold wrath.

CRYSTAL'S CRUCIBLE

'What the hell is wrong with you, ya stupid c**t!'

'*Excuse me?* There is no need for such language!'

'Piss off, bitch! Now give me ya goddamned number so I can sort out the insurance.'

The thought of giving her number to such a horrid man turned her stomach, but the law gave her no choice. They exchanged contact details before he left in a huff.

She was about to move again when another man approached her, this one far more respectable looking in a high-vis tradesman's uniform. 'Excuse me miss, but I wanted to let you know I saw the whole incident. That guy was clearly at fault and I'd be happy to vouch for you as a witness.' He introduced himself as Trevor and gave her his phone number and registration plate.

'Thank you so much, Trevor. You have restored my faith in humanity.'

The sun was setting by the time Crystal got home from reporting the accident at the police station and dropping her car off at a crash repairer. She paid the taxi driver and ambled up the path to her house. The flicker of the television in the living room was the only light showing from the street. A groan slipped out. *Looks like Mum is home, which means that creep might be with her.*

Crystal attempted to sneak in through the front door.

'Crissy, *darrrlll*, is that (hiccup) you?'

Damnit! 'Yes, Mum.'

'Come 'ere would ya?'

She strode up the hall and into the living room, glaring at the drunk skunk who sprawled herself out all over the sofa. '*What?*'

'Where you been? I'm starvin'!'

'I was in a car accident.'

'Ah shit! Is the car okay?' She sat upright.

Inhaling deeply, Crystal clenched her fists. 'I'm fine, Mum. Thanks for asking.'

'Well, I can see *you're* okay.'

'The car got pretty smashed up. It is out of commission for a few days. Where's that man of yours? I figured you'd be with him.'

'Who, Diesel? He's old news. Fairweather friend and all that jazz. Speaking of which, why don't we go out to a jazz club tonight? It's been ages.'

Crystal collapsed into one of the mint green suede armchairs and massaged her tense shoulders.

CRYSTAL'S CRUCIBLE

'Hmm, let me think about this… That'd be a big, resounding *No*!'

'Why not?'

'Are you kidding me? I crashed my car tonight for starters. Oh, and it's a Monday night. Nothing is open.'

'Bummer! We should make plans to do it soon though.'

Feeling her stomach rumble, Crystal grabbed her phone. 'I thought you were hungry? I'm ordering pizza.'

'Mm, sounds good,' Judy agreed.

After feeding and bathing Judy, Crystal retired to her room. She slipped into a clean cotton nightgown, peeled back the crisp linen, and climbed into bed. When her head hit the pillow, she exhaled her relief. *What a night!* Closing her eyes, she pictured Adam and realised transport would be an issue. *Shoot!* Without thinking, she picked up her mobile and dialled Adam's number.

'Hello?' His voice was groggy.

'Adam? Oops! Sorry if I woke you.'

'Crystal?' Adam's tone switched to high alert. 'Are you okay?'

'Um… yeah, I should have called in the morning. I'll let you get back to sleep.'

CRYSTAL'S CRUCIBLE

'What's going on, Crystal?'

She sighed. 'I crashed my car on the way home tonight.'

'*Oh hell!* Are you okay? What happened?'

'Yes, I'm fine. The rain was bucketing down, so naturally the roads were insane. Anyway, long story short, an arsehole in a ute rear-ended me. The fucker even tried to pin the blame on me.'

A chuckle drifted across the phone line, reminding Crystal of feathers floating on the breeze. Infected by his mirth, she suppressed her own laughter, instead focussing on his soft voice, letting it calm her. 'What's so funny?'

Adam cleared his throat. 'Oh gosh! Sorry, Crystal, I'm not used to hearing you cuss. Please promise me you're okay?'

Her cheeks flamed. 'I'm fine, I swear. It's just…'

'Yes?'

'My car is in the shop for a while and without it, getting to work is much harder; so—'

'It's okay, Crystal, I can give you a lift. You live in St. Kilda, right? That's not far out of my way.'

CRYSTAL'S CRUCIBLE

He remembers where I live? 'Wow, um… you're very generous, but I can manage with public transport. I might need to start later if that's okay?'

'Don't be ridiculous. I live in Brighton, so it's no trouble at all.'

Crystal wrestled with the idea. The thought of spending more time alone with Adam stirred her most primal urges, but it also terrified her. *What if I give away how I feel and make a fool of myself?*

'Crystal? You still there?'

'Yeah, I'm here. Just thinking about your offer.'

'Hmm, do I make you nervous?'

'A bit,' she admitted.

'It's okay, I promise I won't bite.'

She imagined Adam's perfect teeth nipping at her skin and a fire flared in her core. Laughing, she resisted the urge to send her fingers south *before* signing off. 'Well, if you promise to behave, I'll accept the ride.'

৩০

Adam

CRYSTAL'S CRUCIBLE

Did I really offer Crystal a lift to work? What the hell was I thinking? After returning his phone to its charger, Adam settled down in bed again. He was hard as a rock. Hearing Crystal talk while he was laying naked between the soft cotton sheets was almost too much to bear. Her voice was like the contented purr of a kitten. With a firm grip on his cock, he closed his eyes and pictured her: plump red lips, hazel coloured doe eyes, and smooth skin. *God, what I'd give to have her here with me now!* He moaned at the thought of her hair spreading across his pillow like a vibrant sunset. Visions of sinking deep inside her brought him over the edge and his whole body spasmed, releasing days of pent-up frustration. Exhaling a gust of breath, he savoured the fleeting moment of bliss.

When his heart rate settled, he grabbed the tissues and cleaned up. He tried getting back to sleep, but Crystal continued to invade his thoughts, bringing on another semi. *Bloody hell!* If he could not stop lusting after her when she was *not* there, how was he going to cope when he got her alone in his car? *Why did I promise her I would behave?*

Adam had a strong suspicion his desires were mutual. He was not oblivious to his effect on women, although he usually paid them no heed unless he was looking for a quick fix. And the office was not somewhere he had ever considered seeking such a distraction, much to the disappointment of a few ladies in admin. *What was that old saying? Don't shit where you eat.* But Crystal was *impossible* to ignore. From the moment their eyes locked, he had developed a severe case of tunnel vision in her presence. Then she literally fell into his arms, forever imprinting her scent and the feel of her milky skin on his senses.

The last woman to leave such a strong impression had been Lucinda. Shocked by the realisation, he jack-knifed in bed. The memory of his ex-wife's betrayal was more effective than a cold shower. With too many disturbing thoughts keeping the elusive Sandman at bay, he decided to get up and channel his energy into work. He threw on a pair of track pants and headed into his study.

A backlog of emails would keep him occupied for as long as it took for exhaustion to overwhelm him. The first few were simple matters to address, so he immediately replied. He flagged the more complicated issues for follow up the next day. After digging through the first page of corporate communication, he scrolled to a personal email. It was from his nephew, Jackson. The nine-year-old boy was wearing his softball uniform and beaming with pride as he held up a trophy. Adam read the following text:

> *Hi Uncle Adam! Look- I won the Most Strategic Player Award. I can't wait to tell you all about it when we catch up in December. How is your tennis hand coming along? Will I get to see you play much this season?*
>
> *By the way, I have some big news. I'm going to be a big brother! Mum told me not to say anything to you about it yet, but writing is not technically speaking, right?*
>
> *Anyway, I look forward to seeing you again soon.*
>
> *Love from Jax.*

How about that! Lucinda has another bun in the oven. At least there would be no doubt about who fathered her child this time. He studied the picture of Jackson, which could have easily been a photo of either Adam or his brother James, from their youth. He typed out a quick response:

CRYSTAL'S CRUCIBLE

Hi Jax,

Congratulations on the award! I'm so damn proud of you, champ. The tennis is going well, and I do hope your Mum lets you come to a few of my matches.
By the way, I promise to keep your secret safe.
I'm looking forward to our next weekend.
Love from Adam.

With a sigh, he clicked SEND. Seconds later, a new message alert popped up. *Surely Jax is not still awake?* But this one was not from his nephew. Sam in IP sent his report to their boss, including Adam in the CC:

Hi Henry,

Adam Fairfax has provided us with evidence of the drug's initial development. We submitted this to the authorities who informed us that Brayzon's data was identical in nature and in timing. I conclude that we have

CRYSTAL'S CRUCIBLE

a mole somewhere in the Company. I suggest a full investigation, starting with the Dandenong Division.
    Kind Regards,
    Sam Whitmore.

The blood drained from Adam's face. *What the? Is Sam for real? Could there be a traitor in my team?*

Chapter Nine

Crystal

The doorbell chimed, bringing a new wave of killer butterflies to the cavity in Crystal's chest. She snatched up her puffer, inhaling two deep breaths of the medicine before answering the door.

Adam stood before her, a picture of perfection in his pristine suit. 'Are you ready? We should hit the road before traffic gets much worse.' His blunt greeting made all the tiny hairs on her skin bristle.

Well good morning to you too! Blinking, Crystal bit back the bitchy retort on the tip of her tongue. 'Um… yeah, I'll get my bags.' She took her backpack from its hook in the hallway, along with her handbag. When she stepped outside, Adam was already waiting in his car with the engine running. Once buckled in, she took a moment to study him.

CRYSTAL'S CRUCIBLE

His attention focussed on reversing and manoeuvring them out of her driveway, but once they were on the open road, a dark cloud loomed over him. 'Are you okay?' Crystal asked. 'You seem… quiet.'

'Sorry. I didn't sleep well last night.'

Recalling the fact she woke him up, Crystal chewed on her inner lip. 'I'm sorry,' she whispered.

Adam sighed. 'It's not your fault. After your call, some other… things came up. So yeah, I'm a bit distracted as well as tired. Feel free to put the radio on if you like.'

Flicking through the stations, she settled on some jazz, but kept the volume low. 'Do you like jazz?'

'It's okay. Not my first pick by any means.'

A shiver drifted across her and Crystal wondered if the cooling was on, but a glance of the dashboard told her otherwise. 'What music do you like?'

'Usually whatever's popular in the charts.'

'Oh, okay.' Crystal had a hard time picturing a refined man like Adam getting into pop music. Closing her eyes, Crystal relaxed into her seat, letting the smooth sounds of Miles Davis wash over her as she breathed in the aroma of luxurious leather mingled with Adam's cologne.

'You play any sport?' Adam's question out of nowhere startled her.

'No. I'm not into sport. My main form of exercise is walking along the beach at sunset.'

'Ick! I detest the feel of sand between my toes. My house in Brighton is about as close as I like getting to the seaside.'

'Wow. Okay.' Bit by bit, the shiny marble pedestal Crystal had put Adam on began to crumble. *How can anyone hate the beach?* 'I guess that rules out my favourite seafood restaurant.'

Idling at a red light, Adam turned his gaze toward Crystal, the hint of a smile tugging at his lips. 'I guess you haven't been to the Atlantic.'

Crystal snorted. 'Yeah right. Until recently that was out of my income bracket.'

'Pity. Their barramundi is to die for.'

'Something to save my pennies for, I guess.'

'Perhaps.' Adam grinned at her before putting the car back into gear. 'Or you could ask one of your many suitors to take you.'

Crystal almost choked on her laughter. 'You're kidding right? It's not like I have men lining up at the door for me.'

'Hmm, I guess you have a boyfriend scaring them off.'

This time she did choke, and it took several sips from her water bottle to soothe the frog in her throat. 'Nope. No boyfriend.'

'I find *that* hard to believe.'

The ambient temperature rose, and Crystal wished the air conditioning *was* on. She pressed her chilled water bottle against her flushed cheeks. 'I guess I'm the one who scares them off.'

'I suppose brainy women intimidate a lot of guys.' He shrugged. 'Their loss.'

'How the hell did we get to talking about my love life or lack thereof?' Crystal mused.

'I think it was all the talk of seafood.'

'Right, because that's such a logical segue.'

Adam let a short laugh slip. 'Sure it is. I assume you've heard about the aphrodisiac properties of oysters.'

'Of course I have, although I am yet to read a valid scientific study proving any such foods can stimulate sexual desire. Most of them claim it is all in the mind, like a suggestive placebo effect.'

'By God, you sound so clinical.'

CRYSTAL'S CRUCIBLE

Mirth rumbled in her belly. 'We are managers in a pharmaceutical company, Adam. Science is our business.'

'I get that, I do, but it doesn't mean I want to invite the MythBusters team into my bedroom and have them debunk the mysteries of romance. That's the one place in my life where I like to shut out the scientific method.'

Unable to cope with the stifling atmosphere, Crystal took the initiative and pressed the AC button, earning a laugh from Adam.

'Feeling a bit hot, are we?'

She hid her blushing cheeks by taking in the view outside of her window. 'I guess summer is here.'

'I figured a chemistry graduate with your skills would know how to read a thermometer.' He tapped the digital display, drawing her eye to the current temperature reading: 14.0°C[9]. 'I would hardly call that summer.' Adam wore a smirk as wide as Australia.

'You are shameless.' She glared at the side of his head.

---

[9] 14°C = 57.2°F

CRYSTAL'S CRUCIBLE

'Comes with the experience and territory I suppose. Although I prefer terms like bold and honest.'

'I think closer synonyms to describe you would be blatant and audacious.'

Adam snickered. 'I see how it is. What would best describe your behaviour, hmm? The words flippant and facetious come to mind.'

'Ouch. I was going to suggest witty and piquant.'

'Mm, fair point. Okay, I concede. Now it's time to put that brilliant mind of yours to work.' Adam parked the car and nodded toward their workplace.

'Indeed.' Crystal glanced back at him. 'Thanks for the lift.'

His face lit up with a beautiful smile. 'My pleasure. Thanks for improving my mood.'

In that moment, Crystal decided she preferred the real Adam to the perfect picture she had painted of him in her mind.

୭୨

Crystal

CRYSTAL'S CRUCIBLE

Walking into the organic chemistry laboratory felt like returning home. The distinct odour of various solvents wafting through the air, despite the fume hoods filling the room with a hum akin to bees buzzing around an apiary. The bright white surfaces glistened under the fluoro lights, a stark contrast to the dank house Crystal lived in. She had decided a daily tour of Aludel's research and development department would be a great way to touch base with her team and keep up to date with everyone's work. But it was also an excuse to treat herself to the welcome sights and sounds of familiarity.

From the literature she had read, Crystal understood the process all started in the Drug Discovery area, so that was where she began her rounds. Shane was concentrating on a distillation set up, so she approached Peter first.

He looked up from his fume hood and smiled. 'Heya, Crystal. What's up?'

'I came to see how you guys are doing. What are you concocting in there?' She glanced toward all the glass bottles he was working with.

'Just mixing up some chemical reference standards.' Peter handed her the procedure he was following. 'That's a monograph from the Pharmacopoeia.'

'Okay, great. I'll leave you to it.' She moved to depart, pausing to add, 'Oh and have a good day.'

'Cheers, Crissy. You too.'

Seeing Katrina working in the adjacent office, Crystal made that her next stop.

As soon as Crystal stepped through the door, Katrina minimised the file on her screen, whipped around on her gas-lift chair and sprang to her feet. 'What do you want?' she snapped with the ferocity of a lashing whip.

Crystal could have sworn she stepped through a portal into some frosty hell dimension. 'I wanted to see how you are doing.'

Katrina crossed her arms. 'Splendid. Are we done?'

Inching closer, Crystal frowned. 'Not quite. I'd like to know what you are working on.'

'None of your business.'

'On the contrary, everything in this department is my business. I need to stay up to date.'

Glaring down her nose, Katrina sent a chill down Crystal's spine. 'How dare you presume to

CRYSTAL'S CRUCIBLE

come in here like you own the place. I have been working here since you were in nappies[10].'

Crystal sighed. 'I need to wrap my head around everyone's projects. I'm not trying to be rude.'

'You don't need to try,' Katrina scoffed. 'I know your type: the young *overachievers*. Let me make myself clear: I abhor micro-managers. You can stop breathing down my neck. I assure you I am good at my job and I work hard. If you want updates, you can wait for the reports I leave on your desk. *Capiche*?' Her sharp voice grated against Crystal's nerves like a knife scraping a dinner plate.

Rearing up to her full height, Crystal scowled. 'Listen, you *insolent woman*! I may be young and new at this gig, but I am still in charge and I will not tolerate such blatant disregard for my authority. I don't know what your problem is, but you better get over it because we have to work together whether you like it or not.'

Clapping erupted beyond the fishbowl windows. Crystal did not realise she had attracted a crowd, yet a glance over her shoulder proved half the men in her team had gathered for the show.

Katrina stormed out of the room in a huff.

---

[10] Nappies are also known as diapers

CRYSTAL'S CRUCIBLE

Hans stood at the front of her cheer squad grinning. 'Way to go putting Sour Puss in her place.'

She resisted the urge to roll her eyes. 'Thank you, Hans.'

Markos came forward a moment later. 'I think you should report her behaviour to Michael. I'd be happy to vouch for you.'

The rest of the group nodded and voiced their approval, all volunteering to sign on as witnesses.

A single rogue tear escaped her fortress and slid down her blushing cheek. 'You guys are the best. Give me a sec.' Curiosity getting the better of her, she ducked back inside Katrina's office to peek at the document she had hidden from Crystal. Unfortunately, the screensaver had come on and when Crystal nudged the mouse, a lock screen came up, prompting her for Katrina's login details. *Damnit! That woman is as savvy as she is savage.* Figuring it was not the time to attempt hacking into a computer, not with the audience waiting for her outside, she decided the snooping could wait. Closing the glass door behind her, she followed Markos to Michael's office. *Christ! It is only my third day here and I am already making a formal complaint to HR.*

Chapter Ten

Adam

Adam looked up at the timid tap on his door. 'Come in.'

Crystal took two reluctant steps into his office. 'I don't mean to intrude, but I wanted to let you know I am ready to leave whenever you are.'

'You are not intruding. Why don't you take a seat while I finish up?' He waved toward the chairs surrounding the small meeting table.

'Um…' Her reluctance prompted him to study her. Crystal was an enigma: all quick wit and dry humour one moment, shy and bashful the next.

'Please, Crystal. Relax for a bit. You're making *me* nervous.'

'Sorry,' she replied before biting her lip and taking a seat.

'Is something wrong?'

CRYSTAL'S CRUCIBLE

'Yeah, kind of,' she muttered.

Adam drew a deep breath, tempering the caveman instinct to clobber whoever had upset this sweet woman. 'What happened, Crystal?'

'I… I don't feel comfortable talking about it.'

Red rage filtered the surface of his skin like molten lava. *Had someone touched her?* His mind flicked through the possibilities. 'If someone here has done something to you—'

'No! It's nothing like that. Just a personal issue.'

Relief was like a fresh breeze on his hot skin, letting him breathe easier with the cool change. 'I won't push you, but I want you to know you can talk to me about absolutely anything. Okay?'

Her cheeks flushed as she nodded.

He shut down his laptop and shoved it inside its case along with a few manilla files containing documents for review. Not wanting to delay Crystal, he had decided to take some work home with him rather than stay late. The walk to the car was silent, along with the first five minutes of the drive.

Crystal eventually broke the mounting tension. 'I did have a run in with Katrina today.'

'Oh? Is that what upset you?' It became impossible to keep his attention on the road. He simply had to sneak a peek at her, to read her expression as she replied.

'No. I dealt with it and Michael is aware of the altercation. I just figured you'd want to know. She seems to have a grudge against me, although I'm not sure what I did to offend her.'

Adam huffed. 'I wouldn't take it personally. That woman doesn't like anyone. She is bitter because I hired you instead of promoting her.'

Crystal burst into a fit of adorable laughter. 'Seriously? I can't imagine the likes of her in any sort of management role.'

He grinned. 'My thoughts exactly. What did she do?' Adam listened attentively as she explained the incident. Hearing how well she responded validated his choice. 'I knew you would be the perfect fit for this job.' Glancing at her, she rewarded him with crimson cheeks again. *God, I love making her blush! I bet she resembles red roses in bed.*

'Thank you,' she whispered.

'Are you getting on okay with everyone else?'

CRYSTAL'S CRUCIBLE

'Yes, actually. The rest of my team are great, especially Markos, Denzel, and Hans. Those guys have been most helpful.'

'Good. I'm glad. Don't let Hans and Peter get up to too much mischief.'

'Ha! Don't worry, Michael already warned me about them. I have started doing a daily patrol of the labs to check up on everyone. It is mostly to keep me abreast of the work they are doing, but I'm also keeping an eye out for anything… inappropriate.'

'See, I knew you were the best.' The words slipped out before he had time to consider their full meaning. But there was no taking them back, even if he wanted to. When Adam parked in her driveway, his eyes locked with hers and the air grew thick with emotion. For a moment, he forgot he was her boss, forgot this was not the end of some date where he had driven his girl home and he was eagerly awaiting her invitation inside. His fingers turned off the engine, their gazes still locked. Crystal's audible intake of breath in response did not escape his attention.

Thump! The moment ended when someone slammed against Adam's side of the car. Turning toward the source of the disturbance, he saw a strange woman pressing her face against the window. The intrusion startled him, and he checked the door locks. After knocking twice, she blew blowfishes against the glass.

Crystal groaned. 'Oh God! Not now.'

'Do you know this weirdo, Crystal?'

Sighing, she replied, 'Yes. That *thing* is my mother.'

Upon closer inspection, he could see the resemblance, especially with the eyes and hair colour. 'Is it safe to open the window?'

'She's mostly harmless. Safe yes, but advisable? Hell to the no.' Crystal got out, attracting the attention of her mother who rounded the vehicle with a drunk swagger.

Seeing the woman's state of inebriation, Adam jumped to the rescue. 'Would you like a hand Mrs. Buchanan?'

Crystal's mother spun around to look at him, although it was more like she was a hormonal teenager checking him out. She grinned widely, licking her lips as her eyes travelled the length of his body. 'I'll take any body part ya wanna give me, honey.' Using the car for support, she stumbled back over to his side and collapsed into his arms, getting a good grope in the process.

CRYSTAL'S CRUCIBLE

Good Lord! How is this vulgar woman related to Crystal? In that moment, Crystal's warning made sense and he wished he had paid it more heed. 'Very funny, Mrs. Buchanan, but I would never take advantage of an intoxicated lady.'

'Such a gentleman. Please call me Judy. What's your name, handsome?'

Looking over Judy's shoulder, he could see Crystal's pallid complexion and wide eyes. He mouthed a reassuring '*it's okay,*' before returning his focus to the drunkard. 'My name is Adam, and I am your daughter's boss. Let's get you back inside before you hurt yourself.' He escorted her to the couch where she passed out.

Crystal followed him back to the front door. 'God, I'm so embarrassed right now.'

'Don't be. You aren't the one who made a fool of yourself. Is she always like this?'

Resignation sagged her shoulders, as though the weight of her mother's burdens was too much to bear. 'Not always, but more often than not these days.'

'And your father?'

'Died when I was eight. Mum hasn't been the same since.'

CRYSTAL'S CRUCIBLE

His heart broke for her. 'Oh gosh, I'm sorry Crystal.'

She shrugged. 'It is what it is. Thanks again for the lift.' Opening the door, she ushered him out with the gloomiest expression he had ever seen.

Every inch of him wanted to wrap itself around her, to blanket her in comfort, but he took her big hint and stepped through the open door.

ഇഝ

Jade

A light drizzle tickled Jade's skin as she walked the few blocks between her dead-end job and the apartment block housing the rest of her boring life. Knowing she was in for another lonely night only exacerbated the gloomy mist engulfing her. *I can't wait for Dieter to finish this goddamn album!*

Shuffling her feet, she kicked a loose stone on the pavement, sending it flying into a parked car on the roadside with a clang. When she glimpsed the Victorian Government number plate, she sighed. *Wouldn't it be my luck if I damaged an unmarked cop car?* After a closer inspection of the sedan, she released the breath she had been holding. There was nothing obvious to pin on her.

She resumed the trudge home, this time paying more attention to her footing. Halting, a sense of being watched overwhelmed Jade. Looking back proved fruitless. There was no one there. *Great! Now I'm paranoid.* Another few metres, and the prickly feeling on the back of her neck returned. Glancing around, she noticed the golden Toyota Supra crawling along the street beside her. The windows were black, concealing the driver's identity, yet she suspected who he was. Choosing to ignore the arsehole who was following her, she made a dash for home.

Panting, she collapsed against the scratchy brick wall of her building. Once she had caught her breath, she stood upright and spied the gold sportscar pulling up in front of her apartment complex. The registration plate came into full view: APOLLO. Rage bubbled through her blood as she marched over to the driver's door and pummelled the window with her fist.

Lowering the glass, he greeted her with a smirk. 'Evening, gorgeous.'

She balled her fists at her sides. 'Why are you stalking me, you creep?'

CRYSTAL'S CRUCIBLE

Apollo grinned. 'Don't pretend like you don't love the attention, sweetheart.'

'You could have picked a less conspicuous car to do it with.' Her eyes trailed over the ostentatious Supra.

'Why? It's not like I'm trying to hide my motives.'

She sighed. 'You need to leave me alone, Apollo.'

The door opened, pushing her back as he rose to his feet. His eyes narrowed on her with dark intent. Squeaking, she stumbled around the vehicle, but did not escape his clutches quick enough. His hulking frame pinned her against the hood of his car, the hot metal searing her flesh through her dress pants. 'Not gonna happen. You and I have unfinished business.'

Jade pushed him away and peeled herself off the hot car. 'If you don't quit hassling me, I'll go to the cops.'

The left side of his mouth curled into a sly smile. 'And what are you going to tell them, hmm? You don't know much about me, not even my real name. Although, I'm sure they'd love to know about the candy you have stashed away up there in unit two-hundred and eight.' His chin jutted out toward her apartment's balcony.

'What the hell do you want from me?' Jade screamed.

He ran a manicured finger along her cheek. 'I want *you*, Jade. I thought I made that abundantly clear the last time we met.'

'Piss off! There is no way in hell I'm sleeping with a pig like you.' She shoved past him, but he grabbed her wrist and tugged her closer.

'Stop pushing my buttons, gorgeous. You'll only turn me on even more. I know you want me; your flirting was off the charts when we first met. There's no denying the chemistry between us. Why don't we head on up to your flat and fuck it out of our systems?'

'Over my dead or unconscious body!' she spat.

He shook his head. 'No thanks. I'm not into snuff and I'm not a rapist.'

Jade gave him a sidelong glance. 'Really? Then why won't you take no for an answer?'

'Because I know you *want* to say yes. Besides, with me, you'd never have to pay for pills again.'

She gasped. 'I'm not some cheap whore willing to spread her legs for free drugs.'

CRYSTAL'S CRUCIBLE

Apollo growled, his deep voice vibrating through her body. 'I never said you were. You only need to open these for me.' His fingers gripped her thigh and sparks shot up her body from the contact. When his thumb pressed against her sensitive spot, she moaned and slumped against him. His breath tickled her neck as he spoke in her ear, 'See what I mean. My touch electrifies your body, Jade.'

Tears pooled in her eyes. 'I… I won't leave him. Dieter is my world; the only good thing in my life.'

'But you want more, don't you baby? You need to embrace your dark side too. I won't ask you to break up with him, just give me a chance to fulfill your deepest desires.'

Meeting his gaze, she peered into the abyss and felt herself getting lost. 'Let me think about it.'

Chapter Eleven

Crystal

A shower was the most important part of Crystal's morning routine. It grounded her after whatever drama her family had put her through the night before. As she watched the warm, soapy water cascade down her body and twirl around the drain, she thought about what had happened with Adam the previous evening. Not the humiliation Judy had put her through. It was his lingering gaze mere moments before her mother interrupted them, and the realisation that struck. *I am falling for this guy.* Crystal had thought he was safe to admire from a distance. She was wrong. This was not like the crushes she had harboured for her university professors for whom she felt nothing but an appreciation for their minds and bodies. She shared a connection with Adam, and it terrified her.

CRYSTAL'S CRUCIBLE

Crystal needed a plan; a procedure for dealing with her feelings and future interactions with him. But she was unsure of the method. If there was a manual for this sort of thing, she had never seen it before. Sure, there were countless Reddit posts and blogs, but she doubted they were substantiated with scientific evidence. That was the problem with relationships. They defied logic.

Groaning, she left the shower, wet feet slapping against the tiles as she pushed all thoughts of Adam aside. She got ready for work in a daze, feeling tempted to try caffeine, but resisting the urge. When the doorbell chimed, her heart rate sped up at the thought of seeing him again. Smiling like an idiot, she opened the door. 'Wow, after last night, I can't believe my mother didn't scare you off. I was half expecting you to fire me on the spot.'

Adam's eyes drank in the sight of her, trailing down to her skirt and heels before wandering back up to her tight blouse. 'Nothing could deter me from driving you to work.' Snapping his mouth shut, his eyes grew wide, and he coughed. 'Seriously though, we all have a difficult family member or two. Your mother's behaviour is not a reflection on you or your work ethic. Come on, let's get going.' He spun around and marched toward the car.

It was strange seeing the self-assured Adam Fairfax lose his cool. *Is that what I witnessed?* Grabbing her stuff, she locked up and hurried after him.

As her seatbelt snapped into place, Adam reversed out of the driveway. 'You okay this morning?'

'Yeah, I guess. As good as any morning.'

'Did your mum give you any more grief last night?'

She sighed, thinking of the battle to feed Judy a decent meal and get her in the bath. 'Plenty. She is like a petulant child. I can't wait to save enough money to get my own place and get her a full-time nurse.'

'The fact that you excelled at uni while dealing with her is astonishing. Do you have any siblings who can help?'

Crystal laughed. 'I have an older sister, but she is almost as helpless as Mum. Although her substance abuse is more illicit than alcohol.'

'God damn. I'm sorry to hear that, Crystal.'

She shrugged. 'At least Jade can hold down a job, even if it is a lousy one. Mum is living off Dad's life insurance and the compensation money, so she has no drive to get up and be productive.'

'Wow! That's awful.'

'It wasn't always this bad. During my childhood and adolescence, she had sober moments where she would make jewellery to sell at markets. That was how she met my old man, hawking her wares at the St. Kilda Market.' Crystal closed her eyes, reminiscing on the beautiful love her parents had shared. 'Dad fell for the carefree hippy she used to be.'

'Hmm, sounds like you got the smarts in the family,' Adam mused.

'On Mum's side I did. I am the only woman in her family to have a university degree. I guess I get that from Dad. He was an engineer.'

They pulled up to a red light and Adam's lips simpered. 'How did he pass if you don't mind me asking?'

She exhaled heavily. 'It was a workplace incident. He was at a construction site and a crane dropped a bunch of steel girders on him.'

'Fuuu…' Adam cleared his throat. 'What a horrible way to go.'

'Yeah.' Crystal took a deep breath. 'What about your family?'

CRYSTAL'S CRUCIBLE

Adam filled the air with awkward silence until he eventually replied, 'Most of them are great. Both my parents are alive and well and I love them dearly. Dad is the Chief Financial Officer of a multibillion-dollar company. Mum sits on the board of several non-profits and is always organising charity events.'

'They sound wonderful,' Crystal agreed.

'They are. My sister, Rebecca is a sweetheart too. She is a solicitor who helps victims of domestic violence.' He paused. 'My brother, however… Let's just say we are not on speaking terms anymore.'

While curious to hear that tale, Crystal decided it was not the time to push him for details. 'Fair enough. I won't ask, but I'm happy to listen if you ever want to tell me why.'

'Thanks.' He fell silent again.

Crystal did not mind the break in conversation. It gave her a chance to tune out and watch the urban scenery flash by, reminding her the world continued to spin with everyone else living out their lives despite what happened in hers.

'How is your induction program coming along?' Adam asked five minutes later.

CRYSTAL'S CRUCIBLE

'Great actually. I aced all the e-learning quizzes and at this rate, I'll finish with the QA training by the end of the week.'

'That's good 'cause I'll be needing you soon.' He gulped, adding, 'with the… uh… work stuff.'

'Yes, of course. The work stuff.'

৪৩

Crystal

Two hours later, a frantic knocking broke Crystal's concentration. Looking up from the document she was reading, she glimpsed Denzel's wide-eyed visage and deathly pallor. She summoned him inside her office with a wave. 'Gosh! What's wrong?'

After closing the door, the stocky Indian man dashed across the room and perched on the edge of a visitor's chair. Tears were spilling from his puffy eyes. 'M-my daughter.'

Crystal felt the blood drain from her own face. 'What happened to her?' she asked in a whisper, recalling the framed picture on Denzel's desk of the tiny darling in her ballet costume, holding hands with his stunning wife, Ariel.

CRYSTAL'S CRUCIBLE

Leaning forward on Crystal's desk, Denzel lowered his voice, stuttering between sobs. 'Sh-she was k-k-kidnapped.'

Gasping, Crystal clamped her hands over her mouth. 'What? When? How?'

'Th-this morning. On her way to school. Th-they sent me a n-n-note.'

'Really? Can I see it?'

Denzel shook his head vehemently. 'No, it is best you don't. I-I need to deal with this alone.'

She frowned at him. 'Denzel, you have to take this to the police.'

'No! No police! They'll kill her.'

Crystal pinched the bridge of her nose and took a deep breath. 'Okay, how can I help? Do you need an advance to pay ransom?'

'They don't want my money.'

'What do they want?' Her mind trawled through the possibilities. Surely if their motives were purely to hurt the girl for their own sick pleasure, they would not have bothered contacting her father with any demands.

'They want my silence.'

The back of Crystal's neck felt like a bed of rose thorns. 'By God! What have you gotten yourself mixed up in, Denzel?'

CRYSTAL'S CRUCIBLE

'I-I can't say, not if I ever want to see Jacinta alive again.'

With a sigh, she slumped over her desk. 'Is there *anything* I can do?'

'I need to take some leave. I know I have accumulated a bit in the years I've been working here. I want to use it all now.'

She gaped at him. 'How much time are we talking?'

He slid his latest pay slip across the desk and pointed to the figure for Annual Leave Accrued: 675 hours.

After taking a few seconds to calculate the sums in her head, she looked up at him. 'That's eighteen weeks, Denzel.'

He nodded. 'I'm sorry. Normally I wouldn't ask, but…'

'I understand. Look, I'm going to need to run this past Michael. I can't make any promises, but I'll see what I can do. In the meantime, you can take the rest of today as sick leave, okay?'

Lurching forward, he grasped her hands in his sweaty palms. 'Thank you so much, Crystal.' He sprang to his feet and bolted for the door.

That poor man. She guzzled some water from her drink bottle before picking up her desk phone and dialling Michael's extension. 'Hi Mike. I need your help with something.'

'Well, hey there, Crissy. What can I do for you?'

She explained the situation, referring to Denzel's dilemma as a family emergency.

'That's a lot of time off, especially with such short notice.'

Crystal sighed. 'I know, but these are extenuating circumstances.'

'I'm sorry, Crystal, but without more details, I can't sign off on his request.'

Her heart sank. She had hoped to keep the nature of his problem a secret for Jacinta's sake. 'Fine, but can I speak to you about this in private?'

'Of course. Come see me now.'

Walking through the open plan office space, Crystal could not fight the feeling someone was watching her, yet whenever she glanced around the room, she found everyone immersed in their work. Michael's door was open when she reached it, so she tapped the plywood with her knuckles before walking in and shutting it.

Michael looked up and grinned. 'Take a seat.' But as he listened to Crystal's explanation, his smile vanished. 'Hmm, okay. I'll approve Denzel's request.'

Crystal let out a breath of relief. 'Thank you.' She rose to leave.

'Be careful, Crissy.'

Turning back, she caught him staring out the window. 'What do you mean?'

When his gaze returned to Crystal, he beckoned her forward and spoke in a hushed voice. 'Given the amount of time Denzel requested, I can't help but think Jacinta's kidnapping relates to work. Keep your head down and stay safe, okay?'

Her brow furrowed. *What the hell?* 'Okay.'

Chapter Twelve

Esme

Curled up on her living room couch, Esme snorted with laughter at the antics of Otis Milburn. Given the show's title, Esme thought *Sex Education* would be enlightening. It did not disappoint. But the slamming of the front door killed her mood and she tensed at the sound of approaching footfalls.

'You better not be playing your childish games.' Her father boomed moments before he appeared, looming above her like a giant brass statue.

'No Daddy. I'm watching television.'

He glanced at the screen and harrumphed before returning his attention to her. 'Jin asked after you today. He is keen to meet you.'

CRYSTAL'S CRUCIBLE

She clenched her fists at her sides and narrowed her eyes at him. 'I told you I would find someone on my own terms.'

'You're clearly not trying hard enough if you have the time to lounge about like a sloth.'

'That's hardly fair, Dad.'

'You want to talk about fair? Where's the thanks I get for everything I do in this family? Do you think I work twelve hours a day because I enjoy it? Now get off your backside and do something productive.'

Esme gaped at him. 'I have been working hard all day too, Daddy. Surely I deserve some down-time?'

Her father huffed. 'That's what sleep is for. Now make yourself useful and go find a husband.' He waved a dismissive hand.

Springing to her feet, Esme stormed out, retreating to her bedroom. She sank into her desk chair, casting her eyes over the half-finished jigsaw puzzle depicting Escher's *House of Stairs*. Picking up a piece, she tried to find a place for it to fit. But her vision blurred with the tears pooling in her eyes. She dropped it back on the pile and ambled over to her bed where she collapsed and wallowed in her misery.

CRYSTAL'S CRUCIBLE

After a good cleanse of the old tear ducts, she sat up and grabbed her phone. She considered calling Crystal but decided to open Tinder first. Several new matches appeared, surprising the hell out of her. There was also a message from a doctor named Charlie: Hi Esme, how are you? You have such a pretty name and sound like a real sweetheart.

Her cheeks were roasting as she opened Charlie's profile to take a better look. Exhaling through pursed lips, she made a whistling sound. *This guy is too sexy to be real!* Her lady parts quivered at the sight of his blond scruffy hair, and designer stubble along a chiselled jawline that could cut through glass. Needing time for her sprinting heart to calm down, she closed the message and looked at the other matches, contacting each of them with a polite greeting.

A few more deep breaths and she was ready to reply to Charlie. Esme did not 'super like' Tinder cards; it was not her style. But when she found Charlie's profile the day before, she had been unable to help herself. He was the sort to get a million women swiping up each day anyway, and she had doubted he would give her a second look, yet there he was, texting her. Hi Charlie, thanks for the message. I'm doing well. How are you?

CRYSTAL'S CRUCIBLE

He replied: A bit average, to be honest, but hearing from you has brightened my day.

Esme felt hot despite the cool air. Oh gosh, you are too kind! Are you sick, or is it a bad mood?

{Charlie} Just exhausted. I've been pulling a few long shifts at work lately.

She sighed, picturing him in a set of scrubs. You're a doctor right? What type of medicine?

{Charlie} I'm a cardiothoracic surgeon. What about you, Esme? Your profile mentions scientific research.

Swoon! He is a brainy hunk. Plus, the pay cheque ought to be enough for her father to overlook the fact he was not Chinese. That's right, I'm a Research Associate at the university, specialising in polymer synthesis.

{Charlie} Awesome. I'd love to pick your beautiful brain on the details, maybe over a drink on Friday night?

Oh my God- oh my God- oh my God! Sounds lovely. After making the arrangements, Esme rang Crystal, bursting the moment she heard her bestie's voice. 'I've got the hottest date on Friday night!'

Crystal laughed. 'Hello Esmerelda, I'm great, thanks for asking.'

Esme squeaked. 'Sorry, I'm just so excited.'

'You don't say. Go on, tell me all about him.'

Relaxing into her bed, Esme switched ears. 'I will, but first, would you mind chaperoning?'

'Of course I'll come. I promised I would.'

CRYSTAL'S CRUCIBLE

'Thanks hun. So…'

'So?'

'He is a surgeon, Crissy. Drop dead gorgeous too, at least in his pics anyway.' She went on to describe Charlie.

'The man sounds like a dream,' Crystal agreed.

She giggled. 'A wet dream at that. Anyway, enough about me and my love life. How are you?'

A heavy sighed travelled down the phone line. 'You know how I had that car crash on Monday?'

Her skin prickled. 'Yeah, but I thought you said you were okay after?'

'I am. Fine, that is. But, well, you won't believe who has been driving me to work while my car is getting fixed.'

Esme gasped. 'No! Not that sexy boss of yours?'

'The very same.'

'Hot damn! How are you coping, having all the time *alone* with him?'

'Mm, it's been good, actually. I enjoy talking to him. I thought conversation would be difficult with how distracting his smile is, but his easy manner helps.'

CRYSTAL'S CRUCIBLE

'Oh gosh! I would die! Or melt into a pile of goop. Either way, they would have to cart me away in a wheelbarrow.'

Crystal burst into hysterics. 'God, I love you! I needed that laugh after the day I've had. One of the guys in my team asked for time off because someone kidnapped his daughter.'

'Wow! Sounds thrilling!'

'More like scary,' Crystal scoffed. 'This is not one of your crime fiction novels. The poor man was in tears and my heart was breaking for him.'

'Ah, geez. I'm sorry, Crissy. I hope the police catch the bastard and lock him away.'

'If only it was that simple.'

෫ඏ

Jade

Dieter's warm arms encased Jade in a sandalwood scented bubble as they sat in one of the VIP booths. She resisted the urge to run her fingers through his spiky hair, knowing how important his image was on performance nights.

CRYSTAL'S CRUCIBLE

When a yawn slipped from her mouth, his eyes narrowed on her. 'You don't have to stay up with me. I know you have work tomorrow.'

Thursday nights at the club were always the hardest. It was all well and good when she was younger. Her body thrived on minimal sleep back then and when it got hard, she powered through her days with a cocktail of amphetamines and energy drinks. But she was nearly thirty and the seven-day party week was taking its toll. She smiled up at him. 'It's okay, baby. I want to be here with you.'

His eyes searched her face. 'Are you sure?'

'Positive.'

Squeezing her thigh, he grinned. 'I'll get some more drinks. What do you feel like this time?'

'A Red Bull, please.'

He arched a brow. 'Did you want any Jäger with that?'

She shook her head. 'No thanks.'

The other brow joined its partner in the race toward Dieter's hairline. 'I think this may be the first time you have said no to alcohol. Are you feeling okay?' He pressed the back of his hand to her forehead.

Jade laughed. 'Don't look so shocked. I'm tired. I need stimulants, not depressants.'

'Okay. I'll be right back.'

She watched his firm backside as he walked toward the bar, sighing when he became engrossed in a conversation with Sargon.

A flash of gold to the right of Dieter caught her attention and her gaze met with Apollo's. She gasped as his hungry eyes devoured her, and the air became stifling. He remained poised in place; a silent sentry simply watching her. Yet his unwavering focus unsettled her because she knew what he was thinking, what he wanted. She imagined what it would be like to let him have his way with her, the feel of his strong hands all over her body, touching her in ways no other man had. Her nerves tingled and hummed at the thought and she felt even more uneasy, twitching as though she was going through withdrawals. *I need to get out of here before I do something I'll regret.*

Apollo's eyes widened as she rose and made her way toward the bar. She could almost feel the waves of disappointment emanating from him when she sidled up to Dieter, wrapping an arm around her boyfriend's waist and planting a kiss on his cheek.

CRYSTAL'S CRUCIBLE

His own arm drew her closer. 'Sorry, babe. I got talking business.'

'That's okay. I think I might head home after all. I can barely keep my eyes open.'

'Okay. I'll see you later.' He embraced her fully and kissed her lips tenderly.

Stepping outside, she relished the cool draught, closing her eyes as it washed over her in soothing strokes.

'Leaving so soon? Your German boy hasn't even started his set.'

Flinching, she whirled around to face Apollo's smirk. 'I'm tired, so—'

He took two long strides forward, bringing him toe-to-toe with her. 'So, I'll take you home and tuck you into bed.' Mischief sparkled in his dark orbs.

'This is not the time or place to make a scene,' she hissed. '*If* we do this at all, you'll need to be more discreet.'

'If?'

'You've only given me a couple of days to think. I need more.'

His fingernail trailed down her bare arm. 'You're driving me wild, sweetheart. I can't stop thinking about all the dirty things I want to do to you.'

A lump formed in her throat and she swallowed hard against it. 'Please…' she croaked.

'Already begging me, hmm? Works better if you get on your knees.'

Jade's skin was pure fire. 'Please give me time.'

He exhaled a gust of breath, tickling her neck, and sending shivers straight to her core. 'Fine. Call me as soon as you're ready. In the meantime, let me drop you home.'

'That's… not a good idea. If anyone sees us…'

Glowering, he nodded. 'Good point. I'll call you an Uber.'

As soon as she got into the car, Jade turned to the driver. 'If you don't mind, I'd like to go to St. Kilda instead.'

The man shrugged. 'What's the address?'

She gave him the directions and slumped into her seat, hoping Crystal would not mind the surprise visit. Jade figured it was safer catching up with her sweet little sister rather than lying in her own bed feeling restless and tempted.

CRYSTAL'S CRUCIBLE

Judy opened the door, slurring her speech as she leaned against the wooden frame for support. 'The hell do you want?'

'Well hello to you too, Mother.' She pushed past the woman-shaped blockade, shoulder checking her on the way through. 'I'm here to see Crystal.'

'She ain't here, so piss off.'

She spun on her heels, copping a nose full of Judy's rancid breath. There were bins full of garbage that smelled fresher than her mother. 'What do you mean she's not here? It's a weeknight.'

Judy staggered closer, jabbing her fingers into Jade's clavicle. 'Crissy's workin' late. Has been most of the week. It sucks the way she's leavin' me here all alone to fend for meself.'

Pushing her back into the wall, Jade growled at the insufferable slob. 'You ought to be more grateful she's working hard to support your lazy arse.'

Slap! Judy's hand came out of nowhere and Jade recoiled at the stinging touch. 'Don't you dare talk to your mother like that!' Judy scowled.

'Oh, I'm sorry, Judy. I forgot you were allergic to the truth.'

CRYSTAL'S CRUCIBLE

'You don't know what ya talkin' 'bout. I bet Crissy is stayin' late at the office to bang that sexy boss of hers. I know *I* would if I were in her shoes.'

Jade snickered. 'You've got to be kidding me! Are we talking about the same girl here? 'Cause the Crissy I know doesn't have sex. Period. Let alone doing the deed at work.'

Judy grinned. 'You didn't see the way they were undressin' each other with their eyes when he dropped her home. It was enough to drench me own panties.'

'Big deal. That happens with every passing breeze anyway. If, by the remote chance, there is something going on with Crissy and her boss, you need to leave them the hell alone. That poor girl has enough hang ups about intimacy. She doesn't need Cyclone Judy barrelling through and making a mess of things.'

Chapter Thirteen

Crystal

Crystal laughed, her heels clicking against the pavement as she followed Esme to her second date along the inner-city streets. 'I can't believe you've organised three dates for the same night!' Most people would rejoice at the start of a Friday night, but Crystal loved her new job. The rest of the working week had been mercifully quiet, and she got her car back.

'It's called being efficient,' explained Esme with a defensive tone.

'Right.'

'You should be thankful I'm not monopolising more of your time.'

'Uh huh.' She did not mind helping Esme, although she did not have a pub crawl in mind when she agreed to it. She thought those days were over when she graduated from university, and her aching feet were reminding her how little she missed them. 'Well after the last creep, I can appreciate your need to vet these guys before spending time alone with them.'

'Ick! He was slimier than the rotten potatoes I found growing in the back of my brother's pantry.' Esme led Crystal into a rustic cocktail lounge full of earthy tones and timber surfaces. 'We have a bit of time before this one shows up. Let's grab a seat and chat.'

Crystal nodded, accepting the mocktail Esme offered her.

After a moment of deliberation, Esme settled on a table toward the back with a good view of the entrance. 'Have you made any matches on Tinder yet?'

'No,' Crystal sighed. 'Honestly, I haven't even opened the app since creating my account.'

Esme furrowed her brow. 'Why not? You promised to give it a go.'

'Because my romantic attentions have been elsewhere.'

Her eyes bugged out and she pursed her lips. 'You don't mean that sex bomb boss of yours?'

Crystal took a long taste of her drink before nodding. 'I think I'm falling for him, Ez. We get on so well and he is such a hunk.' She sucked on her bottom lip.

'Jeepers girl! Has he put any moves on you? Do you even know if the feelings are mutual?'

She shrugged. 'Maybe, I don't know. There have been moments, but it could be my imagination and I am clueless when it comes to reading men.'

Sitting up, Esme inhaled deeply. She kept her gaze locked on Crystal as she sipped her margarita. 'Have you considered the possible repercussions for becoming involved with your boss?'

Crystal narrowed her eyes. 'What do you mean?'

'I mean there is a good chance your employer has policies to prohibit fraternisation. I doubt they will allow you to have an intimate relationship with Adam. In the very least it's a conflict of interest.'

Crystal recalled reading something in her induction notes about managers facing a conflict of interest and everything that entailed. *Why didn't I think the same rules apply to Adam?* 'Damnit! You're right. I got too caught up in my emotions to consider that.'

'Wow, you've got it real bad for him, don't you?' Esme offered half a smile.

CRYSTAL'S CRUCIBLE

'Yeah, I guess I do.'

Esme glanced at her phone when it buzzed. 'He's here.' She tapped out a quick reply before standing to greet the man walking through the door. Date number two was barely an inch taller than Crystal and he wore his mid-length brown hair slicked back with enough cheap product to make the Yarra River flammable.

His eyes lit up when Crystal rose beside Esme. 'Wow, Esme, I didn't realise you'd be bringing your hot friend along for the ride. But that's okay, I'm always down for a threesome with two lovely ladies.' The sleaze offered his hand for Crystal to shake. 'Who might you be, gorgeous?'

Crystal glared down her nose at the greasy hand and crossed her arms over her chest. 'I'm the chaperone and you can go now.'

He gaped at her. '*Excuse me!* I think that is Esme's call.' He glanced at the woman in question with pleading puppy dog eyes. 'You still wanna have a drink with me sweetheart?'

'Yeah right! I don't date arseholes,' scoffed Esme, copying Crystal's pose. She grabbed Crystal and dragged her outside, leaving their drinks half finished. 'Well, that was a disaster.'

CRYSTAL'S CRUCIBLE

'Are you sure you want to bother with the next one?' Crystal was beginning to doubt Esme's taste in men and wondered if Tinder was such a good idea for someone as naïve and innocent as her.

'I have much higher hopes for Doctor Charlie. We've been chatting a bit this week and he seems nice.' Turning a corner, Esme marched on toward the final stop for the night.

Familiarity nagged at Crystal, like a sense of déjà vu, prompting her to stop. 'This hot doctor's name is Charlie? Can I see his profile pic?' Crystal gasped when Esme handed her the phone displaying Charlie's photo. Those intense blue eyes staring back at her had not changed a bit with the years.

'Told you he was a hottie.'

'You're not kidding. I know this guy, Ez.'

'Really? How?' Esme bounced on her heels.

'We were friends in high school.'

The breath of relief gushed out of Esme's lungs. 'Oh, thank God. He must be a decent bloke.'

'I wouldn't go *that* far. Charlie's not a complete jerk, but...' She chewed on her lip again.

'But what? OMG! He wasn't your cherry popper, was he?'

'No, but he was the first boy to break my heart.'

Esme's eyes widened. 'Your first crush?'

Crystal confirmed Esme's theory with a nod. 'What happened?'

Pulling Esme aside, Crystal found a tram stop to sit at. 'After years of torture, not knowing if he felt the same way, I plucked up the courage to ask him to the senior formal. I literally jumped for joy when he said yes.' She paused to process the painful memories. 'He was the perfect gentleman, even when I didn't want him to be, if you catch my drift. At the after party—something he dragged me to despite my protests—I found him making out with my bestie. My tears startled him, so he asked what upset me. Apparently, he thought we only went to the dance together as friends. Anyway, I fled in a huff, running right into the arms of our mutual friend, Brad. *He* was the one who took my virginity and when Charlie found out, he got mad and stopped talking to me.'

'Wow, that's messed up. I'm sorry, hun. Look, I don't have to meet Charlie if you don't want me to.'

Crystal shook her head. 'It's all water under the bridge. You should go for it.'

CRYSTAL'S CRUCIBLE

'Okay, but only if you're sure.'

After several minutes of reassurance, they made their way to the next bar. Crystal was not about to stand in the way of Esme's happiness, and it was ancient history.

When Esme's phone buzzed with a message, she rose to meet Charlie near the entrance. Crystal watched as the charming doctor placed a chaste kiss on Esme's hand before following her back to the table. Charlie's eyes sparked with recognition. 'Crystal?' He grinned as she nodded. 'By God! Crystal Buchanan. How long has it been? What brings you into a crowded bar on a Friday night?'

Hiding clenched fists under the table, she forced a smile. 'I bumped into my friend Esme and decided to join her for a mojito.'

He glanced at her glass. 'Does this mean you eventually came around to the idea of alcohol?'

'No. This one's a virgin.'

Esme spluttered, spraying the remnants of her mouthful over the table. '*Crystal!*'

Charlie laughed in the way that used to make her quiver. It no longer had such an effect, in fact, none of the desire she had ever felt for him remained. 'Crystal was talking about the drink, I'm sure.'

CRYSTAL'S CRUCIBLE

Rolling her eyes, Crystal turned to Esme. 'I'll leave you to it hun. I'm getting tired after such a hectic week.' They hugged and Esme whispered her thanks. On her way out, she grabbed Charlie's arm and glowered at him. 'You hurt my best friend and I'll castrate you with your own scalpel.' With that, she left him gaping in her wake.

ಸಌ

Adam

Sweat dripped from every inch of Adam's skin as he belted the tennis ball with untold fury. In that moment, the yellow felt-covered sphere represented everything wrong with his life: past betrayals, current frustrations, and future trepidations. It was a mild day, yet it felt like the sun was channelling all its heat directly at him. He reared up in front of Greg, swinging again and claiming another point.

'Jesus Christ! Stop hogging the damn ball. What's with you today?' Greg growled.

Adam huffed and returned to his side of the court, bouncing on his heels to await the serve. He smashed it, letting his racket fly when the ball hit the net. '*Shoot!*'

CRYSTAL'S CRUCIBLE

Greg jogged over to him. 'Dude, you have got to cool down.'

'You're right. I'm sorry.' He marched over to the sidelines and guzzled a gallon of Gatorade before accepting a freshly cut wedge of orange from one of the groupies. Biting into the fruity flesh, he savoured the sweet, citrus tang as the juice exploded in his mouth.

The bleached blonde smiled. 'Looks like you could use some tension relief.' She winked at him.

After glancing at the name badge pinned to her pristine, peach coloured dress, he smirked. 'Claudia, is it?'

Her ponytail bobbed as she gave him an enthusiastic nod.

'Tennis *is* my stress release, sugar. But thanks for the offer.'

Greg sniggered as she pouted, slapping Adam on the back as they returned to their set. 'Looks like you need more than a tennis match, bro. Why didn't you take her up on the offer?'

'Because I'm not interested.'

'Seriously? If I wasn't married, I'd be tappin' that fine piece of arse.'

Adam shrugged. 'She's too plastic for me.'

'Never stopped you before,' Greg scoffed.

CRYSTAL'S CRUCIBLE

'Maybe I want a change.'

Stopping in his tracks, Greg gaped at Adam. 'Bloody hell, how did I not see it? Who is she? Do I know her?'

Looking at his feet, Adam suppressed the wry smile threatening to give him away. 'I don't know what you're talking about.'

'Oh come on, man. You're either banging a new bird and this is more than a one-night stand, or you're desperately trying to get in someone's pants. I wanna know details.'

Laughing, Adam rolled his eyes and readied for play. With thoughts of Crystal distracting him, the opposition continued to wipe the floor with them. As soon as the announcer called 'game set match', he wiped his brow and sauntered up to the net to shake hands with the opposing team.

Greg was hot on his tail when they hit the changerooms. 'Details. Now!'

Adam sighed. 'I'm not sleeping with anyone.' He peeled off his polo shirt and flung it on the bench beside his bag.

'Then it's the second option, which could go some way to explain your brutal backhand out there today.' Greg finished stripping out of his drenched clothes and wrapped a towel around his waist. 'So, who is she?'

'Give it up man.'

'Nah uh. After the way your temper lost us that match, you owe me an explanation. Who. Is. She?'

Looking at the ceiling, Adam searched it for answers, for a way out of this interrogation. He returned Greg's gaze. 'My personal life is none of your business. Please quit badgering me.'

'Oh hell. It's *her*, isn't it? That's the only reason why you'd wanna keep it under wraps. I get the attraction, Adam, I do. Everyone at work with a dick is drooling over her, but the two of you have been spending time alone together. Has anything happened?'

'No!' Adam snapped. 'Of course not. I'm not deaf. I heard Michael's warning when we hired her.' Seizing his toiletries bag, he stormed into the shower, slamming the cubicle door behind him. Greg's laughter was bouncing off the tiled surfaces. *Christ, he's infuriating.* He stepped under the stream of warm water, trying to wash away his worries. But he could not shake the thoughts of Crystal. She entrenched herself deep under his skin, firing through his nerves. Groaning as he grew hard for the seventh time that day, he smacked his head back against the hard wall and squeezed himself. Giving in to the urge, he jerked off to mental images of the redhead with the world's most beautiful smile.

Once he finished dressing, Adam looked across the room to see Greg grinning at him. 'What?'

'You desperately need to get laid. Just go for her, man. I won't tell anyone.'

Adam shook his head. 'I don't even know if she wants me.'

'Pfft. All the chicks want Adam Fucking Fairfax.'

'But Crystal is not like most women. She is a puzzle.'

Greg's lips curled into a lopsided smile. 'No wonder you're obsessed with her.'

Chapter Fourteen

Crystal

Monday was gearing up to be a stinker. Their first real hot day of summer and Crystal was thankful for the climate control at work. It was far more effective than the evaporative unit at home, and she even needed her blazer inside. When Michael popped his head into her office to mention the Krispy Kremes he got for everyone, her stomach audibly growled. 'Thank you.'

Michael laughed. 'You're welcome, but you better be quick.'

Crystal beelined for the breakroom. She found a few of the guys huddled around the cartons of sugary goodness. They were not holding back. With a snort, she jabbed Hans in the shoulder blade. 'Save some for the rest of us, buddy.'

CRYSTAL'S CRUCIBLE

Tipping his ginger scruff-covered head back, he looked up at her with a doughnut smile.

Crystal immediately noticed his eyes were more glazed than the pastries he was chowing down. 'Are you stoned?' Clenching her fists, she felt her skin prickle as she frowned. 'In. My. Office. *Now!*' She caught a glimpse of the wide-eyed look Hans exchanged with Peter before she stormed off. It was the first time she had ever raised her voice in public, let alone at work. Closing the door behind him, she ushered him into one of the visitor's chairs before sitting at her desk. 'Do I need to call for a drug testing kit, or will you fess up?'

'It's okay, Crissy. I have a prescription. It's in my HR file, so feel free to check with Michael.'

Her chin almost hit the desk. 'Why do you need it?'

Wriggling in his seat, Hans looked to his twitching feet. After an awkward silence, he returned his gaze to her. 'I have multiple sclerosis. The cannabis helps with my symptoms better than anything else.'

'Oh gosh, I'm sorry…' Her voice trailed off because she had no idea what to say.

CRYSTAL'S CRUCIBLE

'Please don't pity me. I get by okay for the most part, although this heat tends to make things worse.'

'Does it… affect your work?' Grabbing a pen from her desk, she chewed on it.

'The MS or the MJ?'

'Either?'

'The MS can, especially when my arms start flappin' about like a bird, but the cannabis relaxes my muscles and keeps the shakes under control. I avoid using heavy machinery or driving when I have flare ups, so please don't worry about my safety. I am keen to keep working for as long as possible to save retirement money.'

She dropped the pen and twirled a strand of hair between her fingers instead. 'Aren't you afraid of becoming addicted?'

'Not really. I've been taking the stuff for years without feeling any compulsion to keep having more. From what I understand, some people are prone to addiction, while others aren't. I can happily let go on the weekends and manage the following week without any if my MS behaves.'

'Wow. How do you handle the loss of self-control?'

Hans laughed. 'I actually find it liberating to let go. Don't tell me you've never even smoked a single joint in your day?'

She bit her lip.

'Really?'

Crystal nodded. 'I don't even drink. My alcoholic mother and drug addicted sister put me off the idea.'

'That'll do it, I guess. Look, I'm sorry if I gave you a fright. I should have told you about this earlier, but I kind of assumed Michael would've filled you in.'

'It's alright. I'll go have a word with him now. Please take care, okay?'

Nodding, Hans took his leave as Crystal made her way to Michael's office. She tapped on the door twice before barging in. Her cheeks flushed when she found Greg perched on Michael's desk, engaged in a heated discussion before they both gave her startled looks. 'Oops, sorry for interrupting. I should have waited.' She spun around to leave.

'Wait!' Michael called out. 'What can I do for you, Crystal?'

Turning to face them, she caught Greg's leering gaze as he took in the sight of her bare legs beneath her mid-thigh length pencil skirt. Her neck felt under attack by a vicious acupuncturist. Snapping her attention back to Michael, she tried to ignore the sensation of Greg's heated stare. 'I need to discuss some confidential HR stuff.'

'Go on,' Michael prompted.

Her eyes flitted toward Greg for a moment.

'It's okay, Greg can stay. The same non-disclosure clauses apply to him.'

She hesitated, looking at Greg who smirked, highlighting the crow's feet around his close-set eyes. When he licked his lips like a starving man who had discovered the buffet, Crystal almost threw up in her mouth. After taking a deep breath, she sat down. 'I accused Hans of illegal drug use because I did not know he was on a prescription. Is there anything else I should know about my team members?'

'Ah shoot.' Michael furrowed his brow. 'I apologise for the oversight. Things have been hectic lately.'

'Moonlight Serenade' sounded in her jacket pocket. Annoyed, she retrieved her phone, intent on silencing it, but seeing the name on the screen stopped her and she accepted the call instead. 'Hey

Adam, can I call you back? I'm in a meeting with Michael.'

'Of course. Come see me when you're done.' His silky voice soothed her nerves, allowing her to breathe easily again.

'Thanks. See you then.' Hanging up, she observed a change in Greg's visage, reminiscent of the expression on Esme's face when she was considering her next chess move. *Why is he analysing me?* She focussed her attention on Michael. 'Sorry about that.'

'No probs.' Michael smiled warmly. 'Why don't you give me a few hours to go over everyone's files and I'll let you know if there's anything else?'

'That would be great. Thank you.' Crystal could not get out of there quick enough.

৪০০৪

Crystal

Crystal sucked a fork full of noodles into her mouth as she read Katrina's latest research findings.

'Healthy dinner,' remarked Adam from her doorway.

CRYSTAL'S CRUCIBLE

Laughing, she put her ramen cup down. 'Don't worry. This is only a snack to tie me over until I get home.'

He closed the door and took a seat on the edge of her desk. 'Not that I'm complaining, but why are you still here?'

Temporarily distracted by the muscular thighs clad in grey suit pants, it took a concerted effort to lift her gaze to his face. When she did meet his eyes, the mischievous spark within them suggested he knew where her thoughts had gone, and her face caught fire. 'I um…' *What were we talking about? Oh right.* 'I wanted to make a dent in this mountain of reports.' She waved her hand over the pile of papers sitting in manilla folders.

The smooth chuckle slipping out of Adam's lips thrummed her nerves, reverberating through her body like softly plucked harp strings. 'You've been here just over a week and you're already a workaholic.'

Gasping, she frowned. 'I am *not* addicted to work.'

He cocked a brow. 'No? Is something else keeping you here?'

'I just…' She drew her bottom lip between her teeth. 'I prefer the air conditioning here.'

Adam burst out laughing.

'What?' Crystal tried to suppress her giggles.

'I'm sorry, I figured there was more to it.'

Like trying to catch moments alone with you? As if I'm going to admit that. 'Well…'

The humour left his chestnut orbs as they burned into her. 'Well?'

'I might also be avoiding my mother.'

His face sank. 'Oh. Fair enough.' Adam rose to his feet. 'I've got a nasty headache, so I'm ready to call it a night.'

Disappointment dropped like an osmium nugget in her gut. 'Does that mean I need to leave?'

'Do you think you'll manage here on your own?'

'Of course. The security here is tighter than my purse strings and I know how to lock up.'

That gorgeous smile returned to his face. 'Great. Don't hesitate to call me if you have any troubles. Good night, Crystal.'

'Night.'

He paused at the door. 'Oh, be sure to tuck your chair in before you go.'

O-kay. 'Will do.'

Adam grinned before leaving and she watched in awe as he tucked in everyone else's chairs on his way out. *Looks like I'm not the only control freak in this place. Is this why he had insisted I wait for him by the car last week?*

Feeling the need to stretch her legs an hour later, Crystal took her noodle cup and fork to the kitchen. Adam had turned off the rest of the lights throughout the building, but the glow of the emergency exit signs was enough to see by. On the return trip, she noticed the crack of illumination beneath the boardroom door. *Odd. How would someone as fastidious as Adam forget the boardroom?* She approached the closed room. Reaching for the handle, she paused, hearing a muffled voice on the other side. She stepped closer, pressing her ear to the door.

Greg's voice drifted through the timber. 'Those IP guys are hard nuts to crack, but I'm confident Brayzon has this one in the bag. Those guys will need the next lot of preliminary findings much quicker this time, though. Might also be worth messing with the R&D data here, to be safe.'

What the hell? Crystal's skin prickled and her heart pounded against her ribs. Her phone rang a moment later, sending her on a skyward trajectory. *Jesus!* Rejecting the call, she sprinted to her office, turning off the light and locking the door before she dived under the desk. Reaching into her handbag, she grabbed her asthma medication and inhaled two puffs. *Is this what Denzel discovered? The reason for his daughter's kidnapping?* Her stomach churned at the thought. Still holding her phone, she dialled his mobile number, but it went straight to voicemail. She left him a message in a hushed voice, 'Oh, hey Denzel. Crystal here. I wanted to check in to see how you are doing. Any word on your daughter yet? Please call me.'

Time ticked by in painful silence as she tried to calm her breathing. She prayed for Greg to hurry up and leave. As the seconds turned to minutes, she relaxed. *Maybe he didn't hear my phone.* But the sound of keys jingling at her door put her back on high alert. *Please no*. The lock clicked, and footsteps approached. She could barely hear them over her throbbing pulse.

The man rounded her desk, his shiny black shoes and pressed pants stopping directly in front of her.

Afraid to breathe, she held the air in her lungs.

Squatting before her, Greg's hand clamped over her mouth to stifle her squeal. He clicked his tongue three times. 'You are too inquisitive for your own good, Crissy. Like a curious kitten.' He leered at her. 'Just as cute too.' Hovering over her, his breath reeked of whiskey. 'I know you were eavesdropping on my meeting. Let me make this simple for you. Stay the fuck out of my affairs and keep your trap shut or my sadistic son will turn you *and* your cute blue-haired sister into his next playthings. And, for the record, his victims never leave his dungeon alive. Crystal clear enough for you?'

Her eyes almost popped from their sockets as she nodded.

He removed his hand from her mouth. 'Do you understand me?'

'Yes,' she hissed.

'Good. I'd hate to see a pretty, little thing like you come to harm. I will have someone watching you, so don't do anything stupid like blabbing to Adam or the cops.' He brushed the back of his hand along her cheek, stabbing her spine with icicles.

When he left the room, Crystal sucked in a deep breath and closed her eyes. *I knew there was something off about that creep.*

Chapter Fifteen

Crystal

Steam swirled around the rim of Crystal's teacup, wafting up to her in a fragrant plume. She was hoping the chamomile would calm her nerves. After the incident with Greg on Monday, she was violently ill for a whole day. It may have been psychosomatic, but it was still a good enough excuse to stay home and hide. Having recovered, she needed to face the music; to prove she would not cower away in the corner like some hopeless damsel. *It's okay to be scared. Who wouldn't be? But that doesn't mean I can't get on with living my life. If I heed Michael's warning and keep my head down, I'll be safe, right?* She hunched over the breakroom table, losing herself in thought.

Someone snuck up behind her. 'You didn't think you could hide the truth from me, did you?'

CRYSTAL'S CRUCIBLE

Crystal's backside sprung clear of the seat before dropping back to the cushioned chair with a thud. Her eyes darted about the room before settling on Adam. 'Hide what?' she squeaked, feeling woozy from standing too quick.

'Your birthday!' He grinned as the rest of their colleagues filed into the room, singing the dreaded song off key.

With flushed cheeks and a galloping pulse, she felt as though she had finished a marathon. And Crystal hated running.

Hans placed a large chocolate cake on the table and smiled at her.

'That better not be spiked with anything,' Adam warned in a playful tone.

'Pfft,' replied Hans. 'Not on your life. I keep the good stuff to myself.'

The air became stifling as everyone crowded around her with expectant expressions. *What do they want from me?*

'You need to cut the cake,' came a cry from the crowd.

When Greg approached her with a knife, the room started spinning before everything went black.

CRYSTAL'S CRUCIBLE

༄༅

Crystal

A warm embrace was the first thing Crystal became aware of as she stirred awake, followed by the sensation of movement. Upon opening her eyes, she looked up into Adam's face and realised he was carrying her. *So much for not being a damsel in distress!* 'Adam?' Her voice came out in a whisper.

Peering down at her, Adam furrowed his brow. 'You fainted. I'm taking you to my office.' His jaw clenched. 'You should have stayed home if you were still feeling sick.' The hard edge in his tone sent a chill down her spine.

'I was fine this morning,' she rasped.

When they reached Adam's office, he shut the door behind them and laid her down on the carpet. Dragging a chair closer, he propped her feet up on it.

'What are you doing?' She reached down to tug at the hem of her skirt as it rode up her thighs.

'Basic first aid, to help the blood flow back to your brain.'

'Oh. What happened?'

CRYSTAL'S CRUCIBLE

He sat on the floor beside her, worry lines creasing his beautiful face. 'One minute you were sitting at the dining table, about to cut your birthday cake, the next you were falling off your chair. Luckily, I was able to catch you before you hit the ground.'

Shuddering, memories of Greg holding a knife returned, so she pushed the image aside and focused on the man who had saved her. An amusing thought struck her, and she tried to suppress the curl of her lips with her teeth.

Adam's brows shot up. 'What's so funny?'

'That's the second time I've fallen into your arms, but I guess you're used to women falling over you.' *What the…? Did I really say that aloud? Must be the lack of blood in my brain.*

Adam laughed. 'Good to see you haven't lost your sense of humour.' His expression turned serious again. 'How are you feeling now?'

'Okay, I think.'

'What did you eat for breakfast?'

'The usual. A couple slices of toast.'

His frown deepened. 'That's not enough after being sick. I imagine you are low on electrolytes.' Rising to his feet, he moved behind his desk to reach for something. He returned with a bottle of red Gatorade. 'Here, drink this.'

Sitting up, she took the drink and smiled. 'Thank you.'

He shrugged. 'It's nothing.'

'Not just for this, Adam,' she waved the sports drink in front of her. 'I mean thank you for everything.'

Sucking in a breath, Adam brought his hand to the side of her face, gliding his thumb along her skin. 'Anything for you, Crystal.'

Sparks fired through her nerves, igniting a blaze in her blood vessels.

A knock at the door killed the moment and Adam leaped across the room like a guilty child caught raiding the cookie jar. Michael appeared a second later, smiling with pursed lips. 'How's the patient?'

'I'm okay,' Crystal replied.

Pulling a chair out from the meeting table, Adam took a seat. 'I think she is still a bit dehydrated after her bout of gastro.' He turned his attention to Crystal. 'You should finish your drink before getting up.'

CRYSTAL'S CRUCIBLE

Entering the room, Michael placed two small white plates on the table. 'I saved some cake from the vultures for both of you.'

Adam laughed. 'Thanks man, I should make you employee of the month or something.'

After chugging down the Gatorade, Crystal rose. Both men rushed to help her. She accepted their support and got as far as a chair before the room swam again.

'Woah! Take it easy,' insisted Michael. 'Try sitting here for a while before standing upright.'

Grabbing her plate, she woofed down the cake, feeling much better despite knowing it would take at least ten minutes for her blood sugar to rise. While mild dehydration likely contributed to her fainting spell, it was not the sole cause. Propping her head on her folded arms, Crystal took their advice and rested for a while. Adam conversed with Michael about sports, remaining close to her, and his proximity provided comfort. Her mind kept returning to that moment immediately before Michael entered. *Was he about to kiss me?* But another question plagued her even more: *Would I have let him?*

ೞಌ

CRYSTAL'S CRUCIBLE

Adam

Adam's nerves felt strung-out and stretched, like a pair of sneakers dangling over high-tension wires. After the scare with Crystal that morning, he hated the idea of leaving her side, yet he worried about losing control if they spent any more time alone together. It was the only reason he let her return to her own office. He came too damn close during the moment they had shared.

But Crystal was not the only person testing his tensile strength. Brayzon had just won the bid for patent rights. *Could this day get any worse?* His stomach replied with a grumble, so he stormed out of his office and headed for the breakroom. *At least I have lasagne to look forward to.* Retrieving the leftovers from the fridge, he popped them in the microwave. He watched as the container spun around, coaxing him into a trance until something caught his attention:

'Holy shit! Crystal popped up on my Tinder suggestions,' Hans exclaimed.

Spinning around, Adam saw Hans and Peter hunched over their phones at the table.

CRYSTAL'S CRUCIBLE

Peter whistled. 'Hot damn. She looks especially luscious in that photo. Is she topless?'

Lunging at them, Adam seized Hans' phone. 'Gimme that.'

Hans' eyes bugged out of his head. 'Wha—'

Adam clenched his fists, the right one almost crushing the phone he held. 'Show some respect, men! This is not appropriate behaviour for the workplace. If I ever catch you drooling over pictures of female colleagues like a couple of horny teenagers again, I will issue you with formal warnings. Got it?'

They both nodded with gaping jaws.

A snigger sounded from the doorway and Adam met Greg's gaze. 'Like you can talk—'

Seething, Adam pointed a finger at Greg. 'You shut up.' Forgetting his lunch as the microwave beeped, he pushed past Greg and marched straight to Crystal. She greeted him with wide eyes as he threw open her door. 'My office. Now.' Turning on his heels, he heard her scrambling out of her chair and following behind him with the click of her kitten heels. *Those damn shoes will be the death of me one day.*

Once they were alone in his office, Crystal hovered near the entrance. 'What's wrong?'

CRYSTAL'S CRUCIBLE

'Close the door.' He collapsed into his chair.

She gingerly perched her perky butt on the edge of a seat, waiting for him.

'I won't mention any names, but your Tinder profile has become the hot topic of discussion among a few of the guys on staff. You need to shut it down before things get out of hand.'

Crystal visibly tensed. 'Excuse me?' Her tone was severe.

'You heard me. That profile has to go.'

'What I do with my personal life is none of your business.'

His eyes narrowed into a glare. 'Your personal life is just that. Personal. Don't give those arseholes any more fuel for their perve fest. You need to maintain a professional appearance at work and having provocative images on any public forum is a bad idea. Most of the managers here don't even have social media accounts.'

'Have you even seen my Tinder profile picture?'

Adam shook his head. He had been too angry with the guys and upset with Crystal to even look at it.

'I guarantee there is nothing explicit about it.'

CRYSTAL'S CRUCIBLE

He gave her a sidelong glance. 'Why would they think you were posing topless?'

'What?' She dug her phone out of her jacket pocket. A few seconds later she rolled her eyes and handed him the phone. 'I was wearing a strapless dress.'

Taking it, Adam inspected the photo of her glancing downward through her reading glasses. She wore minimal makeup, although vibrant red gloss accentuated her plump lips. The image almost took his breath away and he agreed it was suggestive. Sometimes less is more. *Christ! I'd sell my left kidney for a chance to see her in that dress.*

'It was a candid shot taken of me at a university dinner,' she explained. 'You can't even see a hint of cleavage, so I honestly don't see what the problem is.' Extending her hand, palm out, she made her silent demand. Yet again she had flipped from timid mouse mode to ferocious feline.

He returned her phone. 'Why do you need a dating app?'

'Argh. It was only a stupid deal I made with my best friend to incentivise her. I don't even check the damn thing. Are we done?'

Breathing a sigh of relief, he decided to take this opportunity to bring up the other issue.

CRYSTAL'S CRUCIBLE

'Actually, there is something else I needed to talk to you about.'

Reclining in her chair, Crystal crossed her arms. 'Go on.'

'You remember those IP meetings I had recently?'

She nodded.

'Well, the matter did not end in our favour, unfortunately. You see, one of our major competitors, Brayzon, submitted a patent application for the same drug formula as us at the exact same time. And they had identical research data to back their claim. Head office are certain someone at this facility has been leaking or selling Company secrets to Brayzon.'

Gasping, Crystal sat up, her face turning ashen. 'You don't think I had anything to do with this?'

'Of course not. You weren't even working here when this whole fiasco started. But I am going to need you to keep a closer eye on your staff and let me know if you learn anything.'

Slumping against the backrest, she chewed on her bottom lip.

'Do you know something I don't?'

She shook her head.

CRYSTAL'S CRUCIBLE

'Then what's wrong?'

'Nothing. I'm just processing what you've told me.'

Adam wanted to believe her, but he still suspected she knew more than she was letting on. *Does she have some theories running through her brain?* 'Let me know if you see or hear anything suspicious?'

'Okay.'

Once she had left, Adam closed his eyes and brought Crystal's profile picture to mind. *I need to get myself a copy of that photo.*

Chapter Sixteen

Markos

Taking advantage of the commotion surrounding Crystal's fainting spell, Markos slinked away. While unsurprised Katrina had not bothered to show her face, he did wonder what she was up to. Sneaking through the drug discovery laboratory with expert stealth, he reached the preparation area undetected. Crouching behind one of the benches, he peered through the window into her office. Katrina was doing something on her computer, but he could not see any details, so he shuffled across to the door and tested the handle. *Unlocked. Good.* He carefully rose and crept into the room.

Minimising her window, she spun around and glared at him. 'Don't you ever knock?'

'Don't you ever smile?' he countered.

CRYSTAL'S CRUCIBLE

Katrina huffed, the movement drawing attention to her massive breasts. She looked incredibly good for a hag who was almost as old as his father. Pity about the complete lack of personality. Not that he cared when it came to the women he used for sex, but something told him screwing with Sour Puss would be more trouble than it was worth. 'What do you want, Markos?'

Smirking, he pressed his body against hers.

Her eyes grew wide. 'Markos!' When her nose brushed against his neck, a small moan escaped her lips.

God bless Christian Dior. The woodsy scent of his Sauvage cologne gets the ladies every time. Stooping over her, he reached for the mouse, but she swatted his hand away before he could open any of the files sitting in her taskbar.

'What the hell do you think you're doing?'

'I want to know what you're working on.' He snaked his free arm around her waist and held her tight against him.

She gulped but did not make any moves to escape his grasp, prompting his mouth to grin wider. 'My work is none of your business, Markos. Now if you don't mind.'

'Oh, but I do mind. I know you are doing something fishy and I want to know what it is.'

She gasped. 'How dare you make accusations like that! And take your hands off me before I report you for sexual harassment.'

Squeezing her waist, he sniggered. 'Please, Kat. If you wanted me to stop touching your body, you would have pushed me away or said something earlier. I can hear your withered old pussy crying out for me. How long has it been since you got any, hmm?'

'None of your business,' she spat out.

Stepping back, he crossed his arms and laughed when she stumbled. 'I guess you don't need *me* then.'

'You are so full of yourself,' sneered Katrina.

'Like you and your snooty nose can talk. If you don't prove you aren't doing anything dodgy, I'll have to take this matter up with Adam.'

She scoffed. 'I figured you'd be running back to your precious Crissy with this.'

Markos cocked a brow. 'Why? This doesn't concern her, but I'm sure Adam will want to know if you've been leaking Company secrets.'

'Well I haven't and you can tell Adam what you like, but I have nothing to hide from him.'

CRYSTAL'S CRUCIBLE

Turning back to her desk, she shut down her computer before storming off.

Women can be the most infuriating creatures! Katrina was a hard nut to crack, much like the pretty piece of tail who he had been chasing to no avail. At least he had a plan for her. *Christ! I need to get laid. I know I accused Katrina of going without sex too long, but my own drought is becoming a serious issue.* He would devote the coming weekend to bedding as many chicks as possible, with or without *her*.

In the meantime, he needed to find out what Katrina was covering up. It was time to call on his hacker friends.

ೞಌ

Crystal

The smell of Judy's cigarette drifted in from the backyard while Crystal set the dinner table. 'For the love of all that's good! Close the damn window if you're going to smoke,' Crystal screamed before sliding the glass down with enough force to rattle the frame. When she returned to her task, the doorbell rang. 'I guess I'll get that,' she mumbled as she strode down the hall.

'Happy birthday!' Esme burst into the house and embraced Crystal. Stepping back, her smile faded as she took in Crystal's sour expression. 'Oh gosh! What's wrong?'

'I had a crappy day and Mum's not making it any better.'

'I'm sorry. Do you want to talk about any of it?'

Crystal shook her head. 'Most of it's work related and I'd rather forget about that stuff for now.'

'Fair enough.' Esme followed her back into the dining room. 'Is there anything I can do to help you with setting up?'

'Could you finish laying out the cutlery? I'll go check on dinner.' In the kitchen, she lifted the slow cooker lid and inhaled the rich aroma of the beef stew. Taking a spoon from the dish rack, she stirred the casserole and tasted the gravy, testing the flavour. *Perfect*. Flicking the dial to warm, she returned the lid. She was chopping the fresh thyme for the garnish when the doorbell chimed again.

'I'll get it,' Esme called out from across the corridor.

CRYSTAL'S CRUCIBLE

'Thank you,' replied Crystal, tensing with anticipation of the inevitable battle she was about to face. Putting her sister and mother in the same room was never a good idea, but neither of them gave her a choice on her birthday, both insisting on time with her. According to Judy it was as much her day as it was Crystal's, she had gone through the pain of childbirth after all. Jade used a similar guilt trip to get her way, reminding Crystal who actually raised her when their mother lost herself at the bottom of a brandy bottle.

Voices echoed through the house as the rest of her guests approached. The back door slammed a moment later and Crystal knew the showdown was imminent. When the house fell quiet, she braced herself and hurried into the dining room.

Jade and Judy stood on opposite sides of the table, glaring at each other, and the air was thicker than a supernatural fog. Shivering, Crystal half expected her father's spirit to manifest and scare some sense into the room. Not that she believed in ghosts or anything science could not prove, but it was a nice thought.

Dieter looked up and smiled as she entered. 'Ah, there she is!' Breaking the silence, he shuffled around the cramped space to get his hug from

CRYSTAL'S CRUCIBLE

Crystal. '*Alles Gute zum Geburtstag*[11].' Dieter's accent was thicker when he spoke in his native tongue, and his voice warmed Crystal's heart.

Jade grabbed her next. 'Happy birthday, Pumpkin. Thanks for cooking dinner. It smells delicious.'

'When are we eating?' Judy demanded. 'I'm starving.'

'Christ, Mother! I've seen monkeys at the zoo with better manners than you,' Jade hissed.

'Everything is ready, I just need to serve it,' responded Crystal with a sigh.

'I'll help.' Jade followed her into the kitchen. 'How've you been?' She grabbed the bread while Crystal carefully lifted the ceramic dish out of the slow cooker.

'Honestly? I've been better.'

'Damn. Is Mum giving you grief, or is this work related?'

'Both. Things at work are… complicated.'

Jade's immaculate eyebrows leaped toward her blue and black braids. 'Don't tell me you're banging that boss of yours?'

Crystal laughed as she placed the pot on the bench where she transferred the contents into a

---

[11] Happy birthday.

serving dish. 'Hell no! Although I suspect there is something… brewing between us.'

'Really?' Jade's voice climbed at least two octaves. 'What makes you think that?'

'He keeps touching the small of my back and looking at me funny. Earlier today, he overreacted when one of the guys at work discovered my Tinder profile. He even insisted I close my account.'

'Yep. Sounds like he's got it bad for you girl!' Jade grinned. 'You need to let him know how you feel. Maybe reciprocate the touching.'

Crystal gulped. 'I… I can't. He's my boss.'

'So what? If you like this man, don't let some stupid rules or other people's opinions get in your way of happiness.'

Like it's that simple. Crystal kept the thought to herself though. She was not in the mood to argue. They took the food out to the dining room and everyone busied themselves with dishing up.

'Mm, yum. Is this Grandma Buchanan's recipe?' asked Jade. 'It tastes exactly like it.'

'Yes, it is.' Crystal beamed.

'Fuck! I hated that snooty bitch,' whinged Judy. 'I need a drink.' She stormed out of the room, returning minutes later holding a highball glass filled to the brim with amber coloured poison.

CRYSTAL'S CRUCIBLE

Dieter cleared his throat. 'How is the new job going, Crissy?'

'Fine,' she lied. 'How's your new album coming along?'

'Good actually. I've finished recording the samples. Now I can focus on the mixing.'

'I can't believe you call that trash music,' scoffed Judy.

'Mum, please,' Crystal begged, feeling her cheeks blaze. She did not like the stuff Dieter made either, but she would never openly insult his craft. Glancing at Jade, she could see her sister was steaming like a volcano on the verge of erupting.

'It is okay, Crissy, I know my music is not to everyone's taste. I have a decent fanbase and I am confident my next album will hit the charts.'

'I'm glad it's working out for you.'

'You should get a real job,' Judy spat. 'One that pays enough to get Jade out of that dogbox you call home.'

'With all due respect—' Dieter began.

Springing to her feet, Jade slammed her hands on the table, toppling Judy's drink and spilling brandy all over the place. 'Mind your own business, you insufferable, lazy excuse for a human being! You should take a good hard look at yourself before judging others.'

Ignoring Jade's rant, Judy urgently salvaged what she could of her precious liquor, scooping the puddle to the edge of the table and back into her glass.

Using her napkin, Esme mopped up the remnants of the spill threatening to drip onto her lap. 'Can you please try to get along for Crissy's sake? You're ruining her birthday.'

Judy huffed. 'It's not just *her* day. I'm the one who stretched my vagina to the point of prolapse to push Crystal out into this world. You know—'

'Mum, please stop. We don't need to hear it again.' While she was grateful her mum gave her life, Crystal could have done without the graphic descriptions of her own birth, a story Judy had retold every year since Crystal's thirteenth birthday. 'Hey, Ez, I've been meaning to ask you about your second date with Charlie.' After hitting it off so well, Esme had agreed to go out with him again on Monday night. Turning to Jade, she explained, 'Esme met Charlie Sinclair through Tinder.'

Jade's jaw dropped. 'As in high school hottie Charlie?'

Crystal nodded.

CRYSTAL'S CRUCIBLE

'Oh my God, I remember you having the biggest crush on him. Not that I could blame you. He was cute for a nerd. What's that kid up to now?'

'He's a surgeon,' Crystal explained.

Jade whistled. 'Damn.'

Returning her attention to Esme, Crystal prodded her, 'How did it go?'

'Ugh, it was a disaster. He kept asking about you. When we called it a night, he even wanted your number.'

Gasping, Crystal frowned. 'Did you give it to him?'

'Of course not! No way am I gonna leave you open to more heartbreak from that bastard. I'm sorry. I never should have gone through with it when you told me about him.'

'Hey, it's okay, Ez. I hope you find a suitable match before your Dad kicks you out.' For the most part, Crystal was relieved Charlie did not get her number. She did not need that drama in her life again. But a small part of her was curious to know his intentions.

The rest of the night progressed without any more hiccups. It helped that Judy migrated to the couch where she passed out from drinking the sum of her bottle, leaving the rest of them to converse freely over dessert. When Crystal climbed into bed, her phone buzzed on the nightstand.

It was a message from Adam: I'm sorry for being a jerk today. How was the rest of your birthday? Are you feeling okay?

Her heart fluttered like a manic moth around a lightbulb as she typed her reply. Apology accepted. I'm much better, thanks.

Another message came through a few seconds later. What are you doing now? I hope I didn't wake you.

She felt warm and fuzzy. I just got into bed. What about you?

{Adam} I've been lying awake in bed for the last hour, unable to sleep.

Holy moly! Has he been thinking about me in bed? What's on your mind?

{Adam} Various stuff. But mostly you.

Crystal's heart skipped a beat. I hope you are only thinking good things where I'm concerned.

{Adam} Pleasant yes, but good? I guess that's a matter of perspective 😉

Blushing, Crystal bit her lip as heat pooled in her core. Her own mind took a turn onto inappropriate road and headed straight for deviant town as she slipped her left hand inside her sleep shorts. Are you flirting with me, Mr. Fairfax?

CRYSTAL'S CRUCIBLE

{Adam} Maybe. Is that ok with you? I'm not making you uncomfortable, am I?

Okay yes, but uncomfortable? I guess that's a matter of perspective 😉. Good night, Adam. Dropping the phone, she addressed the ache between her legs.

Chapter Seventeen

Adam

A relentless string of teleconferences and urgent emails kept Adam locked in his office for the better part of the day. He even ate his lunch at his desk while working. Business hours were over by the time he had a moment to spare. Glancing out of his window, he could see most of the cars had cleared out of the employee parking lot. Aside from his own, there was only one other vehicle: A rose-gold Subaru Impreza. Grinning, his thoughts turned to the text messages he had exchanged with Crystal the night before. He picked up the desk phone and dialled her extension.

'Hello?' Her sweet voice went straight to his dick.

'Hi Crystal. Can you please come see me?'

'Sure. What do you need to see me about? Should I bring anything?'

CRYSTAL'S CRUCIBLE

Shoot! Think quick. 'Um…' He glimpsed the conference pack on his desk and grinned. 'It's about the National Pharmaceutical Seminar. Just bring yourself.'

'Okay, I'll be there in a minute.'

Restless legs got the better of him while he waited, wearing a hole in the carpet with his pacing. *What the hell am I going to do?* Adam had not felt this anxious about a girl since losing his virginity to Samantha Bailey in year ten. He was usually confident with women, but this whole situation with Crystal unnerved him and he knew he needed to tread cautiously. When she announced herself with a gentle knock, he perched on the edge of his desk. 'Come in.'

Letting the door click behind her, she approached hesitantly, the blush in her cheeks deepening with each step. 'Hi,' she croaked in a whisper. Her chest rose and fell with shallow breaths from beneath her pastel pink, silk blouse. The colour of the shirt matched the pinstripes in her grey skirt. While conservative, the outfit was also flattering, and his hungry eyes devoured the sight of her. Stopping in front of the meeting table, she was the perfect picture of demure innocence, her head downcast as she peeked up at him. 'So, uh… what was the seminar thing you wanted to discuss?'

He handed her one of the pamphlets. 'The Company has a few tickets booked. I'll be going and I think you should join us.'

She flicked through the booklet. 'This looks great. I'd love to go. Thank you.'

His heart leaped at the thought of escaping to Sydney with her for a few days. 'Oh hey, have you noticed any suspicious behaviour in your department?'

She sucked in a deep breath, easing it out between pursed lips. 'No. Nothing yet.'

'And how was your evening? Did you manage to get comfortable enough to sleep okay last night?'

'Oh… um… eventually.' The fire in her cheeks was hot enough to roast marshmallows.

It unravelled the last threads of his willpower, and he stalked across the room toward her. 'Eventually, hmm?'

Lifting her gaze, she looked at him with wide eyes as he came toe-to-toe with her. 'Adam?' she gasped, her legs backing into the table where she dropped her backside against it.

CRYSTAL'S CRUCIBLE

Right where I want her. He closed the distance, grabbing the table and caging her in his arms. 'I'm only going to ask you this once. If you say no, I promise to back off and leave you alone because I don't want a sexual harassment case on top of everything else. But after last night, I'm confident my feelings are mutual. Am I right, Crystal? Do you want me?' The seconds he waited stretched out toward infinity, despite their regular ticking on his wall clock, deafening in the otherwise silent room. *Or is that my heartbeat?*

'I…' her voice was softer than velvet. 'I'm scared of how much I feel for you, how much I desire you.'

Her honesty floored him. Adam tucked a strand of hair behind her ear and stroked his thumb along the side of her face. 'Is that a yes?'

She nodded.

Brushing his nose against her ear, he inhaled the sweet, musky scent that was partially perfume and entirely *her*. He felt her body quiver against him. 'It scares me too, baby. I know wanting you is wrong in so many ways, but it feels right in those that count.' He pressed a kiss to her pulse point, eliciting a deep moan from her throat. When he nibbled her neck in the same spot, she bucked against him, spreading her legs a fraction wider in the process. A primal part of Adam was dying to know how wet she was, but the more lucid part of his mind warned him not to rush things.

He cradled the back of her head with his left hand, staring at her luscious mouth moments before crushing it with his own. Reciprocating the kiss, she stroked and sucked his lips with hers. She tasted like honey at first, and when he pried her mouth open, slipping his tongue between her teeth and gliding it across her palate, an unusual floral flavour joined the intoxicating mix. His free hand glided down her arm, across her hip, and clutched her thigh. A raw, guttural sound escaped him as he touched her soft, silky skin. When his fingers travelled higher, she flinched, and he drew back to study her expression. 'Are you okay? Did I hurt you?'

'I'm okay. Sorry. It's just…'

Moving his hand from her thigh, he cupped her cheek. 'It's just what?'

'I'm not ready for more yet.'

His mouth gaped open as he tried to process the implication. 'Are you… a virgin?'

Shaking her head, she laughed nervously. 'No, although it's been so long you could call me a born-again virgin. I simply need to take things slow.'

'That's fine. I'm happy for you to set the pace.' His blue balls protested so painfully he imagined them going on strike and forming a picket line. It took immense fortitude to ignore them, but he succeeded, focusing on what Crystal needed. 'Is the kissing still okay?'

She smiled with a radiant glow, lighting up the room. 'Mm, yes, very yes.'

Adam picked Crystal up and moved her to his desk, the sturdier piece of furniture in his office, and they kissed until the last rays of the sun dipped below the horizon.

༄༅

Crystal

After checking the coast was clear, Crystal entered Adam's office, closing the door with her backside. Ever since their first kiss the night before, she felt like a giddy teenager sneaking around with her boyfriend, seizing opportunities for clandestine make out sessions.

He looked up and grinned. 'Lock the door.'

CRYSTAL'S CRUCIBLE

She flicked the latch and crossed the room with the two fast food bags she carried, dropping one on his desk. Crystal salivated at the smell of greasy burgers wafting through the room. 'Here is your lunch Mr. Fairfax.'

His eyes darkened with lust. 'I love it when you address me like that.'

Mischief twinkled in her eyes. 'I know. That's why I do it.'

'Come here.' He reached out a hand, which she accepted, and pulled her down into his lap, kissing her ardently.

Even with the layers of fabric between them, she could feel the impressive bulge in his pants. It empowered her to know how much she turned him on, but it also scared her because she figured he would eventually grow tired of waiting for sex. When his desk phone rang, he ignored it, prompting her to giggle.

'What's... funny?' He spoke against her lips between kisses.

'Aren't you going to get your phone?'

'No.' He squeezed her hips. 'I'm busy.' Encircling her waist with his arms, he deepened the kiss until his mobile rang. 'Argh.' Lifting the offending device from his desk, the name GREG flashed on the screen before he answered it. 'What?'

Crystal heard Greg's voice on the other end, 'Where are you man? Lucinda's here with Jackson.'

'Shoot! Already?' Adam glanced at his watch. 'It's only gone three.'

'Don't tell me you're offsite?'

'No,' he sighed. 'I'm having a late lunch at my desk.'

'Really? I tried your office, but you locked the door.'

Adam exchanged an impish grin with Crystal. 'I wanted some peace and quiet.'

Greg snorted. 'You picked the wrong job for that, bro.' Seconds later they heard the door unlock and the man himself strolled into Adam's office, halting when he locked eyes with Crystal.

She scrambled out of Adam's lap and smoothed down her skirt.

'Shut the damn door,' Adam snapped, rising to his feet. He marched up to Greg, scowling. 'Don't you dare breathe a word of this to anyone.'

'Chill boss man.' Greg directed his gaze toward Crystal. 'Your secret's safe with me.'

A shiver shuddered through Crystal's spine. She could hear what he was not saying.

CRYSTAL'S CRUCIBLE

Adam's mouth formed a hard line as he turned back to her. 'Please excuse me a moment, Crystal.'

When he left the room, she joined Greg near the doorway and watched as Adam greeted a tall blonde woman and a young boy. The adults spoke briefly before Adam exchanged a secret handshake with the kid, both laughing as they bumped fists and slapped palms. 'Who are they?'

Greg hovered close to her ear. 'Adam's ex-wife, Lucinda, and her son, Jackson.'

She turned her wide-eyed expression on Greg. 'Adam has a son?'

He shrugged. 'Possibly. He doesn't know for sure if the boy is his, although Lucinda swears Jackson is James' son.'

'Who is James?' Her heart warmed at the sight of Adam joking around with Jackson, pretending to play tennis with imaginary rackets and balls.

'James is Adam's brother.'

'What?' She spun to face Greg, the blood draining from her face.

'Lucinda had an affair with Adam's brother. It went on for four years before he caught them. When they divorced, she moved in with James.'

CRYSTAL'S CRUCIBLE

'Wow. That's messed up. Poor Adam.'

A sly grin grew on Greg's face. 'Indeed. That's why he doesn't date women anymore. He only has meaningless hook-ups. Lucinda killed his faith in the female population. Be sure to make the most of sex with him because it won't last.' He sauntered across the office to his own room, leaving Crystal reeling from the revelation.

Grabbing the door frame for support, she felt the tears begin to trickle down her face. *You stupid girl! What made you think he would be any different?* She stumbled out of his office and dashed into the storage closet to hide her anguish from the world.

Chapter Eighteen

Adam

Adam left Jackson playing on his iPad and went in search of Crystal. He had been looking forward to having his nephew sleep over, although Lucinda's timing was almost as poor as her communication skills. With the work Christmas party on the next day, he would not get a whole weekend with Jackson. *Would have been nice of her to mention Jax finishing school early today when we made these arrangements.*

He finished scouring the R&D labs to no avail and headed back to the main office for another sweep of the area. As he passed the storage closet, he heard a muffled noise inside. Memories of pulling her into that room a few hours earlier filled his mind and his dick. While it was only for a heated kiss, he knew when she was ready, he would make a point of bending her over against those shelves.

Could that be her now? It occurred to him he might be interrupting another couple getting up to exactly what he fantasised about doing with Crystal, but he did not care. He turned the handle and opened the door enough to peek inside. The sight of her crying on the floor pierced his heart. He rushed inside, locking the door behind him, and kneeling beside her. She recoiled when he placed a hand on her shoulder. 'What's wrong baby?' he whispered against the shell of her ear. Her body shuddered, but she did not answer him. Adjusting his position, he got more comfortable and wrapped his arms around her. He peppered kisses along her shoulder, up the nape of her neck, and along her cheek. 'Talk to me sweetheart. Let me help.'

'Please stop touching me,' she croaked out.

'What?' he jerked back. 'Why?'

Instead of replying, she glared at him.

'You're killing me here, baby. Please tell me what's going on.' He stroked her back, but when she winced, his hand pulled back as if from an electric shock.

Shuffling around, she backed into the rear shelves, hiding her head between her knees.

CRYSTAL'S CRUCIBLE

Determined to get to the bottom of this, he stood his ground by moving into her personal space. Lifting her chin, he looked into her red, puffy eyes. 'Why don't you want me to touch you?'

Her pupils narrowed into slits. 'Because I don't want to be another one of your flings.'

'What are you talking about?'

'I'm not interested in casual sex. I'm an all or nothing kind of girl.'

Things were still new, and Adam had not yet had a chance to define their relationship. He did not understand where this was all coming from. 'What makes you think I only want to sleep with you?'

'Greg. He…' Another sob racked her body. 'He told me about your ex-wife.'

Oh hell. Adam sighed. 'Damn that bastard. I love the guy like a brother, but he can be such an insensitive git sometimes. He told you half the truth.' He paused to take a deep breath. 'Lucinda betrayed me, and I spiralled into a state of despair for years. The only women I took to bed were plastic imitations of her, and after I used them up, I threw them away like the trash I believed they were. I'm not proud of how I treated them. Even when I pulled my sorry arse out of that slump, I struggled with trusting women. I only ever went for the no-strings options. But then you came into my life, Crystal, and I started to feel things here.' He patted his heart, followed by his head. 'And here. The day you stumbled into my office in those kitten heels, you ignited something in my soul that blazes hotter than any flame. I don't know how to douse it and that scares the hell out of me, because I haven't felt this way about anyone since Lucinda, and she destroyed me.'

Her bottom lip quivered as she drew it between her teeth and stared at him.

'I'm sorry I didn't tell you about this stuff earlier. It has been a bit hard to think straight around you lately, and we were having so much fun.' He gave her a lopsided smile earning himself a delicate giggle. *I wish I could bottle that sound.*

Crystal frowned a second later. 'Where do we go from here?'

'Honestly? I'm still trying to work that out, but I know I want something exclusive. You are the only woman I have eyes for, Crystal. I hope you feel the same way because I sense I can trust you, and—'

'Yes.' She leaned forward and combed her fingers through his hair. 'You are the only man I want, Adam.' Her lips touched his in a tender kiss, turning fervent when she straddled him.

CRYSTAL'S CRUCIBLE

Holding her tight against him did not feel close enough. Every molecule in his body screamed out for more contact, to become one with her. Sliding his hand down, he cupped Crystal's arse and reached for her damp panties, but her spring-loaded legs propelled her out of his lap. Gobsmacked, he gaped up at her. 'Shoot! I'm sorry, sweetheart.' He rose to his feet and embraced her. 'Are you okay?'

'Yeah. Sorry, I'm just scared.' She hugged him back.

What exactly is she scared of? Several scenarios ran through his mind, none of them good, and all of them stirred his protective instincts. While he was desperate for answers, he did not feel it was the time to question her. 'Come on. There's someone I want you to meet.' Clutching her hand in his, he led her across the corridor to his office, locking the door behind them. 'Crystal, this is my nephew, Jackson.'

The boy looked up from his seat behind Adam's desk and smiled.

With her left hand still holding Adam's, Crystal extended the other toward Jackson who shook it firmly. Jackson cocked his head to the side and studied her face. 'Did you hurt yourself, Crystal? You look like you've been crying.'

She grinned. 'I did, but your uncle helped me, and I feel much better now.'

'That's good. I'm glad you're okay. Uncle Adam is very smart and kind. He always makes me feel better,' Jackson explained matter-of-factly.

A short laugh slipped from Adam's lips. 'Thanks buddy. You're the best wingman a guy could ask for.'

Jackson looked at their entwined hands. 'Is Crystal your girlfriend, Uncle Adam?'

When Adam glanced at Crystal, she gazed at him expectantly. He turned back to Jackson and nodded. 'Yes, she is, but shh.' He brought his finger to his lips. 'It's a secret, so don't tell anyone okay?'

He mimed zipping his mouth closed. 'My lips are sealed.'

ೞଓ

Jade

Club Commotion always drew a large crowd on a Friday, but that night was especially busy, the extra body heat countering the mild weather outside. DJ Dieteronimo had released the first single from his upcoming album and word was spreading that he was the hottest up and comer in town. Jade was happy for him as she pushed through the crowd, making her way up to Sargon's balcony to get a better view of the stage.

'Evening, gorgeous.' Sargon grinned as he beckoned her, his gold tooth sparkling when illuminated by the strobes. 'Will you have a drink with me?'

'If you're paying.' She winked before taking a seat across from him.

Laughing, he snapped his fingers and a scantily clad bar maid appeared at their table. 'Daphne, sweetheart, would you kindly get a mojito on the house for the lovely Jade?'

'Yes, sir.' The girl turned toward the bar and waited for Sargon to cop a feel of her arse before she tended to the drink order.

'The new favourite?' Jade inquired.

'Ah huh. She's such a doll, don't you think?'

Jade shrugged. 'I suppose. You're going through them quicker than usual these days.'

'I guess my expectations rose since you left me. Why don't you come back to work here, Jade? I'll pay you much better than that godawful supermarket and you'll have much more fun.'

She sighed. 'You know Dieter would never approve.'

Sargon shook his head. 'That man has you more whipped than a submissive in a BDSM dungeon.'

Jade burst out laughing. 'He prefers monogamy and I'm okay with that.'

'Are you though? I see the way you look at other men like they are on an all-you-can-eat buffet, but you are on a diet.'

'I've been there and done that, Sargon. It's time to move on with my life. Besides, it's not like Dieter has put a stop to all of my fun.' She turned her gaze toward the DJ booth, but her eyes fell short when she spotted a familiar gold shirt on the dancefloor. A pair of bimbos flanked Apollo, grinding against him as he alternated between sucking each of their faces. She scowled at the sight of them. *What the hell is wrong with me? I should be happy he is moving on.* 'I guess Apollo has the night off,' she remarked, unable to curb the bitter edge to her voice.

'Nah. He's always working, but that guy knows how to mix business and pleasure. With how the pair of you hit it off, I'm surprised you're not joining them.'

CRYSTAL'S CRUCIBLE

Jade rolled her eyes at him. 'You don't get the concept of monogamy at all, do you?'

''Fraid not, sweets. The word has never been part of my vocab.' He flashed her another toothy grin. 'Seriously though, have you prepared yourself for the lonely nights ahead when Dieter starts touring? Surely he doesn't expect you to behave when he is halfway 'round the world buried balls deep in groupies.'

Narrowing her eyes, she pretended her fingers were scissors cutting something. 'He wouldn't dare.'

He laughed. 'Not if he knows what's good for him, but he is a man, and speaking for my kind, most of us are weak-willed rakes.' Picking up his e-cigarette, he puffed on the sweet-smelling vapour before offering it to her.

Accepting it eagerly, she inhaled a lungful. 'Thanks. I guess Dieter and I will cross that bridge when we come to it. He hasn't even mentioned tours yet.' They watched the rest of Dieter's set, vaping and drinking together in silence. She took her leave of Sargon and headed for the stairs.

Passing one of the private booths, a flash of gold drew her eye, and she stopped in her tracks. The red velvet curtain was partly open, inviting voyeurs to witness the carnal acts taking place inside. Apollo had one girl on her knees as she swallowed him whole. The other sprawled out on the table, moaning from the lip service he was giving her. Jade's core flooded with desire, drenching her panties as she enjoyed the live porn show.

Lifting his head, Apollo wiped his glistening gob with the back of his hand. Catching Jade's gaze, he smirked. 'Would you like to join us?'

Indecision paralysed her, as though trapping her in some form of purgatory. She could not tear her eyes away from the deviant devil before her and return to the ardent angel who warmed her bed at night.

'Or do you prefer to watch?' He pulled out of Hoover's mouth and lined himself up at Table Girl's entrance.

Words failed Jade; the sight of his thick crown gliding along the girl's slick folds mesmerised her.

'This could be *your* sweet pussy, Jade.' He thrust inside the woman and Jade heard herself whimper in unison with Table Girl.

Approaching footsteps broke her trance and she looked up in time to see Dieter headed her way.

CRYSTAL'S CRUCIBLE

She wrenched the curtain closed and hurried into her boyfriend's arms.

Chapter Nineteen

Crystal

'Gosh, I can't believe I've never been through the Dandenong Ranges before. They are stunning.' Crystal drove up toward the function centre along a road densely lined with a mix of ferns and towering gums.

'Yeah, they are,' agreed Esme. 'I can't believe you waited until today to tell me about your new *boyfriend*. Why didn't you ring me the moment you got home on Thursday?'

'Because I was still in a daze. I'm not sure how I got home in one piece.'

Esme laughed. 'Wow, he sounds like a dangerous drug. The police should do random hormone testing.'

'I know, right!' Crystal had almost failed to recognise herself in the mirror earlier that night, not only because of the thick makeup, or the strapless cocktail dress. It was the extra pep in her voice and bounce in her step. 'I'm going to need you to chaperone me tonight, to keep me from running into Adam's arms and exposing our secret.'

'I'll do my best, but you did promise me there would be some eligible bachelors on the menu, hence this ridiculous dress. I don't know why Mum insists on making me look like a Chinese doll.' Esme was attired in a black, knee length cheongsam with a red floral pattern, and her hair was in a traditional updo.

'You look hot in that dress, Ez. Your mum knows what she's doing.' Crystal pulled into the parking lot, her breath hitching when she realised she had instinctively parked next to Adam's BRZ.

Men in expensive suits and ladies in glittering gowns hovered around the entrance to the reception room. Adam was the only familiar face among them, and his eyes lit up the moment they locked with Crystal's. Linking arms with Esme, she approached him with measured steps, whispering, 'That's him.'

'Hello Crystal. You look lovely this evening.' Adam's formal tone contrasted with the lust blazing in his gaze as he admired her outfit.

'Thank you, Adam.'

Esme's throat clearing interrupted their private smile.

'Oh right, Adam, this is my best friend, Esme Kwan.'

'It's a pleasure to meet you, Esme.' He shook her hand.

'Same here,' replied Esme. 'I've heard so much about you and it's good to put a face to the name in Crissy's stories.'

Quirking his brows, he fixed his attention back on Crystal. 'Stories hmm? I hope you've been saying good things about me.'

'I believe the more appropriate word is pleasant,' Crystal reminded him.

Adam laughed. 'Touché.' Slipping a hand to the small of Crystal's back, he led them over to a group of men in tailored tuxedos. 'I'd like to introduce you to our CEO. Henry, this is Dr. Crystal Buchanan, our newest addition to the team. She heads up our R&D department at Dandenong.'

Flashing his pearly whites, Henry took Crystal's hand in a firm shake. 'Ah yes, our youngest manager thus far. I hear you are something of a prodigy, Crystal.' With a full head of thick, grey hair and prominent chin, Henry could have passed as Patrick Dempsey's older brother.

CRYSTAL'S CRUCIBLE

Her cheeks heated with the compliment. 'Thank you, sir.' If Adam had not already swept her off her feet, Crystal could have seen herself falling for the silver fox.

Adam continued introducing the executives and their partners before guiding Crystal and Esme to their allocated table. 'I'm sitting with the bigwigs, but I'll catch up with you later tonight.'

Her heart dipped, but it was for the best. 'No worries. See you then.'

His hand lingered a moment on her back before he composed himself and returned to his place near the door. Crystal inspected the place cards at her empty table, smiling when she realised she would be with most of her team. The only exceptions were Katrina who did not attend social events, and Denzel who was still dealing with his family crisis.

'This place is gorgeous,' remarked Esme as she took her seat and glanced around. The décor was modern and simple, drawing the eye to the breathtaking view. Floor to ceiling windows surrounded the circular room, providing a panoramic view of the forest canopy in the foreground and Melbourne's skyline beyond.

CRYSTAL'S CRUCIBLE

'Sure is. I can't wait to see the city lights once the sun sets.'

The rest of Crystal's department arrived gradually over the next half hour, giving her an opportunity to introduce Esme to each of them. Once they were all settled in, a waiter approached Crystal. 'Which main course would you like this evening, ma'am?'

Glancing at the menu for the first time, she saw there was a choice of barramundi, chicken, or something vegetarian. 'The fish please.'

'An excellent choice. Can I pour you a glass of wine?' He waved toward the selection sitting on the table.

'Just water for me, thanks.'

Markos—who sat next to Crystal in his signature brown suit—tapped her on the shoulder. 'You know the Company are paying for *all* of this, right?'

Crystal planted a smile on her face. 'I appreciate the gesture, but I don't drink alcohol.'

'Like ever?' He gaped at her like she was a foreign life form he had encountered for the first time, while the waiter moved across to take Esme's order.

CRYSTAL'S CRUCIBLE

Laughing, Hans ordered the fish before leaning across Esme's place to join the conversation. 'Dude! She's never even smoked a single joint in her life either.'

Crystal rolled her eyes. 'Dear God, I feel like I'm back at a high school peer pressure party.'

A deep belly laugh bubbled out from Markos. 'Tell me, Esme, how did you and Crystal meet?'

Topping up her glass of chardonnay, Esme glanced at Markos with a coy smile. 'We went to uni together.'

Eyes bugging out, Hans looked from Esme to Crystal and back again. 'Wait! Are you ladies like lesbian lovers?'

'What? No!' Esme's attention shot to Hans. 'Why would you think that?'

'Crystal did bring you along as her plus one tonight.' Hans waggled his eyebrows. 'It's okay if you are. I'm quite partial to a bit of girl-on-girl action myself.'

Crystal sprayed her mouthful of water across the table. 'Hans! That's hardly appropriate dinner conversation, let alone something to say with female colleagues present.'

CRYSTAL'S CRUCIBLE

'Sorry, boss. I forget to use my filter sometimes.'

Timothy, the man who was essentially Hans' supervisor, shook his head in resignation and offered Crystal an apologetic look, as though he was directly responsible for the guy's behaviour.

'To be clear,' Crystal explained with a playful tone in her voice, 'I brought Esme here because I wanted to introduce her to a few nice, single men, but I fear I may have misjudged some of you.' She narrowed her eyes on Hans. 'Sorry, Ez. I should have swapped places with you when I first thought of it.'

Esme's cheeks had turned a pretty shade of pink. 'It's okay.'

Markos steered their discussion to safer topics, like politics and religion, as their meal came out in a series of courses. The tension around the table had dispersed and Crystal relaxed for the most part. It was impossible to unwind completely with a certain pair of chestnut eyes frequently catching her gaze across the room.

༄༅

CRYSTAL'S CRUCIBLE

Jade

There were times when the hair of the dog[12] was the only answer. In her attempts to push Apollo from her mind the night before, Jade had dropped a cocktail of pills and washed them down with twice her weight in booze. She was still buzzing from the high until noon when the mother of all comedowns hit her. Dieter had nursed her through the worst of it, but it still felt like a thrash band had turned her skull into their kick drum when Dieter headed into the club for his sound check. This was why Jade walked into the place at ten o'clock, pre-loaded on half a bottle of Jäger.

DJ Dieteronimo was the headline act, which meant another late one. When she headed up to Sargon's balcony, she found him and Dieter talking business with a bunch of industry giants in suits each worth more than the sum total of her assets. Jade turned for the stairs. Losing herself in a crowd of sweaty, writhing bodies would be preferable to making small talk with a group of gormless hacks who only found their way into the music business because they lacked the necessary moral integrity for a career selling used cars.

---

[12] Hair of the dog means curing a hangover with alcohol.

CRYSTAL'S CRUCIBLE

She got as far as the hallway Sargon had dubbed his 'Carnal Corridor,' when a hand reached out from behind a red velvet curtain, grabbing her wrist and dragging her into a private booth. Strong arms wrapped around her, swinging Jade around to face the table, and bringing her back flush with a hard chest. A wave of tingles, like feathers dancing across her skin, replaced momentary panic when the familiar woodsy scent filled her nose.

Apollo's warm breath caressed her neck as he spoke in his deep, toe-curling voice. 'I'm sick of waiting, gorgeous.' One of his hands plunged beneath her sweetheart neckline, gaining direct access to her braless breasts. Yanking up the hem of the bodycon dress, he cupped her exposed pussy with the other hand. 'Tell me you don't want this, and I'll stop.' He flicked that sensitive bundle of nerves nestled among her folds, applying more pressure to it with his thumb.

She whimpered, unable to summon the words she needed to stop him. A finger stroked her entrance. He was the flint to her steel, igniting a spark as he struck her flesh with his own.

'I'm not hearing any protests. Do you want me to stop?' The words were on the tip of her tongue, but when he bit her earlobe and squeezed her clit, her mind went blank. He rammed three fingers deep inside her, bringing her close to climax, but backing off before she got there. 'Do you want me, Jade?'

Her body quaked, her core quivered, and her voice quavered, 'Y-y-yes.'

'What's that, sweetheart? I didn't quite hear you?' He plucked her bud like a guitar string.

'I-I said yes.'

'Yes what? What do you want from me, Jade?'

'Fuck me, damnit!'

He shoved her forward and she tumbled into the Laminex table, thankful for the bolts fixing it to the floor when she gripped the smooth edge to steady herself. Feeling the loss of contact like a slap to the face, she shivered. But the chill did not last. The unmistakable sound of a zipper, followed by the ripping of foil, sent a rush of heated blood through her veins, and anticipation flooded her body. Seconds later, Apollo's firm hands bent her over, pressing her breasts into the solid surface as he held her down. 'Tell me again, Jade. What do you want?' His voice was gruff as he rubbed the tip of his dick along her opening.

CRYSTAL'S CRUCIBLE

'I want your cock, Apollo. I want you to fuck me, *hard*.' The moment he thrust into her, pain mixed with intense pleasure and Jade's vision blurred. He pulled out and slammed back into her. Again, and again, with unrelenting force. Her muscles clenched and she exploded around him. Before she had time to recover from one orgasm, he drove her over the edge again, and again, showing her no mercy as he turned her inside out.

Once Apollo had finished, he collapsed onto the velvet couch. 'Come here, sweetheart,' his voice was low and husky.

Trembling, Jade turned to face him, perching her butt on the table. 'Why?'

'Please just come here,' he begged, all trace of his usual bossy tone gone.

She stumbled toward him, feeling her headache return as soon as she stood upright. Digging his fingers into her hips, he pulled her onto his lap, enveloping her in his warm embrace.

Grasping her chin with his thumb and forefinger, Apollo lifted her gaze and searched her eyes. 'Please tell me you want more, because I'm already addicted to you, Jade.'

She sucked in a breath, processing the emotions swirling in her chest. 'Yes,' she whispered, and Apollo devoured her lips in an all-consuming kiss.

Chapter Twenty

Crystal

Crystal sat alone at her table, tapping her feet to the lively jazz music as she watched the frivolities, laughing as Hans and Esme tried to outdo each other's stupid swing-dance moves. Along with most of the senior team members, Markos had already taken off, much to Crystal's disappointment. She had secretly hoped he and Esme would hit it off. *At least Ez is having fun.*

A hand clamped onto her shoulder, disrupting her thoughts. 'May I have this dance?'

She looked up into Adam's impish grin. 'Is that wise? What if people suspect something is going on between us?'

Squatting beside her, he spoke in a hushed voice. 'No one is paying enough attention. We have reached the magical time of night when everyone is too absorbed in their own business to care what anyone else is doing.'

Scanning the room, she realised he was right. Everyone else was either dancing or wrapped in conversation. She glanced at the hand he offered her and bit her lip.

'Come on, baby. This may be the closest thing we get to a proper date for a while, and I intend to make the most of it.'

'Okay, fine. Just keep it clean.' She rose and let him lead her onto the dance floor. Truth be told, her feet longed to move with the live band's music. 'The Company has gone all out for this Christmas party.'

Adam placed his right hand on the small of her back, gripping hers in his left as they assumed a closed position. 'It's the main event of the year, and Henry feels we deserve it for working so hard.'

'That's sweet of him. Henry seems like a nice fellow.'

Adam arched his brow. 'He is, but I hope I won't be competing with him for your affections. I saw the way you were checking him out earlier.' His tone was teasing, although there was a hint of worry in his eyes.

CRYSTAL'S CRUCIBLE

Crystal laughed. 'Fear not. He is too old and married for me. I would never get involved with someone else's husband.' Staring into his eyes, she drummed her fingers in his palm. 'Nor am I ever going to cheat on my own partner.'

The music slowed and the singer began crooning the lyrics to 'I've Got a Crush on You,' prompting Adam to tug Crystal closer. Lifting his hand up her back, he brushed her bare shoulders and smiled. 'Thank you.' He held her gaze and the air between them grew thick with desire. When his head tilted forward, she feared he was about to kiss her out in the open, but his mouth moved to her ear at the last minute. 'I'm dying to know if this is the same dress you wore in that photo you put on Tinder.'

'It is, actually.'

A small moan escaped his throat. 'Christ! We need to get out of here before I do something royally stupid. Say your goodbyes, then head outside and wait by your car. I'll meet you in a few minutes.'

'Okay.' Crystal made her way over to Esme. 'Hey Ez, I'm heading home. Do you want a lift with me, or should I call you an Uber?'

CRYSTAL'S CRUCIBLE

Hans sidled up next to Esme and draped his arm over her shoulder. 'I can give her a lift.'

Crystal's wide eyes darted from Hans to Esme who giggled and threw her arm around his waist. 'I'll be fine, Crissy. Don't worry about me. Go, have a good night 'cause I know I will.' She winked.

Laughing, Crystal shook her head. 'Night.' The air was brisk when she stepped outside, and she wished she remembered her cardigan. She looked through her boot and backseat, hoping there was something in there. It was wishful thinking because she never left things in her immaculate car. The sound of central locking beeped beside her, and she bumped her head on the doorframe. '*Shoot!*' Looking up, she met Adam's sidelong glance.

'Are you okay?'

She rubbed her head, feeling a bump emerging. 'Yeah. I guess this sneaking around has me on edge.'

'The fear of being caught doesn't thrill you?' The right side of his mouth quirked up into a sly grin.

'Sorry to disappoint but I don't have a rebellious streak. I think my sister pulled all of those tendencies out of the kiddie gene pool.'

CRYSTAL'S CRUCIBLE

Adam pressed up against Crystal, trapping her against the icy, metal chassis of her Impreza. Stroking her face, he soothed her with his soft, silky words, 'Nothing about you could disappoint me, baby.'

She should have pushed him away or screamed at Adam for risking such an intimate display. They were still outside a building full of the people who must not know about their relationship. Instead, she brought her lips to his, kissing him chastely.

With a groan, he stepped back and adjusted the tent in his pants. 'Come on, let's go. Follow me in your car, I want to take you somewhere nearby that'll be more... private.'

'Okay,' she rasped. They drove for about five minutes before pulling into a carpark surrounded by trees. When she stepped out, Adam was holding his suit jacket as he approached her.

'Here, put this on.'

She let him dress her in the soft cotton blend; feeling it caress her skin. Instinctively, she pressed her nose into her shoulder, inhaling Adam's fresh scent in the fabric. 'Thank you.' There was one other vehicle parked nearby; a silver Corolla with fogged up windows, and Crystal felt her cheeks flush as she imagined what the occupants were doing. Lacing her fingers with Adam's, they walked onto a deck overlooking the forest.

'The view is better at dusk and dawn,' he explained. 'Sorry it's too dark to see much now.'

'That's okay, my eyes are still adjusting, but I can see a bit.' The moonlight helped. Even though it was waning, there had been a full moon two nights ago, and the majestic white light was shimmering on the lake below. As soon as she moved up to the railing for a better vantage point, Adam's arms encased her in his warmth, his hands gripping the wooden beam. Closing her eyes for a minute, she savoured the sensation of Adam's solid body against her back; his hot breath tickling her neck.

When he kissed the crown of her head, she mewled like a kitten and turned to face him. His eyes filled with flickering flames, narrowing on her lips moments before his mouth claimed hers. Pushing up on her toes, she dug her fingers into his shoulder blades and deepened the kiss. The prickly hair of his chinstrap beard had been strange and uncomfortable the first couple of times, but she had grown to love the feel of his bristles scratching her, to crave it even. When their tongues danced together, she could taste his breath mint and a twinge of panic seized her. *Why didn't I think of taking one? I hope I don't have bad breath from dinner.* She pulled back to gather her thoughts.

Adam grinned. 'I have booked a room at a cute hotel nearby. Shall we continue this there?'

She gaped at him. 'Oh, um… I don't think I'm ready for that.'

He sighed. 'We don't have to have sex, Crystal. All I want is to spend the night holding and kissing you.'

Uncertainty played its familiar tune in her mind as she twirled a strand of hair and considered his proposition. *Is it a wise idea to climb into bed with Adam? He is still a man, after all.*

Cradling her head in his large palm, he gave her a serious look. 'I promised I'd let you set the pace and I intend to keep my word. I will not force myself on you, nor pressure you into doing anything you don't feel comfortable with.'

Crystal bit her lip. Hard. After taking a deep breath and heaving it out beneath the weight of her rapidly beating heart, she nodded. 'Okay, but no funny business, mister.'

He simpered. 'Of course not. I am a perfect gentleman. Your virtue is safe with me, Dr. Buchanan.'

CRYSTAL'S CRUCIBLE

※

Adam

Adam had spent the rest of the weekend in a hazy dream state, filling it with as much Crystal time as he could manage. They had made out like a couple of virginal teenagers until the early pre-dawn hours, slept with their limbs wrapped around each other, and woken up for more heated kisses. Keeping his pants on had almost killed him, but he cared too much for Crystal to push his luck. After gorging on a full English breakfast, they had returned to his house and played a few rounds of chess, all of which he had lost, but he relished the challenge. Returning to reality on Monday had been gruelling, especially since he had to avoid the temptation to shove Crystal up against the wall and devour those plump cherry lips whenever he saw her.

Greg barged into Adam's office at lunch time, preventing him from taking the one opportunity he had thus far to get some time alone with Crystal. 'What the heck do you want?' he grumbled as Greg closed the door.

CRYSTAL'S CRUCIBLE

'To caution you. Dancing with Crystal on Saturday night in front of the bosses was daring. If *I* noticed the way you were looking at her, I'm sure Henry did too. And disappearing around the same time? Hardly subtle, man.'

'Shoot! Did any of them mention it to you?'

'No, but I bet they are going to keep a closer eye on you now. Why are you still messing around with her? I get she's hot, but is that sweet young pussy of hers worth the risk to your job?'

'This isn't merely some casual fling, Greg. I have some strong feelings for her, and we haven't even had sex yet.'

Gobsmacked, Greg shook his head before changing the subject to tennis.

Adam did not get a chance to catch Crystal alone until seven PM, when the place resembled a ghost town. Finding her office empty, his heart sank until he glanced out of her window and noticed her car was still on site. He found her in the labs, setting up some glassware. 'There you are.'

She looked up and gave him the biggest, brightest smile. 'Hi. I wanted to test a theory I came up with today.'

He cocked his brow. 'And it couldn't wait for tomorrow?'

CRYSTAL'S CRUCIBLE

Crystal sucked on her bottom lip, making Adam jealous of her teeth. 'I suppose, but I want to get this done before we fly to Sydney on Wednesday, and I won't be able to sleep until I try it.'

Being a self-proclaimed workaholic with a borderline high-functioning brain, Adam knew exactly what she meant. 'I could think of ways to get your mind off work; to help you sleep.' He bobbed his brows for effect.

Her teeth clamped down on her lip again and he lost it. Closing the small distance between them, he pressed Crystal against the bench, grabbed her hips, and kissed her passionately. She moaned into his mouth, stoking the furnace in his loins, so he thrust against her. Gasping, she withdrew and stared at him with wide eyes. One second ticked by. *Two… Three…*

She jumped at him, wrapping her legs around his waist, and clinging to him like a monkey as she smothered his mouth with kisses. He walked her back and propped her arse on the bench, freeing his hands to explore her body. His fingers ventured up her spine and along her collarbone. Ripping her lab coat open, he stood back and stared at the hint of cleavage beneath her white blouse. Lifting his gaze, he sought her eyes for permission while his fingers skirted along the edge of her neckline.

After sucking in a breath, Crystal unbuttoned her shirt in gradual, deliberate movements, keeping her eyes locked with his. Her hand hovered over his for a moment before guiding it inside her bra.

Adam gasped when he found her puckered nipples. 'Can I taste them?'

'Yes.' Her voice was hoarse and breathy.

Tugging the bra cups down, he exposed her hard, pink buds and his dick surged to life. He flicked his tongue against one of them and she whimpered. As he took her sweet, tender flesh between his teeth, Crystal arched her back, pushing into him with wanton desire. He sucked and nibbled on her, eliciting more primal sounds from the depths of her body. When he moved across to her other breast, he noticed she was fingering herself. Overcome by the need to touch her *there*, he thrust a hand inside her pants.

The moment his forefinger brushed her clit, she jerked back, knocking over a retort stand. A crucible crashed onto a heater-stirrer. When the volatile contents of the dish hit the hot element, the chemicals burst into flames.

CRYSTAL'S CRUCIBLE

'God damnit!' Crystal cried as she jumped to action. She dashed across the room and grabbed the fire extinguisher. 'Kill the power, Adam!'

The sound of his name snapped him out of his shock, and he rushed over to the emergency shut-off switch. After punching the big red button, he spun around to watch in amazement as Crystal doused the fire like an expert. They both fell silent as they cleaned up the mess. Adam had no idea what thoughts occupied Crystal's mind, but he did not ask. Thinking of how to report the incident became his primary concern. There was no way to hide the evidence. The fire singed the bench, and the extinguisher would need replacing. *What am I supposed to put on the form? I can hardly write 'foreplay' as the cause. Jesus, what was I thinking?*

When they finished packing everything away, Crystal hung her lab coat on the hook by the door. 'Good night, Adam.'

'Crystal, wait! I—'

'Please don't. Not right now. I'm exhausted and I need to be alone. We'll talk about this tomorrow.' She hurried out of the building before he could protest further.

Adam heaved a heavy sigh. Mental note: chemistry labs are not a safe place for second base.

Chapter Twenty-One

Crystal

Paranoia prickled like a rash across every inch of Crystal's skin. Whenever she caught herself scratching an itch, she inspected the area, expecting to see patches of eczema, but there was nothing more than the red marks from her own fingernails. After the fire she started in the lab the previous night, everyone was giving her suspicious looks, studying her like a specimen under the microscope. She was avoiding all contact with Adam, out of fear and embarrassment.

The only person who appeared oblivious to the whole incident—as he whistled away in the analytical lab—was Hans. Looking up from the HPLC machine, he beamed. 'Yo, Crissy! I've been meaning to thank you for introducing me to my beautiful Princess Esmerelda. You've made me the happiest man!'

CRYSTAL'S CRUCIBLE

'Wait, what?' She stopped in the doorway and gaped at him.

'Ez didn't tell you?'

'Tell me what?'

'We hooked up at the Christmas party and have been talking on the phone every night since. I'm surprised she didn't mention it to you.'

A cinching cramp clamped around Crystal's chest. *Why didn't Ez call me?* She recalled letting her phone go flat, too caught up in her own love life for the last few days to charge it, and a wave of guilt washed away the pain. 'Oh, um, my phone's been out of commission since Saturday night.'

With brows rising, Hans tilted his head and studied her. 'I heard about your fire incident last night. Is everything okay? Something is distracting you lately.'

Damnit! A metallic taste oozed into her mouth, and she realised she was biting her lip too hard.

'Judging by those pink cheeks of yours, I'm guessing you've been getting some action too. You should bring him along to the *Episode IX* opening tomorrow night.'

'Oh shoot! I'm sorry Hans, I forgot! I'll be in Sydney for a work conference tomorrow.'

CRYSTAL'S CRUCIBLE

'Bugger! I was looking forward to seeing you in costume… and meeting your new beau.'

She laughed nervously. 'I never said I had a man in my life.'

'You didn't have to. It's written all over your face.'

'Well, have fun tomorrow night.' Crystal escaped the room before Hans asked for details. She headed back to her office and plugged her phone into the charger. When she turned it on, there were twenty missed calls and a bunch of texts from Esme, Adam, and Jade. Ignoring the others, she checked the messages from Esme. They started out referring to some exciting news she was dying to share, and begging Crystal to answer so she could spill the beans in person rather than text. The thread soon dissolved into snide remarks and angry faced emojis and finished with expressions of concern over Crystal's wellbeing. She typed out a reply:

Sorry for ghosting you. My phone was flat, and I only just got to a charger. Things have been super busy and crazy. I will ring you tonight.

As soon as she hit SEND, a call came through from Adam and she accepted before she realised what she was doing. 'Oh, um… hey.'

'Why are you dodging my calls, emails, *and* messages?' Adam's tone was like sour lemon juice laced with a bitter resentment pill. 'I need you in my office now. And before you argue, this is an urgent work matter.' He hung up before she could respond.

The blood drained from her face. *Time to bite the bullet.*

Adam looked up from behind his desk when Crystal entered. 'Lock the door.'

After complying with his request, she sat in a visitor's chair and waited.

'I get that you're crapping yourself after last night, but I'm still your boss, which means you can't give me the cold shoulder at work. Especially when you owe me an incident report.'

'I… I'm sorry.'

He pushed a form across his desk. 'I took the liberty of drafting this for you. I know it's a big fat fib, but it's the best story I could come up with to absolve both of us and avoid arousing suspicion.'

> *Description of Incident: I (Crystal Buchanan) was preparing an experiment to test my latest theory when Adam's sudden appearance in the lab startled me. Focussing on my task at the time, I did not hear him enter the*

room. As a result, I jumped and knocked over a retort stand. This sent the volatile reaction mixture smashing into a hotplate and igniting. Adam isolated the power while I doused the flames with the appropriate fire extinguisher.

'This is fine,' Crystal lied as bile rose from her empty stomach and burned her oesophagus. None of this was okay. She was about to commit fraud.

'I'll need you to fill out the specifics regarding PPE and the chemicals involved etcetera.'

She nodded as tears pooled in her eyes.

With a sigh, Adam lowered his voice. 'Talk to me, baby. What's going through your mind?'

Crystal met his gaze as a few salty tears dripped onto her lips. 'Our relationship needs to stop.'

Adam visibly tensed. 'I don't think so. We simply have to be more careful.'

She shook her head. 'No. That fire was a sign, Adam. A huge red flag. We shouldn't be together.'

CRYSTAL'S CRUCIBLE

'Nonsense!' He spat the word, rising from his seat, and rounding the desk with the fury of a charging bull. Collapsing to his knees in front of her, he grabbed her hands and peered up at her with pleading eyes. 'I know you don't believe in such illogical, superstitious nonsense.'

'This isn't about omens. What happened last night is proof neither of us have our heads screwed on right and there is too much at stake.'

'You think I don't know that? Let's just play it safer.'

'No. I can't do this anymore.'

He dropped his head in her lap and Crystal combed her fingers through his hair, feeling the rise and fall of his chest against her legs. After several seconds of excruciating silence, he looked up at her. 'What *really* scares you, Crystal?'

'I'm worried about you losing your job.'

His eyes narrowed. 'I know there's more to it. You flinch every time I touch you… intimately. Like when I tried to pleasure you last night. Why?'

Sucking in a deep breath, she held it trapped in her lungs as she considered how to broach the topic with him. *May as well get it over with.* 'Ihaveasexphobia.'

CRYSTAL'S CRUCIBLE

He blinked a few times and furrowed his brow. 'Did you just say you have a phobia? Of sex?'

She nodded.

'But you're not a virgin, so…' His voice trailed off as he turned deathly pale. 'Oh God, does that mean you were—'

'No. It's not what you think. I've never had a meaningful relationship before. The only men I've ever dated in the past lied about their feelings and manipulated me. All they wanted was to get in my pants and as soon as they got their way, they dumped me. I developed a complex and tried to deal with it by having a few one-night stands of my own, but the sex was always lousy. Over time my problem escalated to a full-blown fear.'

Adam stared at her, slack jawed. 'Wow. I'm sorry for how those arseholes treated you. Wait, if you didn't enjoy the sex, does that mean you've never orgasmed?'

She bit her lip. 'Not with a man, I haven't. I manage it fine on my own.'

A growl rumbled from his diaphragm. 'Selfish wankers like that should be castrated. There is no excuse for not getting a woman off. Even when our dicks don't cooperate, we have plenty of other means.'

CRYSTAL'S CRUCIBLE

'To be fair, the last couple of guys did try their darndest. I couldn't get out of my head and relax enough to enjoy it. I'm sorry, Adam, but I don't see how this is going to work for us in the long run. I'm too broken to be fixed.'

Scooping her up in his arms, Adam sat her on his desk, right where they had shared their first kiss. 'You are *not* broken, you hear me. We will work through this, *together*. You have been the first sign of light in my own darkness and I'm not giving up on you. I know being with you risks my job, but I'd rather that than lose my one chance at true happiness. Just please stay with me.'

All of Crystal's pent-up emotions poured out of her tear ducts. Adam wrapped his arms around her, whispering soothing words in her ear.

'I don't know how to do this.'

'It's okay, baby. We'll take it slow. One day at a time. I'm a patient man and I'll do whatever it takes to keep you by my side. Even if that means cooling it down a notch while we sort through things.'

A new sense of hope sparked in her heart, bringing a smile to her face. 'Do you mean that?'

'Yes, Crystal. I meant every word.'

CRYSTAL'S CRUCIBLE

ఠఁ

Crystal

Temptation incarnate would be a large, winged animal, one that could transport Crystal and Adam to a remote island away from prying eyes. The flight scheduled for the next day, however, would take them into the belly of the beast. Having packed a suitcase, Crystal collapsed on her bed and thought about her predicament. Sharing a hotel with Adam and not being able to touch him: the definition of torture. Needing to get her mind off the matter, she grabbed her phone and searched for Esme in the directory of contacts. Before she could make the call, her doorbell rang. Given the late hour, she considered ignoring it and calling her best friend anyway, but the visitor soon progressed to loud, incessant thumping. *Bloody hell. Don't tell me Mum locked herself out again.*

    The woman on the doorstep was not a drunk Judy, but a hysterical Jade, with tears streaming down her face. 'Why haven't you answered my damn calls?'

CRYSTAL'S CRUCIBLE

Crystal felt knots forming in her stomach as she tugged Jade inside, shunting the door with her foot. 'Oh shoot! What's wrong?'

Jade threw her arms around Crystal and wept against her neck.

'Shh, it's okay,' Crystal soothed, stroking her sister's back. 'Tell me what happened?'

'I screwed up big time.'

Ushering Jade further into the lounge room, Crystal sat her on the couch and embraced her tight. 'It can't be that bad if I'm not bailing you out of gaol.'

Jade huffed. 'Getting away with crimes doesn't make us any less guilty.'

Pulling back, Crystal studied Jade. 'What did you do?'

'I cheated on Dieter.' She followed her confession with a fresh bout of tears.

Crystal gaped at her. 'Does he know?' she asked in a whisper. Unable to speak through her crying, Jade shook her head. Crystal pulled her back in for another hug, waiting for the sobbing to subside before asking, 'When?'

'Saturday night. I… I fucked a guy at the club. Sargon's new dealer.'

'Oh boy! Was this a one-time thing?'

CRYSTAL'S CRUCIBLE

When Jade bit her bottom lip, Crystal's heart sank. Emotions swirled together like marbled paint. On one hand, she pitied her sister, on the flip side, she was sad for Dieter. They had always been the perfect couple and she figured it was only a matter of time before wedding bells chimed.

'This guy has pursued me for a while now,' Jade explained. 'He'd tempted me before, but I didn't give in until Saturday, although we did it like five times that night. I thought maybe he'd get me out of his system if we had sex, but I was wrong. He just rang me for another hook up. I don't know what to do, Crissy.'

'I can tell you what you *should* do.'

She gave Crystal an expectant look.

'Tell Dieter, and you can go from there.'

Jade's big, hazel eyes opened wide. 'That would crush him, not to mention his Visa.'

Crystal sighed. 'I know, and that's why I'm torn on this. I've learned there are lots of murky moral ambiguities when it comes to matters of the heart and I'm in no place to advise you, let alone judge you.'

'Hmph. Sounds like my baby sister is all grown up. Do me a favour?'

'Maybe. What do you need?'

CRYSTAL'S CRUCIBLE

'A distraction to keep me from running back to a certain sinful someone.'

'It's a good thing Mum is sleeping at her latest boyfriend's house tonight.' Backing up against the end of the sofa, Crystal placed a cushion in her lap. 'Come here.' She patted the pillow and Jade curled up against it. Once they settled, Crystal considered telling Jade all about Adam, but decided secrecy was too important. Instead, she turned on the television, and scrolled through the Netflix menu until she found *Ultraviolet*, a show they both agreed on.

Chapter Twenty-Two

Crystal

Crystal welcomed the blast of arctic air smacking her in the face when she entered Tullamarine's domestic terminal. It was a relief from the sweltering forty-degree heat of the late afternoon sun. Wheeling her suitcase along the white and grey speckled tiles, she approached the luggage check-in line where Adam was waiting for her. 'Hi.'

His thirsty eyes soaked up the sight of her. 'You look delicious in that outfit.'

She had opted for her strawberry dress. The light pink, figure-hugging fabric floated around her knees, displaying an array of red berries. 'Oh, um, you told me to dress for comfort on the plane, and with the heat, this was the best I had.'

Snaking an arm around her waist, he pulled her closer and grinned. 'I'm not complaining, even with my own comfort compromised.' Adam looked equally edible in his white shorts and pale pink Abercrombie polo shirt.

When his mouth brushed against her, Crystal gasped. 'We're in public, Adam. What if someone we know sees us?'

'I'll risk it for a taste of your sweet lips.' She could feel herself blushing, but the heat in her cheeks travelled south as soon as he kissed her. He pulled back from her with a groan. 'Keeping my hands off you for the next two and a half days will be torture.' They had both agreed further displays of affection in the workplace were a dangerous idea and that included corporate functions beyond the office. 'I can't wait to get you all to myself on Saturday.' He gestured for her to enter the check-in line, hovering close behind her.

Once they passed through security, they headed straight for their gate. Sitting beside Adam in the lounge area, Crystal zoned out, letting her mind drift. It was a shame to be missing the *Episode IX* opening that night and she wondered if Denzel would get a chance to see the movie on the big screen anytime soon.

Adam's hot hand clamped her thigh, yanking her from her thoughts. 'What's on your mind?'

She turned to him and forced a smile. '*Star Wars*.'

His brows ascended heavenward. 'Care to elaborate?'

'The latest film opens tonight. I was going to see it with the guys, but this conference came up. I'll have to make a point of going when I get home.'

'I'll take you. We can make it a date.'

'Really? That would be awesome!'

Sweeping her hair aside, he murmured in her ear, 'Anything for you, baby.'

Bubbles of joy floated in her chest, and Crystal theorised she could almost fly to Sydney without needing a plane.

They spent the rest of their journey discussing *Star Wars* and other favourite movies, while flirting and sneaking covert touches where they could. But as soon as their feet hit the Sydney tarmac, they adopted their game faces and professional graces.

When they entered the capacious hotel lobby, Henry Alden rose from one of the red, armless wingback seats in the lounge area to greet them with firm handshakes. 'Adam, Crystal, it's good to see you both again so soon. How was your flight?'

'Hassle free, which is always a plus,' replied Adam.

'Are you staying here too?' Crystal asked. 'I thought you lived in Sydney?'

'I live in the suburbs,' Henry explained. 'I figured it would be easier to stay at the conference venue, to save the commute. We all have deluxe rooms on the third floor. Why don't you folks go check-in and freshen up, then meet me in the bar for a drink?'

As soon as the elevator doors closed, Adam leaned into the back wall and combed his fingers through his hair. 'Damnit! I think Henry is on to us.'

Crystal's heart skipped a beat. 'What? Why?'

'This is the first time he has stayed on location for one of these things. He usually chooses a fancier hotel nearby or endures the drive. And slumming it with us in the deluxe rooms rather than taking a top floor suite? That can't be a coincidence. Greg was right.'

Hearing that creep's name sent a shiver down her spine. 'What do you mean?'

'According to Greg, our interactions on Saturday night looked suspicious. He said the bosses would likely be watching us.' The lift pinged, opening to their floor. Adam's hand jutted out, holding the door for Crystal.

Stopping outside her room, she offered Adam a sympathetic smile. 'Good thing we already talked about going cold-turkey on the PDA at work.'

'Is it though?' He stood in front of the adjacent room. 'Resisting the urge to touch you around other people is hard enough. But staying here, attempting to sleep right next door to you rather than sneaking into your room, is going to be downright painful.'

'I know, but we have to try.'

He held her gaze for several excruciating seconds before disappearing into his own room. When Crystal stepped into hers, she took a moment to appreciate her spacious accommodation, furnished with warm, neutral tones, and a huge bed. *If this is what Adam calls slumming it, I'd love to see what their idea of luxury is!* She opened her suitcase on the bed, hung up her clothes in the wardrobe, and took her toiletries bag into the bathroom. Her eyes immediately went to the deep, full-length tub calling to her like a siren. Remembering she had pressing obligations, she dismissed the thought, and settled for a quick shower. *The pamper session can wait until later tonight.*

Wearing a conservative black and beige midi sheath dress, Crystal made her way downstairs to meet Adam and Henry. The bar had a strong urban-industrial aesthetic going for it with distressed timbers, brass pipes, and copper features. She found Adam and several other managers at one of the tall, solid tables by the window. After reacquainting herself with everyone, she sat on the stool beside Henry and across from Adam. It was an advantageous spot, offering her a view of the bustling life outside in Sydney's World Square precinct. The vista was a much-needed distraction, saving her from drooling over the sight of Adam in a dark blue button-down shirt and grey chinos.

Henry turned to her. 'Are you hungry?'

'Yeah, I am. The meal on the plane wasn't enough.'

Laughing, he handed her a menu. 'They never are. Here, pick something. Everything is going on the Company card tonight.'

'Thanks.' She smiled, feeling her cheeks flush.

Henry ordered her meal and returned to his seat, moving closer to her. Gesturing to the wine bottles on the table, he asked, 'What's your poison? Red or white?'

'Oh, neither thank you. I don't drink alcohol.'

His brow arched. 'Is that so? Religious or health reasons; if you don't mind me asking?'

'Lifestyle choice, actually. My mum's an alcoholic, and addiction runs in my family, so I prefer to stay stone-cold sober.'

'Fair enough. I have heard lots of people swear off the stuff when they see what it does to their parents.'

'Indeed.' Glimpsing everyone's eyes on her, Crystal shifted uncomfortably. 'So, uh, where's your wife, Henry? Is she staying with you?'

'No. The missus couldn't make it. Too many of her own work commitments.' Henry leaned in closer, resting his hand on hers. 'Why do you ask?'

Sucking in a sharp breath, Crystal choked on her tongue and spluttered. 'I was thinking it would be nice to have another woman here to balance the testosterone.'

His fingers traced patterns along her hand. 'Are you sure that's all there is to it?'

ഩଔ

CRYSTAL'S CRUCIBLE

Adam

A red haze filled Adam's vision, as his eyes burned figurative holes into Henry's hand. Beneath the table, he clenched his fists together until he felt blood oozing from eight small crescent shaped wounds.

Fingers snapped in front of his face. 'Hello? Earth to Adam.'

'Ah, what?' Brows pinching at the bridge of his nose, he looked into Henry's partially glazed eyes.

Henry laughed. 'I asked you what you think Crystal's motives are, asking me if I am sleeping alone tonight. Do you think it's an innocent question, or does she have some ulterior motive?'

When he met Crystal's gaze, she gulped, but kept her countenance otherwise neutral. *Is this some kind of test?* Schooling his own expression, he turned his attention to Henry and shrugged. 'Hell if I know, although you don't strike me as her type, old man.'

A devilish smirk formed on Henry's face. 'On the contrary, that's not what I've heard from Professor Ashbury.'

CRYSTAL'S CRUCIBLE

What the…? Don't react. Don't react. Don't react. 'With all due respect, Henry, I doubt that's any of our business.'

'Hah! You're probably right.' Henry threw his arm across her shoulders. 'My apologies sweetheart, I didn't mean to dredge up your sordid past.' When he whispered something in her ear, Crystal gaped at him, her face ghostly pale.

The food arrived a moment later, giving Henry something else to occupy his filthy hands, and the conversation shifted to lighter topics. The night progressed and their party dwindled, one person at a time, until only Crystal and Adam remained.

After ordering two double shots of top shelf whisky on the rocks, Adam took the tumblers back to the table, putting one in front of Crystal. 'Here, I figured you could use a stiff drink after that, 'cause I sure as hell can.'

'I don't drink, remember?' She pushed the glass over to him.

'Oh right. Sorry, my mind was elsewhere. Have you ever been drunk?'

'No. I've never tasted a drop of alcohol.'

'Hmm.' The gears began turning in his brain, albeit sluggish and clunky from the numerous drinks he had imbibed to help take the edge off. There was only so much one man could endure when he was made to bear witness to a slimeball fondling his woman, while he was powerless to stop it.

'What?' Crystal's forehead creased.

'I theorise your inability to enjoy sex stems from your need for control in much the same way you refuse to drink a drop of alcohol.'

Her hazel eyes bugged out. 'That's preposterous!'

'Is it though? As a control freak myself, I recognise the signs and I think it's fair to say you have a strong need for control. More so than me, I'd wager. I can enjoy the occasional beverage,' he held up his whisky for effect, 'and I love losing myself during sex. Yet you can't bring yourself to do either.'

'It's an interesting hypothesis, but you're forgetting something. I can still get myself off.'

A mental image of Crystal pleasuring herself slipped into his mind, stirring his dick from its slumber. Adam forced the picture from his head by clearing his throat. 'The supposition still holds because when you bring yourself to climax, you still have control over the situation. You're not surrendering yourself to another or trusting anyone else by letting them see you at your most vulnerable. Intimacy opens us up to strong emotions and the possibility of heartbreak.'

Crystal was chewing her bottom lip. Without thinking, he reached across the table and pulled the abused flesh from her teeth using the pad of his thumb. 'Adam!' she hissed, eyes darting around the room.

He slumped back, making a concerted effort to maintain his balance on the backless stool. 'Sorry. I've been losing my mind tonight. I've never seen Henry behave like that before. The cruel bastard must have been testing me.'

'I don't think that was about you, or even us,' she whispered, leaning over. Her cleavage peeked out from beneath her V-neck dress.

Appreciating the buxom display, he licked his lips before lifting his gaze to her eyes. 'Why not? It took every ounce of my willpower to avoid reacting like a possessive caveman and clobbering the arsehole. He was clearly trying to get a rise out of me.'

She shook her head. 'Henry either wants me for himself, or he's testing *me*.'

'What?' The red haze returned.

CRYSTAL'S CRUCIBLE

'When he whispered in my ear, he told me his room number, inviting me to join him later.'

'What did you say?'

'Nothing. I was too shocked.'

'Good. Best tactic is to ignore his advances. If he touches you anywhere inappropriate, tell him to stop or kick him in the nuts, then report him, okay?'

She nodded. 'Don't worry, I won't let things get out of hand.'

Adam breathed a sigh of relief. 'So, who's this Professor Ashbury?'

෩෬

The Thief

Sneaking into the labs was a lot easier with the cats away. Even so, this rat was not about to take any extra risks. He had become accustomed to finding his way by the dim light of the exit signs and saw no need to turn on the overheads. Once the computer booted up, he typed in his associate's password and inserted the thumb drive. After the last breach, the head chumps had become extra vigilant about cyber security, which meant the most sensitive data was no longer saved on the main server. They used a separate closed network in the R&D labs and limited access to a selected few. He snickered, thinking how easy it had been to bypass their new safeguards. All it took was one mole to burrow their way into place and Bingo!

Using the secret file path the mole had given him, he found the gold he had been digging for, and copied the files across to the external drive. He opened a couple out of interest, but they were encrypted. *No matter, the family has ways and means around this.* Leaning back, he laced his fingers behind his head and relaxed while the data transferred.

A flicker of light beyond the window caught his attention. *Fuck!* He switched off the screen and dropped below the desk. *Who the hell is that?* He heard the click of a door and soft footfalls across the lab floor.

'I know you're in here. I can hear the hum of the computer's motor.'

Katrina?

Rounding the desk, she kneeled beside him, grinning like the cat that got the cream.

Huh. I guess I was wrong about all of them being away.

CRYSTAL'S CRUCIBLE

She ran one of her long talons along his face. 'You have been a bad boy, haven't you Gregory?'

He glared at her, remaining silent and refusing to admit anything.

'Why don't we make a deal? Use your position of power and influence in the ranks to have Crystal removed and put me in her throne, and I won't show the police all the evidence on you and your boy.'

'You've got shit,' he scoffed.

'Do you honestly want to test that theory? Because getting pinned for a drug racket like yours comes with some pretty heavy penalties.'

Greg shoved her up against the wall and wrapped his hands around her throat. 'You sure you wanna threaten me? Little piggie can't squeal if she's dead.' He tightened his grip, applying enough pressure to block her windpipe. He normally despised getting his hands dirty, leaving the wet work for others, but desperate measures and all that. Rather than struggle, she stood there with a smug grin. 'Damnit!' He pulled back, releasing her.

Her voice came out hoarse when she spoke, 'You are smarter than you look. Of course I wouldn't confront you without life insurance. Now, do we have a deal?'

CRYSTAL'S CRUCIBLE

Pausing for thought, he decided getting rid of Crystal could work in his favour since she knew some of his secrets. 'Okay fine. How long do I have?'

Chapter Twenty-Three

Crystal

The knots in Crystal's shoulders unravelled, gradually dissolving into the lavender scented bubbles surrounding her. She had survived the conference and another dinner with Aludel's executive managers with her dignity intact. Having an early flight the next day was the perfect excuse to avoid socialising more than necessary. The worst that had come of Henry's flirting was having to tell Adam about the embarrassing encounter with her third-year chemistry professor. Thankfully, Ashbury had acted with the necessary professional decorum, turning down her advances, else she might have done something truly regrettable. Even so, she did not expect him to mention it to Henry Alden.

With hands gliding across her bare skin, her mind turned to Adam. As one of her arms dipped between her legs, she heard a faint tap on her door. *Should I get that? It could be Henry and I don't want him barging into my room, but if it's Adam…* That thought alone prompted her to climb out of the tub and don a white, fluffy bathrobe. Easing open the door a crack, she found Adam and breathed a sigh of relief. She beckoned him inside, wrapped her arms around him, and pressed her lips to his.

Groaning into her mouth, he took charge of the kiss, walking her backwards until her legs hit the side of the bed. The impact, while slight, was enough to make her aware of the situation. Blushing, she broke the kiss and tugged at the seams of her robe to ensure they did not fall open. For a moment, Adam's eyes widened as he took in the sight of her, then they grew dark and heavy. 'Are you… naked under that?' He spoke with a husky voice.

Biting her lip, she nodded. 'I was in the bath.'

He sucked in an audible breath. 'I came in here to talk about a work issue, but seeing you like this… God, I'm holding onto my self-control by a thread. If you don't want me to make you lose yours all over that bed, I suggest putting some PJs on ASAP.'

CRYSTAL'S CRUCIBLE

'Okay,' she squeaked. 'Take a seat over there.'

Adam sat in the desk chair she had pointed to and watched as she retrieved a set of sleep shorts and camisole from her suitcase.

She caught his gaze and felt her cheeks flush again. 'I… uh… don't mind if you see me, but you might want to close your eyes to temper the torture.'

'Proceed,' he replied gruffly, keeping his eyes open.

Shoot. I didn't think he would take it as an invitation to watch me strip. Crystal held his stare for a few seconds before diverting her attention to the task at hand. In a deliberate motion, she untied the cord around her waist. When she began opening the robe, she heard his breath hitch, and looked up to see him gripping the arms of the chair with shaking hands. Lifting the garment from her shoulders, she let it drop to the floor. Her face was on fire as Adam's eyes scanned her body from head to toe. Not wanting to prolong the torture, she spun and grabbed her shorts, bending over the bed in the process.

CRYSTAL'S CRUCIBLE

'Oh hell!' The murmured curse slipped from Adam's mouth. 'You have the most incredible arse, baby.'

Glancing over her shoulder, she smiled. 'Um… thanks?' She noticed Adam's hand had moved inside his pants. Seeing the effect she had on him was empowering and arousing; liquid lust pooling between her legs. Forgetting her pyjamas, she dropped to the bed and resumed what she had started in the bath. 'Take your pants off, Adam. I want to see you pleasure yourself.'

He complied with her request, letting his engorged dick spring free. His thumb grazed across the tip, spreading precum down the long shaft. Crystal licked her lips, wondering what he tasted like. She had never had the courage to take a man's cock into her mouth before, and the sudden curiosity surprised her. With four fingers plunging between her folds and a thumb pressed against her clit, Crystal worked herself into a sexual frenzy, spurred on by the view Adam offered. Her vision blurred, and her body trembled, plummeting over the edge within half the time it usually took to make herself come. When her senses returned, she heard Adam grunting and looked across the room. His eyes closed and clenched as his own orgasm took hold.

Adam's lids fluttered open, and he gave her an impish grin. 'Best work meeting ever.'

Laughing, she rolled her eyes. 'That was *not* a work meeting.'

Swiping some tissues from the box on the desk, he cleaned himself. 'Not yet, but work was the reason I came to see you in the first place.'

'*Sure* it was,' she scoffed. 'You totally came to my room in the middle of the night, rather than waiting to see me back at the office, for the sole purpose of a business meeting.'

'Yeah, okay, I guess you got me on a technicality there. Now, would you mind covering up? I've already got another semi and it won't be long before things escalate.' Lifting his navy-blue flannel pants from where they had fallen around his ankles, he fastened them with the drawstring.

Crystal followed suit, dressing in the sleepwear she had picked out.

Closing the distance between them, Adam pulled her in for another kiss. Brushing her hair aside, he whispered in her ear, 'Thank you for such a special, intimate moment, Crystal. Trusting me like that was a big step, and it fills me with hope for all the things to come in our relationship.'

Wow! I orgasmed with a man! It had not even occurred to her until he put it like that. Sure, it may have been her own hands touching her, but she had let Adam witness the whole scene. It counted as significant progress in her opinion. Simpering, she lured him down onto the bed, kissing him more before curling up in his arms. 'What did you need to talk to me about?'

'After dinner, Henry called an urgent meeting with a few of us to discuss another security breach. I don't know if you were aware of this, but when IT recently isolated the sensitive data at each of our sites to department specific servers, they also set up monitors to track activity on these networks.'

'Obviously I knew about the restrictions, but I was unaware of the tracing.'

Adam sighed. 'They were able to identify some suspicious activity last night. Someone downloaded encrypted documents pertaining to the latest drug research to an external drive.'

'Shoot! That's not good.'

'No, it's not,' Adam agreed. 'It does mean, however, we can narrow our list of suspects to someone in your team.'

CRYSTAL'S CRUCIBLE

'What?' She jack-knifed, sitting upright in the bed. 'How can you be certain one of my guys or girls are responsible?' Crystal already knew Greg was the culprit and it pained her to keep his secret, but there was nothing she could do. There was no evidence to pin on him, and even if she could dig up something, there was a murky death threat cloud hovering above her whenever she considered spilling the beans.

'Only your team can log in to those computers, Crystal. Not only that, but they hid the files on the system. Meaning whoever stole those documents last night was either R&D personnel, or they were assisted by someone who is.'

Holy moly! Greg has an accomplice in my department. She thought back to the night she overheard him talking in the boardroom. Only discerning his voice, she assumed he was on the phone, but in hindsight, it was possible the other party in that conversation was right there in the room with him. 'What happens now?'

'Henry wants you and me to crack this case wide open. He sends his apologies for the flirting, by the way. Apparently, that was a test, but not the sort I had suspected. He was assessing your morality, to ensure he could trust you with the trials ahead.'

'*Seriously?* What a lughead.'

Adam shrugged. 'At least he doesn't suspect anything is going on between us.' Clutching her arm, he pulled her down against his chest and stroked her head. 'When we return to Dandenong tomorrow, we need to focus on this investigation, but you can't let anyone know that's what we are working on.'

'I may have a science degree, but I'm not a sleuth. Why can't they hire a private detective for this?'

He sighed. 'Because we can't afford the expense. If you and I can't figure this out before Brayzon patent any more of our trade secrets, Aludel Pharma will go bankrupt. Besides, you are technically a genius with a hardon for logic puzzles. This should be a cakewalk for you.'

She dismissed his praise with a nervous laugh. Discovering the mole would be the easy part. Blowing the whistle is what worried her.

༺༻

CRYSTAL'S CRUCIBLE

Adam

Oppressive heat smacked Adam in the face the moment he alighted from the taxi onto the pavement in front of Aludel's Dandenong facility. The smell of smoke drifted across from the East Gippsland bushfires, and he spared a thought for the poor souls who had already lost their homes and livelihoods.

'Christ! What a scorcher,' Crystal complained as she joined him.

'Yeah, I heard they even cancelled the Melbourne cricket game.'

She gave him a blank stare.

'Oh right, you don't follow sports. My bad.' He opened the building's front door for her, following close behind with his luggage in tow.

Jessica greeted them with a warm smile. 'Welcome back. How was the trip?'

'Good,' Adam replied.

'Very informative,' added Crystal.

When they entered the main office, Greg emerged from his room, ambushing them at Adam's door. 'Hey boss, I need to talk to you.'

'Not now, man,' Adam grumbled. 'Can't you see I just got back?' Shoving his key in the lock, he opened his office, flicked on his light, and turned on the air conditioning unit. He wheeled his suitcase across the room, stowed it in a corner behind his desk, and collapsed into his chair.

Pushing passed Crystal, Greg barged into the room and marched up to the desk. 'This can't wait.'

With a huff, Crystal placed her own luggage in the opposite corner, crossed her arms over her chest, and stood there tapping her feet.

Adam narrowed his eyes on Greg. 'Yes. It. Can.'

'Fine! But don't blame me when shit hits the fan!'

Crystal snorted, attracting one of Greg's prize-winning dagger stares. The colour drained from her face the moment their eyes connected, and Greg stormed off, slamming the door behind him.

'Don't worry about Greg. His temper tantrums are the stuff of legend around here,' Adam explained. She nodded and sat at the meeting table while Adam picked up his desk phone and dialled Michael's extension. 'Hey Mike, Crystal and I need to prep the performance reviews in her department. Can you please bring us all the relevant personnel files?'

CRYSTAL'S CRUCIBLE

'Yes, of course. How was the conference, by the way?'

'Tiring, but good.'

Michael delivered a stack of manilla folders in four neat piles on the round table in front of Crystal. 'Good luck.'

Moving from his desk, Adam locked the door and sat across from Crystal. He picked up one of the folders and flicked through the pages. 'I'm still not sure what you hope to achieve by looking through these.'

Retrieving her laptop from her carry-on bag, Crystal set the computer up beside a pile of paper. 'Think of this like a jigsaw puzzle, one with thousands of pieces scattered throughout the building. We have all we need to solve this, but we have to make it all fit together.'

'And how are these,' he waved over the folders, 'part of the puzzle?'

'How do you normally start a jigsaw puzzle?'

'With the corners and edges.'

'Exactly. The information in these files will give us a timeline and some background intel on each of our suspects. I used the return flight to design a spreadsheet for collecting data. Here's a copy for you.' She handed him a USB stick.

CRYSTAL'S CRUCIBLE

Seeing her in full Sherlock mode was awesome. Arousing even. Adjusting the bulge in his pants, Adam rose and grabbed his own laptop. When he opened the spreadsheet template, he exhaled with a whistle. 'Impressive database you've built here.' She had even programmed several macros to help them.

'What can I say? I love Excel.' She smiled coyly, stirring another rush of hot blood through his veins. Opening the dossier on the top of her pile, she skimmed the page while chewing on her pen. 'Hmm. When was the initial leak for the last drug?'

'About two and a half years ago.'

'According to this, Hans has only been here for a year. If he wasn't even working here at the time, we can rule him out, right?'

Adam shook his head. 'I wish it were that simple. We can't discount the possibility of multiple culprits. While unlikely, there is still a chance the initial thief hired him to help infiltrate the network.'

'Oh.' She fell silent and returned to chomping on her pen while reading.

He tried to concentrate on the job, but his eyes kept returning to the biro in Crystal's mouth. 'Could you please stop eating the stationery?'

CRYSTAL'S CRUCIBLE

'Sorry,' she mumbled, dropping the ballpoint as she typed something.

Forcing himself to focus, he soon slipped into a rhythm of scanning for each item of information and entering it into the spreadsheet. Hours passed and Adam's muscles began to cramp. After a stretching break, he returned to the tedium, but noticed the pen in her mouth and groaned. 'You're doing it again, Crystal.'

'Doing what?' She lifted her gaze to him.

Leaning across the table, he plucked it from her fingers.

Her forehead creased as she tilted her head. 'Is this one of your control freak things, like with the chairs?'

He huffed. 'No. It's distracting because you keep drawing attention to that kissable mouth of yours.'

She giggled, but soon stopped, reading the intent in his eyes. 'Oh, you're serious.'

'Very.' His attention returned to her lips and she sucked in a sharp breath. The air sparked and sizzled between them. He glanced at the clock on the wall behind her. Business hours were not quite over, and other people continued to work beyond his locked door. Taking a deep breath, he raked his fingers through his hair and got back to work.

Chapter Twenty-Four

Jade

Balled up on her couch beneath the wall mounted air conditioner, Jade channel surfed until she had flicked through all of them a dozen times. There was nothing interesting. She picked up her phone and shot Crystal a text:

{Jade} Can I use your Netflix? I need a distraction. Stat. Oh and your password.
{Crissy} LOL. Go for it. Password is Gambit.
{Jade} You wanna join me?
{Crissy} Can't soz. Working late.
{Jade} Is that code for banging the hot boss on his desk?
{Crissy} NO! Although I am alone with him 😊

Laughing, Jade sent her best wishes before closing the message app and opening the streaming service. About five minutes into the first episode of *Ultraviolet's* second season, someone knocked on her door. She peeked through the peephole and froze. It was him. He thumped against the door a second time and she silently recited her mantra. *Stay strong! Don't give in!* Her phone rang and she startled before snatching it up from the coffee table. It was him. *Damnit!* With the closed door providing a barrier between them, she answered.

'I know you're home, sweetheart. I can hear you inside your flat. Why don't you let me in, hmm?'

'I'm not feeling well.' Her voice sounded so pathetic she doubted her excuse fooled anyone.

'Dieter told me as much. The bright flickering light of a TV screen is an odd migraine treatment. Even so, I brought a shit tonne of pharmaceuticals with me. Whatever ails you, I'm sure I have the fix you need.'

Oh hell! She touched her forehead against the hollow timber barricade standing between her and a night of bliss. 'We shouldn't be doing this, Apollo.'

'I think that ship sailed by about the third or fourth time we fucked on Saturday night. Stop beating yourself up over it and enjoy the time you get with me.'

CRYSTAL'S CRUCIBLE

Spoken like a true devil. Unfortunately, he made a valid point. With a sigh, she ended the call and flung the door open.

He stepped inside wearing his usual gold shirt over brown chinos, capping it off with a smug grin. His dark brown eyes scanned the apartment. 'Cosy.'

'Cut the condescending crap and show me what you got already.'

'Which one's the bedroom?' He gestured toward the two doors leading from the open plan living area. Jade pointed to the room on the right and he made himself at home on the edge of her bed. He unzipped a large pouch, displaying an impressive assortment of pills, powders, and vials. 'I've got all the good stuff. Do you want something to perk you up or would you rather chill out?'

'Since you're *here*,' she wiped her hand over the bedspread for effect, 'I'm assuming sex is also on the cards, so I'll take the molly.'

He withdrew a baggie and dropped it on the bed. Jade inspected the contents, finding four bright orange pills, each stamped with the impression of a capital A. When she rose, Apollo grabbed her hand. 'Where do you think you're going?'

'To get my wallet.'

CRYSTAL'S CRUCIBLE

'Forget it. You can have this lot for free if you share them with me here and now.'

She let him pull her into his lap. 'Thank you.'

A sly grin crept onto his face as he unsealed the plastic bag. 'Open wide.' When she did, he placed two of the tablets onto her tongue and handed her a bottle of water. She swallowed the candy and returned the drink which he used to take his own dose. A moment later, his mouth was claiming hers between the frantic removal of clothes.

…

Their limbs tangled together for the second time that night as the drugs set in. Jade's intense climax convinced her there were actual stars on the ceiling. She was riding him at the time, throwing her head back when the orgasm tore through her. The twinkling lights were so pretty. 'Do you think they'll burn me if I touch them?' she asked him as she reached for the stars.

Digging his fingers into her hips, he yanked her down on his cock. Hard. 'What are you talking about?'

With a guttural cry, she shattered to pieces all over him. Again. 'The stars,' she rasped. 'On the ceiling.'

CRYSTAL'S CRUCIBLE

He laughed. 'You're so fucking wasted.'

'Yeah, well you're so fucking hot. Like the sun. Is that why you go by the name Apollo? What is your real name anyway?'

Smirking, he flipped her onto the bed, bringing her legs up over his shoulders. 'I'll never tell.' He bobbed his brows and thrust into her.

೫০৫

Crystal

Sensing his irritation from the way he was fidgeting, Crystal looked at Adam across the small round table. 'Have you found something?'

'No. That's the problem. So far there is nothing in these files to implicate or exonerate any of them.' Lifting his gaze, Adam's eyes narrowed in on the biro in her mouth. Those warm chestnut orbs turned dark as they focused on her lips, his hand returning to his head.

The light cotton blouse, she usually found comfortable in hot weather, clung to her sticky chest, and she wished she could rip the thing off and fan herself. 'Well, if I can't chew my pen, you should stop raking your fingers through your hair.'

His brows leapt sky high. 'And why is that?'

'Because your tousled hair looks too damn sexy. Oh, and stop jiggling your leg. It keeps drawing my attention to your muscular thighs, and—'

'Christ!' Adam dropped his handful of papers on the table as he sprung to his feet. 'This is too hard with so much sexual tension in the air.' He stalked toward her with a fire blazing in his eyes.

She gulped hard against the lump in her throat. The scared, timid part of her wanted to run for the hills, but she froze in place, giving Adam an opportunity to trap her in a cage of hulking arms.

Pinning Crystal in the chair, he stooped above her, filling her nose with his delicious fruity scent as his hot breath tickled her skin. 'Either let me ravish you, here and now, or take your half of the project to your own office.'

'Adam, I—' She lost the words when his thumb rubbed against her nipple, sparking a fire in her quivering core. The only sound she could muster, a garbled mewling noise.

'What's it gonna be, Crystal? Stay or go?'

'Stay,' she squeaked.

Without a moment of hesitation, he pulled her out of the chair and shoved her up against the wall. His mouth crashed against her lips in a frenzied kiss, teeth gnashing at her flesh and tongue clashing with hers in a battle for supremacy. The onslaught was rough and brutal, yet she had never felt more adored in her life, especially when he dropped to his knees to worship at her shrine. He peppered her legs with playful bites and chaste kisses, trailing them along her thighs while hiking her skirt up around her waist. Gasping, she winced when his fingers hooked into the waistband of her panties and tugged them down.

Holding her gaze, he stared at her in reverence. 'There is nothing to be afraid of, baby. I want you to feel good and I am not going to stop until you see stars.'

Sucking on her bottom lip, she nodded her consent.

He parted her lips with one slick swipe of the tongue, pressing his nose against her bud. 'Mm,' he hummed against her opening, sending a seismic tremor through her bones. 'You taste like milk and honey.' His deft tongue continued licking and flicking at her sensitive flesh; his fingers following in its wake.

Palms laid flat against the wall, she tried to hold herself up, but as the intensity increased, her knees buckled. Before she collapsed, Adam wrapped his arms around her and carried her to the desk, the same spot where they had shared their first kiss. Kneeling once again, he resumed feasting on her. Crystal had no idea how many minutes passed—time became meaningless in her altered state of consciousness—but she got there. Arching her back, with fingers clutching the edge of the desk, she let a deep moan ascend from her belly as the shockwave took hold.

    As the mind fog settled and her vision cleared, she saw Adam standing before her, naked from the waist down, hand gripping his erection. She met his eyes, and they shared a moment, an understanding of each other. 'Make love to me, Adam.'

    His eyes bulged. 'Are you sure?'

    'Yes,' she rasped. 'That's if you want—'

    'Shh,' he hushed her with a finger to the lips. 'Of course I want to bury myself inside you. You are the most beautiful woman I have ever had the pleasure of touching. But you are more than that to me. I don't want to rush you because what we have is too important. That's why I need to know you are truly ready for this.'

    Tears tingled her eyelids. 'I'm ready.'

CRYSTAL'S CRUCIBLE

A beautiful smile lit up his face. Retrieving the wallet from his discarded pants, he produced a foil packet, ripping it open with his teeth. He hovered at her precipice, giving her one final chance to back out. When she nodded, he sank into her, groaning the moment he fully immersed himself. Dropping his forehead in the crook of her neck, he took a deep breath, the rest of his body motionless. He whispered in her ear, 'It's okay to let go with me, sweetheart. I promise to look after you, now and always.'

ಸಿಂ

Jade

After hours of mind-blowing sex, Jade collapsed beside Apollo, utterly spent. 'You have the most insatiable appetite.'

Laughing, he pulled her against his side, mirth rumbling through his ribs. 'You're no slouch either, sweetheart.'

Her hand glided across his skin, wet with perspiration, and her fingers knotted in the thick mat of hair adorning his chest. 'I don't think I can go again though. Not if I want to walk tomorrow.'

CRYSTAL'S CRUCIBLE

Turning his head to face her, mischief sparkled in his eyes. 'What on Earth would you want that for? If you can still use your legs, we have *not* finished.'

'Don't even think about it. Unless you want my boyfriend to castrate you, I suggest allowing me the wherewithal to change the sheets and hide the evidence before he gets home.'

'Hm, good point.' Apollo rose from the bed and made his way into the adjacent bathroom. He returned with a smirk on his chiselled face. 'You might want to change the bin bag in there.' Searching the mess of clothes on the floor, he found his gold satin boxers, bending over to pick them up and giving her an eyeful of his toned cheeks. As he stepped into the shorts, something on her dressing table caught his attention. He picked up the photo in its silver frame and whistled. 'Cute picture. Who's the other hottie with you?'

'That's my younger sister. Trust me when I say you are not Crystal's type.'

Glancing at her, he cocked his head. 'Why? Is she a lesbian?'

'Do you honestly think all straight women would fall for you? Like you're God's gift to women or something?'

'Something like that.' He waggled his brows. 'If she doesn't bat for the other team, why wouldn't she be into me?'

Jade giggled, attempting to hide the pang of envy twisting her gut. 'Crystal prefers… older men. Like uni professors. She totally crushed on a few of them when she was studying her chemistry degree. I think she's got a thing for her boss now.'

'Curious.' He returned the photo and dug out the rest of his outfit. Even dressed in wrinkled clothes, with ruffled hair, he looked like a Greek god. 'Will you meet me at the club tomorrow night?'

She nodded.

'Good. Dress like you did last Saturday. In fact, don't bother wearing panties around me ever again.' He demanded, with a toe-curling air of arrogance. 'Understood?'

'Yes.' Her own voice came out husky.

The bed dipped beneath his weight as he kneeled beside her, bending over to plant a chaste kiss on her lips. 'Night, sweetheart.' He waltzed out of the room, out of her flat, leaving her tangled in the sheets, a dishevelled mess of mixed emotions.

Chapter Twenty-Five

Crystal

It was almost midnight when Crystal got home on Sunday. Flicking on her bedroom light, she glimpsed a figure on her bed and jumped out of her skin. 'Jeez Mother! You scared the hell out of me.'

'Where've you been all weekend?' She slurred her words, and as Crystal drew closer the scent of urine, brandy, and marijuana assaulted her nose.

'My recent whereabouts are none of your business. Why are you waiting up for me? On my bed no less?'

'I need help bay-thing.' Judy scrutinised her and clapped her hands together. 'Oh. My. God! You've been messin' 'bout with a *man*, haven't ya?'

Crystal's cheeks flushed. She never could hide her sexcapades from her mother. The woman had an insane sense for telling when either of her daughters were getting some. It was the only motherly instinct remaining after she had lost her husband.

'Knew it!' Judy screeched, snickering. 'You filthy hussy!' Crossing her legs, she sat up on the bed like an attentive school child. 'Tell me all 'bout it. Was it good? Does he have a big cock?'

'Mum! I am *not* talking to you about this stuff. Come on, let's get this bath over with so I can get some sleep.' She helped Judy stand, ignoring her pouty face, and guided her into the bathroom.

'Please,' Judy begged from the tub.

'No,' Crystal replied from her seat on the lidded toilet. 'Hurry up and clean yourself.'

With a huff, Judy splashed about, spilling water all over the floor in her frenzy.

Once Crystal had tucked her mother into bed, she closed the door and heaved out a sigh. Her own bed felt empty and foreign after sleeping in Adam's all weekend. Rolling over, she saw her phone light up with a notification. She grabbed it from the nightstand and unlocked the screen. There was a text from Esme: Lost my virginity tonight. I can't wait to tell you all about it!

Holy moly! Crystal sat up and called her best friend. 'OMG, congratulations girl!'

Esme laughed. 'Um, thanks.'

'What was he like? Wait! Not too much detail, I still need to face the guy at work. I'm assuming this is still Hans we're talking about?'

'Wow. What's with the oral diarrhoea, woman?'

'Sorry, I must have caught it from Mum. So?'

She laughed again. 'Yes, it was Hans, and he was fantastic. So caring and gentle. At first anyway. Each consecutive time got more heated and frantic.'

Sounds familiar. 'That's awesome, Ez.'

'I am so high on the fumes of our love tonight I doubt I'll get any sleep. I'm also nervous and excited about tomorrow.'

'What's happening tomorrow?'

'Hans is coming to dinner, to meet my family.'

Crystal sucked in a sharp breath. 'Things sound pretty serious with you two.'

'They are, Crissy. I think he might be the one.'

Yikes. Something niggled at the back of her mind. 'Please be careful, Ez.'

'What do you mean, be *careful*?'

CRYSTAL'S CRUCIBLE

'I'm not sure you should trust Hans, especially not with something as precious as your heart.'

'What?' Esme shrieked. 'Why would you say something like that? I know Hans has a bit of a potty mouth, but he is kind and—'

'I know he seems like a nice guy,' Crystal cut in. 'And I hope he is, but some bad stuff is going down at work that has Adam and me questioning the loyalty of everyone in my department. I worry about you getting mixed up in this mess.'

'Hans would never hurt me,' she huffed. 'Why can't you be happy for me? Just because *you* can't enjoy sex doesn't mean that *I* can't.'

Crystal sighed. 'I *am* happy for you, Ez. But I'm also worried. For the record I am not jealous either, not after spending the whole weekend in Adam's bed.'

'Wait, did you…?'

'Have amazing, mind-altering sex with him? Yes, on repeat.'

'Wowsers. Why didn't you tell me earlier?' She laced her tone with sadness, possibly even disappointment.

'Because I just got back from a weekend of amazing, mind-altering sex with Adam.' Pausing, she gave some thought to the situation, the whole story as it were. 'Look, I haven't been neglecting you on purpose, Ez. Things have been crazy at work. I'm glad I have the next two weeks off for Christmas and New Year's. Between the trip to Sydney, the whole corporate espionage conspiracy, and this new relationship I have with Adam, I've barely had time to fart, let alone keep in touch with anyone. My own sister got angry with me for ignoring her calls recently when she had her own meltdown.' Everything hit her like a crushing weight on her shoulders and the tears sprang free. 'I'm sorry.' She sobbed. 'I have (sob) too much (sob) on my plate right now.'

'Hey, shh. It's okay,' Esme assured her. 'I'm sorry for letting my crazy pants show. I guess I've been a bit emotional too.'

Crystal snorted. 'That's sex for ya.'

'I know right! Ha! I never thought I'd get what all the fuss was about, but here I am.' Esme laughed a moment, then her voice turned serious, 'What's this conspiracy business going on at your work? Why do you think Hans might be involved?'

After debating the pros and cons of telling Esme, Crystal decided it might help to have another savant on the case, especially one who might be sleeping with the enemy. She explained everything to the best of her ability, even Greg's death threat, although she did not mention his name.

'Good God! You have to go to the cops about this, Crissy!'

'I can't. Even if they lock this creep away, his psycho son will come after me. Esme, promise me you will *not* breathe a word of this to anyone. Especially not Hans.'

'My lips are sealed, I swear. Is there anything I can do to help?'

'Actually, there is. Can you monitor Hans for suspicious behaviour?'

ಸಿಡಿ

Crystal

Aludel Pharma may have closed their doors for the holidays, but Crystal was not at leisure. She still had an urgent project requiring collaboration with Adam Fairfax. *Gosh darn, what a shame!* Entering his driveway, she smiled to herself. He had promised her a surprise. *The challenge will be doing any work behind these walls.* She parked in front of the two-story Art Deco masterpiece. The white building had more curves than the latest Victoria's Secret catalogue and Crystal had fallen in love with it at first sight.

'Morning, beautiful.' Adam answered the door wearing nothing more than grey track pants and a glowing grin.

Christ! He may as well be naked. Not that I'm complaining, but… 'Morning.' Her teeth clamped down on her bottom lip. Once inside she hung her handbag on a coat hook and dropped her laptop on the hallway sideboard, freeing her arms to embrace Adam.

His mouth claimed hers in a heated kiss as he walked her backwards through the house, bumping into a few walls and items of furniture along the way, until they found the couch. Sitting down, he pulled her into his lap, allowing her to straddle the growing bulge in his pants. 'I still have that surprise for you,' he whispered against the shell of her ear.

'Hmm, you mean greeting me dressed like this wasn't it?'

'Like that, did you?'

Her cheeks heated as she nodded.

'I'll keep that in mind.' His fingernails trailed along her bare arms, eliciting goosebump tipped tingles. 'I have some awesome news for you.'

CRYSTAL'S CRUCIBLE

'Oh? Have you made a breakthrough in the case?'

His hands moved up to cup her face. 'No, baby. This is more personal.'

Her heart hammered in her chest. 'Go on.'

'I know we haven't voiced our feelings yet, so this may be presumptive of me, but I believe we have something special.' His gaze scanned her face, drinking her in, as though memorising every feature, every freckle. 'When I tell you this, I don't want you to feel pressured to reply in kind. The words should come naturally.'

'Adam what—'

He hushed her with a finger to the lips. 'Let me finish. An opportunity has presented itself at work. One that will allow us to openly date.'

She stared at him with wide eyes. 'How?'

'You know our QA Manager, Felicity, recently went on maternity leave?'

'Yes.'

'There were plans to hire a temp, but she has handed in her letter of resignation because she wants to focus on motherhood for an extended period. The job used to be mine. It makes sense for me to fill the vacancy and let someone else step up.

No longer being your boss removes the conflict of interest.'

Crystal gasped. 'Won't you take a huge pay cut though? You can't sacrifice so much for me.'

He brought her forehead down to rest against his. 'Crissy babe, I'm so madly in love with you that I'd give it all up. At least this way we can still work together, and I'll have a job I don't mind.'

She needed to pick her jaw up from the floor before replying. 'You're… in love with me?'

'Yes, I am. I have been for a while, but I didn't want to scare you off by saying it too soon.' The fact he waited until after sleeping with her lent more credence to the sentiment. This was not some thinly veiled attempt to get into her pants like with her exes. 'I've given it a lot of thought, and I—'

This time Crystal cut him off, pressing her lips to his to show him how she felt about his declaration. She did not need words to tell him his affections were mutual. The warmth in her chest soon escalated to a fire in her blood, fuelled by the way Adam was grinding against her. Newfound confidence took root deep within, inspiring her to take charge of the situation. When she pulled her summer dress over her shoulders and threw it to the floor, his hooded gaze darkened. She removed her bra next, followed by her knickers. Tugging his pants down, she looked up at him, gaping. 'Going commando, huh?'

'Is there any other way to wear grey trackies?' Winking, he reached into the cushions and produced a foil packet. He laughed as she gaped at him, handing her the condom. 'Pays to be prepared for all situations. Would you like to do the honours?' Blushing, she took it and peeled the packet open. He threw his head back and groaned as she took extra care rolling the latex over his shaft, down to the hilt. Similar noises slipped from his lips as she lowered herself onto him. 'God, Crissy. You feel *so* good.'

Rocking back and forth, her body merged with his in a synchronised rhythm, their whimpers harmonised. As she placed her hands on his chest, she realised even their hearts were beating in unison. The tempo increased and soon she was riding the crescendo of their passion.

Collapsing into him, Crystal breathed in his scent and exhaled her contentment. 'I love you too, Adam.'

Wrapping her in his arms, he kissed the crown of her head. 'What are your plans on Christmas Day?'

CRYSTAL'S CRUCIBLE

'Binging on microwave pudding and watching old movies.' She yawned against the crook of his neck.

'With your mum or sister?'

'Neither. They'll be doing their own thing, either high or drunk. We haven't come together as a family since Nanna died and even then, it was strained.'

He gasped, gazing into her eyes with furrowed brows. 'I'm sorry to hear that, Crissy. Would you like to be my date?'

'Date for what?'

'My family dinner.'

She sat up. 'Are you serious?'

'Absolutely. Nothing would make me happier than spending Christmas with you, my love.'

Chapter Twenty-Six

Crystal

Crystal ran her thumb and forefinger along the silken strands of red hair, twisting and fraying them as she bit chunks out of her inner cheek.

Reaching across the console of his sporty Subaru, Adam clamped his hand on her thigh. 'You don't need to worry, baby. My parents are going to love you.'

She took a deep breath, inhaling New Car Smell. *I know this thing is several years old. Why does it still smell like this?* 'How can you be sure? I was raised on the wrong side of the tracks. And the age gap—'

'Firstly, my folks may be wealthy, but they aren't snobs. Secondly, I am certain because they are going to see all the qualities I fell in love with.'

CRYSTAL'S CRUCIBLE

Warmth filled her chest and flowed through her body. *How did I get so lucky?* She stopped fidgeting and relaxed into the chair until they reached his family home. A new wave of panic seized her limbs and stole her voice when she looked at the grand manor. The wide frontage boasted large, panelled windows, and thick, geometric columns. It looked like something out of a Jane Austen novel. Snapping her gaping jaw shut, she turned and looked at Adam. 'You grew up *here*?'

He shrugged. 'This property has been in my family since Toorak was established in the mid nineteenth century.'

Yep, no big deal. She studied him. *How is he only in middle management? Men like him usually own companies.*

'You ready?'

No. She nodded. Adam opened the car for her and took her hand. They crossed sparkling granite pavers and climbed the steps to the veranda. He unlocked the front door, punching in a code on the keypad, and led her inside. Halting, she took a moment to admire the sweeping staircase and elegant marble statues of Greek heroes.

CRYSTAL'S CRUCIBLE

He squeezed her hand. 'Come on, we have lunch out back.' The echo of his voice faded into the click-clack of her heels on the tiles. A small party assembled beneath a marquee on the sprawling lawn. The sounds of Christmas jazz, laughter, and cheerful voices filled the air.

An ageless woman in an ivory power suit, with blonde hair pinned in an updo, looked at them, springing to her feet and grinning. 'Adam darling! Merry Christmas.'

Slipping his arms around her, he kissed her cheek. 'Merry Christmas, Mum.' Pulling out of the embrace, he pressed a hand against the small of Crystal's back. 'Greetings all. This is my girlfriend, Crystal.' Gesturing to each of them in turn, he made the introductions, 'My mother, Michelle, my father, Daniel, Rebecca here is my sister, her husband is Troy, and their children are Rachelle and Toby.'

Each of the smiling adults shook her hand and the kids, who looked about nine and eight respectively, jumped up and hugged her. Next thing she knew, they were flanking her, tugging at her hands, and dragging her over to their side of the table.

'Hello Crystal! Will you sit with us?' Rachelle begged.

CRYSTAL'S CRUCIBLE

She looked to Adam for guidance. When he nodded, she accepted the invitation to sit between Rachelle and Toby.

'You have a pretty name, Crystal,' Toby declared. 'It suits you.'

Her cheeks flushed. 'Thank you, Toby.'

'Smooth, kid,' Adam commented. 'Looks like I might have some competition for my girl's affections.' He winked while handing her a glass of sparkling apple juice before pouring himself a French champagne.

Michelle clapped her hands. 'It is delightful to meet you, sweetheart. Please tell us how my son chanced upon such a lovely young lady.'

She gulped. 'We met through work.'

'Crystal is a certified genius,' Adam explained, bringing more heat to her blazing face.

'Is that so?' Daniel inquired. 'What is your IQ score, if you don't mind me asking?'

By how she choked on her drink, anyone would think he was asking for her bra size.

Rebecca moved around to pat her back. 'Stop embarrassing the poor girl.'

'It's okay,' Crystal assured them. 'I'm not used to discussing my merits outside of a job interview. My IQ is one seventy-nine.'

CRYSTAL'S CRUCIBLE

Michelle, Daniel, and Troy gaped at her, prompting Adam to laugh. 'Told you.'

'I got straight As on my report card,' Toby boasted.

'Me too,' Rachelle chimed in. 'I can recite the alphabet backwards and count to one-hundred in three languages.'

Crystal giggled. 'Sounds like I might not be the smartest girl at the table.'

'We can both solve a Rubik's Cube in under two minutes,' Toby added. 'What's your best time, Crystal?'

'Gosh. I never timed myself and it has been a few years now.'

Toby tapped his mother's arm. 'Can we do Cube races after lunch?'

'If Crystal wants to,' replied Rebecca.

'Sounds like fun,' Crystal agreed.

A few caterers approached the table with trolleys full of food. They distributed the seafood cocktails, carved the cold meats, garnished the salads, and restocked the bottles of wine and soft drink. Crystal soon eased into the conversation while enjoying a sumptuous meal. As the sun set, they moved inside for supper by the Christmas Tree, where Adam donned a Santa hat and gave out the presents. Watching the joy and wonder on the kids' faces as they unwrapped their goodies brought a tear to Crystal's eye. It occurred to her she wanted to be part of a family like this, to bring her own precious babies into a loving home and lavish them with gifts that lit up their faces.

'Hey, are you okay?' Adam asked in a soft whisper, breaking her reverie.

'Yeah.' She wiped her eyes. 'Just feeling sentimental.'

Kneeling before her, he pressed a kiss to her forehead and presented her with a small parcel, neatly packaged in glossy, white paper with gold curling ribbon. 'Merry Christmas, baby.'

She sucked in a sharp breath. 'You didn't need to get me anything.'

'Maybe not, but I wanted to give you this even before you surprised me with that thoughtful gift.' He was referring to the porcelain, art deco styled chess set she had given him when he picked her up.

Carefully, she untied the bow and peeled back the clear tape, taking care not to rip the paper. When she unravelled a small jewellery box, her heart pattered. She took a deep breath and opened the lid. Gasping, she looked at Adam, emotion brimming in her eyes. 'It's beautiful.' Crystal lifted the delicate rose gold necklace out of its cradle, inspecting the swan shaped charm a moment before releasing the clasp.

'May I?' Adam reached for the ends of the chain.

Nodding, she let him take it as she turned her head and lifted the hair from her neck. Her skin sparked and tingled when he touched her. The pendant bounced against her chest, dropping to the opening of her cleavage. Pressing it against her clavicle, she smiled. 'Thank you, Adam. It's perfect.' They shared a chaste kiss before he returned to his *Santa* duties.

೫๏ಌ

Adam

Two days after Christmas, Adam managed to tear himself away from Crystal's side, albeit reluctantly. He wanted her to join him for lunch with Greg, but she insisted he should have some quality 'guy time' while she continued working on the case *without distractions*. He strolled into the bustling bistro to a soundtrack of seasonal music, clattering crockery, and lively chatter.

Greg, who was already waiting, rose from their table to give him a one-armed hug and slap on the back. 'So glad I could pull you away from that hot, red-headed piece of arse for a few hours.'

'Show some respect man!' Adam snapped.

'Woah!' Laughing, he threw his arms up in a show of peace. 'I didn't realise you were so pussy-whipped already.'

Adam took his seat across from Greg. 'I hope you realise being in love is different to being whipped.'

The blood drained from Greg's face as he stared aghast. 'Tell me you aren't confessing to being in love with a woman who is not only thirteen years your junior, but also off-limits.'

'The age-gap doesn't bother us, and I'm about to change the work situation.'

'How so?'

'I'm stepping back into my old job as QA Manager. That will put me on equal footing with Crystal and remove any conflict of interest.' A waiter approached, disrupting the look of abject horror on Greg's face. After ordering the salt and pepper squid, Adam handed his menu to the young, bearded hipster. Greg took a sip of the table water and narrowed his eyes on Adam. 'Whatever happened to climbing the ranks and filling Henry's shoes?'

Adam shrugged. 'I guess I've had a change of heart since meeting Crystal. My priorities have shifted.'

Greg shook his head. 'You can't do this, bro. She's not fucking worth it.'

Fed up with Greg's bull, Adam rose. 'I can't do this. I'm sick of you talking trash about the woman I love.'

'Wait!' Greg tugged at Adam's shirt. 'You have to hear me out. Crystal has been lying to you.'

Adam froze. Hairs bristled across his skin as he swivelled around to meet Greg's gaze. 'What are you talking about?' he ground out through clenched teeth.

'You might want to sit down for this one.' Greg waved toward the chair Adam had vacated.

'Spit it out,' Adam demanded as soon as his backside hit the seat.

'I have good reason to believe Crystal knows more about this IP theft than she is letting on. She might even be the mole you are looking for.'

Bile churned through his stomach and climbed his throat. 'Do you have any evidence?'

'No, but Katrina does.'

Unable to hold it any longer, Adam rushed to the bathroom and emptied the contents of his stomach into one of the toilets. After flushing, he stumbled out to the sink to wash his face and rinse his mouth. Taking a long, hard look in the mirror, he asked himself, 'Have I fallen for another traitorous whore?'

Chapter Twenty-Seven

Crystal

Crystal dropped the heavy bundle of papers on the desk to her right with a loud *whack*. *It figures Katrina has one of the largest files on record.* Picking up the last folder from her pile, she scrunched her brow at the name: ROBERT LANDON. 'Who the hell is he?' Flicking through the pages bound by a tube clip, she soon discovered he was her predecessor. *Curious. I wonder what happened to him.* Searching further she learned he was in his fifties, much too young to retire. *So why—*

Thump, thump, thump. Someone knocked furiously on her study door.

Removing her reading glasses, she rolled her eyes and rose to see what her mother wanted. Her eyes grew wide when she met Adam at the threshold of her private domain. She thought he had lunch with Greg, making his presence an unexpected, yet welcome surprise. 'Um, hi.' She reached up to kiss him, but he pushed her aside and strode into the room, sending her heart plummeting into the floorboards. That was when she noticed the tension in his clenched jaw and fists.

He glanced at her workstation before turning his fierce gaze on her. 'Was this all a farce or was there a nefarious reason for digging through everyone's personal details?' Adam waved a hand toward the stack of files.

'Adam, what—'

'Are you the mole, Crystal?'

'What! No, why would you think that?'

Squaring up in front of her, his expression oozed malice. 'Apparently Katrina has evidence of your involvement in this racket. I thought I'd do you the courtesy of asking first. What does she have on you, Crystal?'

She gulped, taking a moment to carefully consider her answer. 'Either she has nothing, or she has forged something because I swear to God I am innocent.'

Adam shook his head and scowled at the ceiling. 'You leave me no choice.' Turning, he approached the doorway when something occurred to Crystal.

CRYSTAL'S CRUCIBLE

'Wait!'

'Remember something did you?' he spat, spinning around to face her.

Crystal sighed. 'It's possible she discovered I have kept something from you. I know who one of the crooks is, but I can't tell you any more than that…' Lowering her voice, she added, 'Not yet.'

'Un-ba-lievable. The spider spins more lies to trap me. Forget it, Crystal. You and I are done and don't bother coming back to work.'

Tears stung her eyes and trickled down her cheeks. 'Adam, please don't do this. I'm not lying, and I promise I am not the mole.'

'Prove you are not involved. Tell me who is!'

'I can't, not without substantial evidence to lock them away.'

'Fine! You have a week to come forward with all the names and evidence you can dig up, or you can kiss your job goodbye.' Storming out of the room, he slammed the door.

Pens rattled in the stationary caddy on her desk and Crystal slumped into her chair, crying big fat blobs of salty grief that splashed onto the page in front of her. Sympathising with Adam was the worst part of her predicament. She could not entirely blame him for reacting the way he did, for tearing open her chest and ripping out her heart. While she had not intentionally deceived him, concealing the truth was still a lie by omission. *How can I make Adam understand my situation?*

Wiping her eyes, she returned her attention to Robert's employment record, the first few documents now soaked in her tears. *Oops!* With a sigh, she closed the folder, thinking there was no point wasting time reading through intel that should have been archived. When she lifted the dossier, a loose leaf fell to the floor. Picking it up, she found an employment termination form with a yellow sticky note attached. As she read the scrawled comments, her skin crawled:

> *Official cause of death: suicide.*
> *Timing is suspicious.*
> *Did he discover something?*
> *Foul play?*

It looked like Michael's handwriting. Recalling what he said the day Denzel requested leave, she wondered if his warning was a threat or made in genuine concern. '*Keep your head down and stay safe, okay?*' The more she thought about it, the more likely the latter became. The reason for

CRYSTAL'S CRUCIBLE

Michael giving her an obsolete file clicked into place. If his suspicions were correct, she needed to shift her focus to investigating a much more serious charge, one that would see Greg rotting in prison for the rest of his life. For that, she would need to get the police on board.

෩෨

Crystal

Spending the last twenty-four hours cutting through red tape, and getting the police on the case, left Crystal feeling like she had been beating her head against a brick wall, and the expression finally made sense to her. The pain and futility of it all. She had taken a cautious approach, convinced someone was trailing her. After instigating a slow speed collision in a car park, she had used that as her reason for entering the police station. There was no serious damage, but the law still required her to report the incident.

Soaking in a bath and rubbing her aching temples did nothing to alleviate the stress and she was too antsy to attempt sleep. Besides, it was a Saturday night, and eight PM was far too early to be dragging her twenty-six-year-old backside to bed. Picking up the phone, she attempted to call Esme, but it rang through to voicemail. *She is likely hanging out with Hans.* With a sigh, Crystal dialled Jade's number.

'Hey chica, what's up?' Jade's voice was brighter than usual, and Crystal guessed she had already started pre-loading her system with alcohol.

Maybe I should have a drink too. 'Hey, I need to blow off some steam. Can I go out with you tonight?'

'Of course you can, hun. Wear something sexy and drive over to my place. We can Uber into the city together.'

Not having many options, Crystal slipped into the strapless number she wore to the work Christmas dinner and slapped on some makeup. Several times during her twenty-five-minute drive, she considered turning back home, until the twinge in her neck reminded her she needed to unwind. She could not even check her blind spot without cringing in pain. *Hmm, maybe I can hook up with someone who will give me a full body massage tonight*. The thought made her laugh. It had been years since she had gone clubbing, something she only ever did during her one-night-stand phase.

CRYSTAL'S CRUCIBLE

Letting her into the apartment, Jade inspected Crystal's outfit and nodded. 'It'll do.'

'Gee, thanks,' Crystal drawled.

'Just being honest. As you can see, I prefer to show a lot more leg, but I suppose the extra skin you are showing up top ought to compensate.'

Crystal rolled her eyes.

'Don't worry, you still look hot enough to start a fire. You won't have any trouble picking up tonight if that's what you want. So why the urge to let loose?'

'Everything's gone to hell in a handbasket, and I'm sick of taking the high road all the time.' The tears returned and Jade pulled her into a hug.

'What happened?'

'I discovered something I shouldn't have and this arsehole at work swore me to secrecy. Long story short, Adam learned I'm hiding something from him and dumped me. He may even fire me.'

'Wowsers and wait up, did you say Adam dumped you? That implies the two of you were in a relationship. When did that happen and why am I only hearing about it now?'

Crystal's stomach cramped with regret. 'Sorry, I was keeping things under wraps until he stepped down from his position of authority over me.' She let out a clipped laugh. 'I guess that won't happen now.'

Nodding, Jade strode into the kitchen. 'Want a shot of something to take the edge off?'

'I don't know, Jade...'

'Come on Pumpkin, a few drinks won't hurt, and I'll watch your back tonight.'

She sighed. 'Fine. Just tonight. What have you got?' Her eyes travelled along the bottles lining Jade's kitchen bench.

'How about tequila?'

'Yeah, okay.' Crystal took the tiny glass of amber liquid Jade offered and threw the bitter drink down her throat. 'Ick! How can you stand this stuff?'

Jade shrugged. 'It's an acquired taste, I guess. Maybe stick to vodka cocktails for the rest of the night if you want more. The sweet flavours of the mixers will mask the alcohol.'

'Thanks.' Already feeling a slight buzz, Crystal followed Jade outside, firmly holding the rails as she descended the stairs in her heels.

'Mm, looking good tonight, Hakeem.' Jade winked at their driver before climbing into the backseat.

CRYSTAL'S CRUCIBLE

'Evening ladies. Who is your friend, Jade?' he asked in a playful tone.

'This is my sister, Crystal. Would you believe, she only just tried her first ever tequila shot? At the age of twenty-six?'

Hakeem laughed. 'Well, you know I don't drink at all.'

'Yeah, but you have God as an excuse. This girl's simply uptight.'

'Jade!' Crystal snapped, trying to appear offended, but failing as she burst into a fit of giggles.

'Sounds like the tequila is working,' Hakeem commented as he continued driving, eyes focussed on the road.

'Ye*p*,' Jade replied, popping the p. 'This is gonna be a fun night.'

Bright, flashing lights and a pounding bass assaulted Crystal's senses when she entered the club. 'I think I need another drink.'

Laughing, Jade linked arms with Crystal and dragged her to a set of roped-off stairs with a VIP sign. 'Hey Harvey, this is my sister, Crystal.'

'Welcome, Crystal.' The burly bouncer winked at her before granting admission.

CRYSTAL'S CRUCIBLE

'I guess being the resident DJ's girlfriend has its perks,' observed Crystal.

'Actually, I used to fuck the Club's owner, that's how I met Dieter in the first place.'

Crystal winced. 'Does Dieter know about your sordid past?'

'Of course. Until recently, I was always honest with him about everything I got up to. On that note…'

'Don't worry, I'll zip my lips. Apparently, keeping life-altering secrets is on trend now.'

They approached a bulky man, with slicked-back hair, and arms covered in ink, who sat alone at a table by the balcony railing, and Jade made the introductions.

While he contrasted with Adam in almost every way, Sargon oozed sex appeal through musk scented pores. Licking his lips, he gave Crystal a lecherous grin. 'Sister huh? I can kind of see the resemblance.' His gaze lowered to her cleavage.

Jade smacked him upside the back of the head. 'Behave, mister. Her man just lickety-split. She's in a vulnerable place right now. Full disclosure Crissy, this one's a complete cad.'

Crystal laughed. 'It's okay, Jade.' Biting into her bottom lip, she weighed the pros and cons of some hot, nasty rebound sex. *Not a smart idea to jump into bed with my sister's ex though. I'm not even sure how I would go with anyone other than Adam.*

'What can I get you to drink, Crystal?' Sargon kept his gaze fixed on her.

'Oh, um…' she glanced at Jade. 'A vodka cocktail, please.'

When Sargon moved to the bar, Jade whispered in Crystal's ear. 'It's okay if you wanna sleep with him. Don't hold back on my account. That man is the bomb in bed, but he is also totes kinky and will likely fuck you fifty different ways into next Sunday.'

'That sounds like a malapropism. Don't you mean *six* ways *from* Sunday?'

Grinning, Jade sat at the vacant table. 'Nope.'

'Oh.' Crystal took the seat across from her.

Sargon handed her a bright pink drink, brushing her hand in the process. Despite her better judgement, Crystal's body trembled, and heat pooled in her core as their gazes locked together.

'Hallo *Liebling.*' Dieter's voice caught Crystal's attention and she looked up to see him embracing Jade. 'Oh, hey Crissy.' His brows furrowed as he noticed the lack of space between

Sargon and herself. More so when he spied the drink in her hand. 'Ah—'

'Crissy had a bad break-up and she wanted to party,' Jade explained.

Dieter cocked a brow. 'What possessed you to introduce her to Sargon? You know his rep better than anyone.'

Sargon groaned. 'Worst wing-man ever.'

Crystal laughed. 'You guys need to relax. Maybe a wild night in the sack is exactly what the doctor ordered.'

They all turned and stared at her, two sets of wide eyes, one hooded.

ಸಂಡ

Apollo

Entering Club Commotion, Apollo snickered to himself, seeing the faces of his regular customers light up with excitement, like kids on Christmas morning. *Maybe I should change my street name to Santa*. He dismissed the idea as soon as it came to him, thinking gold suited him more than red.

CRYSTAL'S CRUCIBLE

Blaze, one such client who always wore tie-dyed shirts he made himself, approached Apollo. 'Hey man, 'sup?'

'Yeah, I'm pretty good, thanks. Yourself?' He considered putting sunglasses on to shield his eyes from the bright colours swirling on Blaze's chest. *Yeah, nah! Even if I have enough street cred to get away with it, I don't want to look like a tool.*

''Ts all good an happ'nin', ya know?'

Having no idea, he nodded politely.

'Ya scorin' plenty of pussay, bet yeah?' Blaze nudged him in the arm and winked.

Glancing up at his blue-haired beauty, he grinned. 'The best.'

Jade caught his gaze and smiled before returning her attention to the pesky boyfriend who had his arm around her. Seconds later, Apollo noticed the other chick who sat at Sargon's table. *Fuck.*

'Man, that's lit.' Blaze's voice drew Apollo's focus back to the current business deal.

'You trippin' tonight?' A sense of urgency prickled all over his skin, as though he had rolled over a lawn covered in three corner jacks. It was time to wrap things up.

CRYSTAL'S CRUCIBLE

'You hook me up right, man, and I'll be trippin' for the rest of the weekend.'

'*Noice*. Double the usual then?'

Blaze gave him a yellowed toothy grin. 'Yeah man.'

To the casual observer, their transaction would have appeared like nothing more than a firm handshake. With that settled, Apollo sank into the shadows to type out a message to his associate. Hey bro, I need backup 2night. Worlds are colliding and it might be time to manage the risk. When I say the word, give it to the chick with blue braids in space buns.

{D Man} On it.

Exhaling sharply through pursed lips, Apollo spied Jade's group from the safety of his hiding spot. *What the hell is she doing here?* If she sat any closer to Sargon, she would be grinding against the filthy bastard's lap. Not an image he fancied getting an eyeful of. It was harrowing enough seeing her fawn all over Adam Fairfax. *Although, according to Patéras[13], Crystal is as good as mine. It is merely a matter of time.* Still, he would rather Sargon kept his paws off the merchandise. That man had a reputation for breaking women almost as much as Apollo did, and he would rather have the honours.

---

[13] Father (Greek)

CRYSTAL'S CRUCIBLE

Watching Jade's beaming face, he wondered if it would be possible to keep her, because it would be a real shame to let her go. Apollo enjoyed the firecracker's company, more than he cared to admit, and the sex was out of this world. Once again, she looked in his direction, as if sensing his eyes on her. Their gazes locked. *Surely not.* He thought he hid himself well in the alcove leading to the bathrooms.

Licking her lips, she began to rise.

In a moment of panic, he ducked into the men's room, shutting himself in a cubicle. His phone buzzed.

It was a text from Jade: Surely you don't expect to fuck me in the toilets when there are perfectly decent booths up here?

His body hummed and moaned with anticipation as he replied. Of course not. It is too early to fool around. Your DJ hasn't started his set. Besides, it looks like you have company tonight. Wouldn't it be rude to leave her alone, at Sargon's mercy no less?

{Jade} Good point. What if I got her to join us? 😉

His semi-hard dick turned to steel at the thought of having his way with both Buchanan girls together. But that would be an epically stupid idea. I thought you said I wasn't your sister's type.

{Jade} With how much she has drunk, I'm pretty sure most guys are her type tonight.

CRYSTAL'S CRUCIBLE

God damn! Crystal drinking alcohol and looking for hook-ups? What has the world come to? Maybe this was his opportunity to get to her. *Screw waiting for approval from Patéras.*

Chapter Twenty-Eight

Adam

Two episodes into *The Witcher*, Adam was growing restless. Not being one to binge on television, he usually preferred keeping busy with work or exercise. He had given up on trying to work after too many intrusive thoughts. Turning off the screen, he tossed the remote aside and headed towards his home gym, halting when the doorbell chimed. He glanced at his watch with a furrowed brow. *Almost ten, a bit late for visitors. Unless…*

With quick strides, he reached the door and threw it open. Recognition struck immediately, chilling his blood. The police detectives on his doorstep were the same ones who turned his world upside down with news of Robert's demise.

Detective Edward Draper flashed his badge. 'Mr. Fairfax, sorry to disturb you at this late hour, but we have an urgent matter to discuss with you.'

CRYSTAL'S CRUCIBLE

'Come in.' Adam opened the security screen and led them into the living room. 'What's the problem, detectives?'

'A colleague of yours recently filed a report concerning the death of Robert Landon. She had reason to believe his death involved foul play, possibly at the hands of those responsible for stealing Company secrets.'

'What?' Adam sprang to his feet. 'Who reported this?'

'We are not at liberty to say,' replied Draper.

'What we can tell you,' added Hammond, 'is her suspicions were warranted. After further studies of the evidence, we have concluded someone else kicked the chair out from beneath Robert, which means we are looking at a murder case. One tied to the IP theft you have been investigating. We are going to need Robert's file again, along with the rest of the personnel records from your office.'

'I thought you already had Robert's file?'

Draper sighed. 'We returned it after closing the initial case.'

'Okay, well I have half the R&D employee records here. The others are at Crystal Buchanan's house, so you'll have to pay her a visit after.'

CRYSTAL'S CRUCIBLE

'We already tried, but she's not home,' replied Hammond, prompting a huff from his partner.

'Wait, how did you know to approach Crystal…' *Click.* 'Shoot! She reported this, didn't she?'

They both remained tight lipped, the younger Hammond looking sheepish under Draper's glowering gaze.

Adam's stomach flipped and churned. 'Did those arseholes threaten her life?'

'Again, we are not at liberty to say,' Draper replied coolly.

'You morons better be doing everything in your power to keep her safe. Do you know where she is right now?'

Draper remained stoic, but Hammond gave the game away by hanging his head like a guilty child.

With a growl, Adam stormed off to his study and bundled up the dossiers the detectives had requested. Returning to the living room, he shoved the papers into Draper's arms. 'You'll have to contact Michael for access to the records in the office. I'll try to get a hold of Crystal.'

CRYSTAL'S CRUCIBLE

He nodded, handing half of the folders to Hammond. 'Thank you. Oh and one final word of advice: don't trust anyone at your work.'

Once the detectives had left, Adam collapsed on the couch and tried ringing Crystal. Straight to voicemail. *Crap on a cracker! If anything happens to her…* Dread coiled around his spine in thick knots, tensing all his muscles. He had been so quick to accuse, to unleash the brunt of his fury on her. His instinct was to call Greg for help, but Draper's voice echoed in his mind. *Damnit!* Thinking of his best mate getting tied up in this mess tipped his nauseous gut over the edge. He ran to the toilet with half a second to spare. Having wasted the risotto that was more enjoyable going down than coming up, he wiped his face and brushed his teeth.

Returning to the sofa, he tried Crystal again, to no avail, before ringing the one person he knew he could trust.

Daniel answered with a yawn. 'Evening Son. Is everything okay?'

'Hi Dad. I hope I didn't wake you.'

'I was dozing in front of the telly. Still, it is a bit late for polite conversation. I assume something is the matter.'

CRYSTAL'S CRUCIBLE

'You're not wrong. I made a huge mistake and I need your help.' Adam explained as much as he could about the conspiracy at work and Crystal's involvement. Tears swelled in his eyes as he finished. 'I can't get hold of her, and I'm worried her life is in danger.'

The following silence was tense.

'You still there, Dad?'

'Yes. I'm just thinking. I'm not sure if I can do much right now, but I'll get in touch with some of my contacts and go from there, okay?'

'Yeah, okay. Thanks Dad.' Feeling about as impotent as a eunuch, Adam resigned himself to listening to Crystal's voicemail on repeat.

༺༻

Crystal

Staggering over to Jade, Crystal whispered at a less than subtle volume, 'I need to break the seal.'

Sargon chuckled while Jade snorted. 'Yeah, okay, lightweight. I'll help you get to the bathroom and back in one piece.' Hooking an arm around Crystal's waist, she guided her along the velvet-lined hallway. Knocking, accompanied by moans, groans, and whimpers filled the air.

Crystal giggled at the noises. 'It sounds like people are having sex.'

'That's 'cause they are,' Jade explained. 'This is Sargon's Carnal Corridor. Those curtains lead to private booths where his VIPs get it on.'

She gaped at Jade. 'Have you ever?'

'All the time.' Jade's candid tone never ceased to amaze Crystal.

'With Dieter, or…'

'Both. Not together of course, but yeah, this was where both relationships started and continue to this day.'

The stairs loomed before them, threatening to swallow Crystal whole with one misplaced step.

Jade waved for the bouncer to help her. 'Thanks Harvey. She's had a bit to drink.'

'I can see that.' He gripped Crystal tightly, biceps bulging in the process.

Crystal felt herself drooling at the display of manly muscles as they helped her down the stairs. Once her feet stood firmly on the ground floor, she smiled at Harvey. 'Thank you, sexy man.'

Harvey's cheeks turned pink, and Jade laughed. 'Naw, big scary Harvey's blushing.'

CRYSTAL'S CRUCIBLE

He shook his head, trying to suppress his own amusement.

'The bathrooms are through here,' Jade explained when they entered an alcove.

'Cheers. I can manage on my own from here,' Crystal assured her.

Jade gave her a sidelong glance.

'I'm okay, promise. I don't need you holding my hand the *whole* way. I'm not as bad as Mum.'

'Fine. I'll meet you at the main bar over there.' She pointed to a large, curved counter topped in speckled steel.

'Got it.' Crystal joined the gaggle of girls queueing for the restroom, crossing her legs to stop the dam in her bladder from bursting. The pain was becoming unbearable, and she regretted sending Jade away because the distraction would have helped. Instead, she focused on the familiar grooves Dieter spun on the decks and bopped in time with the rhythm. She barely made it to a vacant cubicle in time and relief washed over her the moment she was able to let go.

As she left the bathroom, Crystal collided with a wall of solid muscle. 'Oh God! Sorry.' Looking up from the half-buttoned gold shirt, her eyes bugged out when they met a familiar face.

CRYSTAL'S CRUCIBLE

'Markos? Wow, I didn't pick you for the clubbing type.' He looked much hotter dressed as he was, not that he had ever been unattractive. Far from it, in fact.

'Oh, hey Crystal. I could say the same for you. I thought you preferred jazz?'

'I do. Prefer jazz that is. EDM nightclubs are not my thing, but I needed to blow off steam, so I came here with my sister.' Maybe it was the vodka talking, but she could imagine how much better he would look naked, on top of her… inside her. *Mm. Adam would blow a gasket if he knew.*

Markos cocked his left brow. 'Sister?'

'Yeah, this is more my sister, Jade's scene. That's her over there with the blue hair. Anyway, it looks like she is waiting for me, so I should get back to her.' Crystal gestured toward Jade who was watching them. 'It was good seeing you though. Maybe we can chat more later tonight?' she offered.

Reaching into his pocket, he tapped at his phone before replying, 'Why don't we get a drink now? It looks like your sister is busy.' When she turned her gaze toward Jade again, Markos hovered close to her ear and whispered, 'That's Drake, a local drug dealer. Not the sort of guy a sweet girl like you wants to be mixing with.'

CRYSTAL'S CRUCIBLE

Crystal frowned. She knew drugs were Jade's thing, but she had hoped this night would be different. 'Fair enough. I know the owner of this club, let's join him for a drink.' Grabbing his hand, she led him up the stairs.

Tugging on her arm, Markos ushered her into a private booth and closed the curtain. He sat her on the edge of a table that had been bolted to the floor. 'What's going on Crystal? Why are you drinking and acting so out of character tonight?'

She sighed. 'I'm dealing with a lot of personal issues at the moment, and I just needed a night off from the world.'

His gentle hand brushed her face, tucking hair behind her ear. 'You wanna talk about it?'

'Not really. I'd rather forget my troubles for now.'

A sly grin tugged at the left corner of his mouth. 'I know a great way to help you forget.' His lips crashed against hers.

She pressed her hands against his chest in a feeble protest before the heat of the kiss overwhelmed her. Yielding to his touch, to the rush of hormones sparking through her veins, she moaned into his mouth. He tasted like exotic spices and his woodsy cologne swirled around them, enveloping her in a dark cloak of sinful temptation. Markos pushed Crystal back against the table, breaking the kiss briefly until his weight bore down on her. As they made out, her dress rose, and he thrust against her partially exposed core. The friction drove her fragile mind crazy, and she reciprocated the action, inviting more. *How has this man reduced me to a wanton floozy? Is this the alcohol lowering my inhibitions?* A jolt of pleasure surged through her body as she screamed in ecstasy. *Or is he just that good?*

With a wide-eyed stare, he sat back on his haunches. 'Fuck. Did you just come?' His gaze lowered to her panties as he licked his lips. When his fingers followed, she jerked at the intimate contact, but he ignored her reaction. 'Mm, you are soaking wet, gorgeous. I can feel how much you want my cock.'

Crystal gulped and bit her lip. Her mind was at war with itself.

Taking her silence as consent, he tucked her panties aside and plunged two fingers deep inside. Within seconds he brought her to climax again.

'Oh God!' she cried out.

CRYSTAL'S CRUCIBLE

Growling, Markos sprang to his feet and pulled her into his arms. 'I'm taking you home with me so that I can fuck you good and hard.'

Chapter Twenty-Nine

Crystal

'Markos!' Crystal protested. A heated make-out session was one thing, but she was not sure about going home with him. Ignoring her again, he dragged her with him.

The moment they stepped out of the booth, Sargon hurried toward them, a wide-eyed expression on his face. 'Crystal! Thank fuck I found you! Come quick, it's your sister.'

'What happened?' she shouted over her hammering heart, rushing after him.

'She collapsed. I think she OD'd on something.'

Sobriety was like a lightbulb turning on with the flick of a switch. 'Did you call an ambulance?'

'Yes, they're on their way. Through here.' He led her behind the stage, into the green room where

CRYSTAL'S CRUCIBLE

Dieter straddled Jade's unconscious form, administering CPR.

'Oh God! What happened?' Crystal dropped beside her sister, stroking her clammy face.

'Dodgy pills,' Dieter explained with a raspy voice between chest compressions.

She looked to Sargon who shrugged. 'I don't know where she got them, but they weren't from my guy.'

'Wait! I saw her with someone shady. My friend said his name was Drake. Does that name mean anything to you?'

'Shit! It sure does.' Sargon's face paled.

'Well?' Crystal glared at him.

'Drake is a mobster, with the Greek mafia.'

'Are you for real?' she screeched at a higher than usual pitch. 'I didn't know we had any mafia in Melbourne.'

Sargon nodded grimly before stepping out the side door to greet the paramedics in the loading dock.

Dieter rose, pulling Crystal up from the floor to clear a space for the stretcher. He trembled as he pulled her into his arms. 'Do you mind if I ride with her?'

CRYSTAL'S CRUCIBLE

'Of course not. Go. I'll meet you there.' Crystal squeezed Dieter's hand before releasing him. Standing in the doorway, tears trickled down her face while she watched them load Jade into the ambulance. Sirens blared a moment later, and she prayed the ominous sound was not also Jade's death knell. Once the flashing lights turned onto the street, beyond her field of view, she began to crumple, but strong arms caught her, pulling her into his chest.

'Hey, shh. I'm sure she'll be okay,' Markos assured her. 'Do you want me to drive you to the hospital?'

She glanced up at him through blurry eyes. 'Yes please.'

'Oh, hey man,' Sargon greeted Markos. 'You taking her to the hospital?'

'Yeah. I'll keep you posted.' Markos ushered Crystal to a carpark behind the club and helped her into the passenger seat of a gold sportscar. Even his vehicle was different tonight.

They travelled in silence, Crystal rested her head against the cold glass pane, unable to form the words necessary for conversation. Upon arrival, she sprinted through the glass doors beyond the red wall. There was no sign of Dieter, so she approached the desk. 'Hi, an ambulance brought my sister here. Her name's Jade Buchanan. Can I get an update on her condition please?'

'Take a seat and a doctor will see you when there is news,' the woman droned.

Nodding, she turned and found a chair next to Markos. 'Hey, thanks for the lift. You don't have to wait with me.'

'I know, but I want to.' He smiled warmly.

Her cheeks flushed. 'About what happened…'

'We can talk about that later. Right now, you have other concerns. Let me do what I can to comfort you, okay?'

'Okay. Thanks.' Crystal curled up against his side, immersing herself in his scent: a woodsy cologne mingled with the natural musk of his perspiration. Uncertainty clouded her mind; a heavy fog making it impossible to decide what she wanted from the man who sat beside her. *Is it wise to keep him close in my hour of need? What if that was a one-time thing and I start catching feelings? What if he wants more and I don't?* Pushing all thoughts aside, she tried to calm herself with some deep breathing.

An eternity later, a doctor approached them. 'Miss Buchanan?'

CRYSTAL'S CRUCIBLE

'Doctor Buchanan,' Markos corrected him.

'My apologies.' The man's expression turned coy. 'I have been treating your sister, Jade.'

Crystal jumped to her feet. 'How is she?'

'Still unconscious and in a critical condition, I'm afraid. I performed an endotracheal intubation to help with her breathing, and we are running a tox screen to see what she took. Once I get those results, I'll know what medicine to treat her with. Would you like to see her?'

'Yes, if that's okay?'

'It is, but her partner has already glued himself to her side, so I ask that only one of you see her at a time.'

Crystal nodded and turned to Markos. 'I won't be long, but if you want to go—'

'I'll wait.'

'Thanks.' She forced a smile before following the doctor into a cramped bay surrounded by curtains.

Dieter looked up as she entered, his eyes red and puffy. 'Hallo Crissy. Have you phoned Judy yet?'

'No. I was waiting for word on Jade's condition.'

CRYSTAL'S CRUCIBLE

He heaved out a sigh. 'The prognosis is grim at the moment. Might be worth giving your mum a heads up.'

Taking a deep breath, she inhaled the pungent odour of disinfectant as she lowered her gaze to Jade's limp body. A tube protruded from her mouth, and another was drip feeding her fluids intravenously via a cannula in her hand. Choking back a sob, Crystal nodded. 'Okay. I'll contact Mum.'

༺༻

Adam

On the fifty millionth attempt to call Crystal, Adam got through.

'Seriously Adam? Do you know what time it is?' The sound of her voice filled him with a sense of relief, even if she was chastising him.

'I'm sorry, but this couldn't wait.'

'Well it's gonna have to, because I'm at the hospital right now!'

That respite was short lived. 'Wait, what? Are you okay?'

'Physically, I'm fine, but ask me again if I'm okay when I get another update on my sister's condition.'

'What happened, Crissy?'

'Jade took some dodgy pills. She's critical.'

'Shoot! I'm sorry, babe.'

'Babe again huh?' she huffed in an angry tone.

'Look, Crissy, I'm sorry for the way I reacted. The police told me about Robert. I didn't realise your life was in danger, but I'm still pissed you didn't ask me for help with—'

'Hang on a sec, Adam.' A crackling noise filtered down the line and Crystal's voice became muffled. 'Hey, Markos, would you mind getting me a coffee?'

Markos? What the…

'Just a moment.' She spoke clearly into the phone again, 'Can we talk about this tomorrow, Adam, I need to go and ring Mum.'

'Crystal, wait—' The call disconnected, and dread curdled like sour milk in his gut. 'Damnit!' Adam hollered as he tossed his phone aside. *Bloody Markos swoops in to comfort her when I should be the one holding her in my arms. Why the hell is he there anyway?* The gears in his head began to turn, and he could virtually hear the clicking sound in his brain as pieces of the clockwork puzzle began to slot into place. *That son of a gun!* Leaping to his feet, he grabbed his jacket and bolted out the door.

As soon as he sat in the driver's seat of his car, Adam realised he did not know which hospital to go to. He smacked the wheel, sounding the horn and setting off the neighbourhood's dogs. *For Christ's sake!* Typing Melbourne hospitals into his browser's search field, he dialled the number for the first result. Naturally, they put him on hold the moment they answered. The sputtering hold music only added to his agitation, and he drummed the fingers of his right hand on the steering column in double time to the tempo.

'Emergency department, how may I help you?' A gruff woman's voice greeted him.

Finally! 'Hi. I'm looking for a patient who you may have admitted there tonight.'

'Name please.'

What did Crystal say her name was? 'Uh, maiden name is Buchanan, I'm not sure if she changed it.'

'One moment.'

He could hear the clicking sounds of a computer keyboard in the background.

CRYSTAL'S CRUCIBLE

'I have a Jade Buchanan.'

Yes! He almost threw his fist into the air. 'That's her.'

'What is your relationship to the patient?'

'Oh, um, I'm a family friend.'

'Sorry, but we only give out details to immediate family.'

Could she sound more bored? 'Okay, no worries, thanks for your help.' Hanging up, he started the ignition and headed for the city, all the while praying Crystal did not leave the hospital with Markos.

༄༅

Crystal

Crystal watched Markos leave the waiting room to embark on his mission to get coffee. Having never drunk the stuff meant she was not fussy, but he had insisted on getting something half decent. Her first taste should not be out of a hospital vending machine. There was even a joke about him taking her caffeine virginity. Biting her lip, she indulged in memories of the night spurred on by the view of his firm, shapely backside. Once he was out of sight, she slumped into a chair and dialled her mother.

'Crystal?' Judy slurred. 'What are you doin' up at this hour? Don't tell me you finally got a social life?' She sniggered along with a few other voices in the background, most of which sounded masculine.

'I'm at the hospital,' Crystal replied with a sigh. 'Jade is in a coma.'

'Who?'

'Jade. Your other daughter.'

'I don't have another daughter. You're my only child and it's way past your bedtime young lady.' She burst into raucous laughter.

'Christ, mother! Are you high?'

'Maybe,' she replied between giggles. 'Would you mind bringing us a truck load of cheeseburgers?'

'NO!' Crystal snapped. 'Jade is in a coma and may not ever wake up. You should put your petty grievances aside and come to see her because this might be your last chance.'

Judy huffed. 'Nah. I'll pass thanks.'

Crystal gasped as tears trickled from her eyes again and she took a deep breath before replying. 'Fine. If you won't have the decency to come here for Jade, you can forget seeing me again anytime soon.' With that said, she hung up and dropped her phone into her bag. Closing her eyes, she pressed her head back against the wall, attempting to stifle more crying.

'Hey, you okay?' Markos' deep voice pulled her out of her head. 'Did you get hold of your mum?' He stood in front of her, holding two large take-away cups of steaming coffee.

She salivated at the rich, bitter aroma. 'Yeah, but she refuses to come. She wrote Jade off years ago.'

Handing Crystal one of the cups, he sat beside her. 'I'm sorry to hear that.'

With a tentative sip, Crystal tested the temperature of her drink. *Still too hot*. As soon as his arm draped across her shoulder, she climbed into his lap, seeking more warmth. A deep growl rumbled in his chest as he embraced her, but he remained quiet otherwise. It was a comfortable silence that she was not inclined to break.

Another familiar voice broke the peace. 'The pair of you look awfully cosy.' When compared with Adam's acrid tone, the coffee's aftertaste was as sweet as fairy floss.

CRYSTAL'S CRUCIBLE

Lifting her gaze, Crystal met his intense glare. 'Adam? What are you doing here?'

'I came to offer my support,' he ground out between clenched teeth.

'As you can see, I've got that covered.' Markos tightened his grip on her.

Adam stepped closer, towering over them. 'Surely I don't need to remind you of the ramifications of such fraternisation? You are his boss, Crystal. You could lose your job over this.'

She let a short, sardonic laugh slip. 'Are *you* really going to lecture me on the Company's Conflict of Interest Policy, after everything *we* did?'

His eyes widened and he shot a wary look at Markos.

'Wait. Did you both hook up?' Markos asked.

'It was a lot more than that,' Crystal confessed. 'But Adam dumped me and broke my heart.'

'Worst mistake of my life, and you'd better keep your mouth shut if you still want a job, Markos.'

Markos sniggered. 'Now I see why they call it a conflict of interest.'

CRYSTAL'S CRUCIBLE

Adam glared at him before turning his gaze to Crystal and softening his tone. 'Baby, can we talk, please?'

'I'm listening.' Her own brow furrowed into a scowl.

'I'd rather talk in private.'

'Too bad.'

Markos rubbed her back. 'It's okay, go and resolve things with Adam. I'll wait for you here.' He kissed her forehead before releasing her.

Rising to her feet, she hesitantly followed Adam outside. 'What the hell, Adam—'

'I don't trust that arsehole.' He gestured toward Markos through the window.

'Why, because he is the one comforting me after you turned your back on us?' she spat with more venom than a brown snake.

He heaved out a sigh. 'Firstly, I came to make amends for that. As for Markos, I suspect he might be the mole and I'm worried about his intentions with you.'

Crystal smirked. 'He made his intentions pretty clear when he kissed me at the club tonight.'

Adam's cheeks flushed with red hot rage. 'Did he fuck you?'

CRYSTAL'S CRUCIBLE

Keeping her smug grin, she shook her head. 'Not yet. But he did make me come. *Twice.*' She waved two fingers for effect.

The astringent rage flowing from Adam was tangible enough to be bottled. 'Don't push me, Crystal. I already want to murder the bastard; I don't need more fuel.' He took a pause breath. 'When the police told me about Robert's death and the threat made to your life, I realised how badly I messed up. I spent the rest of the night freaking out, worried something had happened to you because no one knew where you were, and I couldn't get in touch with you. I am *extremely* sorry, babe.' Moving closer, he reached out for her, but she backed away.

'Your arrogance knows no bounds, if you think that pathetic apology is enough to make me run back to you.'

Hurt flickered in his eyes. 'I'm trying. I want to make it up to you, baby. Tell me what I need to do to set things right.'

'Give me some time. My emotions are a mess right now, and my love life is the least of my concerns. Go home and I'll call you when I'm ready to talk.'

CRYSTAL'S CRUCIBLE

He nodded gradually. 'Stay the hell away from Markos, though. His sudden interest in you is highly suspicious given the circumstances.'

She gave him a sidelong glance. 'What do you mean by *sudden* interest?'

'I'm not blind to the ways other men perve on you. Markos was one of the few men at work who didn't feast on you with hungry eyes.'

Crystal shrugged. 'Maybe he's skilled at masking his emotions.'

'If so, that makes him even more dangerous. Promise me you won't go home with him,' he pleaded with puppy eyes.

'Fine,' she sighed. 'I promise.'

The muscles in his face relaxed. 'Thank you. I'll leave you to it.' He turned and dragged his feet away but halted, looking over his shoulder. 'Oh, and I hope your sister recovers soon.'

She nodded and watched as he walked away before returning to her seat.

'What was all that about?' Markos inquired.

'He was begging for my forgiveness and trying to win me back.'

Markos studied her features. 'You were using me for a rebound fuck, weren't you?'

Flinching at his vulgar language, she felt her cheeks flush. 'No… I don't know…'

He brushed his knuckles along her cheekbone. 'It's okay if that's all you needed. I'm just sorry I couldn't give you more before all this…' His hand waved around the hospital waiting room. 'While I'd love to take you back to my house and continue what we started, I'm content being your friend for now.'

Crystal forced a smile. 'Thanks, Markos.' Returning her attention to the coffee in her hand, she drank it while her mind drifted. *I hope Adam is wrong about Markos.*

Chapter Thirty

Apollo

Apollo was a less than fitting nickname for the man who stormed into the hospital, a dark tempest swirling around his mood. Perhaps Zeus would have been more suitable. A day after her admittance, the hospital moved Jade to a private room. Her condition had stabilised, but she continued to slumber like the beauty she was. Crystal was dozing in the chair next to the bed, snoring faintly when he entered. Apparently, she had talked Dieter into taking alternating shifts with their vigils because he was usually more of a night owl. This fact didn't help her, however, after the sleepless night she had just endured. It also gave Apollo the opportunity he needed to finish cleaning up his mess.

Closing the door, he crept over to Jade's drip. The dose of Fentanyl in the syringe he carried would be enough to finish the job before the doctors could save her. He was within an inch of ending her life when he caught a glimpse of her pretty face and wavered. *Shit! What am I doing?* Dropping the needle back in its case, he perched on the edge of her bed and took in the sight of her. A foreign sensation clawed at his chest. The pain was sharp, cramping the muscles around his lungs, smothering his breathing.

It occurred to him he had almost lost the only woman who had ever touched his black soul; the only person who had brought light to his darkness. While his hand had not forced those pills down her throat, she had only taken them because of him. Pressure swelled behind his eyes and his cheeks grew damp with the salty fluid seeping into his mouth. *The fuck? Am I weeping?* His ribs trembled with a silent snigger at the irony of the situation. *Everything Patéras and I have worked for, all we have wanted is within reach and this is when I catch feelings for someone.*

Apollo was a selfish man, he craved it all. The promise of power and possessions meant nothing if he could not share them with a companion. He did not just want the playthings in his dungeon, but the love of a woman who understood him, who made all his fantasies come true. *Jade*.

He stroked her cheek with his knuckles and leaned over to kiss her lips chastely. 'Wake up for me, sweetheart,' he begged in a whisper. 'I promise I'll find another way to fix things. Please come back to me.' A knock sounded at the door, startling him to his feet.

Crystal stirred as a nurse strode into the room to check Jade's vitals. 'Oh hey, Markos.' Her voice was groggy when she addressed him. 'Did you manage to find a change of clothes for me?'

'Yeah, although I bought you some new stuff because your mother was not home.' He handed her the paper shopping bag.

Eyeing the boutique store's logo, her eyes widened. 'I'm not sure I can afford this stuff.'

He smiled. 'My treat. I hope they fit okay.'

Pulling the garments out, she gasped. 'They're gorgeous, thank you.' She turned to the nurse. 'Is it okay if I use my sister's shower?'

The middle-aged woman nodded. 'It's not like Jade can use it yet.' When Crystal disappeared into the bathroom, the nurse laughed. 'You sound like quite the catch, young man. I hope your woman realises how lucky she is.'

CRYSTAL'S CRUCIBLE

'Oh, Crystal and I aren't a couple,' Apollo corrected her. 'Not yet anyway.'

Returning the clipboard to the base of Jade's bed, she smiled. 'Most men start with flowers and chocolates, so you're already on the right track. Keep up the good work.' After winking at him, she left the room.

Crystal emerged amidst a plume of steam dressed in the silky, rose-gold blouse and matching dress pants, and his breath hitched at the sight of her. He would have opted for a dress or skirt combo, but she had insisted on comfortable pants, so this was what she got. 'You look stunning.'

She blushed. 'Thanks. I feel overdressed for the occasion, but this fabric feels soft and comfy. I love it.' Her words mirrored his thoughts exactly.

He approached her with open arms, and she accepted his embrace. 'Is there anything else I can do for you?'

'You've already done so much. I couldn't possibly ask for more.'

Drawing back, he cupped her face in his hand. 'Nonsense. Tell me what you want and it's yours.'

A real smile lit up her features, the first hint of happiness she had shown since learning of Jade's overdose. 'Where have you been all my life, Markos? For now, I just need more hugs.'

Fuck! These Buchanan girls were going to be his undoing. He sucked in a breath, inhaling her sweet, musky scent as he held her firmly against his body. *Is it greedy of me to want the two most beautiful women in the world? Likely.* But he did not care.

෨෬

Adam

It was New Year's Eve yet celebrating was the last thing on Adam's mind as he spent the day in a restless limbo, alternating between Netflix and the gym. When his phone buzzed with messages, he launched for the device like a starving man, hungry for an update from Crystal. It had only been a couple of days since he had talked to her at the hospital, and he still held out hope for them.

It was five in the evening when she texted him: Hi Adam. What are your plans for tonight?

His heartbeat doubled in speed as he replied. I've been invited to a few parties, but I don't feel like going to any of them. How are you? Any news on your sister?

CRYSTAL'S CRUCIBLE

{Crystal} Jade is stable, but still in a coma. I'm too depressed to party, but I was hoping we could talk. Is it okay if I come over?

{Adam} Yes, of course. Head straight over as soon as you're ready.

{Crystal} Thanks. As soon as Dieter gets here around 6pm, I'll go home and freshen up. Should get there around 7.

Adam spent the next two hours manically cleaning away the evidence of his recent bachelor phase, washing dishes, dumping take-away boxes and wrappers in the bin, recycling the empty gin and tonic bottles, and relocating the dirty clothes from his bedroom floor to the laundry hamper. With about ten minutes to spare, he sniffed his armpits and winced. A shower was *not* optional at this point. The doorbell rang as he walked from the ensuite to his bedroom. He slipped into a clean pair of grey track pants.

Crystal's jaw dropped when he opened the door. 'Are you trying to kill me, dressing like that?' He could have said the same for her with the figure-hugging black V-neck dress she wore.

'Sorry, I was in a rush to finish getting ready.' He gave her a lopsided grin. 'I almost answered wearing nothing but a towel, but I didn't want to scare you off before giving you a chance to talk.'

CRYSTAL'S CRUCIBLE

Snorting, she followed him through the hallway, into the living room. 'Mind putting a shirt on? You'll distract me too much otherwise.'

'Sure.' Adam turned to hide the smirk forming on his face as he walked back to his bedroom. It was thrilling to know he still affected her. He threw on a white sports brand tee and hurried back. 'Can I get you anything to drink?'

She made herself comfortable on the couch. 'Got any softies[14]?'

'Only cola and tonic water, I'm afraid.'

'The cola sounds good; I could use the caffeine hit.'

Adam's brows hit the ceiling, but he bit his lip to stifle the remark on the tip of his tongue. Grabbing two cans of Coke from the fridge, he handed her one and popped the top on the other before sitting beside her. 'Crystal, I'm—'

'Adam, I'm—' They both started at the same time.

'You go first,' he insisted, placing a hand on her knee.

Glancing at his grip on her, Crystal gulped and lifted her gaze to his. 'I'm sorry for keeping secrets, but I guess you know why I did it now. The

---
[14] Soft drinks

thing is, I still can't tell you who threatened me because I'm fairly certain he has someone watching me and I wouldn't put it past him to tap my devices and bug our homes. If I so much as hint at his identity, he will send someone after me. Even telling you this much is a risk, but you figured most of it out on your own anyway.'

'When you say he, are you talking about the mole in R&D?'

She shook her head. 'No. I'm thinking the mole works for this guy, or they might be a victim of blackmail. I still have no idea who they are and without evidence, we have nothing to pin on anyone.'

He sighed. 'I didn't get a chance to finish going through my half of the files before the police confiscated them.'

'I guess we have to put our faith in the criminal justice system now.'

'What—' He was about to ask what she told the police but stopped himself when he remembered the possibility of bugs in the house. *I'll have to sweep for listening devices later.* 'What happened with Markos?'

Her cheeks turned a beautiful shade of pink, one he usually loved seeing, but given the context, he felt his stomach churn. She averted her attention to the drink in her hand, chugging down a few mouthfuls before looking at him. 'Aside from one night of making out in a nightclub, he has been a good, supportive friend during this whole Jade ordeal.'

'So, you're not dating?'

'No.'

Adam braced himself before asking, 'Do you have feelings for him?' The way she lowered her gaze told him all he needed to know. 'Shoot!' He rose, but Crystal tugged his arm, pulling him back to the seat.

'Wait. Listen to me, Adam. Yes, okay, I may have developed some feelings for Markos. It was hard to avoid with all he did for me, but I'm not in love with him, not like I am with you. I love *you*, Adam. Only you.'

His breathing hitched at her words. 'It feels so good to hear you say that again. I never stopped loving you either, baby. Even while upset and angry, thinking you had betrayed me, I couldn't shake your hold on my heart.'

Her eyes brimmed with tears as she climbed into his lap, lifting the hem of her dress to straddle him. 'Where do we go from here?' she asked in a whisper. 'Do we start over?'

'I'd rather pick up where we left off,' Adam admitted, feeling the first stirrings between his legs. 'That okay with you?'

Nodding, she kissed him deeply, smothering him with her softness.

God, I miss these lips and the feel of her skin against mine. The moment she began grinding against him, all the blood in his body rushed into his erection, leaving him dizzy. Pushing aside her panties, he slid one finger between her folds, moaning when he discovered how wet she was. 'I need to be inside you, baby.' This time he welcomed the blush in her cheeks as she freed him from the confines of his pants. Holding his gaze, she hovered above Adam for one excruciating second before impaling herself on him. They both cried out upon the moment of impact, and within minutes they were coming together.

As soon as Adam had caught his breath and regained his composure, he carried Crystal to his bed, where they spent the night making love and eating pizza. Having lost track of time, they only knew the new year had started when the distant crackle and boom echoed the fireworks exploding between them.

Chapter Thirty-One

Jade

White light filtered in through her closed eyelids. The rhythmic beeping that had been Jade's constant companion continued, although the sound was less muffled. Awareness crept back, and she realised her parched throat hurt like a bitch. Squinting, she tried to take in more of her surroundings. Even without seeing him, she knew Dieter curled up next to her. Everything about his presence was familiar, from his sandalwood cologne to his slim, toned body that was too tall to fit on the bed he had squeezed into. *The bed is not ours.* That was her first clue, the second being the pungent odour of antiseptic. *I'm in a hospital.* She reached out and brushed her fingers along the facial hair lining his chiselled jawline. It was easily more than one day of growth.

CRYSTAL'S CRUCIBLE

He stirred, his long lashes fluttering as he opened his blue eyes. '*Liebling*? Oh thank God!' Dieter peppered her face with kisses, only halting when an inhuman sound escaped her gravel-lined gullet. 'What's wrong?' he asked with a frown.

She pressed a hand to her throat, and he nodded.

'I'll get help.' He sat up and pressed the CALL button.

A male nurse arrived a minute later. 'Morning, Jade. How do you feel?'

'Th-thirsty,' she rasped, feeling her speech slur.

'Understandable. You haven't drunk anything for days. We've kept you hydrated with a drip, but your throat has been out of use.' He handed her a glass of water. 'Start with small sips.'

'Days?' She gave him and Dieter a wide-eyed look.

Dieter nodded grimly. 'Happy New Year, my love. I'll explain everything in a moment.' Once the nurse had finished checking her vitals, he left them in peace. Savouring the cool liquid with small mouthfuls, Jade listened to Dieter's explanation. She had overdosed on MDMA pills laced with Fentanyl.

CRYSTAL'S CRUCIBLE

'It was touch and go there for a while. You had me worried, *Liebling*.'

Knowing she had tapped death on the shoulder and returned alive, rendered her speechless for several minutes. Her mind buzzed with conflicting thoughts until she made two difficult decisions. 'I need ta quit takin' tha' shit, but I'm gone n-need ya help.' *Why is talking so damn hard?*

Dieter clasped her hand and squeezed it. 'Of course, my love. I'll do anything for you.'

Hearing those words made her next resolution much harder and tears welled in her eyes. 'I'm s-sorry, baybe.'

'Shh, it's okay. We'll get through this.'

Jade shook her head. 'N-no, you don' unerstan'. I'm s-sorry 'cause… (sob)… I ch-cheated.'

Dieter stiffened. 'What?'

'Wif Apollo.'

His breathing quickened. 'Was this a once off, or…'

'Weeks. I'm s-sorry. I swear I'll cut ties wif him an—'

'Stop it! I have heard enough! I think you'd best ask Crystal to be your sober sponsor.' Rising from the bed, he left her with those parting words.

CRYSTAL'S CRUCIBLE

Jade wept pitiful sounds of anguish, too weak to summon the gut-wrenching cry the occasion deserved. She knew this would be a risk if she told Dieter the truth, but she honestly thought there was more chance he would try to work through the mess with her. *Is he really willing to throw away four years of love and happiness? With any luck he'll come around to the idea of reconciliation after he had had time to reflect on the situation.* After a few deep breaths, she closed her eyes and settled back to sleep.

Jade had no idea how long she slumbered, but when she awoke, Crystal sat by her bed, reading something on her Kindle with sullen eyes betraying fatigue. 'C-Crissy?' Her voice was still hoarse and slurred.

Jumping up, Crystal dropped the e-reader on her chair. 'Jade! You're awake!'

'Yeah. Secon' t-time t'daay. Luckay me,' she droned.

'What? Why didn't Dieter let me know? Or was it after he left this morning? Oh Gods, I'm sorry if you woke up to an empty room. I kind of slept in after last night…' Her rambling trailed off when she dragged her bottom lip between her teeth.

Jade sighed. 'Dieter was 'ere, ba lef me.'

CRYSTAL'S CRUCIBLE

'What do you mean he left you?'

'Na sure where we stan' right noow, but I tol him 'bout ma affair, and he didn' take it well.'

Crystal's eyes bugged out. 'Are you insane? Why didn't you wait until you had recovered? You obviously need a bunch of rehab to get you through this and it's going to be tough without him.'

Turning her head, Jade hid her shame from Crystal.

'Oh God! Jade, I'm sorry. I didn't mean to snap; I've been so stressed and worried about you.' The bed dipped as Crystal perched beside her, grabbing her hand, and caressing it with circular thumb strokes. 'I'm here for you hun. Whatever you need.'

Redirecting her gaze, she smiled at Crystal. 'Thanks, Pump'in.' … 'I f-felt too guiltay.'

Crystal nodded. 'I totally get it. My own guilt has plagued me for a while now. Vastly different circumstances, mind you, but I understand how it feels.'

'P-please help me go soba?'

Her face lit up as she clapped her hands. 'Yes! Absolutely!' Crystal paused for thought before adding, 'You wanna get a flat together?'

CRYSTAL'S CRUCIBLE

'Fa real?' Jade's own heartrate picked up. 'What abou ma?'

'To hell with that bitch,' Crystal sneered.

Jade cracked up laughing. 'F-finally come ta ya s-senses eh?'

'Let's just say our mother showed her true colours when I told her about you coming here. I have no desire to speak with her again.'

With a sigh, Jade nodded, understanding what Crystal meant. As a teenager, she had seen Judy at her worst, a side of their mother she tried to hide from Crystal while taking on the role of parent herself. 'I'd love ta live wif ma sista. S-should be a blast.'

'Amen to that.' Grinning, Crystal moved closer and embraced her.

The gesture bought fresh tears to Jade's eyes. *At least I still have my Pumpkin.*

ಸಿಜ

Crystal

Closing the door behind her, Crystal leaned against it with a sigh. She was grateful to see her sister awake at last, but the cognitive impairment worried her.

'How is she?'

Startled, she looked down at the seats lining the hallway. 'Oh hey, Markos. I didn't see you there. How long have you been waiting?'

'About an hour.'

'You should have come and met Jade. She woke up this morning.'

He rose. 'Yeah, I heard you talking to her, which was why I didn't want to interrupt. I figured you had a bit of catching up to do. How is she?'

Crystal sucked in a deep breath. 'Jade has a rough road ahead of her. The overdose caused some brain damage, like a stroke. I'm not sure if she will recover fully with rehab, but I guess we can only hope.'

'I'm sorry, Crissy.' A medley of emotions swirled in his dark, deep-set eyes, not all of them readable, but genuine concern clearly showed in his expression. 'You look exhausted. Wanna grab a caffeine hit, my shout?'

'Um…' Recalling Adam's warning, she almost declined, but gazing upon Markos, she decided there was nothing malicious about the man. If they stuck to public locations, she would be fine. 'Yeah okay. I need to use the bathroom first.'

Nodding, he returned to waiting on the corridor chairs while she ducked into the nearby restrooms.

Crystal leaned against the vanity bench and shot a quick message to Adam, letting him know she was about to have coffee with Markos, *as friends*. She did not need the facilities but thought it would be rude and suspicious if she texted in front of her companion. Dropping her phone back in her bag, she washed her hands and joined Markos.

'I know a great café nearby,' he explained as they left the building. 'With the weather being perfect, I thought it would make for a nice stroll, but if you're not up for it, I'd be happy to drive you there.'

'The walk sounds lovely, thank you.' Like the rest of her, Crystal's legs were tired after a wild reunion with Adam, but she did not fancy pushing her luck by getting in Markos' car.

'I know the last few days have been hard on you, but that hot mess look you've got going on suggests more than a few restless nights and some sisterly concern. Did you have a big New Year's Eve too?'

CRYSTAL'S CRUCIBLE

Arching her brows, she looked at him askance. 'Hot mess huh?'

'Emphasis on the *hot*, of course.'

'Markos—'

He threw his hands up in resignation. 'Friend zone, I know. But I reserve my right to complement you as much as I like.' Halting his steps, he pressed his lips to her ear. 'You did treat me to some of the best almost sex I've ever had, after all. A night like that is impossible to forget.'

Her cheeks flamed. Clearing her throat, she continued walking in silence.

'What did you get up to last night?' he asked again.

She sighed. 'Would you get upset if I told you I spent my night in bed with another man?'

'Hmm… Maybe, if it was serious, and only if the other guy is opposed to sharing you.'

Spluttering, Crystal stumbled, catching her foot on the tiniest crack in the pavement. A strong arm caught her around the waist, bringing her back flush with his solid chest. She gulped and twisted in Markos' embrace. His gaze trapped hers, golden embers flickering amidst dark, penetrating orbs. 'What are you implying?' she whispered.

CRYSTAL'S CRUCIBLE

'I don't do monogamy, Crystal, and I don't expect it from my lovers either. You can fuck who you like so long as you return to my bed on the regular.'

With a hammering heart, she inhaled shallow breaths, employing every ounce of willpower she possessed to resist his allure. 'I'm sorry Markos, but the man I'm seeing is big on monogamy and loyalty, so I won't be returning to your bed. Not that I was ever technically in it, but you know.'

'That is a shame.' He loosened his grip but did not release his hold of her. After studying her face, he tickled her pulse point with his hot breath. 'I guess I'll have to try harder to win you back.'

She gaped at him, which he took as an invitation to assault her lips with the pad of his thumb, sending shivers through her spine and liquifying her core. It was clear Markos was highly skilled in the art of seduction. She would need to be careful with him because no matter how talented he was in the sack; she would not risk betraying Adam. 'We should go get that coffee.'

'Aha.'

'That means letting go of me, Markos.'

CRYSTAL'S CRUCIBLE

Mischief twinkled in his eyes. 'Nope. Not gonna happen.' He tucked her against his side, keeping his arm around her waist as he guided her forward.

Crystal huffed. 'I get the impression you don't easily take no for an answer.'

He laughed. 'I am aware of the word, but I don't hear it often. In my experience, most noes become yesses with enough persuasion.'

'Wow. I thought Adam was arrogant.'

His ribs shook with more mirth. 'I guess that means I *am* your type. Was Adam the one you spent last night with?'

She fell silent.

'It's okay, Crissy, I won't tell anyone. I figured it had to be him after that run in we had the other night.'

'Once he steps down into the QA Manager role there won't be a need for secrecy. Can you please keep your knowledge of our prior relationship hush-hush?'

He squeezed her hip. 'Of course. I'd hate for him to spill the beans on us and put your job in jeopardy, not that I can see him doing so if he truly cares for you, but still.' As soon as they reached the café, he released his arm and opened the door for her.

Smooth. She sat in the chair he pulled out for her and watched as he lined up at the counter to order their drinks.

Her phone buzzed a second later, and she read the reply from Adam: Be careful. Watch your drink like a hawk and do NOT get in his car. Love you xxx.

She rolled her eyes. *Talk about paranoid.* Nothing about Markos suggested he wanted anything more than getting into her pants. She had her own reasons for avoiding a drive in his car and they had more to do with trusting herself. After typing out a brief reassuring response, she looked up and smiled at Markos as he sat down across from her.

'Tell me more about Jade,' Markos insisted.

'Why? Did you fall for my comatose sister?' she gibed, catching a strange flash of something in his eyes. 'I'm joking, although she would totally be your type.'

'I was asking because I'm interested in you, and by extension, your family life. Besides, doesn't Jade have a devoted boyfriend?'

Her brow furrowed as she shook her head. 'Not anymore. He broke it off with her after learning she recently cheated on him. Apparently, she's not suited to exclusivity either, which makes sense considering the nature of her prior relationships.'

'Curious,' he mused.

'I kind of feel sorry for Dieter, but at the same time I think dumping her at this critical time was a jerk move, especially since she wants to clean up her act and swear off the drugs.'

His eyes grew wide. 'Is that so?'

'Yeah. That means she will need a lot of support from me. I'm going to get an apartment with her and help with her rehab.'

'That's generous of you, especially with your full-time workload.'

'She'll have a nurse helping during the day while I'm at work, and trust me when I say, she'll be less of a burden than my alcoholic mother who I've been looking after for years.'

Their coffee arrived and Markos stirred a sachet of sugar into his short black, while Crystal decided she preferred her latte unsweetened. Glancing at her over the lip of his cup, a sly grin curled one side of his mouth. 'I have plenty of space for both of you at my house, and I won't charge rent.'

CRYSTAL'S CRUCIBLE

Crystal snorted. 'Nice try. I doubt Adam would allow that sort of living arrangement.'

Markos cocked his brow. 'What? Are you telling me he would be too jealous to let you sharehouse with another man?'

'You're not simply some random guy, Markos. Given our history, I think he would be adamantly opposed to the idea.'

He laughed. 'Nice pun.'

'What?' Thinking back, she realised what she said and shook her head. 'Not intentional.'

'Pity. About the pun, and your refusal. Maybe I should try to talk Jade around to the idea.'

She gasped. 'You wouldn't dare?'

Markos replied with a smug grin as he sipped his shot of espresso.

৸০৻

Apollo

After walking Crystal back to her car and watching her drive away, he turned back toward the hospital with a renewed sense of hope and a spring in his stride. Not even the sterile stench of bleach dampened his mood as he traversed the corridors to

Jade's room. *Dieter is out of the picture!* He knocked and opened the door.

'Aypollo?'

'Evening, gorgeous.'

'I almos' din recognise ya wif out ya gold s-shirt.' She clamped a hand over her mouth and frowned.

He perched on her bed. 'What's wrong, sweetheart?'

She sighed. 'I s-sound stoopid. You s-should go.'

Clutching her hand, he shook his head. 'I'm not going anywhere. I heard what a dick Dieter was by dropping you when you're already down.'

'Yeah, well tha 'cause of *your* dick.'

He laughed. 'Touché, my dear.' Leaning in, he brushed his lips across her forehead, feeling her shiver as he moved down, kissing her nose, and her lips. She mewled, granting his tongue access to her sweet mouth, tasting of jelly and ice cream.

Pressing her hands feebly against his chest, she hissed the word, 'Stop.'

Recoiling, he stared at her. 'Shit! Did I hurt you?'

'No.'

He released the breath he was holding and move back in for another kiss.

'Wayt. We canno do th-this.'

Narrowing his eyes, so they pinched the bridge of his nose, he sat upright. 'Why? You don't even need to feel guilty about Dieter anymore. Let me show you I'm the better choice.'

She shook her head. 'This's nah 'bout Dei'er. It's tha drugs. I need ta quit.'

'I understand, sweetheart. I really do. I promise I'll keep that shit away from you.'

'No. I'll s-stil be temp'ed wif you.'

'Not if I stop making and dealing all together. I'm prepared to give it all up for you.'

Her jaw dropped. 'S-ser'ously? Wha 'bout money?'

He shrugged. 'I'm a resourceful man. Dealing is one of the many ways I earn money. Believe it or not, I do have a day job. A well-paying one at that. Plus, I've already cleared my mortgage, which is why I want you to come live with me.'

Jade's eyes bugged out so much she resembled an anime character, complete with blue hair and huge tits. It was incredible how delicious she looked, even in a frumpy hospital gown. 'Bah I agreed ta s-share wif Crissay.'

CRYSTAL'S CRUCIBLE

'She can move in with you. I have plenty of space. You can each have your own rooms, you can sleep with whoever you like,' he licked his lips, 'and if you get lonely, my bed is big enough for both of you.'

Silent laughter rumbled in her chest. 'Ya dir'y perve. 'Sif she'd go fa tha.'

'You'd be surprised what she's up for. We had a wild time at the club the other night. I'm keen on that threesome suggestion of yours now.'

'I s-still doubt she'd go fa tha livin' arran'ment.'

A cunning idea occurred to him. 'Don't tell her it's my home. Pretend another friend offered up use of the place while they are abroad. Make it out to be a house-sitting deal with a more permanent option upon their return. Then I'll surprise her, and I bet she'll give in after falling in love with the house… and me.'

She shook her head. 'Unbalievable.'

'Come on. It's a genius idea. Worst case scenario, Crystal moves out and you get more of me. What do you say?' He gave her a toothy grin.

'F-fine.'

'Yess!'

This time she yielded to his deep kiss.

Chapter Thirty-Two

Crystal

Crystal spent the rest of the week helping Jade during her intense physiotherapy and speech pathology. While her talking had significantly improved during this time, she was still unsteady on her feet, which meant a wheelchair and walking sticks would be essential for a while yet. Still, the progress she made gave Crystal hope.

Adam had granted her an extension to her annual leave—before he resigned from his role as her boss, moving back to the QA Manager position—which gave her extra time to help Jade move into the 'A-mazing' house she kept bragging about, hyping it up to be some big mansion or castle. While the sweet deal her sister had scored on the property impressed Crystal, a dog box would make her happy if it meant being free of her

CRYSTAL'S CRUCIBLE

mother—the trollop *(emphasis on troll)* who kept getting underfoot as Crystal packed her stuff.

'Please don't leave me,' Judy pleaded from Crystal's bed.

Ignoring her, Crystal continued emptying the contents of her wardrobe into canvas shopping bags.

'Crissy, honey, how will I live without you?'

Hmm, how to pack the hangers so they don't end up in a tangled mess?

'Why do all the people I love leave me?' Judy whinged.

Retrieving her phone from the dressing table, Crystal searched the internet for moving hacks and coat hangers, eventually finding a simple method that appealed to her. She walked into the study and grabbed the rubber bands, using them to wrap the hangers in stacks. As she tucked an old blanket around them, her phone chimed with a text.

{Adam} How goes the moving prep?

Crystal smiled as she typed her reply. Good. Nearly finished packing. Although, it would be better with your company rather than Judy's.

{Adam} Wouldn't a grizzly bear make better company than your mother?

She burst out laughing. Yes! Absolutely! Still, I miss you. How is work?

CRYSTAL'S CRUCIBLE

{Adam} I miss you too. This place is dull without you. What's your new address going to be?

Biting her lip, she hesitated before revealing the truth: I don't actually know. Jade insisted on surprising me with a big reveal. Apparently, this is some hot shot dream home. She rolled her eyes thinking about it.

{Adam} Hmm, okay. Strange girl. Message me as soon as you get there. Love you xxx.

Love you too xxx. She tossed her phone aside and moved into the bathroom to pack her toiletries.

'Crissy?' Judy hovered by the door. 'Crissy, *please*.' The incessant nagging was annoying, like a buzzing fly.

No, the whining of a mosquito is more accurate.

'Maybe I should have a drug overdose to win back your attention!'

Crystal spun on her heels and stomped up to Judy, jabbing a finger into her collarbone. 'Listen, you insufferable cow, Jade is legitimately trying to clean up her act. She deserves my support. What have you ever done other than inflict pain and misery on those around you? If you want to OD, be my guest. With any luck you'll rid the world of the horrid woman you have become.'

Judy gasped, tears brimming in her eyes. Turning about, she stormed down the hall, into her bedroom, where she slammed the door.

CRYSTAL'S CRUCIBLE

Good riddance to bad rubbish. A second later the doorbell rang, and Crystal rushed to answer it.

Bouncing on her toes, Esme squealed with delight when the door flung open. She pulled Crystal in for a hug. 'This is so exciting!'

'Thanks for helping, Ez.'

'No probs, hun. I would've been insulted if you didn't ask.'

Crystal's eyes grew wide, her brows shooting off her face when she spotted Markos helping Jade out of the small moving truck parked in Judy's driveway. The place they were moving to was furnished, so they did not need to cart much. 'Um, hi. What are you doing here? Don't you have work today?'

He grinned. 'Nope. I'm helping with the move. Figured you'd need some manly muscles to move the heavy stuff.' There was something strange about his voice she could not identify.

She observed the way his arm slung over Jade's shoulder. 'I take it you've met my sister.'

Jade snorted. 'Pumpkin, he is the guy from the club I was tellin' you 'bout.'

Crystal felt close to straining a facial muscle. 'The one you cheated with?' She turned her gaze back to Markos. 'Why didn't you tell me about your relationship?' His interest and concern for Jade's welfare made sense, another piece clicking into place within the puzzle of life.

He shrugged. 'It was her secret. I'm not one to kiss and tell.' After ensuring Jade firmly clasped her walking stick, Markos embraced Crystal. 'Cute nickname, by the way.'

Stepping back, she narrowed her eyes on him. 'Call me by it and I'll castrate you. Only Jade gets to use that name.'

'Hmm, what should I call you then…'

'Crissy is fine.'

Mischief sparkled in his eyes as he grinned. 'Yes, you are fine.' He clicked his fingers. 'I know! How about Peach? I love peaches, they are so sweet and juicy…' He leaned in to whisper against the shell of her ear, 'Just like you.'

Crystal cursed her pale complexion for revealing the blush in her cheeks. 'No, not Peach.'

'I think yes.'

'Yo, bitches!' Esme called from inside the house. 'We gonna start loading these boxes into the truck, or what?'

'Yeah, coming!' Crystal cried.

Markos cocked a brow.

CRYSTAL'S CRUCIBLE

'Quit it, you.' Crystal pointed an accusing finger at him.

'What? I didn't say anything. Let's get to work, Peach.' He strode inside the house.

Jade was leaning against the side of the truck with an amused expression painted on her face. 'You got it bad for him too, don't ya? At least now you know why I was powerless to resist him.'

'Shut up! It's not happening. I'm back with Adam now.' Crystal would have slapped Jade if she were not so fragile. Instead, she helped her into the house.

'Mhmm. Where's Mum?' Jade asked.

'Sulking in her room. I doubt we'll see her again today.'

Jade squeezed her arm. 'I'm so proud of ya for moving outta here.'

Going from caring for one needy relative to looking after another was not exactly what Crystal had envisioned when she secured the funds for independent living, but the sacrifice would be worthwhile if it meant keeping her sister alive and healthy. 'Cheers, Sis. Here's to new beginnings.'

※

CRYSTAL'S CRUCIBLE

Crystal

Bang! The doors of the truck closed on the last of Jade's belongings, and Crystal averted her eyes, wiping away the drool on her chin before Markos turned to catch her in the act of perving. They assembled on the street outside Jade's old Fitzroy apartment building, where Dieter had made himself scarce for the day, leaving instructions for Jade to drop her key in the letterbox. Crystal jingled her own keys on her finger. 'I guess I'll follow you guys there.'

Markos shook his head. 'Nope. You're coming in the truck with us. Esme can drive your car there.'

'What? No way!'

'Gee thanks for putting faith in my driving,' Esme scoffed.

Crystal shook her head. 'It's not that, Ez. I just…'

'Can't keep your hands off me?' Markos suggested in a playful tone.

She glared at him.

'*Please*, Crissy,' Jade begged, batting her lashes. 'I wanna see your face when you first look at this place.'

CRYSTAL'S CRUCIBLE

'Fine,' Crystal conceded with a huff, dropping the keys in Esme's palm and marching up to the truck's cabin.

'You'll need to get in first,' Markos explained. 'I'll lift Jade into the seat once you're buckled in.'

'This sounds like a ploy to get me in range of your grabby hands.'

'Something like that.' He gave her a sly grin, his eyes full of dark promises.

Sighing, Crystal climbed up onto the bench seat, taking her spot in the middle. *Adam's going to have a fit when he finds out about this.* She thought it curious Markos was not the least bit scared of Adam, the taller of the two. They were both strong, athletic men, but she had no idea who would be more skilled in a fight. She could not imagine Adam in a brawl, whereas Markos frequented nightclubs, giving him a streetwise edge.

Markos sat next to her, pressing his thigh against hers. The contact was enough to jolt her hormones into overdrive. She closed her eyes and bit her lip, focussing on thoughts of Adam and trying to ignore what the devil in the driver's seat was doing to her body. 'Are you tired, Peach?'

CRYSTAL'S CRUCIBLE

Prying one eye open, she peeked at him. 'I am, actually.'

'We have a bit of a drive ahead of us. Feel free to take a nap.'

Brilliant idea! It was the perfect strategy for avoiding the volatile chemistry simmering between them. 'Sounds good to me.'

'This should help.' He handed her a red blindfold.

Her eyes darted from the mask to his face and back again. 'I don't think I want to know why you carry that thing in your pocket.'

'Then don't ask.'

Crystal snatched it from his hand and covered her eyes, leaning against Jade's shoulder to maximise the distance between Markos and herself. The engine started and the movement of the vehicle soon rocked her to sleep.

Jade roused her with a nudge. 'Wake up, Pumpkin. We're here.'

'Wha?' Crystal rasped blearily, wiping drool from the corners of her mouth. It felt like a few short minutes since she had drifted off, but when she glanced at the dashboard clock, she realised they had been on the road for over an hour. The truck trundled along an extensive gravel track lined with topiary hedges. Turning a bend, the driveway opened onto a granite-paved ring road circling an enormous three-tier fountain. Gasping, Crystal stared in awe at the building.

Jade giggled. 'Impressive huh?'

Speechless, Crystal nodded. She scrambled out of the driver's side, desperate to see more of the magnificent sight. The white stucco mansion was more of a sprawling villa, with ocean blue window frames and shutters. Mounting a few steps, she entered the courtyard, enclosed on three sides by towering walls and several sets of stairs with blue railing, leading up to balconies. The central feature of this area was a large swimming pool shaped like an elongated quatrefoil with a border of blue and white mosaic tiles. With the hint of sea brine in the air, Crystal lost herself in the beauty, imagining for a moment she was somewhere along a Mediterranean coastline.

She snapped a selfie in front of the house and sent it to Adam with the caption: Postcard from the Greek Islands, LOL. Seriously though, this place is breathtaking!

{Adam} Wow, I had no idea they made buildings like that in Australia. Where are you? Got an address for me yet?

Oops! In the excitement she had forgotten to ask for details. Glancing around, she looked for

Jade, but everyone had disappeared. She replied to Adam: Not yet. Will get back to you on that one. I fell asleep on the drive, so all I know is we are somewhere over an hour from Fitzroy.

Descending the steps, it occurred to her Jade would find access to the house difficult in her condition. *Maybe they found another entrance?* Circling the left side of the house, she glimpsed the expansive grounds. There was nothing but gardens, vineyards, and scrub for miles. She could not believe she was about to call this picturesque property her home. Laughter drifted on the breeze and she found a wide door on the side of the house. *Bingo!*

Esme had joined the party, the three of them chatting around a stainless-steel bench in the centre of an industrial kitchen. 'There you are!' She ran up to Crystal, throwing her arms around her. 'I am so jealous! I totally want to live here too.'

'I'm sure that would be fine,' Markos suggested.

Crystal furrowed her brow. 'You can't invite random people to live in someone else's home.'

He smirked. 'No, but I can confer with the guy who owns this place. How do you think I got the okay for you and Jade?'

'Wait! *You're* the one who's friends with the owner?'

'Something like that.'

She tapped her fingers on the counter. 'Jade, this place has lots of stairs, how are you going to get around here?'

'There are service elevators all over The Villa,' Markos pointed out. 'Come on, let's celebrate.' He produced a bottle of bubbly from a nearby fridge.

'Jade is going stone cold sober, remember? That means no mind-altering substances of *any* kind.' She yanked the bottle out of his grasp.

'Read the label, Peach. That's sparkling grape juice. Zero alcohol.'

'Oh.' She checked the bottle, confirming the truth. 'Good.'

Markos took it back and poured them each a glass before moving into an adjacent living room. 'Hey, let's get a moving day pic.' He handed his phone to Esme. 'Would you mind doing the honours?'

'Sure,' Esme replied with a smile as she laid her glass to rest on a nearby bookshelf.

CRYSTAL'S CRUCIBLE

He put his own drink down and pulled Jade to his side. 'You're in this one too, Crissy. Get over here.'

Reluctantly, she ambled over and stood next to Markos who snaked his arm around her waist, tugging her closer, the jerking motion tipping her glass and splashing juice down her top. 'Damnit!'

'At least it's not one of your good shirts,' Esme offered, stifling a laugh.

'Here, let me help,' Markos insisted, yanking the tee over her head before she had time to realise what he was doing and tossed it aside.

'Markos!' she squealed with red hot cheeks while Esme and Jade doubled over with laughter. Before she could escape to hide her shame, he grabbed her, eliciting another shriek.

'Fuck, I love hearing you make that sound.' Seizing her, he tickled her exposed flesh, setting off a wave of hysterical noises.

She collapsed to her knees. 'Mercy. Please grant me mercy.'

'Well, since you begged so nicely.' Picking Crystal up, he tucked her into his right side and summoned Jade to his left. 'Photo, now!'

The click of a camera sounded before Crystal was able to escape his clutches and run for cover.

CRYSTAL'S CRUCIBLE

She found a clean shirt in her bags of clothes and slipped it on before returning. 'We should unpack.'

Jade blew a raspberry. 'Party pooper!'

'Crystal's right,' Markos conceded. 'I still need to get the truck back to the depot tonight.'

Jade unpacked her clothes while everyone else lugged gear inside. As the afternoon wore on, the playful banter continued, although Markos eased up on the groping, because his hands were too busy working. After he left to return the truck, Crystal put her finger on what was bugging her about Markos' voice. He spoke with a modulated pitch rather than keeping it monotone. Bit by bit, the man she thought she knew was morphing into someone else. *Or is he shedding a false persona?*

෨෬

Apollo

A familiar black Mercedes waited outside his suburban apartment, prompting him to close the door of his gold Supra with more force than necessary. Time was of the essence and he had hoped to clear the last of his stuff from the flat before heading back to The Villa. Approaching the sedan, he found it empty. *Great, he plans to ambush me inside*. He rode the lift, shifting his weight from side-to-side as he tapped the rail with a manicured fingernail.

Predictably, *Patéras* was waiting on the sofa, one leg crossed over the other, ankle-to-knee. A cigar smouldered between his fingers, filling the air with an earthy leather aroma. 'You've made quite the mess of things, boy. Do you realise how close I am to closing this deal with Henry? Aludel will be mine within a month, two at the most.' He pinched his thumb and forefinger. 'We are *this* close to cornering the drug market in Australia. I'm sure I don't need to remind you what that means for the contra side of business.'

'No, I know.' He tossed his keys on the kitchen bench. 'I'm also extremely busy right now, can I take a rain check on this arse whooping?'

Snickering, *Patéras* stubbed out the cigar in a crystal ashtray on the coffee table. 'I thought the days of belt lashings were long gone, but if you keep pushing my buttons, I'll be sure to send Alex your way later.' He gestured toward the hulk lurking in the corner of the room. 'I promise it'll be a lot less fun than the kinky shit you normally get up to.'

CRYSTAL'S CRUCIBLE

One glimpse of the bodyguard come hitman was enough to send shivers through all his nerve endings. 'Fine. What do you want, *Patéras*?'

'Tell me what happened with Crystal's sister. Why isn't she dead yet?'

He slumped into an armchair facing his father. 'I couldn't do it. She's grown on me and I can't harm her.'

Patéras shook his head. 'Love turns you soft, boy. You can't afford such weakness in our world. What happens when she tells her sister about your alter ego? Crystal is a bright spark, she'll put the puzzle together in no time. Deal with these girls before one or both go squealing to the cops, *again*.

'If either of them show up dead now, it will make me appear more suspicious. Besides, I'm dealing with them, okay? I have the situation literally contained.'

'Explain,' *Patéras* demanded.

'Well, they say a picture speaks a thousand words. Here.' He brought up the moving day photo on his phone and showed *Patéras*.

'Was this taken at *I kryfí víla*[15]?'

'*Naí*.[16]'

---

[15] The Hidden Villa (Greek)
[16] Yes (Greek)

CRYSTAL'S CRUCIBLE

'Good work, Kyriakos. Send me that image with a caption strongly implying they are living with you. It should help keep the other sharks at bay if you catch my drift.'

'Hmm, that should work well, especially if I make Markos disappear.'

Patéras arched his brows. 'Is that why you are moving out of here?' He swept his arm around the room full of moving boxes.

Kyriakos nodded. 'I've already handed in my resignation at Aludel. I intend to return my attention to Brayzon. Our Ops Manager there is a bit of a flake.'

'Suits me fine. Keep a lid on those Buchanan girls.' *Patéras* rose, summoning Alex with a wave. When he reached the door, he paused and glanced over his shoulder. 'Jade's pussy better be worth all this trouble you're going to.'

'Oh, it is.' Kyriakos gave his father a sly grin. 'So is Crystal's.'

Chapter Thirty-Three

Crystal

Darkness surrounded Crystal when she awoke in the throes of an orgasm. *What the hell?* Taking stock of her environment, she realised her breasts pressed against the bed she had claimed, and her left cheek rested against the pillow. Long, skilled fingers toyed with her sensitive bud, filling the room with the scent of her arousal. She tried to move but failed. He pinned her legs and her hands… *Oh God!* Fear and lust intertwined, coiling around her like the rope binding her wrists. She wanted to scream, yet only a pathetic whimper slipped out.

The man trapping her shifted, pressing his erection against her bare backside and bringing his mouth to the shell of her ear. A familiar woodsy cologne wafted through the air as Markos spoke,

CRYSTAL'S CRUCIBLE

'Tell me Peach, who were you dreaming about when I made you come just now?'

'What do you think you're doing Markos?' she asked feebly.

'Answer my question, Peach. Was it me, or Adam?' He pressed his thumb against her clit.

Crystal bucked involuntarily from the jolt of pleasure shooting through her. Hoping he would think it was from her struggling to break free, she continued writhing and tugging at her restraints in a legitimate attempt to escape. It was no use. All she managed was chafing her skin against the rope. Tears pooled in her eyes, and she swallowed against the hard lump in her throat. 'Are you going to rape me?'

'It's not rape if you give me consent,' Markos explained in a deep, husky growl.

'Not gonna happen!' she snapped.

His chest quavered against her back. 'You say that now, but by the time I'm done with you, you'll be begging me for a sweet release.'

'I thought we were friends. Why are you doing this to me?'

'We *were* friends, but I got sick of waiting.'

'I am so firing you for this.'

CRYSTAL'S CRUCIBLE

'Too bad I already quit, and you're as good as gone, which means I have all the time in the world to make you mine.' He thrust his fingers deep inside her and she hated how easily he strummed the strings of her desire. Crystal trembled beneath him, close to climax when he stopped. 'That first one was a free sample, but I'm not letting you come again until you submit to me.'

'You're dreaming if you think *that* will ever happen.'

'We'll see.' Stretching across the bed, he reached for something on the floor. A buzz sounded behind her when he returned to straddling her legs. As the pulsing plastic pressed against her nub, another shock frayed her nerves.

Lust trickled along her thighs, her body betraying her. 'Please,' she pleaded.

'Please what?'

'Please stop.'

He slammed his body against her. 'No, not until you give in.'

'How is this any different to rape if you won't give me the option to say no?'

'Fine, you wanna do this the hard way?' Markos shuffled down and tied her ankles to the posts at the base of the bed. 'Keep refusing me all you want while you lie here and rot.' He stormed across the room, the absence of his heat sending a chill of goosebumps dancing across her flesh.

'Markos, wait! Let's talk about this. Please.'

With a few quick strides, he returned, kneeling beside the bed and flicking on the lamp. He stared at her with frosty eyes. 'Markos is dead, sweetheart. From now on, you can call me Apollo.' Holding her gaze, he tucked a loose strand of hair behind her ear in a surprisingly tender gesture. 'When you seduced me at Club Commotion, I had hopes for us, Peach. But when Adam waved his bone, you ran back to him and humped his leg like a good lap dog. You left me with no other choice. I can't have you and your sister running free, telling the world about me and my old man. At the same time, I can't bring myself to end your miserable lives either. That leaves me with one final option.'

Blood drained from her face as the grey-matter gears turned. 'Confinement,' she murmured. 'You don't plan on letting us leave this house, do you?'

Markos, or rather, Apollo smirked. 'You always were the smart one. A curious kitten landing yourself in a world of trouble.'

CRYSTAL'S CRUCIBLE

And click! 'It's you, you're the mole! Does that mean… Oh God! Did you murder Robert?'

He sighed. 'You need to learn when to keep your mouth shut, Peach.'

She glared at him. 'Did. You. Kill. Him?'

'No. Dad leaves most of the wet work to his hitmen. You're lucky I took an interest in you, else you'd have a bullet in your brain by now.'

'Lucky?' she scoffed. 'Not bloody likely. Being tied up and held against my will is not my idea of a holiday Mar—Apollo.'

'You might not see it that way now, but if you give me a chance, I could make you and your sister extremely happy. You will both be princesses here in my castle.'

'You are truly sick in the head!' Crystal spat. 'This is not some fairy tale, you creep. Nor are we in some twisted mafia romance where you can make me fall in love with you by holding me captive.'

'Maybe not. But regardless of how you feel about me, you're stuck here now. I suggest you learn to make the most of it.' Bending over her right shoulder, he planted a chaste kiss on her lips before taking her phone from the nightstand. Turning off the light, he left her alone in the dark, still secured to the bed.

CRYSTAL'S CRUCIBLE

༄༅

Jade

Everything was strange that morning. Jade was home but she was not. The trill of songbirds told her the day dawned, yet thick curtains blocked the familiar rays of first light. The scent on the sheets was different, earthy rather than spicy, and the arm draped across her was more muscular than Dieter's. It took her a few minutes to process the changes, to appreciate everything she had gained in the face of all she had lost. Snuggling into Apollo's heat helped to some extent, but when she realised he was too out of it to reciprocate her affection, she rolled over with a sigh and rose from the bed.

She slipped into her wheelchair because walking had become too mentally taxing for her morning brain. After riding the service lift down to the ground floor, she trundled into the kitchen, hoping to find signs of life, but it was empty. *Where's Crissy?* Given how early her sister went to bed, Jade had expected her to be up and bustling about before anyone else. In contrast to herself, Crystal had always been a morning person. She explored the lower levels of the main house, occasionally stopping to admire beautiful features or gasp at expensive electronics. *Living in the lap of luxury will take some getting used to*. With a smirk, she thought about the man's lap she was living in.

When her search yielded no results, she returned to the upper floor bedrooms, wishing she had paid more attention to Crystal's room choice. There was still no sign of her, and Jade's heart hammered. She took a few deep breaths and tried to put herself in Crystal's shoes. *Where would she be?* The girl had gone on about wanting her own place for years, to escape the tethers of responsibility for their ungrateful mother. It stung to think she had become the burden in Crystal's life. With that in mind, she crossed the rooftop garden connecting an adjacent guest house.

The aroma of culinary herbs swirled around her with the light breeze, stirring a growl from her empty stomach. Pushing aside the urge to give up and make herself some toast, she peeked through the first door on the right: nothing. Two more doors proved fruitless, but when the fourth door opened, she laughed at the scene within. 'That kinky fucker.'

Turning her head—the only part she could move—Crystal faced the doorway. 'Jade?'

CRYSTAL'S CRUCIBLE

She wheeled closer to the bed. 'Hey Pumpkin. I'm s-surprised to see you getting into the bondage already, 'specially when Apollo hasn't so much as blindfolded me yet.'

'I didn't want this,' Crystal replied in a frail voice.

'What?' Switching on the bedside lamp, Jade inspected Crystal's expression: red puffy eyes, crusty nose, and pale cheeks. 'Shit! What'd he do to ya? Did he…' She trailed off, unable to utter the word aloud, partly because she could not bear to think Apollo was capable of such perverse cruelty. Such an act did not fit with the man she knew. *But how well do I know him, really? He still hasn't told me his real name, after all. Have I misplaced my trust in this man?*

'Not entirely,' Crystal rasped. 'He took some liberties with my body, but he admitted he would not take things further until I…' She sniffled. 'Begged him for it.'

Scanning Crystal's body and spotting the vibrator on the nightstand, Jade's jaw clenched as the penny dropped. '*That bastard*!' Her voice lowered, becoming vicious. 'Lemme guess, you didn't put out, so he left you tied up out of spite.' It reminded her of one of the scumbags who used to work at the Club back in the day. Thankfully, Sargon had known where to find her on mornings after Chad had tried to impose his will upon her.

'Sort of, but there's more to it than that. Can you give me a hand with these ropes, then I'll explain?'

'Yeah, course,' Jade replied with a nod. Starting with the right wrist, she recognised the simple, yet effective single column tie Apollo had used. *Figures he'd know his stuff.*

When Jade undid the knot, Crystal breathed a sigh of relief and shook her hand. 'Thank you. If you can get my other wrist, I'll do the ankles.' Several minutes later she was free and sitting up with a glass of water in hand, her second after sculling one in the bathroom. 'Firstly, did you know Apollo, as you call him, worked with me at Aludel?'

Jade, who sat beside her, felt her eyes pop. 'No! I s-swear I had no idea.'

Crystal nodded. 'Figures. He went by the name Markos, although I suspect that is a fake name, after something he said last night. Anyway, we were good friends at work, nothing seemed off about him and even immediately after I made out with him at the club, he was kind to me, a perfect gentleman and all that jazz. But since then, he

CRYSTAL'S CRUCIBLE

upped the flirting and became more persistent about me leaving Adam for him. He showed his true colours last night.' Tears trickled from her eyes.

She gave Crystal a one-armed hug, pulling her close. 'Hey, shh, we'll ditch this jerk and get our own place. Not the end of the world.'

'Thing is, Jade. I know too much about him. He told me you and I can't ever leave this place and he confiscated my phone. I bet he did the same to yours.'

'Ah hell.' The blood drained from her face as she recalled the massive gates that had greeted her at the property's entrance, and all the surveillance cameras she had teased Apollo about. *This place isn't just a fortress, it's a prison*. Closing her eyes, she felt a dense ball weighing down her stomach. But that sense of dread paled in comparison to the sharp pang in her chest. *Is this how Dieter felt about my betrayal?* 'There must be a way to get outta here. I'm not givin' up hope, not yet.'

'There might be a way. I didn't see the front gate when we arrived, but I'm guessing security is tight.'

Jade nodded. 'Fort fuckin' Knox.'

'But there must be a key of some sort?'

CRYSTAL'S CRUCIBLE

She cast her mind back to the moment they approached The Villa. 'Yes! There's a fob on his keyring with a button that opens the gate. But how do we get our hands on it?'

'That should be the easy part. The trick will be getting out there undetected.'

'Hmm.' She tried to come up with a plan, but forward thinking had never been her forte, and since the OD, the fog in her brain made it much harder.

'We need a way to distract him, to catch him unawares and knock him out,' Crystal suggested.

'You're a bloody genius, Crissy! I'm glad one of us got Dad's smarty pants genes.'

Crystal blushed. 'Yeah, but how do we distract Apollo?'

'Sex. I'll do what I do best and s-seduce the arsehole. When he is fucking me, you can whack him on the head with a blunt object. We can get you into the room under the pretext of a threesome since he's been keen to have us both at once.'

'Now who's the brainiac?' Crystal smiled. 'Are you sure about having sex with him again though?'

Jade laughed. 'Oh hun, I've slept with men for less virtuous reasons. This will be a cakewalk for me.'

Crystal sighed and fell silent.

'What is it?' Jade inquired.

'He'll smell a rat unless I sleep with him first.'

'What? No way! You don't need to do that, Crissy. What if we leave you tied up, then I free you after knocking him out?'

Crystal shook her head, twirling hair between her fingers. 'Won't work. With your body still on the mend, you simply don't have the strength and agility to take him out on your own. I'm going to need full use of my limbs.' She gulped. 'If you can do this, Jade, so can I.'

Tears threatened to flow from her eyes as Jade's heart expanded to fill her chest. She plucked the strand of hair from Crystal's hand and tucked it behind her ears. 'You are the most selfless person I know, and I'm so damn proud of you, little sis.'

Chapter Thirty-Four

Adam

Adam slammed his desk phone back on its cradle. *Why won't Crystal answer?* It had been almost two days since she moved, since their last communication, and he could not fight the uneasy feeling in his gut. The timing of Markos' recent resignation did not sit well with him either. He eyed the sandwich taunting him from its plate. Even though his stomach groaned, he found it hard to fathom eating, so he threw his lunch in the bin and stuck to drinking his Gatorade.

After three short knocks, Greg barged into Adam's new, yet old office. 'Hey man, how's it feel to be back in that chair after all this time?'

He shrugged. 'It's a job.'

Greg slumped into the visitor's seat. 'I still think you made a mistake. No pussy in the world is worth hamstringing ya career over. Speaking of which, how is that cute redhead of yours doing?'

Adam scowled, but decided not to push the issue. *We'll have to agree to disagree*. 'I don't know what's going on with Crystal. I haven't heard from her in two days and I'm getting worried about her. She won't answer her phone either, it keeps going straight to voicemail.'

'Hmm.' Greg stiffened and glanced out the window. 'Have you heard the latest on this Brayzon fiasco?'

Perched on the edge of his seat, Adam gripped his desk with white-knuckled hands. 'What do you know, Greg?'

'There's talk of a buy-out.'

'I don't give a damn about Brayzon. Tell me what you know about Crystal.'

'I hate being the bearer of bad news, but I did warn you about her. You should have fired her traitorous arse when you had the chance. Although I'm sure Henry will—'

Smack! Adam thumped his fist on the desk. 'Stop rambling and tell me!'

'A little birdie told me about the thing she had with Markos. I wouldn't be surprised if she fell for his charms again.'

CRYSTAL'S CRUCIBLE

No! Adam refused to believe Crystal would betray him like that. She had been honest about all her interactions with Markos, reassuring him everything was platonic because she knew about his insecurities. 'They spent one night together and didn't even take things all the way. Crystal wouldn't cheat on me.'

'You have a lot of faith in her considering she moved in with the man.'

'What?'

Greg handed Adam his phone, showing him a photo of Markos standing in front of an expensive leather couch, flanked by Crystal and Jade, his arms wrapped around their waists. The picture caption read: Look who acquired the two sexiest housemates. #Ménageàtrois. 'Maybe Crystal's busy enjoying a private housewarming, if you catch my drift?'

The thing that made Adam's blood boil was seeing his girl scantily clad within another man's arms. *Is this why she was cagey about telling me the address? She didn't want me to know she moved in with Markos?* The more Adam thought about it, the less it made sense. It was not like she could hide the truth forever, not if she intended to let Adam visit her home. *Then again, it wasn't like we ever hung at her last place. We always use my house.* 'How did you get that photo?'

'Markos sent it to me.'

'I didn't know you socialised with the guy outside of work. Has he told you anything else about his relationship with Crystal?'

Greg took his phone back. 'I know Markos was banging her older sister and he bragged it was only a matter of time before he got a threesome with them.'

Adam shook his head. 'You think you know a man…'

'Indeed.'

'Do you know why he quit?' Adam asked.

'Not explicitly, but if I had to guess, I'd say it was for similar reasons to you stepping down. To remove the conflict of interest.'

Adam had not thought of that possibility, but it made too much sense to ignore, which brought him right back to the cloud of doubts darkening his mood. 'Can I ask a favour?'

'Anytime, bro.'

'Can you give me Markos' number? I'd like to have a chat with that sleaze bucket.'

'Sure thing.' Greg retrieved the contact details in his phone and handed them to Adam.

CRYSTAL'S CRUCIBLE

After writing down the number, he returned Greg's phone. 'Mind giving me some privacy for this?' As the door closed behind Greg, Adam took a deep breath and dialled.

'Markos speaking.'

'Put Crystal on the phone,' demanded Adam with a bitter tone.

'Oh, it's you. Sorry Adam, but Crissy doesn't want to talk to you.'

He clenched his jaw. 'Then hand her the phone so she can tell me herself.'

Markos sighed. 'Fine.'

Adam heard muffled mumbling in the background and seconds later Crystal spoke, 'Now's not a good time. I'm sorry.'

'Crystal, wait—'

But Markos was back on the line. 'Sorry, dude, but she's made her choice.'

'What's going on, Markos? What are you doing to her?'

He snickered. 'Do you *really* want to know?'

'Yes.'

'Fine, but you asked for it.' The call ended, followed up with a media message, a picture with the caption #Nooner.

CRYSTAL'S CRUCIBLE

It was too much. The pain in his chest reached critical mass and Adam hurled his phone at the wall, watching with wide eyes as it smashed and dropped to the floor. 'Fuck!'

ೋ಄

Crystal

Crystal looked up in horror as Apollo snapped a sex selfie, one capturing his dick in her mouth. 'What are you doing with that?'

He gave her a lopsided grin. 'Getting Adam off our case.'

God no! He will never forgive me for this.

'As you were.' He rammed himself back into her mouth.

'Is this a private party, or can I join too?' Jade's husky voice was a welcome relief.

'Mm, please do, gorgeous.'

Jade crossed the room, her walking stick clicking against the timber floor. She propped it against the dressing table and eased herself onto the bed.

With a grin, Apollo emptied himself down Crystal's throat. Grabbing her hair, he pulled her up

CRYSTAL'S CRUCIBLE

from her knees and shunted her onto the mattress. 'I want to watch you undress your sister.'

Crystal gaped at him.

He laughed. 'Quit the innocent act, Peach. I know how filthy your mind and body can get.'

Kneeling behind Jade according to Apollo's instructions, Crystal lifted her sister's dress above her head. Apollo's hungry gaze drank in the sight and Crystal noticed his cock springing to life again.

Apollo moved to the bed beside Jade. He pressed a tender kiss on her lips before pulling her up to straddle his lap. She threw her head back and yelped as he entered her. A moment later she began riding him, shooting Crystal the look that told her to be ready.

'Come sit on my face, Peach, and give Jade a kiss.'

She crawled up the bed, but rather than moving into the requested position, she grabbed Jade's walking stick and whacked his temple with as much force as she could muster. His head lolled to the side, facing away from her.

Jade sprang from his cock and sat on his chest, clicking her fingers in his face. 'Hey arsehole, can ya hear me?'

Nothing.

CRYSTAL'S CRUCIBLE

Crystal shoved Jade's dress back over her head before donning her own. She searched the mess of clothes on the floor, finding Apollo's chinos. 'Where are his keys?'

Jade stared at her with wide eyes. 'Damnit! We've got one shot at this.'

'I know. They must be in his room. Come on.' After grabbing her backpack and stealing his phone, Crystal helped Jade into the hall where the wheelchair waited.

'I'll call the cops.'

Crystal nodded, tasting inevitable freedom. But dread and logic sucker punched her in the gut. 'Wait! Apollo won't stay down for long and he has Greek mafia connections,' she explained, recalling Drake at the club. 'He'll sniff the police a mile away, giving him time to alert said mafia and send a hitman here sooner than the police can find us. Let's get out first.'

'Damnit. You're right.' Jade sighed.

'Hold on tight, hun, because this is going to be the ride of your life.' With a shove, she sent Jade sailing down the hallway towards the main house, running after her. Crossing the rooftop garden was more arduous, the friction too high between the pavers and the wheels to maintain momentum for long, but once they got to the next corridor it was a short trip to Apollo's room. She found his keys on the dressing table and tossed them into Jade's lap.

'Thank Christ!' Jade cheered. 'Let's get out of this Godforsaken place.'

They made it to Crystal's car without any further issues but lost precious minutes in the battle to fold the chair so it would fit in the boot, all while Jade insisted Crystal forget it. 'And what happens if we break down before reaching civilisation, huh? You can't keep up with me if we have to run on foot.'

'Okay fine.'

Crystal found the trigger release and wrangled the thing into the boot. Less than a minute later she turned her own key in the ignition and exhaled the breath she had been holding when the car fired to life. Reaching across for the gearstick, she felt Jade's hand clamped down on her arm.

'Um, Crissy, look.' She gestured toward the guest house upper floor window where Apollo stood watching them.

'Oh hell!' She yanked the shift into first, moving through the gears as fast as possible to speed down the driveway.

CRYSTAL'S CRUCIBLE

'Fuck me, sis, when did you become Speed Racer?' Jade roared.

Crystal winced at Jade's choice of words. 'Remember that douche I had a crush on in school?'

'Charlie? Yeah, I remember him.'

'His dad taught us a bunch of defensive driving techniques.'

'At least he was good for something,' Jade sneered.

As they approached the gate, Jade tapped the button on the fob. 'Why isn't it working?' Her voice was on the edge of hysterical.

'I guess we need to get closer. Keep pressing it.' The impossibly tall gate loomed before them, an equally high steel fence flanking it, with razor wire covering the lot. 'Now would be great!' Crystal shrieked. If the gate did not open soon, they were going to crash into it.

'I'm trying!' Jade snapped, 'But it won't fucking work!'

Slamming her foot on the brake, Crystal skidded to a stop, mere seconds from collision. She snatched the fob and pointed it at the gate, pressing it hard. Still no response. 'Crap! He must have disabled it.' A second later, Apollo's phone rang from the cup holder. She glanced at it, noticing her

CRYSTAL'S CRUCIBLE

own name requesting a video call and exchanged a worried look with Jade before answering. 'H-hello?'

Apollo's face came into view. 'Hey Peach. Forgetting someone?' He adjusted the camera to show Esme's battered face, tears streaming from her eyes, and duct tape covering her mouth.

'Oh God! Ez!' Crystal's heart leaped into her throat and she gulped. 'How? Why?'

When the creep's face popped up behind Esme, he clucked his tongue. 'Silly Peach. I honestly thought you were smarter. Why on Earth would I let your friend leave when she knows where to find you? I locked her away in my dungeon for safe keeping. You should have known I'd have multiple contingencies up my sleeves. You didn't honestly think I reserved those surveillance cameras for the perimeter, did you? Besides, even without hearing your plan come together, I would have been suspicious when you willingly gave yourself to me without further incentive.'

She cursed herself for blowing their best chance of escape with a rushed, poorly conceived plan. 'Fine. You win. We'll come back if you promise not to hurt Esme anymore.'

Esme shook her head wildly.

CRYSTAL'S CRUCIBLE

'Oh, I know you'll come back since you have likely hit a dead end anyway. I just wanted you to know there is a lot more on the line now. And trust me when I say, you will pay for that nasty bump on my head.' He disconnected the call.

She heaved out a heavy sigh. 'I'm sorry Jade.'

'You should go. Try and find a hole in the fence or brave the wire and climb it. Anything to get out of here.'

Crystal shook her head, tears trickling down her face. 'I can't leave Esme, or you. There's no way you'd make it over the fence.'

'I know, but you could go get help.'

'You're kidding right?' Crystal scoffed. 'He would kill Esme and possibly even you if I escaped alone. I'm not willing to risk your lives.'

'Stop being a damn martyr, Crissy. Ez wouldn't want you to sacrifice yourself for her, and I sure as hell don't. Besides, Apollo loves me in his own twisted way. I doubt he'll kill me. I can buy you some time, keep him sexed up. You know this is our best chance.'

The left side of her brain told her Jade was the voice of reason, but her emotions made a strong case against the idea. 'I don't know, Jade.' Closing her eyes, she thought strategically and picked up

CRYSTAL'S CRUCIBLE

Apollo's phone. 'What do you suppose his PIN is? I need a six-digit number.'

'I know it's not a number, but Apollo is six letters.'

'And letters correspond to numbers on a keypad.' Crystal grinned at Jade before punching in the code 276556. 'Bingo! That moron is too predictable.' She found the mobile number she was looking for, typed out the message and deleted the conversation from the phone's memory. 'Done.'

'Now what?' Jade asked.

'Now we go back to the house and wait for help to arrive.'

Chapter Thirty-Five

Adam

Staring at the gin in the bottom of his glass, Adam wondered if this was where addiction began: Driven to drink by Crystal Buchanan. The irony was not lost on him. He needed to rid his mind of the image that was haunting him and numbing it with alcohol was the most effective option. He took another sip and startled when the doorbell rang. Sauntering over with a drunken swagger, he greeted his best mate with a grunt as he flicked the latch on the security screen.

Greg held up a fresh bottle of gin. 'Thought you could use a drink, although I see you've already started without me.'

'Can always use more.' Adam snatched the offering before Greg could renege, returning to the living room. 'Help yourself.' He gestured toward the open bar.

CRYSTAL'S CRUCIBLE

After fetching himself a beverage, Greg sat in an armchair, facing Adam. 'You wanna tell me about the incident with your phone earlier?'

'Not really,' Adam huffed.

'Could be therapeutic.'

He glared at Greg. 'What the hell would you know about therapy? It's over between me and Crystal. End of story.'

'Is this because of the pic I showed you? We don't know for certain—'

'She was sucking him off, Greg. The bastard even sent me photographic evidence.'

He laughed, something akin to a Bond villain. 'That's my boy.'

Adam narrowed his gaze on Greg. 'Excuse me?'

'All I'm sayin' is, that man knows how to make his father proud.'

'What are you talking about bro?' His fuzzy head hampered Adam's ability to make sense of Greg's dribble.

'Why don't you have another drink?'

'Why don't you tell me what the hell you're talking about?' He shifted his weight, perching on the edge of the couch.

CRYSTAL'S CRUCIBLE

'I ought to give my plastic surgeon a raise. He did such a swell job of hiding the family resemblance.'

'Resemblance to who, Greg?'

'My son, of course. The man you call Markos, although that's not his real name.'

Adam's jaw hit the floor. 'What the actual… Wait, did Markos, or whatever his name is, orchestrate the IP theft at Aludel?'

He let out a raucous laugh. 'No, Adam. He's a smart kid and a devoted son, but he doesn't have what it takes to plan for the big picture. Thinks with his dick too much.'

'Does that mean you…' Adam felt the alcohol churning in his empty stomach, threatening to resurface.

'I must say, I'm impressed Crystal kept her mouth shut all this time. Makes me wonder if her loyalties have always been with my boy. She looked pretty happy on her knees sucking his dick.'

Wanting to wipe the smug grin off Greg's face (if that was even his name), Adam rose.

With lightning reflexes, Greg aimed a pistol at Adam. 'Sit down and don't do anything stupid.' He released the safety catch. 'Someone wants you dead, Adam. Now I usually send my minions to do this sort of dirty work, but I thought I'd make an exception with you. This is more personal after all.'

Adam gaped at the barrel of the gun.

'You have no idea how long I've wanted to shut your snooty mouth, to make you choke on that fucking silver spoon. Thank the Lord I'm a patient man, I know how to play the long game. You were useful when you had power in the Company, Adam. But you threw it all away over a bitch who can't even keep her legs closed outside your bedroom.' He snickered. 'Fuck, you really know how to pick 'em don't ya?'

With his hands raised in a show of submission, Adam took a deep breath. 'What do you want, Greg? Let's cut a deal.'

'Hmm.' Greg tapped his chin. 'Nope, I don't need you anymore. Aludel is as good as mine and you're too much of a liability. Besides, someone put a hit out on you. You won't be leaving here alive.' He stood, keeping the gun steady as he grabbed the fresh bottle of gin and offered it to Adam. 'Now drink up.'

'Why?' Refusing to take the liquor, he eyed it suspiciously.

CRYSTAL'S CRUCIBLE

'Because shooting people is not my MO, although I will put a bullet in your brain if you don't cooperate.'

'So what? You're going to poison me?' Adam scoffed.

Greg shook his head. 'No, *my friend*. You're going to poison yourself. With alcohol. Less suspicious that way.'

'Screw you. Shoot me and be done with it.'

As Greg slammed the bottle down on the coffee table with a thud, the adjacent crystal tumblers rattled and chimed. 'Fine. If that's how you want to play it. But if you don't do this my way, I'll be sure to pay Lucinda a visit and send that boy to the grave too. Did you know he was yours all along? She lied about the paternity test. I caught a glimpse of the results.'

'*You bastard!*' Adam screamed, jumping at him, and reaching for the gun. As Greg's arm shot out, the weapon fired as it sailed through the air, silent but for the shattering of a window. Greg shoved him to the ground, kicking him in the ribs before moving toward the pistol lying abandoned on the floorboards. Before Greg reached it, Adam tackled him, and they wrestled. The men exchanged punches for what felt like an eternity, but Adam knew he was slipping away. The alcohol he had already imbibed, along with the concussive blows to his head, were taking their toll. *At least I'll make the arsehole hurt before oblivion takes me.*

The door burst open, and he heard cries of 'Police' amidst the commotion before everything faded to a chaotic blur.

ಸಂಧ

Sargon

Visiting the cop shop always made Sargon's skin crawl. He was like an unholy presence on sanctified ground. It did not matter that he had half the City's force in his pocket. Entering the shrine of justice still took him too close to those who could turn his world upside down with the flick of a pen. But his friends needed him and that meant putting his own issues with the law aside. He was small fry, after all, and dangling the big game in front of their trigger-happy faces was bound to keep them distracted from his little operation. *How had I not made the connection between Apollo and the Greek mafia?* Shaking his head, he followed the officer into an interview room.

CRYSTAL'S CRUCIBLE

'Here you go.' He opened the door for Sargon. 'Buzz me when you're done.'

'Cheers, mate.' Sargon waited for the door to close before moving to the seat opposite the shirtless, rich toff with a broken nose and two black eyes. The man reeked of booze and appeared to be nursing the mother of all hangovers. 'Adam Fairfax?'

'Yeah, who's asking?' He scowled. 'You don't look like a police detective.'

He snorted. 'Far from it. The name's Sargon. I'm a good friend of your girl's sister and I recently had the pleasure of making Crystal's acquaintance.'

'Crystal's not my girl,' he sneered, vitriol dripping from his tongue.

'You might want to rethink that stance on the matter. She's the reason you're still alive. If it weren't for Crystal reaching out to me, I wouldn't have known to send the pigs to your house.'

Adam's mouth gaped open. 'Why? How...'

'I don't know all the particulars yet, but I know she's in serious trouble and she needs our help, as does my sweet bluebird. A man with strong ties to the Greek mafia has them captive. You know him as Markos, but I knew him as Apollo, and I bet neither of those names are real. I mean, what arsehole names their kid Apollo? Anyway, Crystal figured the tosser would order a hit on you and it looks like she was right.'

'Good God!' exclaimed Adam.

'Indeed. She asked me to relay a message to you.' He retrieved his phone from his pocket and read the text aloud. 'Here it is. "Tell Adam, I still love him, that I never wanted Markos, and not to believe everything he sees." Not sure what that last part means, but I assume you do.'

Adam turned as white as Sargon's satin bed sheets. 'It means I want to kill that creep.'

'Join the club, mate. Your girl's not the only one he put his filthy paws on. First, we gotta find him. I've got the coppers scouring the records for all properties connected to the Stavros family and cross referencing with the recent phone tower activity on Crystal's account. Her idea by the way, not mine. Wish I was half as smart as her.'

'Stavros family?'

'Oh right. You didn't know. The man that was trying to put a cap in your arse got arrested, obviously. They ran his DNA and found out he is the long-lost son of a mobster from Greece. A Stavros.'

'I had no idea.'

CRYSTAL'S CRUCIBLE

'Clearly. Don't feel like a fool though, mate. They had us all duped. Will you help me take that fucker down and rescue the girls? Once we know where they are?'

Adam nodded. 'Yeah, of course.'

'Good. I suggest laying low until then. The cops are still rounding up Stavros' men, so it might not be wise to make your presence known while some of them are at large. I have a safehouse you can use if you don't have anywhere else to go.'

'That would be great. Thank you. Is that for me?' Adam pointed to the hoodie Sargon held.

'Yeah, the cops asked me to bring you a shirt and I figured this would help to keep you incognito.' He tossed the jacket to Adam who rose to put it on, flashing bruised ribs in the process. 'Yikes man, they look nasty. Has a doctor checked you out yet?'

'No. Just a paramedic who suggested they might be broken. Mind if we visit the hospital on the way?'

'No probs. There's one other stop we need to make too. Got to enlist more help and I have a feeling convincing this next bloke is going to be more difficult.'

Chapter Thirty-Six

Dieter

Bill, bill, and look at that, another bill. Dieter dropped each of them in the mail basket on the kitchen counter, wondering how the world managed to go on spinning as though the most Earth-shattering thing did not happen to him. It was not like he was a complete egotist. *Not like the jerk who stole my girl.* But he thought a few more people would have noticed. He continued sifting through the letters, pausing when he reached one addressed to Jade. She had not left him with a forwarding address. Picking up his phone to text her about the issue, he spotted the envelope's sender: The Department of Home Affairs. He still needed to let them know about the change to his relationship status, which likely meant deportment back to Germany. *Might not be such a bad thing. What's left for me here?*

CRYSTAL'S CRUCIBLE

A heavy knock at the door intruded upon his thoughts. Sargon's timing was uncanny, reminding Dieter he still had a job and a potential recording contract. 'Shit. I am sorry, Sargon, I forgot to ring in tonight.'

The club owner waved his hand in a dismissive gesture. 'All good. I figured you'd still be moping. I'm not here about work.'

'Then why?'

'Can we come in for a chat?'

For the first time, Dieter noticed the other man standing behind Sargon, hidden in the folds of an oversized hoodie. 'I would like to know who I am inviting into my home.'

'Oh right.' Sargon stepped aside, letting the other guy through. 'This is Adam, Crystal's ah… what are you exactly?'

'Her boyfriend,' replied Adam.

Dieter gasped at the man's bruised face. 'What happened to you?'

'The Greek mafia,' Sargon explained, 'which is why we are here.'

He let them both into his flat. 'Can I get you anything to drink?'

'Coffee would—'

CRYSTAL'S CRUCIBLE

'We don't have time,' Sargon interrupted Adam with his eyes fixed on Dieter. 'You are in danger, my friend and I'm glad I reached you before they sent a hitman to *your* door. Seems Fairfax here was their primary concern, which was just as well, since I doubt you'd appreciate protective detail from a bunch of pigs.'

'Fairfax?' He directed his attention to Adam. 'Wait, you are the boss Crystal was talking about?'

Adam nodded. 'Or at least I was.'

'We gotta get you outta here, mate,' Sargon continued. 'Pack your valuables and come with me.'

'Why would these mobsters come after me?'

Sargon heaved a sigh. 'Because Apollo is one of them and he has Jade and Crystal.'

Dieter scowled. 'Jade made her bed.'

'No.' Sargon shook his head. 'She had no idea what she was getting herself into and now both of those girls are at that sadistic freak's mercy. Against their will, mind you. Jade still loves you, which makes you a target. He can hurt her by harming you. Now *move*.'

'Fine.' Dieter dashed into his room and threw his stash of drugs in a backpack, along with his passport and cash savings. Locking the apartment, he followed Sargon downstairs. 'How do you know all this?' he asked once settled into the front passenger seat of a V8 Commodore.

'Crystal messaged me from Apollo's phone when their escape attempt failed. Those girls need our help getting out.'

'So, send the bloody cops,' Dieter spat. 'I'm done cleaning up Jade's messes.'

The engine roared to life and Sargon flew down the street. 'Look mate, I know you have fresh wounds and all, but can you honestly tell me you don't care about her anymore? And what about Crystal? If memory serves, you loved her like a sister. And I bet you'd like nothing better than serving that wanker his just desserts[17].'

'What if I do care?'

'This is a delicate matter, Dieter. One sniff of bacon and Apollo will do something drastic. We need to go in there ourselves.'

'Don't you think he will smell a rat when he sees me and Adam?'

'Not if you guys stay hidden as we approach the property.' After locking Dieter's stuff in his safe, Sargon headed south along the highway.

Half an hour into the drive, silent except for Adam's snoring, Sargon spoke up again, 'Our

---

[17] What one deserves

bluebird needs her wings to fly. That's why she did what she did.'

Turning from his study of the passing view, Dieter furrowed his forehead. 'What are you talking about?'

'The monogamous lifestyle does not suit Jade. It stifles her, like nails pinning her pretty, little wings to a board. You trapped her in a relationship she could not deal with. Her love for you won't diminish if you give her the freedom to express her sexuality with others.'

'It's not that simple, Sargon.'

'Sure it is. I've seen plenty of successful poly couples.'

'Jade never hid her past from me. I wasn't the one imposing this on her. She chose to give it up for me, for the sake of my residency. It was the only way I could apply for a partner VISA.'

'The government love sticking their nose in people's personal business,' Sargon sneered in disgust. 'Don't let a bunch of bureaucrats dictate who you invite into your bed. If you're not hurting anyone, it's none of their damn business.'

Adam snorted. 'Amen to that.'

Sargon laughed. 'Welcome back, sleeping beauty.'

CRYSTAL'S CRUCIBLE

After another fifteen minutes, the car turned onto an exit ramp and Sargon pulled over to the side of the road. 'Time for you guys to assume your hiding places.'

Tucking himself into the rear footwell was not an easy task for Dieter and his long legs, even with the front seat shunted forward as far as it goes. Sargon handed him a pistol before giving Adam a machete.

'Why does he get a gun and I only get a knife?' Adam complained.

Arching a brow, Sargon waved his own Glock in the air. 'Have you ever fired one of these?'

'No, but I'm sure it can't be *that* hard.'

Sargon sniggered as he threw blankets over each of them. 'Arrogant toff.'

Dieter lost track of time as they travelled toward the monster's lair. His legs began to cramp, and he worried they might seize up before he got a chance to introduce his fists to Apollo's face. When the car stopped, he heard Sargon lower the driver's window, followed by the buzz of an intercom.

'Apollo, my man! It's Sargon.'

'How the hell did you find this place? And what are you doing here?' the crackly voice asked through the speaker box.

CRYSTAL'S CRUCIBLE

'Your dad sent me here on business.'

'Why is this the first I heard of it? He should've alerted me.'

'Yeah, well he can't. The poor bastard's holed up in a prison cell and needs your help bailing him out. He called me because he didn't want to alert the cops to your whereabouts.'

'Fuck! Okay, come on in.'

A moment later, the Commodore rolled on through the gates, tyres crunching against gravel as they approached the unknown.

෨෬

Crystal

The shallow gashes in Crystal's skin oozed, the stinging turning to an insufferable itch as the wounds began to scab. She could not even scratch them because Apollo had cuffed her arms and legs to some horrid contraption within his so-called dungeon. The cellar furnished with red velvet did not meet Crystal's expectations when he said the word 'dungeon'. She had envisioned medieval torture devices, not plush couches, or the enormous four-poster bed, complete with canopy, taking pride of place in the middle of the room.

Jade was dozing on the bed, spread eagled and tied to each post by red ropes. Crystal envied her sister's reprieve, even though she knew Apollo induced Jade's sleep with drugs, setting her rehab back to square one. Esme, on the other hand, was chained to the opposite wall and her state of unconsciousness was far more concerning given the severity of the head injury Apollo had inflicted upon her. The psychopath had re-enacted the blow to the temple Crystal had given him using the same walking stick, but he used much more force. The only sign of life in Esme's battered body was the shallow rise and fall of her naked chest. Another faint whimper sounded from the adjacent room, reminding Crystal they were not alone. Apollo had another captive, one who sounded much younger than herself, and the thought of what he had done to her sent chills down her spine.

Crystal had never felt such bitter hatred toward another living soul. Even her mother's sins paled in comparison. She let the tears flow, wondering if any of them would see the light of day again. *Will I ever feel Adam's warm breath against my neck and his strong arms wrapped around me?* Her stomach somersaulted when she considered the possibility that Sargon would be too late to save Adam.

A gun fired somewhere in the house and footfalls thumped across the floorboards. Crystal exhaled sharply, knowing help had arrived. Moments later a man in a black tracksuit entered the room, slinking across the stone covered ground toward her. A hood covered his head, hiding his face until he reached her. When he did, she gasped. 'Adam! Oh my God—'

'Shh.' He pressed a finger to her mouth. Tears pooled in his bruised eyes when he took in the sight of her. 'Markos is a dead man,' he ground out through gritted teeth. Finding a small key on a nearby chest of drawers, Adam dropped the large knife he had been carrying to unlock the metal cuffs from her wrists and ankles.

She collapsed into his embrace. 'I love you so much, Adam.'

'I love you too, baby,' he rasped. 'I'm sorry he did this to you.'

'Hey.' Lifting his chin, she focused his gaze on her eyes. 'It's not your fault.'

'It is,' he countered. 'I should have trusted you. If I never left you in the first place—'

CRYSTAL'S CRUCIBLE

Crystal clamped his lips shut with a kiss. 'You are not accountable for that creep's actions. Stop blaming yourself. Okay?'

He nodded and devoured her mouth with another kiss, much deeper this time.

'Isn't this the most cinematic moment,' Apollo sneered from the doorway. 'Get your hands off my woman, Fairfax.'

Adam spun around to face Apollo, tucking Crystal tight against his side. 'Crystal never was, nor will she ever be yours, you sicko.'

'She will be, once you're dead.' Apollo aimed a gun at Adam's head.

The clicking of the safety catch prompted Crystal to spring to action. Grabbing the abandoned knife, she charged toward Apollo in a frenzied rage.

He dodged her with a laugh and grabbed a fist full of her hair, yanking her back against him. 'You should know better than to bring a knife to a gunfight, Peach.'

Bending over, screaming as strands of hair tore away from her head, Crystal showed Apollo how effective a knife could be. She plunged it into his thigh.

The gun slipped from his hand as he fell back, bellowing. '*You fucking bitch!*'

CRYSTAL'S CRUCIBLE

Crystal snatched the gun and handed it to Adam who gaped at her with wide eyes. Blood dripped from the machete in her right hand as she straddled Apollo, pressing the blade to his carotid artery.

Apollo snarled at her. 'You don't have what it takes to kill someone. If you slit my throat, the guilt will destroy you.'

'Perhaps.' Crystal shrugged as she pivoted one-eighty degrees on his stomach and unzipped his fly. 'Maybe death is too merciful a punishment for your crimes against women.' She gripped his flaccid dick, not surprised in the slightest when it hardened in her hand. She sliced the vile organ clean from his body with a determined strike and sprang to her feet, leaving him writhing and screaming on the floor.

Adam drew closer. 'Um, Crystal? Are you okay?' He kicked Apollo in the head, knocking him out cold.

She panted heavily as the adrenaline rush subsided. When Crystal caught Adam glancing at her hand, her own gaze followed, and she yelped. Shocked by the dismembered body part and all the blood, she flung it aside, doubled over and emptied her stomach.

CRYSTAL'S CRUCIBLE

Strong arms picked her up and hugged her tight. 'It's okay, baby. The nightmare is over. Everything is going to be okay.'

Chapter Thirty-Seven

Jade

Blurred shapes moved amidst the cacophony of muted sounds and it took Jade several minutes to recall where she was. *The Dungeon*. Her skin was hot and sweaty, and the urge to vomit was growing by the second. She closed her eyes against the harsh, cruel world. *I hope Apollo doses me up again soon*. Being out of it was preferable to witnessing the horrors around her and it made the sex more tolerable.

When he tugged at her restraints, she took a deep breath to control the stammer in her voice. 'I-if you are going to fuck me now, can I have some more juice first?'

'No, *Liebling*, I would never do that to you. You are going to be sober the next time I make love to you, and we will do so in *our* bed.'

'Dieter?' She sighed. If he was here, she must have drifted back to sleep. 'I don't know what's worse. The pain and misery of my waking hours, or these dreams torturing me with a sense of hope. I should have been stronger. I should have resisted him. I should have—'

He pulled her up into a sitting position, cutting her off with a firm embrace. 'This is not a dream. It is time to go home.'

'That's what you always say in my dreams.'

'There might still be some junk in her system,' a familiar voice explained.

'Sargon? What are you doing here?' she asked when his face came into view beyond Dieter's shoulder.

'Crystal messaged me, remember? I could hardly resist the opportunity to swoop in all gallant and whatnot to save you, but it looks like the German Giant beat me to it.'

'Strange,' she mused aloud. 'You're not usually in my dreams.'

Sargon followed Dieter's laugh with a huff as he clamped a hand over his chest. 'Oh, my wounded heart.'

'Hey Sargon, can you get Esme?' a third man asked.

CRYSTAL'S CRUCIBLE

Surprised by the alien voice, Jade turned to see a thug in a black hoodie holding Crystal who appeared to be sobbing. 'Who are you and what are you doing with my sister?'

'Relax, Jade.' Dieter ran his hand up and down her back in soothing strokes. 'That's Adam, Crystal's boyfriend.'

'But—'

Crystal stirred in his arms, glanced her way, and nodded reassuringly. 'Sorry you guys couldn't meet under better circumstances. It's okay, babe, you can let me go now.'

Gripping her tighter Adam shook his head. 'I'm not letting you go again for the foreseeable future.'

'Well, someone needs to free the little girl, and Sargon has his hands full with Ez.'

'What little girl?' Adam asked.

Crystal pointed to the red door that had concealed the child's identity and muffled her cries. During her more lucid moments, Jade had noticed the voice too, and it made her skin crawl. When Adam released Crystal, she stumbled across the room and flung the door open. The girl shrieked and hollered when Crystal carried her out, but the poor thing was too weak to struggle in Crystal's arms.

As the light revealed the girl's face—her naturally brown skin made darker from a build-up of grime—Adam gasped. 'That's Denzel's daughter, Jacinta. I guess Denzel discovered Greg's secret too.' He joined Crystal, helping her soothe the young girl as they carried her out of the dungeon.

'The police should be here soon. Let's get out of here.' After covering her with his jacket, Dieter helped Jade to her feet, supporting the weaker left side of her body. She hobbled toward the door and up the stone steps leading out of the cellar. They emerged into the cool night air where bright lights flashed, and sirens blared around them. Pulling her into his chest, Dieter shielded her from the mayhem. His lips found her ear and he whispered to her, 'I will never leave you again, *mein Liebling*.'

When the paramedics arrived with a stretcher and bundled Jade up in a blanket, Dieter hovered nearby, refusing to let her out of his sight even as they carted her off to hospital.

As soon as they had a moment alone, she squeezed his hand and cleared her voice. 'I'm so sorry for everything I did with—'

'Don't. I never want to hear that man's name again. He did foul, unspeakable things to you and your sister, not to mention Esme and that poor child, and I am sorry I gave him the opportunity.'

'I was the one trying to apologise here.'

'No need. I understand why you did it. I hope you can forgive me for leaving you, especially when you were vulnerable.'

'Of course I forgive you. I love you so much, Dieter. Thank you for… everything.'

'I should be thanking you. I mean it this time when I say I'll do anything for you.' He sealed his promise with a deep, passionate kiss, ignoring the cheers and wolf whistles from their audience in the emergency department.

༄༅

Two years later: Crystal

Crystal carefully turned each page of the newspaper, in pursuit of the crosswords. She paused when a headline caught her attention: 'Notorious Stavros Gangsters Sentenced for Life.' Taking the paper into the living room, she smiled at Jackson who sat on the couch, scoffing down a bowl of sugary cereal while watching Saturday morning cartoons. 'Hey champ.' Milk dribbled from his mouth as he waved. She curled up beside Adam on the adjacent sofa and handed him the open broadsheet. 'Check this out.'

He put his science journal aside and plucked the page from her hand, a sly grin curving one side of his mouth as he read the article. 'About time those bastards got what was coming to them. I just hope they can pin that blackmail charge on Katrina.'

Crystal gaped at him.

'What?' Adam asked.

'You pulled the paper apart.'

Glancing at the damage he had done, he shrugged. 'There's going to be a lot more mess and chaos in my life pretty soon. Figured I'd start getting used to it.'

She knew he was downplaying the enormity of his efforts in curtailing the need for control. 'True that.'

'Did you see the postcard on the coffee table?' He pointed to the unsorted stack of mail.

'Not yet. By the time I got home from that impromptu office party last night, I was too exhausted to do anything but climb into bed.' After

CRYSTAL'S CRUCIBLE

failing to reach the table when she attempted to bend over, she let Adam retrieve the postcard.

He pressed a chaste kiss to her lips before dropping it in her hand. 'Hans looked stoked last night. I'm sorry I couldn't stick around.'

'That's okay. Your time with Jax is precious and it warms my heart seeing you guys together. Besides, Esme mentioned something about a big engagement party at her Dad's house, so we can celebrate with them then.' Returning her attention to the tattered card, she studied the glossy photo of Saint Basil's Cathedral, admiring the brightly coloured building with its various onion-shaped domes, before flipping it over to read the scrawled message:

Hey Pumpkin,

I hope you and your sexy husband are well and that you are popping plenty of vitamin pills. Dieter and I are having a blast in Moscow. We even ran into Sargon while he was visiting family. I'll save all the juicy details for when I get home, but let's just say my German Giant has embraced the poly lifestyle

CRYSTAL'S CRUCIBLE

*(wink wink). This is the last leg of his
tour, so we should be back soon.
     Big sister hugs from Jade.*

Brushing away a stray tear from Crystal's face, Adam lifted her gaze to his. 'Is everything okay?'

Gulping, she nodded. 'Damn hormones.'

He beamed at her and lowered his eyes to her belly, laying his hands on her bump and staring at it with reverence. 'Judy phoned me last night, by the way. She panicked when she couldn't get hold of you directly.'

'Neurotic much? It's odd how her maternal instincts took this long to kick in.'

Adam laughed. 'Yeah well, it helps that she is fully sober after how many years?'

'Nearly eighteen. What did she want?'

'She was checking in to make sure you and the baby are okay. I assured her you were both fine.'

'Is the baby kicking?' Jackson sprang from the couch and hurried over.

'He is,' Crystal replied. 'I think he might be a soccer or footy player with those strong little feet of his.'

CRYSTAL'S CRUCIBLE

Jackson screwed up his nose. 'Softball and tennis are much better sports, aren't they Uncle Adam?'

'They are,' Adam agreed. 'And I'm sure learning them from both of us will make him happy.'

'Phew!' Jackson wiped his brow. 'That's a relief. I love my little sister, but I look forward to having a baby brother too.'

Adam sputtered and Crystal's eyes bugged out. After composing herself, she asked, 'Why… How… What makes you think this child is your brother?'

'Mum explained that because Uncle Adam is my bio dad, his baby boy is my brother. I assume this is the baby she was talking about?'

'Yes Jax.' Crystal smiled at him, then at her husband. 'Adam is definitely the father of my baby. Lucinda telling you the truth without consulting us first came as a surprise.'

Tears brimmed in Jackson's eyes, so Adam kneeled in front of him. 'Hey buddy, I'm sorry I didn't tell you sooner. I wanted to, believe me, but your Mum wasn't ready. Honestly, I'm glad she told you, but like Crystal said, we are surprised she did.'

CRYSTAL'S CRUCIBLE

Jackson stared at his bare feet a moment before meeting Adam's eyes. 'I kind of worked it out for myself and asked her about it.'

This time Adam's eyes popped. 'How?'

'I have a couple mates with single mums who visit their dads. When I learned my cousins don't come here much, I got suspicious. Then, while looking at some old photos on the computer, I saw the wedding pics of you and Mum, so I asked her.'

This kid never ceased to amaze Crystal. Jackson resembled his father so much she knew he had a great future ahead of him. Yet she also pitied all the poor souls who were bound to have their hearts broken when falling for his charms.

'Is it okay if I call you Dad?' Jackson asked.

'Absolutely!' Adam grinned so wide he flashed his perfect white teeth. 'If that's what you want, I would love nothing more, son.' He embraced Jackson, who returned the sentiment.

'I love you too, Dad.'

Crystal's heart melted as she watched the exchange. 'Hey you guys, mind the emotional pregnant woman up here. The floodgates are about to open.'

Adam and Jackson shared a mischievous look before they both surged forward, flanking her in a group hug. 'We love you too, Crystal.' They chimed in unison.

Tears of joy poured forth and when the guys released their hold, she felt another kick. With a smile she thought about the months and years to come. Crystal's next trial by fire was about to start, but unlike most of the others she had suffered through, she welcomed the challenge of motherhood with open arms.

The End

What's Next?

Thank you for reading *Crystal's Crucible*. I would be most grateful if you could show your support by leaving a rating or even a review.

Up next will be a prequel to this one, telling the forbidden love story of Adam's ex-wife, Lucinda, and his brother, James Fairfax. It will also feature some characters from a previous book. While you can read *The Phoebe Braddock Books* in any order, if you intend to read *From Prying Eyes*, it is best to do so prior to this one to avoid spoilers. Keep an eye out for:

Undeniably Wrong: A Phoebe Braddock Fiction

Keep reading for a sample…

Bonus Content

Jade's Menage in Moscow
Read all the juicy details from Jade and Dieter's tour of Europe. **Warning:** this short story features some hot polyamorous content.

Crystal's Deleted Scene
Remember Crystal and Jade's dark, steamy threesome with Apollo? I initially wrote more for this scene, but decided the details were too gratuitous, so they did not make the final cut. **Warning:** this scene involves some dub-con F/F interaction between the sisters.

You can find these and more exclusive content on the FREEBIES page of my website:
www.starlaarts.com

Acknowledgements

Wow! This book has taken me on such an emotional roller coaster. As soon as the idea came to me to write Crystal's story, I sat down and pushed myself to the finish line in record time. Pulling several all-nighters and giving up on my social life for two months may not have been the healthiest thing to do, but the results rewarded me in ways I had not experienced before. Typing The End and hitting PRINT on my first draft gave me such a high! I could not have done this without the loving support of my beloved Jason who fuelled my insane writing binge with caffeine, laughs, and inspiration. He is my biggest fan and my favourite critique partner. Thanks also to my brother George and my dear mum for celebrating over a bottle of bubbly with me that night.

I owe a debt of gratitude to my bestie, Sarah, to whom I dedicate this book. I haven't always been

ACKNOWLEDGEMENTS

the most reliable and present friend, especially when I'm deep diving into the minds of the characters I create. Yet she has stood by me through thick and thin and supported my writing profession as my second biggest fan. Our history traces back to a previous life when I still possessed grand ideas of taking the science world by storm. Our career paths started along similar lines, then veered apart as I pursued other interests, but our friendship has prevailed through dedication, a passion for fancy garb, and a mutual love of Buffy the Vampire Slayer.

Kudos to my beta readers! You guys are fabulous for deciphering my early scribbles and helping me transform them into this coherent and cohesive novel I am proud to publish. Thank you so much Amanda Mashburn, Ariel Mareroa, Breen Rodriguez, Elli Morgan, and Felix Staica.

Last, but not least, I'd like to acknowledge my awesome ARC readers and Street Team who contributed to the success of this book by sharing their love of it with the world.

The Phoebe Braddock Books
(Taboo Romance & Forbidden Love)

The Phoebe Braddock Books started as a budding idea while L. Starla drafted ***I Heart Mr. Collins***. The protagonist of this story published a novel of her own, inspiring Starla to write the book that Phoebe wrote. The series has since grown into a rich universe of taboo romance, forbidden love stories, and reflections on difficult issues. While each book can be read as a standalone, existing characters will return in fourth title of the series and beyond.

I Heart Mr. Collins: Phoebe Braddock's Love Story

From Prying Eyes: A Phoebe Braddock Romance

Crystal's Crucible: A Phoebe Braddock Romance

Undeniably Wrong: A Phoebe Braddock Fiction
(August 2022)

Undeniably Wrong
A Phoebe Braddock Fiction

There are many sides to every story and Lucinda's tale is no exception.

Lucinda's affair damaged Adam Fairfax and it took him years to recover. Most painted her as the villain, but did anyone think to ask her why their marriage collapsed? Why did she cheat on him?

I dare you to turn back the clock and delve into a warped web of high society schemes and veiled threats. This is a world where people poison everything they touch and make a blood sport of betrayal. With all the lies and deception swirling around her like a murky swamp, it is no wonder Lucinda bought into it, letting it taint her soul and relationships. Yet none of them pose a greater risk than the shadows of her past.

> AVAILABLE AUGUST 2022
> Keep reading for a sample…

Undeniably Wrong

Chapter One

Innocence is such a fleeting phase, yet even now society prizes a woman's virtue as a treasured commodity. Lucinda once valued the ideals of saving herself for marriage, but in the blink of an eye, she let a stranger pluck the precious pearl from her oyster. She never even knew his name. Looking back on the deed, she questioned her reasons and came up with a plethora of excuses: the guy's sex appeal, peer pressure, alcohol, hormones, growing tired of behaving. They all seemed valid, but one truth shone brighter than the rest: she wanted *him*. Undeniably. It all started with a stupid game…

'Let's play truth *and* dare,' Erin Higgins declared from on high, perched precariously in her pillow throne.

Lucinda groaned, exchanging a look with Nicole who offered a sympathetic simper, but

UNDENIABLY WRONG

neither of them vocalised their protests. Denying Erin was top on the social suicide list, right next to double denim and listening to Aqua. The other four girls giggled, passing a French Champagne between them. *How do they not see the irony of drinking their "classy" drink straight from the bottle?* Shivering, Lucinda wrapped herself in the sleeping bag on her bunk.

Wicked intent gleamed like sapphires in Erin's blue eyes. 'Just for that show of enthusiasm, I think Lucy should go first. Does anyone have a question for her?'

'I do!' Sally waved her hand in the air and Lucinda narrowed her eyes on the daft girl. 'Last I heard, you were a virgin. Is that still true?'

A sigh slipped out as Lucinda's shoulders deflated. 'Yeah, still true. I told you I'm saving myself.'

Zoe Bristow giggled. 'That's like so archaic. No one *really* waits for marriage anymore, do they? I mean, who's gonna check?'

'But God knows all,' Erin mocked, impersonating their religious studies teacher, Sister Josephine, with hands held in a sign of prayer. Everyone except Lucinda and Nicole sniggered. The Queen Bee returned her attention to Lucinda. 'I dare you to get off with someone tomorrow. Find a hot single guy on the slopes and flirt with him, then in the evening, make your move.'

Lucinda gaped at Erin. 'I… I can't.'

'For Christ's sake, girl, I'm not insisting you have sex with the guy, unless you *want to*.' Erin's lips curled in a lopsided grin. 'You just need to get as far as second base, bonus points if you do so in his bed.'

'I'm still not sure.' Lucinda bit her lip, debating the pros and cons of defying Erin.

'Refuse the dare, and I'll let the records show you slept with Terrance Bristow.'

Bile climbed Lucinda's throat at the thought of such a horrid rumour spreading. Zany Zoe's brother was one of the vilest men to walk the Earth and he would happily support Erin's claims, especially given their history. She shuddered as the memories pushed their way out of the locked recesses of her mind. Gulping down the bitter taste, Lucinda nodded. 'Okay. It's only second base right?'

Erin smiled wide enough to show her sparkling teeth. 'Right.'

Zoning out as the girls continued, Lucinda's mind reeled with the prospect of intimacy. Aside

UNDENIABLY WRONG

from the French kiss she had shared with Erin's cousin, Michael, during another party game, the only guy she had done things with was Terrance, and those were times she would rather forget. The trauma had been enough to put her off dating anyone else. Boarding school had been a convenient excuse, "sheltering her from the corrupting influence of the male species" as her mother had put it. She still had another year and a half of seclusion to savour, although holidays were another matter. There was no avoiding the school's requirement to return home during the term breaks.

'Are you seriously daring us all to make out with a guy?' Nicole's voice brought Lucinda back to the moment.

Erin laughed. 'Damn straight! Need I remind you we are free of the parentals? We've got to make the most of mid-year break, bitches. I'm making it my personal mission to find a hottie to keep me warm for the next five nights. I suggest you all do the same.'

Ick! On the bright side, I won't have to share a room with her again if she's busy shacking up with a winter fling. Lucinda held her tongue despite the urge to voice her thoughts.

UNDENIABLY WRONG

'Please don't bring any hook-ups back here,' Nicole begged. 'I don't need to see that shit. I'll carry through with my dare, but I can't promise to get lucky every night, so when I am sleeping in this room, I want a dick free zone.'

'Of course,' Erin agreed. 'This is our safe space. No guys allowed. Now let's get our beauty sleep. We all need it for tomorrow...some of us more than others.'

ʚɞ

Crisp snow sparkled in the morning light, the sun ducking between wispy white clouds. The slopes of Mount Hotham glowed with the same pristine purity Lucinda brandished. *But for how much longer?* Leaving her novice friends behind, she headed straight for Brockhoff, one of the longer black trails down Heavenly Valley. While there was less snow than on most of the other resorts her family had taken her to around the world, Hotham still boasted the best powder Australia had to offer.

She paced herself on the first run, learning the terrain. On her third descent, she noticed someone in a camo print tracksuit watching her from the trees. The man was still there on her fourth go, so she carved across the snow in a tight turn to approach him.

Pushing green goggles up onto his head, he revealed dark eyes set deep in his hooded gaze. 'I'm impressed. Where'd you learn to ski like that?'

Feeling her face flush, she silently thanked her mother for the full coverage her pink balaclava provided. 'Switzerland.'

He whistled his approval. 'Is that where you're from?'

'No, I'm local, but I travelled lots with my parents.'

'Nice. When you say local…' His voice trailed off as he inched closer, stepping out from the shade of the Eucalypt he had been leaning against.

Lucinda sucked in a breath as she took in his sculpted face. In the light, his eyes were more of a deep reddish-brown and stubble lined his chiselled jaw. *What had he asked? Oh right, he hadn't technically phrased it as a question.* 'I'm Victorian. Grew up in Barwon Heads.'

A cheeky smile lit up his features. 'Does that mean you're a beach girl too?' His eyes scanned her body, and she wondered what he was thinking.

'Yes, of course. I *live* at the beach in summer.'

UNDENIABLY WRONG

Licking his lips, he stared shamelessly, lust blazing in his eyes. 'Fancy a race? Loser buys the winner a drink at the bar tonight.'

The suggestion caught her by surprise, and she laughed. 'Um, sure. Sounds like fun.'

'Indeed.'

They waddled to the summit together and the gorgeous guy counted down from five. On 'Go!' he pushed off at break-neck speed, gaining the lead by a considerable margin. Lucinda pushed herself but failed to gain on him. He waited patiently for her at the base, clutching his skis in one arm and grinning as she reached him. After catching her breath, she extended her hand. 'Congratulations. I'm glad you didn't hold back. I hate it when guys let me win.'

He shook her hand, smirking. 'Trust me sweetheart, I'm all for gender equality, but you have to earn your wins. There's only one activity where I *let* a woman come first and then I pretty much guarantee it.'

Lucinda's cheeks burned and it took several seconds for her to realise he had not released her. She glanced at their joined hands, drawing her bottom lip between her teeth as her eyes returned to his heated stare. 'I—'

UNDENIABLY WRONG

A hulking oaf charged into the back of her sexy stranger and slapped him on the back. 'Come on man, let's grab some grub!'

'Be right there, Russ.' He kept his eyes fixed on Lucinda while dismissing his friend. When the giant stomped off toward Snake Gully Hut, mystery man leaned in to press his lips to her ear. 'You owe me a victory drink, so what do you say to meeting at The General tonight? Say around nine?'

Instinctively, she attempted to tuck a strand of hair behind her opposite ear, forgetting it was all tied back in her ski mask, so her fingers hovered awkwardly against her face. 'It's a date.'

'I wasn't game to make any such presumptions, but if you insist.' He winked and strode away, leaving Lucinda's heart in a flutter.

Wow! That was easier than I expected. She had succeeded with the first half of her dare without even trying. Then again, Lucinda never had difficulty attracting attention from the opposite sex, unwanted as it often was. The next stage of her challenge would be the true test.

ಸಂಡ

UNDENIABLY WRONG

The girls drew every eye as they entered the bar at quarter past nine. 'Fashionably late' according to Erin who paused to survey the room while Lucinda sought one man in particular. And… bingo! The unmistakable smile greeted her. He sat alone at a table near the front windows wearing jeans and a grey knit sweater.

Erin nudged her. 'Is he here?'

'Yes, there he is.' She nodded toward her date whose grin widened.

'Hubba Bubba!' Erin patted Lucinda's back. 'Good choice. Go get him tiger.'

Golden waves of freshly coiffured hair bounced around her as Lucinda sauntered toward the man of the hour. Accustomed to the attention her friends attracted, she ignored the wolf whistles and crass remarks other guys directed her way as she passed them.

He rose to meet her, planting a chaste kiss on her cheek and filling her senses with his spicy cologne. 'Hey. It's so good to see you again.'

'Likewise.' She smiled warmly.

'I've got to ask though, what's with the entourage?' He glanced over her shoulder.

'Don't worry about my friends, they won't bother us. They're just here to find their own fun.'

UNDENIABLY WRONG

'I hope so because the redhead is wigging me out.'

Lucida giggled. 'Yeah, Erin freaks everyone out. Seriously, forget her.'

He placed his hand against the small of her back, touching her ever so lightly, yet sparking something deep and sensual within her. 'Okay. What can I get you to drink?'

Blinking, she tried to break the magnetic pull between them. 'I believe the first round is on me. That was the deal, right?'

'Hmm, no.'

She gaped at him. 'But—'

'You changed the rules when you said those three magic words.'

'What words?' She felt her brow creasing as she thought back to her previous encounter with him.

'It's. A. Date. What sort of gentleman would I be if I let you pay for anything here tonight?'

'Ha! So much for gender equality.' Not that she was complaining.

'Some old school values are worth keeping, don't you think?'

Lucinda nodded, relieved she would not need to take her fake ID on a test drive.

UNDENIABLY WRONG

'Good. Now that's settled, what would you like to drink?'

Beverage choice was the furthest thing from her mind. 'Surprise me. Anything but gin,' she quickly added.

With eyes bugging out he chortled. 'Brave woman. Have a seat, and I'll be right back.' Tugging a chair out, he helped her into it and brushed his fingers over her shoulder before walking away. Tingles trailed down her back from the contact.

After taking a deep breath, she looked around the room. Erin and the other girls caught her attention, grinning manically and offering thumbs up. Lucinda smiled as she shook her head before turning her attention back to her *date.* She admired the firm form of his backside while he stood at the counter and chuckled to herself when "Crush" by Jennifer Paige started playing over the sound system.

With drinks in hand, he turned and caught Lucinda perving on his arse, a knowing smirk lighting up his face. The rest of the room faded from view as he approached, filling her vision with his radiance. A tall glass appeared in front of her and after glimpsing what she assumed to be cola, she cocked her head. 'A Coke?'

UNDENIABLY WRONG

Taking the seat opposite her, he offered her a lopsided grin. 'Try it.'

Sucking through her straw, she almost choked on the burning sensation. 'Woah! That's… strong. What is this?'

'A Long Island iced tea. Five different shots topped with cola. Although I got them to double up on the triple sec in place of the gin.'

She laughed. 'Are you trying to get me drunk, sir?'

Mischief glimmered in his beautiful brown eyes. 'You wanted a surprise.' He chugged down a mouthful of his own deadly concoction without any trouble. 'Do you like it?'

With the advantage of hindsight, she took another taste, enjoying the tang on her tastebuds. 'Yes, actually.' A few more sips and a buzz began to set in. 'So, what do you occupy your time with?'

'Aside from skiing and surfing, you mean?' He waited for her nod of acknowledgement. 'I also love camping and travelling the world, searching for *daring adventure*.' Lowering his voice to add emphasis, he sounded like David Attenborough.

She cracked up laughing and they enjoyed a moment of mirth before she clutched at her sore ribs. 'Sounds awesome. Do you work?'

UNDENIABLY WRONG

'Not yet. I'm still studying at uni, finishing up my degree in business management.'

'Business, really? That sounds so… dry for a thrill seeker like you.'

He snorted. 'It's not so bad, plus I'm also majoring in tourism. I have ambitions to open my own Outdoor Adventures company. The sort where the tour guides can also offer instruction, whether it be abseiling, bungee jumping, kayaking, scuba diving, you name it.'

Her eyes grew wider with every death-defying activity that rolled off his tongue. 'Have you done all those things?'

'Of course.'

'What about sky diving?'

'That too. What about you? Have you jumped out of a plane?'

'Not yet, but I'd love to.'

'Then you should.'

'There are so many things I want to try.'

'What's stopping you?'

She shrugged. 'Study.'

'That's a lame excuse. I'm still at uni, remember. What's your major?'

'I'm working toward architecture.'

UNDENIABLY WRONG

'Yeah, that sounds intense, but still, you need to make the most of your holidays.'

'Tell me about your adventures, perhaps you'll inspire me to get out there more.'

As the night wore on, he regaled her with tales of his exploits. Halfway through listening to his account of hiking along the Inca Trail, Lucinda realised she had no idea what his name was. Blushing, she bit her lip.

His gaze lowered to her mouth. 'What?'

Too embarrassed to ask so late into their conversation, she wondered how she could find out. 'Nothing.'

'Sorry, I've been talking your ear off, I must be boring you by now.'

She shook her head adamantly. 'No, not at all. I just…' Searching for a way to dig herself out, she spotted the bathrooms. 'Need to use the ladies' room.'

'Oh right.' Springing to his feet, he helped her rise from her chair. His arm snaked around her waist, and he led her to the amenities. She did not need the support to walk even though she felt tipsy, but there was no way in hell she was letting go of him until they reached the threshold he could not pass.

UNDENIABLY WRONG

Erin burst through the door a moment later. 'You better not be chickening out. I swear to God if you waste this opportunity—'

Lucinda giggled. 'Hell no. I'm all in.'

If brows could fly, Erin's would have made it halfway across the world. 'Like all the way?'

'Maybe. He is amazing and so… yummy.'

Squealing, Erin attempted to hug Lucinda who ducked into a cubicle. 'Sorry hun, I'm busting to pee.'

Erin huffed. 'Okay, fine. Take these. I bet you'll need them.' A box of condoms slid under the door and Lucinda shoved it into her clutch bag. 'I'll leave you to it. I want a full report in the morning.' The outer door closed, leaving Lucinda in peace.

When she returned to her mystery man, he dragged her onto the dancefloor. Grooving to the first few R&B tunes, he held her at arm's reach, maintaining a polite distance between them. But then "Pony" by Ginuwine started and his lascivious grin invited her to sample sin. She stepped closer, bringing their bodies together and conceding to the music. Letting herself go felt liberating and she relished the freedom. No one stood around judging her, no one told her what to do, and no one stopped her claiming the man's lips in a deep, passionate kiss. He tasted like memories of winter: drinking chai beside a wood fire; smoke, spice, and sensuality. Hot blood coursed through her veins, and she mewled into his mouth.

Reciprocating her sentiments with a grunt, he spoke gruffly in her ear. 'You want to get out of here? My room's not far.'

'Yes,' slipped out in a breathless, needy voice. She followed him outside and down the path to her purgatory, the road to her ruin.

I Heart Mr. Collins
Phoebe Braddock's Love Story

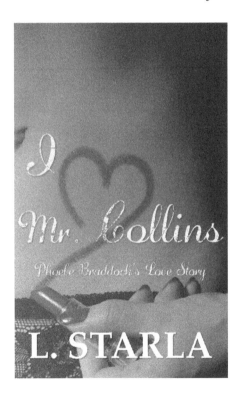

Is it possible to find love without boundaries?

I might have described myself as innocent a few months ago, but that was before my schoolgirl crush

I HEART MR. COLLINS

turned into something real and passionate beyond my wildest imagination. Now my lustful appetite has awoken and there is no going back.

The problem is, no one else can know what I do when alone with Mr. Collins because it would jeopardise his career. Other people wouldn't understand what we have.

At least graduation is just around the corner, and I will strike off lying and deception from my current list of sins. That is my hope, but will I find the courage to be completely honest with everyone?

From Prying Eyes
A Phoebe Braddock Romance

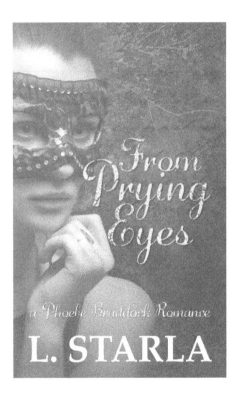

Is the true expression of love really a sin?

Haunted by visions of a mysterious stranger making love to her in the dark, Sophie is torn between affections for the guy she's had a crush on for years and strong yearnings for the man of her dreams. And she can't shake the feeling that there is something familiar about her fantasy lover.

Then one fateful night, her dreams come to life at the debutante ball where Sophie is swept off her feet for several blissful minutes. But when the masks come off, she is forced to accept the shocking truth: her enigmatic lover is no stranger.

Does she deny her deepest desires or pursue a forbidden passion?

Winter's Magic Series
(Magical Realism / Paranormal Romance)

Winter's Maiden 1

Winter's Maiden 2 (November 2021)

Winter's Thrall (May 2022)

Winter's Mother 1 (November 2022)

Winter's Mother 2 (May 2023)

Winter's Bride (November 2023)

Winter's Crone 1 (May 2024)

Winter's Crone 2 (November 2024)

Winter's Maiden 1
Winter's Magic Part 1

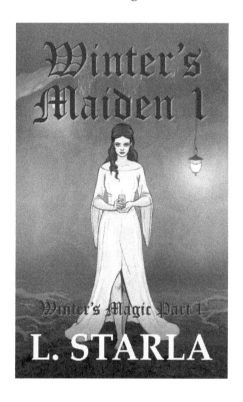

Do you hide from the monsters, or embrace your magical destiny?

WINTER'S MAIDEN 1

Alannah Winters: hedonist. Impulsive, precocious, and dangerously drawn to mysticism. Whisked away from her hometown at a young age and raised ignorant of her close ties to the pagan Gods.

When tragedy strikes her family again, she is forced to return to the small Irish settlement of Gaeilge Shores, a town shrouded in secrecy. At least she has her beloved cousins by her side, helping to unravel the mysteries of her heritage.

Alannah had always harboured feelings for Liam, the eldest of her two cousins, and seeing the man he has grown into only serves to intensify those desires. But when she rocks up at her new school, the captivating blue eyes of a tall, dark, and handsome senior virtually consume her. Not to mention the unsettling way things have changed with Brendan, her other cousin.

Can Alannah survive her inevitable transformation? And what is to be done about the three hot guys vying for her attention? Alannah's early signs of hedonism will prove to be much more than a passing phase…

About the Author

Laelia Starla is an Australian author who often raided her mother's shelves for any form of fiction she could get her hands on. Her first love was the horror genre, but she owes her love affair with the romance novel to her high-school English teacher, who started her on the classics. Given her earlier reading, magical realism and paranormal romance were a natural progression. Along with steamy romance, these are the genres she writes.

Laelia also loves spending her spare time playing tabletop and video games, paper crafting, singing, dancing, and watching anime.

Access Exclusive Content

Join my newsletter to access free stuff like short stories, deleted scenes, fan art, and invitations to future launch events.

Newsletter: www.starlaarts.com>freebies
Facebook Group: groups/l.starlareadersgroup

Follow me Online:
Website & Blog: www.starlaarts.com
Goodreads: Laelia_Starla
BookBub: www.bookbub.com/profile/l-starla
Amazon Author Profile: author/l.starla
Instagram: laeliastarla
Facebook: StarlaArts
Twitter: Laelia62498118

Printed in Australia
AUHW011749240621
347634AU00003B/4